Splendid Morning

SPLENDID MORNING

Robert F. Casemore

G.K. Hall & Co. • Thorndike, Maine

First published by Angus and Robertson LTD 1944

Published in 1999 by arrangement with Robert Casemore.

G.K. Hall Large Print Romance Series.

The text of this Large Print edition is unabridged.
Other aspects of the book may vary from the original edition.

Set in 16 pt. Plantin by Rick Gundberg.

Printed in the United States on permanent paper.

Library of Congress Cataloging in Publication Data

Casemore, Robert F.
Splendid morning / by Robert F. Casemore.
p. cm.
ISBN 0-7838-8474-5 (lg. print : hc : alk. paper)
1. Cuba — History — Revolution, 1895–1898 — Fiction.
2. Spanish-American War, 1898 — Fiction. 3. Florida — History — 1865- — Fiction. I. Title.
[PR9619.3.C389S65 1999]
823—dc21 98-49016

TO
THE MEMORY OF
MY FATHER

AUTHOR'S NOTE

In *Splendid Morning* I have deliberately tried to avoid historical analysis. This is a book designed to entertain rather than to instruct. Certain events in it are, of course, historically true, others are entirely fictitious. The battle of San Juan Hill and the siege of Santiago de Cuba are, I believe, as accurately chronicled as they were in the newspapers of that day. I have shunned history books, especially those written in the light of the present day, for their accounts of the Spanish-American war are combed and sorted with the cold mackerel eye of analysis. By reading newspapers of that era and talking over personal experiences in the affair with still keen-eyed oldsters of Tampa and Key West, I have endeavoured to capture the mood of the day. It is useless to write about the past with one's heart in the present.

Outside certain historical figures who played grimly against the dark background of Cuba's fight for independence, the characters in *Splendid Morning* are entirely imaginary and do not represent any living person.

R. C.

CONTENTS

1

The New Horizon

The companion-way was steep and narrow. Sharon Douglass steadied herself with one hand on the thin guard-rail as she ascended from the saloon to the upper deck of the *Grover Cleveland*, riding one day out of Galveston. She gazed at the few passengers with mild interest, wondering how any of them, including herself, could have been senseless enough to sail on this miserable little tub to the West Indies. Yesterday when these people had boarded the ship they were complete strangers to her, without name or personality and now, before they had cruised twenty-four hours into the Gulf of Mexico, she regarded a few of them almost as intimate friends. For shipboard travel induces man to carry his life story at the tip of his tongue like a sapid morsel; it leads him to wear his emotions on his sleeve like chevrons; it makes him more intimately concerned with his fellow man than he has ever been before.

The *Grover Cleveland* was a small, compact ship, narrow of beam and slightly unstable. She was a coal-burner, built at Philadelphia in 1864 and now in her thirty-first year of service. Her engine and boilers, installed when it was fashionable for vessels to carry both motor and sails, were far too big for the size of the hull. They caused her to shudder frequently as though she had a chill, and every now and then she plunged into the waves, apparently hell-bent for Davy Jones.

After dinner, Sharon retired to her berth for an afternoon siesta. She slept well enough, the weather being unusually calm, and when she awoke the orange sun was setting at the far point where the sky caressed the water. For the first time since her departure from Galveston she was disturbed by vague misgivings. For the past twenty-four hours she had tried to be gay, but when she had laughed aloud at one of the captain's jokes that morning at breakfast, Hilary Edgecomb had shot her a glance that stabbed her conscience.

Her father's death had not really struck her a mortally cruel blow, but she realized with a touch of irritation that she was expected to act as though it had. So she slipped on her taffeta dress because it was the only thing in black she had — and because black was rather becoming to her. Perhaps, after all, mourning wasn't going to be such a hardship. Still, if there was ever a term she loathed it was "weeds".

The upper deck was narrow, and Sharon headed quickly for the rail. She had to admit, wryly, that she wasn't entirely at home on a boat. The rolling plains of Texas with cattle grazing in great herds, and she on a horse to punch them —

that was her life. The tremble of the ship made her giddy, and her smile, as she greeted Hilary Edgecomb and Carlos Menendez at the rail, was a trifle forced. The admiration in their glances pleased her.

She knew she was not beautiful, but there was a look of vitality in her face that was striking. Her eyes were set too closely together, making the bridge of her slightly-tilted nose seem very narrow. Under lamp-light they were dark blue, but by day they looked grayish. Her lips were not full, and their straightness and thin lines expressed determination. Her bosom was full and well rounded, her hair auburn with little dark tints, and the contrast of the black dress against her fair, lucid skin was dramatic.

Hilary Edgecomb was a tall, slightly bald man, slightly effeminate, who liked to call himself a student of Shakespeare. A barber who had set up shop adjacent to an army post in New Jersey, he had accumulated a comfortable sum in trimming the beards and cutting the hair of innumerable captains, majors, and colonels, and was going to Havana to open a café. A heavy gold chain was draped across the waistcoat of his English tweeds, and on his long and slender finger glowed a cameo ring.

Sharon searched the upper deck for Eric March, whom she found the most interesting of her fellow travellers. He was an ensign in the United States Navy and had been on furlough to Galveston where his grandmother lived. Now, he had informed Sharon, he was on his way back to the naval base at Key West. When he first spoke to her a few hours out she thought him a trifle bold, but he was the only passenger near her age. His probable twenty-five or twenty-six wasn't too far removed from her twenty.

It had never once struck her as strange that the only friends she had made on shipboard were men. She never seemed to get along well with women, and she wondered if her Aunt Phoebe in Cuba would be shocked to hear that up to now she had moved in a social circle consisting entirely of cattle-men and meatpackers.

"Have a nice nap, Miss Douglass?" Edgecomb inquired amiably.

Sharon smiled at him. "Yes, I slept quite well."

"What a charming dress you're wearing."

"Oh, this?" she said deprecatingly. "Why, it was a present from my father." Now, by God, she had said the wrong thing. That suggestion would set Mr Edgecomb off with his precious sympathy again.

"Oh, my dear girl," he cried, conscience-stricken, "I am indeed sorry. I didn't mean to say anything — anything at all — that would hurt you. Really I didn't!"

Hurt! Sharon felt herself almost cold to the word. She was no more hurt than if she had never lost her father. She could barely recall him as a parent, but only as a grotesque and unreal being who had moved dimly through her life.

His passing had left her less grief-stricken than awed. To announce this fact would be damning, she knew, so she smiled gently and forgave Hilary Edgecomb, wishing to high heaven she had worn her green and lavender calico. It was cut low enough to reveal the soft, milk-white curve of her shoulders.

"I wanted to come on deck sooner so as not to miss the sunset," she announced to the two at the rail, "but it took me so long to hook myself up." She smiled at them a little embarrassedly and they looked down. They were gentlemen, she thought, perfect gentlemen and terribly dull. She felt sure that Eric would have flashed his eyes straight at her, impudently.

"Where's Mr March?" she asked in her soft Texas drawl. Hilary Edgecomb knocked his pipe against the heel of his boot as gently as if the pipe were made of crystal.

"I believe he's down in the hold telling the engineer what's wrong with the boilers."

"Oh, bother! I wanted to hear some more about the Navy."

"Young March is a nice enough chap," Edgecomb agreed amiably, "but his boundless enthusiasm for Mr Roosevelt annoys me. It shows a decided lack of intelligence — equal to that of, say, a congressman — to profess admiration for Mr Roosevelt's policies. Lord, what fools these mortals be!"

"It would seem only natural to me, inasmuch as Señor March is in the navy," Carlos

Menendez drawled, cautiously looking about as if afraid of offending someone. His voice was naturally mild and he always indicated his commas with a slight clearing of the throat.

"Mind you, I have nothing against the man myself," Edgecomb continued, twisting his cameo ring. "As the bard would say, 'the elements so mix'd in him that Nature might stand up, and say to all the world "This was a man!" ' I'm a republican too. Yet I think he wastes too much time arguing in favour of a bigger navy. He should stick to the civil service. Land's the thing these days, I tell you. Our frontier is ever pushing westward. We'll need troops to take care of that. That's where an army comes in. Isn't it so, Miss Douglass?"

"Why, yes — of course — I suppose so," Sharon murmured inattentively. She was wishing that Eric March would come up from the boiler-room. Why did men always have to be fascinated by machinery? But at least Eric wasn't talking politics all the time. She liked the yarns he told her of life aboard a battleship, some of which frankly shocked her. Somehow the shocking things always seemed the most interesting.

"I have yet to see a more stupid class than the military," said Carlos Menendez quietly, "save possibly the clergy."

"Suppose we leave the cloth out of this," Edgecomb growled. "I see no need to discuss religion."

"I don't either." Carlos humoured him. "I was merely using it as a point of comparison."

Menendez's voice, soft as the purring of a kitten, annoyed Hilary Edgecomb, who liked a man to speak up. A small man, who liked to call himself a Cuban patriot, Menendez was dark and wrinkled, with short, clipped hair. As a planter at Siboney he had lost everything because Spain exacted taxes far beyond his ability to pay. His hands were coarse and his knuckles resembled knots in tough hickory. Across his cheek and chin extended a white machete scar.

"I see nothing stupid about the army," said Edgecomb, the dilletante, whose knowledge of military affairs had been gleaned from a reading of Gibbon's *Decline and Fall.* "To my mind, the larger it is the better. I see your point though, Señor Menendez. As a Cuban you're dominated by the military despotism of Spain." Hilary Edgecomb had also absorbed *in toto* the various opinions of certain chiefs of staff as he had shorn them of their hair.

"Dominated? I believe crushed would be a better word," Menendez replied bitterly.

"Tommy-rot!" said Edgecomb, jocularly. "It isn't as bad as all that. I've been around a few places myself, and I say spare the rod and spoil the child. I think Spain should take any measures to quell an insurrection. You talk as though it were the second Dark Ages, Señor Menendez."

"It's Cuban slavery," answered Carlos doggedly.

"Oh, come off now. Slavery went out with the Civil War." Edgecomb laughed good-naturedly. "I propose we go below and I'll play you chess."

"Yes," Sharon agreed suddenly. "I do believe you exaggerate, Señor Menendez. Nothing could be as terrible as you describe."

During her wakeful hours on the ship she had heard of nothing except the struggles of Cuba against the mother country, Spain. Only when she had been with Eric had the talk flowed into different channels. "Soon," she reflected, "I'll know all I want to know about precious old Cuba. Uncle Clay and Aunt Phoebe will see to that. Well, I hope they haven't forgotten how to dance there." At that moment she felt that she would cheerfully give her life for one more glimpse of the broad floor in the ranch house living-room where she had so often danced reels and cotillions with her father's cow-hands.

"I'm afraid Miss Douglass is bored with our little dissertation on foreign affairs," observed Edgecomb.

"Fiddlesticks, Mr Edgecomb, I'm nothing of the sort," Sharon objected. "You make me feel a perfect simpleton."

It was then that Eric March came up the companion-way. His jeans were soiled with oil and grease; his brown hair hung uncombed into his eyes. Despite his appearance, a joyful smile lighted Sharon's face.

"Oh there you are," she cried buoyantly. "I was beginning to think you were going to be stand-offish and never come up from that stuffy old engine-room."

"The engine's far too big for this tub," Eric announced bluntly. Sharon admired his sureness. His voice was vibrant, young, strong. She liked the way he formed words with his lips — a little carelessly so that they sometimes cascaded from him. He had a habit of glancing at her every time he drove home a sentence as if his eyes sought approval for what he had spoken. They were brown eyes, spaced far apart and filled with a quiet good humour. When he laughed he threw his head back and laughed with his whole body. His hands were calloused from tarred rope. Slim of hip, he had the build of an expert swimmer.

All the boys of twenty-five in Sharon's past acquaintance had been cattle-men who knew a great deal about feed and branding and marketing. Eric was different, and she wished suddenly that he was going all the way to Cuba. She brought her mind back to what he was saying — he was still on the subject of the engine.

"If they don't put in a smaller one she'll eventually shake herself to pieces."

"That's what I've been thinking," agreed Edgecomb. He made a note of the fact on his mental cuff so that he might repeat it to his friends in Havana.

"It always makes me feel a trifle sad," Carlos sighed, "to see the day of the sailing vessel at its twilight. I believe there is nothing more beautiful than the sight of a ship with sails unfurled against the setting sun."

"But we must be practical, my dear Señor Menendez. This is 1894! Come along, there's just time for that game of chess before supper."

The two of them nodded to Sharon and Eric and descended to the lounge. Eric turned to Sharon. She looked up at him eagerly as he brushed the hair back from his eyes.

"We're passing the first of the Dry Tortugas," he said a bit gruffly. "I thought maybe you'd like to look at them through my glasses."

"I'd love to," she said. "Thanks for rescuing me from that session of history."

"We can see the islands better from the bridge. I think Captain Larribee will let us up there if I ask him."

He stepped aside and gave her his hand as she ascended the few steps to the long platform extending across the deck, above the rails, and just before the pilot house. She accepted it, thrilling to his warm touch, and noticing that his eyes were fixed on the cameo curve of her neck and the slight line of bare shoulder before it ended abruptly at the edge of black taffeta. She let fall her hand and lifted her skirts to ascend the steps, conscious of his searching gaze. "Come along, Mr March," she called out gaily, to hide her momentary confusion, "we mustn't keep the islands waiting." Then she stepped upon the bridge. The last sunlight splotched the deck like yellow paint and the deep blue of the Gulf Stream seemed deeper yet in the sunset. She gazed eagerly at the thin line of dark green land that lay off the bow on the starboard side, and her mind went back to the events that had led to this voyage across the Gulf and her meeting with this fascinating young sailor.

Two weeks previously, Sharon's father, Fred Douglass, had been shot and killed across a gaming table.

Standing now on the bridge of the *Grover Cleveland*, she was somewhat bewildered, though unafraid. Her future was insecure: yet, characteristic of her heritage, she had hastily said farewell to her past without regret. It was as if she was voyaging through space, uncertain of her destination and equally uncertain that she would ever return to her point of departure. At the moment she didn't much care, one way or the other.

Fred Douglass, a fabulous figure, had come from Saint Louis to take his part in the great "Oklahoma run", later drifting into Texas with his pockets full of greenbacks realized from the sale of his claim. During one of his infrequent visits to a place of worship he had met Grace Arms, a Sunday-school teacher, induced her to leave the service before it was finished, and married her the next day. Their first-born, a son, they lost by scarlet fever; then came Sharon. But before she was a year old her mother died of consumption.

Fred Douglass bought cattle — great herds of cattle — and sold them at fat prices to the Chicago markets. He strode about the town of Cardenas in great leather hip boots, a Prince Albert coat, and a flowing black tie. His splendid, ox-like body shouted with the lust for living. He carried a gun loosely strapped to his flank, though no one had ever heard of him using it. He and Sharon lived at the Pinto House where from childhood on she did the best she could to entertain her father's somewhat dubious friends.

With the profits from his shrewd cattle deals Fred Douglass bought land along the Rio Grande on which to breed more cattle. There he built a great rambling rancho, made great sums of money, and let slip casually through his fingers even greater sums — at the gaming tables.

On a certain Saturday evening in 1887 in the Apache Saloon he lost his entire fortune — herds, feed, everything — at faro, and by 3 A.M. on Sunday morning had won it all back again. Not a drop of perspiration was seen on his broad forehead in the meantime, nor a frown of apprehension. He came to be known along the back gambling alleys of the countryside as Lucky Fred Douglass.

Two weeks prior to Sharon's sailing he had made a trip north to Cardenas to put some cattle on the market. There he had the sudden impulse to play faro. He stepped into the Apache Saloon, his old haunt where as a youth he had earned his sobriquet.

At the bar were a number of his old friends, each with a foot on the rail and a hand on a hip pocket. The talk was loud and raucous, smoke hung heavy about the ceiling. Henry, the bartender, having served everyone present, leaned indolently beside one of the pink cupids which supported the fly-specked mirror, his hand idly patting Eros's rump.

As Henry recognized Fred and snapped to attention the others turned to see who had come in. "How're ya, Fred?" . . . "If it isn't Lucky!" . . . "How's ranchin' these days?" . . . "How many head o' cattle this time?"

"Three fingers of the old stand-by!" Fred called out to Henry, who had a large whisky glass ready. Gulping his drink and wandering over to the green felt-covered table in the corner, he said, "Deal me in, boys. I got a hankerin' to double my kale."

With a knowing nod the dealer proffered the cards to him. "Care to look over the deck, Lucky?" another asked.

"Hell! I don't need t'. I got a knack with cards. I could draw aces out of a stacked deck, even if there warn't a goddamn ace in th' pack."

Fred took his place and they played in silence for a few hands. Finally Fred leaned back in his chair. "Anyone in here interested in an A1 good cattle buy?" Thumbs in his arm-pits, his big hat pushed back, he awaited an answering bid. "I got some prize longhorns." That was Fred's way of starting a business deal.

"How many and how much?" inquired a quietly dressed gentleman at his left who was smoking a long cigar. "I might be interested." This unassuming man with a small clipped moustache and goatee was a stranger to Fred. He looked him over critically.

"I got five hundred head and my price is two hundred a head."

"We might do some business, Mr Douglass, but I haven't the money with me. Here's what —"

"You know my name, eh?"

"Doesn't everyone in these parts know you?" The stranger maintained his quiet dignity.

"All right. Spit out your proposition."

"I'll give you a five-year franchise for free transportation of your stock on my railroad. That's my proposition."

"Your railroad?" Fred snorted in contempt.

"The C. S. & T. You've heard of me I believe — Morgan Graham?"

"By God, yes!" Fred exploded. "You're th' sheep-herdin' bastard that's been chargin' me sky-high rates fer haulin' my beef. I been wantin' t' meet you." His broad grin showed that he meant no offence.

The two shook hands as the other men and a scantily clad woman, the Apache's singer of bar-room ballads, gathered about to watch Fred Douglass put over another deal.

"Tell you what I'll do," Fred said, oblivious to everyone in the room except Mr Graham. "Bein' a gamblin' man first and foremost I usually let th' fifty-two pasteboards do my decidin' fer me. Are you willin' t' leave it up t' them?"

Morgan Graham smoothed his moustache and caressed his goatee, his very finger-tips deliberating. He looked at the man who was nearly twice his size and gave a quick glance at the onlookers.

"What's your proposition?" he asked with caution in his tone.

"I put up all my land, all my grain an' feed, all my shares in the Chicago Packing House, and every head of cattle I own agin' your railroad — and I mean outright ownership down to the last tie and spike. Th' winner is th' one that draws th' highest card in this deck."

Tense waiting followed for what seemed minutes. Morgan Graham stopped stroking his goatee. Apparently no one was even daring to breathe when he looked at Lucky Fred Douglass and said, "On one draw?"

"Ain't you game?" Fred taunted. "I'm damned sick 'n' tired of linin' your pockets. A five-year franchise wouldn't do me no good five years from now. With your railroad and chargin' th' rates you do I ought t' be a millionaire by that time. I been hankerin' t' travel over my own tracks anyway. How about it, Graham, are y' game or not?"

"I'm game, all right, but I want it in writing.

And I want a new deck." The ligaments in Morgan Graham's throat were taut, the muscles in front of his ears twitched, his eyelids narrowed.

"Bring me a piece of paper and a new pack of cards," Fred called to Henry, and there was a noticeable movement among the spectators. The tension was released. A fellow gambler handed out an order book from which Fred tore a sheet, and by the time Henry was on hand with the paper and the deck of cards the terms were written and signed. "This ain't a new deck," Fred roared at Henry. "Bring me a new deck, you she-goat!" Henry grumbled and found a deck which was satisfactory to both parties.

Fred tossed them on the table and said to Graham. "You first!" Graham cast aside his half-smoked cigar, ran his hand smoothly down the pack of cards, spread them fanwise and turned a card face up which had been buried in the middle. It was the jack of diamonds.

"Draw your ace on that," he challenged confidently.

Fred Douglass chose the card next to the one Graham had drawn. It was the ten of spades. He turned a sickly colour and rose unsteadily to his feet. "Let me see that deck." Leaning on one hand he reached for the cards with the other but a quicker hand than his obliged and there all the cards lay, face up.

"It's all right, Lucky," said one of the men. And another corroborated the statement. Lucky himself could see it. Beads of sweat stood out on his forehead like great drops of dew. The reckless self-assurance of his youth had betrayed him. The luck he thought would never give out had failed. He stood rocking slightly before the table. He blinked his eyes. Suddenly he seemed old. All eyes were upon him as he fumbled hesitantly at his hip.

"Look out!" Henry cried. "He packs a gun!"

But Morgan Graham was already pulling a six-shooter from his own hip. It barked twice, swift and sharp. The woman screamed. Fred stared at her absurdly for a trice, swayed, and closed his eyes. His magnificent body crashed to the floor. In his hand he clutched, not a gun, but the polka-dot handkerchief he had taken from his hip pocket.

"Sweet Jesus! He only wanted to wipe the sweat from his face," a man said grimly.

"I — I thought —" Graham faltered, then spoke with desperate sureness. "You men are witnesses. You saw me shoot in what I was given to believe was self-defence. You've witnessed that I won the property too." He grasped the signed agreement from another player's hand and flourished it in their faces. Leaving Lucky Fred Douglass to the ministrations of those who were willing to help if they only could, Morgan Graham hastened away to collect his debts.

And the heritage left to Sharon was entirely characteristic of her father. One home in which she could no longer reside because it belonged to a gambler just one card luckier than her father had been, a score of debts that she could never hope to pay, and a confusion of memories — nights in railway cars, the acrid odour of burnt hide on freshly branded cattle, the tinny and discordant music in Texas saloons, and a blurred portrait of her father as he strode through all this heritage-pattern in his hip-boots and Prince Albert coat like an off-colour thread in a tapestry.

Sharon's only living relative was Clayton Arms, her mother's brother whom she had never seen. She wired him in Cuba, where he and Aunt Phoebe lived, and the reply came back promptly, with enough money for her passage, but little more than enough. Having no children of their own, Uncle Clay explained, they would be glad to have her come and live with them. She wondered if they would really be glad, or if her American ways would shock them. And idly she wondered if Cuba would be as bloody as everyone tried to picture it.

"Captain Larribee says it's all right for us to stay up here for a while," Eric grinned, emerging from the pilot house, "providing you join him for supper."

"I think that can be arranged," Sharon murmured while she watched the bow of the *Grover Cleveland* cleave the water into two great walls like the parting of the Red Sea for the flight out of Egypt. "I love to watch the water, Mr March.

It makes me want to go in swimming."

"You're a strange girl," said Eric simply.

"Why do you say that, Mr March? Am I?"

"You sure are! You're different. You've got real nerve. And suppose you get used to calling me Eric. I'm used to hearing it. And I'm going to call you Sharon whether you permit me to or not."

"You're very bold." Sharon tried to be very severe.

"Yes, and you like me that way, don't you? I haven't been fooled for a minute, not since we first met. That's why I think you're pretty fine. Most girls shrink away in their petticoats and expect to be coaxed all the time."

"Do they really?" This was hard for Sharon to imagine. "But how do you know so much about me?"

"Captain Larribee and I have talked about you behind your back. I know that you're facing a new world and that you aren't making any fuss about it. I know how much courage you've got and I like you for it."

"He told you why I'm going to Havana?"

"Yes. I made him tell me all he knew. I think you're a very brave girl, the way you've held up after the death of your father."

"The truth is, I hardly knew him, Eric. He never was at home very much. I guess he wasn't suited to being both ma and pa to me. I'm wearing black simply out of respect for convention. He'd blow clear across the Rio if he thought I'd wear black for him."

"And your mother?"

"Ma was a lunger," Sharon replied bluntly. "I never knew her."

"Tell me something more about your father." Eric was soberly sympathetic. "Judging by you I wager he was a pretty swell fellow."

"He was a gambler, Eric. He gave me everything when he had it to give but he threw it all away on the turn of a card. Even his life. That's all I can honestly say for him. It was his way."

"Do you stay in Havana or — ?"

"I go to Santiago. That's where my uncle and aunt live."

"Should I write to you there?" Eric asked.

"Do you want to?" Sharon countered.

"It would be next best to talking to you and I do like a good listener. I know ships and I know the Navy and maybe I don't know much else, but I never get tired of talking about them. It's been swell meeting someone who doesn't get tired of listening." He took her hand in his and she let it lie there, her small white hand looking smaller still across his large, calloused fingers as he studied the shapeliness of it. Abruptly he lifted it to his lips and kissed the backs of her fingers a little roughly.

"Why did you do that?" Sharon withdrew her hand.

"Because I wanted to. And what I want to do, I go about doing."

She turned her shoulders to him and looked

out across the water. Land stretched long and low in the Gulf. Strange tropical vegetation, lush and tangled, was faintly luminous in the gathering dusk. Overhead a pelican dipped in wide circles about the ship's masts, and a flying-fish leaped and sailed across the sea in a long, fast glide.

"Loggerhead Key," Eric explained, pointing to the land. "That's our southernmost lighthouse there in the Dry Tortugas. Here! Look through the glasses." A tall, slender, white shaft rose from the water's edge and stood bleakly silhouetted against the rose-tinted sky. Near the top a railing encircled it, and through the glasses Sharon could dimly discern the figure of a man rising and stooping at regular intervals.

"That's old Bayard Cole," Eric informed her. "He's filling the lamps with kerosene. Next he'll put them in front of the reflectors in the top of the tower and light the wicks. There's an engine down in the base that makes the lamps turn. I see old Bayard about twice a year. He's a queer old coot with only one leg. A barracuda got the other one."

Sharon shuddered. Eric casually placed his arm about her shoulders and drew her close. Accepting his gesture of affection, she let her head rest on his chest. His chin touched her hair, the sweet and heady fragrance engulfing him in a wave of emotion. His words were scarcely more than a breath:

"We'll be in Key West before midnight,

Sharon. I don't have to report to the commodore until six o'clock in the morning. The *Grover Cleveland* doesn't sail until ten. I'd like to take you to midnight supper and for a walk on the beach. Just the two of us."

Sharon was silent.

"Say yes," Eric urged, his voice just above a whisper but vibrant with pleading. Sharon only turned her head a bit as if to listen more intently. Eric's words came fast and compelling. "We're young, Sharon, and it's right that we pair off. You've got to pack into a couple of hours, when you're on a sea trip, what you'd take two months to do on land." Sharon drew his hands from about her waist and, still close to him, turned and let him embrace her candidly; yet she did not speak, and Eric sensed that she was not quite ready with her answer.

"We may never see each other again — at least not for a long while. We owe ourselves this one last evening together. I know a little place where we can get food you've never tasted before. It's in a palm grove where the Bahamans have settled."

Sharon twisted away and leaned against the rail again, Eric's arm about her waist, her hand on his, caressing it thoughtfully; letting him know without any words that she must have a little time to say yes, that she knew what yes might mean.

A mischievous breeze that had come out to play when the sun was gone teased the water into little white crests and tossed fine, cool spray into Sharon's face. One by one the lamps in the beacon on Loggerhead Key were lighted. As it turned, the broad beam of light, intensified by the thousand reflectors, swept across the water bringing into radiance the tiny whitecaps, making them sparkle like myriads of rhinestones. Sharon looked up at Eric and found him waiting for her answer, his eyes serious. With her own eyes and the pleading of her face she asked him for one more word — perhaps of assurance.

"Come on," he said, tightening his arm about her. "Don't be afraid."

"All right, Eric. I will. I'll go with you. Why pretend? I like you very much and I like what you said a few moments ago. What I want to do from now on I'm going to go about doing."

Both his arms were about her. "Bully girl, Sharon," he murmured softly in the darkness. And again after kissing her, "Bully girl."

In the distance, dark, grim, and foreboding, Fort Jefferson on Garden Key squatted in the ocean like a giant watch-dog of the sea. It seemed to be keeping vigil over the two.

Sharon and Eric, together with the other passengers, were gathered in the saloon listening to tales of the sea as only Captain Larribee could tell them. No one thought of retiring, for they were due in Key West in half an hour. Captain Larribee was a stunted, corpulent man who seemed as broad as he was long. Perhaps his mutton-chop whiskers contributed to this effect. His neck was so creased and burnt it looked like Morocco leather. He seldom buttoned his coat because it was so much more comfortable unbuttoned. His florid face and blue-veined nose gave the impression that he was a heavy drinker. Captain Larribee was not a heavy drinker — only a steady one.

"No more stories to-night!" He rose ponderously. "Time to go on deck and see the sights." The guests followed his lead, some briskly, some reluctantly. Hilary Edgecomb donned his ulster. Even in these near-tropics the nights were too chilly for comfort. Eric placed his pea-jacket over Sharon's shoulders. It had a strong, sweaty, masculine odour about it and this, combined with the pungent aroma of pipe and tobacco, set her blood tingling.

The soft yellow light of gas-lamps on the pier spread a diffused glow over the pitch waters, and lanterns bobbed about like fire-flies.

"Jove!" Edgecomb exclaimed between his teeth. The embers of his pipe glowed dull and warm in the darkness.

"It is a splendid sight at that," said Carlos Menendez who happened to be standing near.

Although Edgecomb had made his exclamation to no one in particular he was pleased to elaborate on the scene when he found that Menendez was there to listen. "There is nothing quite so beautiful as harbour lights at night — dotting the sea in the distance like carelessly scattered diamonds on black velvet." His voice rose as his fervour heightened. "I am reminded of Keats — 'A thing of beauty is a joy for ever'. Or is it? Beauty is such a transient thing — or perhaps I should say, we observers are such transients to beauty."

"Perhaps one sees so much of loveliness" — Carlos Menendez looked towards the harbour, yet he was seeing far beyond it, not caring about an audience — "that each successive thing of beauty drowns out the memory of those seen in the past. Cuba was once a beautiful island, but it is not a joy for ever."

Eric dropped his hand from the railing and his fingers brushed Sharon's in the darkness. She gave him her hand, "Careful now . . . you mustn't lose your head . . . you may never see him again . . . better shut your eyes to his smile . . . remember, he said it himself, you may never see him again . . . don't lose your head." The warning pulsed and throbbed and beat upon her consciousness like a legion of drums.

"I've seen this sight often," Eric said. "What do you think of it, Sharon?"

"I like it." The very simplicity of her answer showed more appreciation of the view than did all of Hilary Edgecomb's panegyric. Sharon had always been brief in her speech, because her thoughts were concise. Her curtness sometimes caused older people to regard her as ill-mannered, but it wasn't that. She simply had a wholesome contempt for empty phrases.

Eric, unable to express himself eloquently at any time, was a little self-conscious among flowery speakers like Hilary Edgecomb. They annoyed him. And the soft-spoken visionary and Cuban patriot, Carlos Menendez, puzzled him. Usually when Eric tried to say something colourful to a girl he ended by being gruff and getting himself misunderstood. But Sharon never failed to perceive the essence of what he was trying to express, the true feeling his gruffness obscured. Sharon and he spoke the same language and it was not always a language of words.

Eric brought Sharon's hand up to his chest and held it a little tighter. She smiled and gave his hand an answering pressure.

As if the enchantment of the harbour lights and lanterns was not enough, the moon rose, large and luminous. Eric whispered to Sharon, "Did you ever see such a moon?"

"Never! It's three times as large as the Texas moon."

"Wait until you see it over the water from the beach!"

Sharon's answering smile disappeared and she dropped her head. Carlos Menendez was watching them closely. She just noticed it. But she did not move away from Eric. Together they gazed at the harbour. The engines were quieter now, and the distance between land and boat was steadily diminishing.

Hilary Edgecomb, tapping his pipe against the

rail, watched the embers fall into the water and die. "I want to spend a few hours ashore," he announced. "I may wander down to the sponge fleet if I can locate it."

"I can easily get a Bahaman to take you there," Eric said. "I've offered to show Miss Douglass some of Key West by night and if you care to go ashore with us —"

"I'll be glad to join you," Edgecomb agreed, a little too readily. "And can you direct me to an eating place at this time of night?"

"I'm taking Miss Sharon to La Mantilla. It isn't very fancy, but it's interesting. It's in the Bahaman quarter where the natives speak with a British accent. Their 'a's' are broader than their shoulders."

"That's mighty decent of you, March. I'll meet you here before we dock." Turning, he descended the companion-way with the others.

"I'll have to go below too and gather up some of my gear," Eric said to Sharon. "I'll come back on deck as soon as I've finished. That's a promise." His heavy pea-jacket had a tendency to slip down from her shoulders and, arranging it higher for her, he gripped her arms for an expressive moment before their eyes said to each other, "Yes, a promise." Eric turned on his heel and ran down the companion-way, Sharon's gaze following him and lingering there after he was gone.

Carlos Menendez was the only other passenger left on deck. Turning to him, Sharon asked, "You're going to Havana too, aren't you?"

"Yes. I'm returning home," he answered softly, "where I belong." He strolled nearer to her. "It's good to be young, isn't it? I wish I were as young as your friend, Señor March. I could do so much more." He laughed at himself in his quiet way. "But I can do nothing at all by standing still and yearning for my lost youth."

Sharon suddenly realized that she knew almost nothing of the country which was so soon to be her home. The shipboard conversations she had heard were tiresome — so many words and so little substance. Now she recognized Carlos Menendez as the one person on the boat who could paint a true picture for her. Whom could she ask more logically about Cuba? A little ashamed of her earlier indifference, she felt that this was an excellent occasion to make up for it.

"Tell me something about Cuba!" Her request was so abrupt that Menendez was a little startled, but there was genuine eagerness in her voice.

"Are you really interested, Señorita Douglass? I was under the impression earlier this afternoon that you were — how do you Americans put it — bored? Isn't that the word?"

"Yes, frankly I was — with Mr Edgecomb's views. But I'm travelling to Cuba and I really ought to know something about it, don't you think? We have a few moments now and if you would be so kind —"

"Ah, if I could only tell you what is in my heart in but a few moments; Señor Edgecomb will learn of it in a short time, I fear. My fellow Cubans are in a sorry state, but these futile attempts to win independence will not last for ever. Some day they will be successful! It will all happen so quickly — like powder going off with a direct match and not a fuse. Señor Edgecomb's restaurant will have a hard time prospering in such a state as we have now. The taxes will be so exorbitant."

"But the Cubans — why do they rebel all the time? I have been told they may vote, that there are no slaves. Isn't that what Mr Edgecomb said?"

"The Government is a military despotism, Señorita Douglass. I'm afraid you don't understand exactly what that means. Let me explain it to you."

"Do please!" Sharon rested her elbows on the railing and held Eric's coat close around her. Only for a fleeting moment now and then did she let her mind race ahead to the moon from the beach. She followed the dissertation on Cuban history with close concentration.

"You see, away back in the early eighteen hundreds, when the first wars of independence were being fought and won and lost and won again, Spain found that all that remained to her were two islands in the Caribbean — sole remnants of the once proud and mighty empire created by her early conquistadors. These were Cuba and Puerto Rico. Suppose we say that Spain was an over-maternal parent, unwise and lacking understanding; and suppose we say that Cuba and Puerto Rico were two naughty children, not really bad, but needing proper handling. Do you follow me?"

Sharon nodded. "Quite easily, Señor Menendez."

"Mother Spain learned nothing from the revolt of her other children who at maturity wanted to sever the apron strings. We know that children must go alone into the world and stand upon their own feet if they are to be strong and have character."

"But you're humanizing land, Señor."

"Is not a country made up of humanity, Señorita Douglass? Spain continued to be an unwise mother to the two remaining children of her brood. She was proud, and because of her pride her parenthood was aristocratic. When she exploited the natives of Cuba and Puerto Rico, economically and politically, she honestly believed she was behaving like a mother who takes candy from her children because she does not think it is good for them before dinner. Only in this case the children never got the dinner," Carlos added bitterly.

"Why do you speak to me in parables, Señor Menendez?"

"Do you think you would like my story,

Señorita Douglass, if I gave you cold facts?"

"Perhaps not, but I'd have a greater respect for the storyteller."

The Cuban gave her a grateful look. "It is hard to believe that a girl so young can be so sensible, even in these times. Very well, I shall give you the facts — unpleasant as they may be.

"Spain's aim has always been to collect, simply yet ruthlessly, silver, gold, tobacco, sugarcane, and all other products from her colonies for one purpose only — to make the mother country rich. She was not at all interested in helping her islands to prosper for their own sake. But if you do not help the source to prosper, the source cannot continue to pay back dividends for long. It is the age-old law of supply and demand. One must not kill the goose that lays the golden eggs.

"Could you blame any colony for being discontented with such treatment — especially when this unstable system of economy is coupled with the arrogant and overbearing manner of the Spanish officials sent to govern and to collect the blood from this very dry turnip? I give thanks a thousandfold, Señorita Douglass, for my opportunity in America, for my chance to study at Harvard, for my early introduction to Karl Marx."

Having never heard of Karl Marx, Sharon kept discreetly silent. In the darkness the boat glided ever nearer to the dock at Key West. But the life on the pier and the movements of the black stevedores no longer held Sharon's interest. She turned her back to the water and the nearing lights on shore.

The narrator continued. "Please do not misconstrue my words, Señorita. For Cuba is still beautiful and haunting and full of exotic mystery. You will discover that for yourself. It rises like an exquisite emerald from the sea. But this charming place has always been victimized and exploited — century after century, decade upon decade. The Spanish officers — those whom Señor Edgecomb would hold so dearly to his heart — have monopolized every position of authority, have stolen from and beaten the natives, besides forcing them to endure every manner of indignity. Can you honestly blame these people — my own fellow Cubans — for revolting?"

"I didn't understand before," Sharon cried quickly. "But please go on. If you think me stupid, instruct me; if you find me eager for facts, give them to me."

"You seem to be a very rare young woman, one who wants to know the why and how of things. Maybe I am a fool to enlighten you; but as you are going to live in Cuba, to be forewarned is perhaps most wise.

"My Cuba — soon to be your Cuba — has been governed for a long time by a Captain-General, assisted of course by many well-paid officials, all sent there by the Spanish Crown. There is no self-government. I'm afraid that by this time a Cuban would not know what to do with such a luxury. These Spaniards possess virtually unlimited and absolute power. Our taxes are exorbitant, and none of the revenue is used for social work or improvements or education — not even for medical service. It is a thoroughly corrupt administration.

"Spain finally did one good thing in freeing the negro slaves. They comprised about one-third of the population. But she has always hampered rather than helped the development of sugarcane, Cuba's chief source of wealth. Spain has acted the fool by imposing high duties on American exports into the islands until she provoked America into placing high duties on Cuban sugar. In that blundering way we lost our best market."

"My uncle, Clayton Arms, owns a sugar plantation," Sharon volunteered. "It is with him that I am to make my home."

"Then I am sure, señorita, that he will find much to tell you that I, having been absent so long, cannot." At Sharon's serious and somewhat troubled look Carlos smiled. "Now I have granted what you asked. You will probably forget most of it, because you are a young girl and there will be men like Señor March to occupy your thoughts. That is but right. However, not many more years will pass before unbelievable hell will break out in my land. It is bound to happen. Remember France and the heads that fell? Perhaps you will be an important part of it all. I am not often given to prophecy, but I predict that before another quarter of a century has slipped by, women will have become a very important factor in the political scheme of things."

Eric came bounding up the companion-way and approached them, his canvas bag slung carelessly across his shoulders.

"But one important thing," Carlos cautioned rapidly. "Even though I ask you not to forget what I said, I urge you to forget my name — even me. Guard your tongue well against the name Carlos Menendez. Please!" With this he slipped quietly away, spoke to Eric as they passed, and disappeared down the companion-way.

Eric stood beside Sharon as she looked out towards the shore again. "He's a funny bird," he remarked. "What was he spilling so many words about?"

"Oh just — things," Sharon replied cryptically.

On the deck the crew was now busy with the ropes. The hoarse shouts of deck-hands floated up to them, mingled now and then with a hearty oath. Everywhere was motion. From the bridge Captain Larribee bellowed his orders. The *Grover Cleveland* slid gently into the slip, her sides nudging the piles, while ropes creaked and strained and timbers groaned. A strong, cold wind sprang up and lashed across the island. Signboards over the shops and hotels swung violently back and forth, casting weird shadows on the ground and the white stucco walls, creaking and groaning like crude doors on rusty hinges. The palm fronds rustled and crossed each other like ghostly scissor blades, making an ominous crackling sound against a background of whispering sighs — an eerie, phantom symphony, played with skilled, sharp fingers of wind on a harp of palms and tamaracks. To Edgecomb this cacophony was the chanting of a thousand unfriendly tongues.

Sharon admired the sure way Eric strode down the street, turning familiarly as they came to cross-roads. She clung to his arm, running a little and hopping now and then in order to match his broad stride. To Sharon the discord of the tropical night was a prelude to adventure. A city girl would have been frightened, but not Sharon, who had ridden through many a Texas north-wester — not Sharon with Eric at her side.

The three of them had left the ship together, and it was Eric's idea to explore the deserted streets of Key West for an hour. Sharon's enthusiasm overrode Edgecomb's growing reluctance. He might have followed Eric's directions for finding the sponge fleet himself, but he wanted to see the café Eric and Sharon were headed for — if they ever got there. The city nauseated him, and there was an air of melancholy and desolation about it that depressed his fastidious spirit. He wondered how Miss Douglass could tolerate it.

There she was, walking into the wind as if she

actually enjoyed it, and not caring at all that she made an odd spectacle in her black taffeta and Eric's pea-jacket. There was something about her own velvet cape being a treasured gift from her father, and Eric had insisted that it be left in safety on the boat. It might be stolen from her very shoulders, Eric had warned.

Walking behind the pair and watching closely lest he stumbled into one of the frequent holes in the board sidewalk, the disgruntled Edgecomb concluded definitely that "the new woman of the nineties" was a lamentable creature. He feared that Sharon Douglass was all too typical of this species. They were unafraid to speak their minds, the presumptuous females. They possessed social consciousness — alarming. They talked of getting the vote — ridiculous. In short, they were striving to place themselves on a level with man, and that in itself was little less than disgraceful. It was a reckless forfeiture of woman's sacred right to wear skirts and be dominated. A woman should be a fragile, Dresden china figure, to be delicately handled — and kept in her place.

In Eric's own good time, and with Sharon still enjoying the walk in the wind, the three arrived at La Mantilla in the Bahaman quarter. Situated beneath tremendously tall Royal palms on the edge of the Atlantic, it was a low, rambling structure of rough boards, thatched with straw. There was no floor; patrons walked and spat upon the uneven ground. The walls were half open to the sky and the salt mists that blew in from the sea. The driftwood tables were sturdy, but rough, and there was no sign of any napery.

Edgecomb sat down heavily with an audible sigh of relief, Eric and Sharon regarding him humorously. He was out of breath and out of sorts and their attitude only irked him the more. It was not until he had regained his breath and laid his ulster on a bench close by — well within his range of vision — that he took a good look at the café. It was the filthiest place he had ever seen. An odour of food and the incessant clatter of dishes and cutlery came from the partly closed door at the rear, most of the patrons were slatternly natives. In Havana he, Edgecomb, would show those Cubans what a real café should look like. He would insist on cleanliness above all things.

"What time is it?" he asked Eric.

"One o'clock." Eric glanced briefly at his watch and back to Sharon. He was enjoying her reaction to the place — that look of adventure. Novelty was the main feature of La Mantilla at the moment — sanitation could be taken up later.

"One o'clock," she laughed. "This is fun! I don't suppose I'll be staying up until one o'clock when I'm at Uncle Clayton's. I don't care if—"

"But," Edgecomb cut in disapprovingly, "I think we — you and I — had better be getting back to the ship."

Eric laughed away that idea. "Miss Douglass

has no intention of going back to the ship — until she is ready to go."

"And I surely won't be ready until I've had something to eat. I'm enchanted with La Mantilla."

The late patrons were leaving. Eric looked for a waiter and, cupping his hands, called, "Manuel! Manuel! How about some service?"

"You know the waiter?" Sharon asked, her eyes glowing.

"Manuel is my good friend. I eat here often." Eric placed his index fingers between his lips and whistled shrilly. Edgecomb, clapping his hands to his ears, gave a pantomime of patient despair.

A young man, dark skinned and with jet black hair, came from the kitchen and looked blandly in their direction. Instantly his face came to life, and before he had finished speaking he was at the table. "Señor March! It is good to set eyes upon you again. You had a happy furlough?"

"Very happy!" said Eric, still looking at Sharon.

Manuel grinned his broadest. "Ah, señor. I understand."

The incongruity of Manuel's speech and appearance was astounding. He spoke like a gentleman from London greeting a friend at his fashionable club in Half Moon Street. He wore a pair of trousers which, under the layers of grease-encased dirt, must once have been white. The jacket seemed to be made of the same material and it was white — that is, the back of it was fairly white. It lay open in front, exposing the dark, glistening chest and belly, smooth and, to Edgecomb, quite revolting. About his waist was knotted a flowered bandana.

"How about something to eat?" Eric asked. "We're hungry as all hell. We've walked up our appetites coming out here."

Manuel grinned again showing the straightest, whitest teeth Edgecomb had ever seen. But they did not redeem him for being so slovenly. He promised to bring meals for three immediately, and walked back to the kitchen, treading cat-like on the balls of his bare brown feet.

The supper was excellent. Even Edgecomb conceded that it was palatable, though Sharon had to tease him into admitting even that. Following a refreshing drink which, Eric explained was made of orange juice and coco-nut, there were generous portions of grouper fish fried in cornmeal, sweet potatoes candied in brown sugar and molasses, and black-eyed peas which to Sharon tasted like peanuts. There was no dessert, but later Manuel brought in small slices of dark bread thickly spread with guava jelly. Edgecomb was amazed at the number of them Sharon ate. Hers was no Dresden doll appetite.

Eric told his guests something of the history of Key West and of the many Bahamans, like Manuel, who lived there. He pointed out the direction of the biggest cigar factory, one place they had not included in their tour on foot, his naval base, and the *Grover Cleveland.*

"I'm glad you know where it is," Edgecomb observed tartly. "That's more than I know." The last patron had slouched out leaving the three of them alone in the beastly place. Why had he wanted to see the sponge fleet or any of Key West at night? Why hadn't he stayed sanely and comfortably on the boat? He felt grimy just from being in this hell-hole. "Is there a place where I can wash my hands?" he asked gingerly.

"Sure. Right through the kitchen. Manuel will show you."

The sight confronting Edgecomb when he pushed open the kitchen door made him clap his hand to his mouth. With a manly effort he gained control over his rebellious stomach and asked Manuel for some soap and a towel. Out of the wild disorder Manuel brought forth and graciously extended to Edgecomb a greasy sliver of soap and a ragged towel which could never have been near a laundry.

The sink to which Manuel directed him so obligingly was filled with utensils and unwashed dishes. Flies feasted industriously on the clinging, dried particles of food. The putrescent odour from the pump nearly brought about the upheaval that his first sight of the kitchen had threatened to start. He moistened his finger-tips and dabbed them on the towel, and not forgetting that he was a gentleman, thanked Manuel as he returned to the dining hall.

Eric and Sharon were gone. His ulster lay where he had left it. He grabbed it as he hurried to the door, looking frantically in every direction. "Damn that sailor!" It didn't occur to him that Sharon could have any part in the despicable affair. Only a sailor would lure a woman off after midnight in a town like this. But if he had any concern for Sharon's safety it was quickly dispelled in his own anxiety. The dilemma in which he found himself was something serious to contemplate. The things that could happen to him! Robbery, assault — how was he going to find his way? Damn that sailor! God damn that sailor!

Captain Larribee had gone ashore when the others did. As always when in Key West, he visited Arita in her little cabaña. Arita was a dark-skinned, black eyed Cuban girl who made a precarious living from the sale of conch shells and coral bouquets which she gathered on the beach. Their relationship was uncomplicated. She asked her *capitan* no questions; he told her nothing. But whenever the *Grover Cleveland* docked Arita was the first person Captain Larribee sought out.

Returning shortly after two, he had lain down on his bunk, fully clothed. Drifting into a warm, pleasant drowsiness he beheld the enticing Arita before him. Nude, except for a wreath of hibiscus blossoms in her hair, she danced and whirled and beckoned, coaxing him to join her. It was a dance of primitive abandon and the little imp, now ignoring her *capitan,* gave herself to it completely, every muscle of her lithe bronze body eloquent of ecstasy.

But abruptly she wheeled upon him, stamping furious feet. Captain Larribee stirred into semi-consciousness. Arita vanished. The stamping sounds continued. Were those engines playing up again? He awakened fully to a pounding on his door. Cursing and muttering, he flung himself heavily out of his bunk and opened the door. It was Edgecomb. And on the bridge below was Thor Edmundson, the first mate, with a feebly flickering lantern in his hand. He had a firm grip on the black arm of Manuel who, bowing and deferential, was saying between his white even teeth, "I bring the white señor back now like boss sailor says." Considering his obligation fulfilled, he jerked away from the mate, backed down the companion-way, scurried across the lower deck, and fled down the gangplank into the darkness.

"Jove!" muttered Edgecomb. "What an experience! What an experience, captain! I felt I simply had to get somebody up and tell him about it. I tried waking Señor Menendez, but he doesn't seem to be about. Hope I haven't disturbed you."

Disgruntled, Larribee invited him in and let him have the old-fashioned wicker rocking-chair that always travelled with him. From a raffia-covered bottle, which he took from the locker beneath his berth, he poured his passenger a short glass of brandy. Edgecomb gulped it down, made a wry face and settled himself in the chair. As he told his harrowing experience he twisted at his cameo ring.

Once fully awakened Larribee cast aside his grouchiness. "I rather imagine a Northerner would consider a walk at night through the streets of Key West something of an experience." He poured himself a glass of brandy. Perhaps he needed it more than Edgecomb did. As he drank it down he loosened another button of his waistcoat.

Edgecomb was painstaking in his report of the long walk and the midnight meal at La Mantilla. He spared the captain no sordid detail of the imbroglio — the filth, the food, the dirty sink, the foul odours. Captain Larribee dared not even smile, though he was tempted to laugh in his visitor's face. He could easily imagine Edgecomb the fastidious at La Mantilla and he wondered if Eric took him there for a joke. The captain was enough of a trencherman to ignore the surroundings in which he ate if the food was good. He had often eaten at La Mantilla, sometimes alone, sometimes with Arita, and he liked the food, and did not question its preparation.

Edgecomb, however, could not dismiss a deplorable condition so lightly. Nor could he toss off his rage at that damned sailor for deserting him at such a god-forsaken hour in such a god-forsaken place. He said, with an overtone of polite sarcasm, "I am alarmed about Miss Douglass, Captain Larribee. Though undoubtedly she is in good hands with Mr March, nevertheless she is a young girl and there is no telling what might happen to her on the streets of Key West."

"Oh, I don't know," Larribee replied, enjoying the bouquet of his second glass of brandy. "I think we can trust the girl with young March. I'm a seafaring man myself and I'll admit my mind's been saturated with brine for twenty years, salted down, so to speak; but I like to think I'm a pretty shrewd judge of people. You're just overwrought, Edgecomb, because March played a prank on you. But I gather what you mean."

He tried to stifle a yawn, but viewing the situation from various angles he began to regard it with some seriousness. Apparently Miss Douglass was with March. And as far as he knew, that was her choice. He did not imagine that the girl had been coerced or kidnapped. She was probably having the time of her life. With what the pair might be occupied he didn't allow himself to be concerned. After all, he was responsible for the safety of his passengers — only on ship of course — but still —

It was annoying. He wished Edgecomb had wakened someone else to tell his troubles to. He wanted to go back to sleep. Dawn came damned soon enough without getting up to meet it.

"I'd have looked for her myself," said Edgecomb self-righteously, "but it would have seemed as if I was pursuing her — God forbid! And then that greasy nigger — Manuel, I think

March called him — insisted on bringing me back to the ship through the darkest and dirtiest alley-ways. His English accent may be very impressive to some, but I tell you frankly, I was afraid for my life every minute. You're in a responsible position, captain, and I think you ought to take measures to assure us of Miss Douglass's safety."

"I can't think it's as bad as you infer, Mr Edgecomb." Captain Larribee rose, smiling. He took a long Tampa cigar from an oak humidor, clipped off the tip with his pocket knife and rolled it about in his mouth. He thought, "I wish this whited sepulchre would take a walk around the deck." He said, "Tell you what I'll do. I'll relieve Edmundson from his watch and send him out to look for Miss Douglass. He knows these native haunts like a book."

Edgecomb, rising, give the captain a look of deepest gratitude and followed him out on to the bridge. But he would have been shocked out of his English tweeds had he known what the captain was thinking at that moment.

The first grey streaks of dawn were lighting the eastern sky like strata of mother-of-pearl when Edmundson returned with the lost Sharon. She was in great spirits and granted a warm smile to both Edgecomb and Captain Larribee, who sat over black coffee and wafers in the saloon.

"I found her walking along the beach by herself, sir," the first mate reported. "I'll return to duty now."

Edgecomb was relieved to see Sharon and, truthfully, Larribee was too.

"Coffee, Miss Douglass?" asked Larribee.

"Yes, do join us, Miss Douglass," urged Edgecomb. "You must be tired and chilled. Some hot coffee will do you good. We were a little worried about you. Are you sure you're perfectly all right? You're rather young to be staying up the entire night."

Sharon choked back a ripple of amusement. All night! Up all night! She felt like telling these two men that being up all night was nothing to her. She felt like telling them that many were the times she had ridden the lines of her father's ranch, alone and out of doors for days, and with no companion save her horse. But she held her tongue.

"Why, of course I'm all right, Mr Edgecomb. I'm splendid. I'm sorry you were worried. And you didn't need to send Mr Edmundson to hunt for me. No coffee, thank you. I think I'll retire now. I'll probably be up in time for dinner."

As she turned from them Edgecomb spoke confidentially to the captain. "I certainly was disappointed in Mr March." His words halted Sharon at the door. "I didn't think he would turn out to be so — well, ungentlemanly. It only shows that what I've said about the Navy all along is more than ever true. The Army's the thing. An officer and a gentleman, you know."

Sharon was back in the room, ready for battle. "Mr March is a perfect gentleman, thank you. I've never had a more wonderful time. I'm sorry for the way we left you alone in the café, if that's what annoys you so. But I see you got back safely."

She gave Captain Larribee a look that was a rebuke in itself and flounced out of the saloon. Hilary Edgecomb, shocked and discomfited, sat gaping at the doorway through which she had departed in such unseemly indignation. Captain Larribee laughed aloud. Sharon locked her door and undressed in the grey light of dawn, now tinged with rose. She slipped a salmon-coloured night-gown over her head, exulting as it dropped in satin loveliness to the floor, and climbed between the stiff sheets. But sleep was impossible. Her mind reeled with the events of the past few hours, and she could not shut out the picture of Eric laughing as he sat across from her in La Mantilla — Eric as he looked at her in the cabaña that moment just before he swept her into his arms.

She had protested when Edgecomb had retired to wash his delicate hands and Eric had jumped up saying, "This is our chance. Come on!"

"But, Eric! What will he think?"

"Who cares what the meddlesome old fool thinks? Quickly now!" He threw his pea-jacket around her shoulders and almost lifted her to her feet. "I shouldn't have asked him in the first place. But I never thought he'd take me up." Then, at the look on Sharon's face and her reluctant hanging back, "Oh, all right. I'll give Manuel a dollar and he'll take him back to the boat."

It was but a few swift steps from the café to the beach. The tropical moon was brilliant — a great silver plate from the fabulous table of an Oriental palace. The sand was fine and soft and whiter than any Sharon had ever seen. Back home the sand at the lakes was coarse and yellow. The wind had died down leaving the sea calm and serene. The tide crept a few inches at a time up the slope of the crescent shore, the waves rolling in lazily. No turbulent pound of water, just the steady quiet murmur of wave overlapping wave.

She and Eric strolled along the beach in silence, drinking in the radiance of the tropical night. The soothing sound of the waves, the caressing softness of the breeze lulled their senses. In the distance Sharon discerned a small hut facing the Atlantic, quiet, deserted, fascinating.

"Look at that cute little cottage!" she cried.

"Cabaña," Eric corrected her.

"Well, whatever it is, whose is it?"

"Mine." He laughed at the almost childlike wonder in her eyes. "Why so surprised? When I'm off duty I like to come out here and be by myself. That's why I built it. It isn't much, I know, but —"

"But I think it's wonderful!" In her eagerness, Sharon ran on ahead of Eric to admire his handiwork more closely. The cabaña was constructed of rough boards and driftwood, thatched with the fronds of coco-nut palms. A stray breeze rustling through the thatching set up a chattering, like gossips across a backyard fence. The cabaña presented an unbroken wall on three sides. The door, opening on a diminutive porch, faced the sea. Eric took a key from his jeans. There was difficulty in opening the padlock.

"The damned thing sticks from the salt spray and the sand blowing into it," he explained. But he forced it into obedience and lighted the lantern that hung from the rafter.

Sharon tried to look everywhere at once. Eric excused the meagre furnishings with a grin. Hinged to the wall and hooked up to two chains was a square shelf of rough boards, which when let down made a serviceable table. Beside it was a huge block of wood to serve as a stool. On the floor were several thicknesses of grass matting, so soft to the step that they reminded Sharon of the carpeting her father had brought to the rancho from San Francisco.

A shelf across the rear wall held Eric's few books, a humidor made from shells, a pipe rack, a *nargileh* and a framed picture of a grey-haired lady.

"My grandmother," Eric said bluntly.

Sharon looked over the books. How like Eric, she mused as she read the titles: Melville's *Moby*

Dick and *Typee*, *Famous Quotations and Speeches by Our Presidents*, *How to Tie Twenty Sailor's Knots*, a log book, a biography of Stephen Decatur and a well thumbed copy of *Robinson Crusoe*.

These things were all the cabaña boasted. Having seen them, Sharon looked at Eric. He was regarding her with almost pleading eyes, as if asking earnestly for approbation. She smiled.

"I think it's wonderful. I'm absolutely in love with it."

Their eyes met and spoke. What they said only Eric and Sharon knew. Something in his gaze made her falter, but he held his hands out to her and she was in his arms, clinging as if afraid she would be torn away from him. His hands were hungry upon her body, rough and groping on her back, her hips. Hers were upon his shoulders, her nails digging into the flesh. The door stood slightly open and the sea breeze, exploring the interior of the cabin, found the lantern. The flame fluttered and went out. The two lovers neither noticed nor cared, for their lips had found each other.

Eric's words came haltingly in a hoarse whisper, "Sharon! This — this something that's come between us — it's bigger than we are. You — I don't have to tell you that, do I?"

Sharon had no words. She had but a fierce clinging desire which she expressed by pressing her cheek hard against his. Her ear she held close to his lips that she might not miss one nuance of his whispered avowal.

"It's hit me amidships. I've tried to fight it, but I gave up, even before we left the ship. I swear it, Sharon, by all the admirals in the Navy, I did try at first." His voice was steadier now; he spoke as if half expecting a rebuff. "I'll be honest. I brought you out here for just one purpose."

Sharon drew away from the intimate proximity of his body, but remained within the circle of his embrace. Dispassionately she said, "Eric, do you really mean that?"

"Are you afraid of me now?"

"Oh, Eric! No!" She was back in his steel-band arms, gripping at his shoulders, uttering her words against his cheek. "Not afraid of you! Perhaps a little afraid of it. I've never —"

"Sharon! I shouldn't have done it, but I'm not asking you to forgive me. All I say is that I've still got time to take you back to the ship, right now — if you say so — but oh, Sharon, please don't say so. I've been honest with you. I didn't try to fool you —" He waited for an answering caress. Words would not be necessary. She was hesitant, as if wishing to hold her fate in abeyance. "Sharon, what is it?"

"It's just that — well, Eric, is this because I'm me — really me — or would any girl have done?"

Before he could speak she kissed away the protest that struggled for expression. His teeth hurt her, but a weakness as if she had been drugged came over her and obliterated the hurt. Eric was on his knees and Sharon sank to her knees beside him on the palm matting. They rocked to and fro for a moment and then she knew they were lying side by side — and there were tears in her eyes.

Eric kissed the tears and laughed softly, reassuringly. Sharon stroked his hair, brushing the unruly locks back from his forehead, tracing his brow with her finger-tips. He kissed the palm of her hand. Then, with a little sob in his throat; he hurled his face in her bosom and fumbled for the clasp of her gown.

The shrill notes of a bugle reveille floated across the sand, faintly, yet shrilly.

"Oh, sweet Christ!" Eric muttered, sitting up. "I should be at the commodore's diggings now. I must have fallen asleep."

"You did, darling," Sharon said and helped him get ready to go while reflecting, "He talks to me as he would talk to a man, but he treats me like a woman. I hate to see him go, but I mustn't be a weakling."

With one last, all-inclusive look around, Eric stepped toward the door, Sharon's hand in his. He stopped and looked at her. "But you — how are you —"

"How am I going to get back to the boat? I'll get back all right. Really I will. I'll lock the cabaña. You hurry on. You must hurry, Eric. You mustn't think of me now. Please don't get into trouble on my account."

"To hell with getting in trouble. I'm taking you to the boat."

"Don't start off by being stubborn. I'll find the boat all right. I'm not Hilary Edgecomb. Good-bye, Eric." She pushed at his arm and snapped the padlock shut as if closing up shop for the day. Nothing in her manner or even in her eyes disclosed that she longed to stay right there in the cabaña until Eric could be free again. "Please, hurry, Eric! You mustn't stand there looking at me like —"

He took her into his arms again, kissed her and, taking a ring from his finger, said, "It may be a long, long time. I want you to have my ring. Keep it to remember me by."

She clutched it in her palm, tightly. "Always, Eric. Now promise you'll write."

"Of course, honey."

They kissed again and he streaked down the beach, never once looking back at her. Soon he was lost to her sight. She wondered, with a little catch in her throat, "When will the long time end?"

The ring was far too big for Sharon to wear, but she slipped it on her finger and held it there to admire. It was of heavy yellow gold, set with an onyx inlaid with a gold anchor and chain adorning the brave letters, U.S.N. "As if I needed anything to remember him by." She clutched the ring again and followed in the same direction, walking slowly and breathing greedily of the pungent salt air.

She knew that if she followed the shore line she was bound to come upon the *Grover Cleve-*

land sooner or later. There was time until ten o'clock to find it. Being alone had never frightened her. She had tasted too much of that in Texas. Being molested did not even occur to her. All she knew was that she was glad to be alive, that she was intoxicated with love, and that she was happy in the dawn.

She had walked barely a half hour when she saw a man approaching. Upon sighting her he broke into a fast trot, running with the rolling gait of one accustomed to the pitch and toss of a ship's deck. Soon she saw who it was — Thor Edmundson, the first mate. She laughed aloud at the look of relief that spread across his broad Scandinavian features when he recognized her.

Sharon tossed for hours in the narrow berth. The oppressive atmosphere in her state-room prevented rest. The afternoon heat beat down upon the *Grover Cleveland* like a blast from a brick kiln as she steamed sluggishly down the channel to Havana Harbour. It was Sharon's first experience of this tropical climate. How glad she would be when the boat docked and she would go ashore once and for all.

She dressed slowly, choosing her cool flowered calico in preference to the taffeta. "The devil take mourning!" she thought. "Lucky Fred Douglass would understand." She descended the companion-way to the saloon, hungry and perspiring.

The heat had driven all the passengers from

the decks into the lounge, as dark and cool a place as could be found on board. Hilary Edgecomb and some of the others were sipping cool lemonade. Carlos Menendez, hands thrust deep in his pockets, stood apart looking out on some far horizon of his own, his face lighted with a sort of spiritual joy.

Captain Larribee, too, stood apart. He contemplated his glass of lemonade and tried not to look too deprecating; but he did wish it was something stronger. "Trip's almost over," he said. He had never made it with so few passengers. His crew was almost as big as his passenger list — with the trouble in Cuba Americans just didn't travel in the Caribbean. "I trust that you —"

He was interrupted by Thor Edmundson entering the lounge. "We're about to break into the harbour proper, captain," the first mate said respectfully.

"Be right up!" Larribee turned back at the doorway and said to his passengers, "I'm glad I got out of making that speech. We'll dock in fifteen minutes."

Hilary Edgecomb, viewing the complacent Sharon, was lost in resentment of her easy dismissal of the adventures of the night in Key West, her contempt of his concern for her, and the ridiculous position in which it placed him. With an effort he repressed the shameful wish that something might have happened to her simply to justify his anxiety. Coming forth from his meditations he addressed the small group:

"I hope you can all attend the opening of my new café El Americano. It's on the Calle de la Reina. I hope to have it in readiness by fall. A perfect spot! Everyone of importance in Cuba will sooner or later visit El Americano. That is why I am extending this invitation to all of you."

"I should be most pleased to attend, Señor Edgecomb," Carlos said when the general buzz of acceptances had died down. "You may expect me. And if Señorita Douglass would allow me, I shall be happy to be her escort when she visits El Americano."

"I'm afraid I'll be living in Santiago by then," Sharon said.

"That is too bad, Señorita," Carlos said, and abruptly changed the subject. "In a moment we shall pass Morro Castle. Would you care to come on deck and look at it?" He proffered his arm to Sharon.

Nodding graciously she accepted. Carlos Menendez interested her and she wished to know him and his beloved Cuba better. From the deck they could barely discern the shores of the island because of a fog-like haze. But when her guide pointed out Morro Castle Sharon focused her eyes and saw, rising from a dark green background, the haughty old fortress standing high on a rock, stern and forbidding. As the *Grover Cleveland* drew a little nearer Sharon could see the battlements, the bridges, the ramparts, as Carlos pointed them out. She could also hear the bitterness in his voice.

"I can't think of it in any other manner but as a symbol of Spanish autocracy."

Sharon had no answer to this so she offered none. Instead she asked, "Why is everything so foggy?"

"It isn't exactly fog," Carlos explained carefully. "It is the action of the intense heat on the water. The two do not mix well and the water sends up this vapour. It is like this all the time, but one gets used to it. Only on very clear days can you view Cuba in all its emerald beauty."

Sharon drank in the scene with eager interest. About the *Grover Cleveland* there appeared a fleet of smaller craft — flatboats, rowboats and skiffs — swarming about the larger ship like minnows around a shark. On a little flat-bottomed boat flying a frayed and dirty sail of duck canvas from its stubby mast, were some four or five absolutely naked Cuban lads. They were about twelve to fourteen years of age, and as innocent of embarrassment or modesty as they were of clothes.

Sharon turned her head away and Carlos smiled at her. He said, "You must get used to sights like this, Señorita Douglass!" Leaning over the rail he barked a few words in Spanish to the boys. They grinned, set up an animated chatter, and gripping the edge of the boat with their toes they plunged one by one into the waves, their brown buttocks glistening in the sun as they disappeared, to emerge a little later with a great show of splashing and play.

Sharon looked foolishly at Carlos. "Silly of me, wasn't it?"

"Yes!" Carlos surprised her. "Considering last night."

She blushed. "What do you mean?"

"The ways of a man with a maid are not well disguised, señorita," he answered cryptically.

Whatever rebuke she might have brought to her lips she immediately forgot. The *Grover Cleveland* was out of the channel and in the harbour proper, a great blue lake, bustling with activity. Steamships plied their various ways grunting, coughing, and spitting great jets of black smoke; sailors shouted boisterously; whistles blew and bells clanged. In contrast to the diligent steamers, schooners and sloops rode majestically through the blue water escorted by the west wind in their half-furled sails.

Carlos's eyes shone. "Tell me, señorita, is it not beautiful?"

"Breathless," Sharon murmured. "Where do we dock?"

"On the lee side. See, the ship is veering in now."

The *Grover Cleveland* had put about to starboard and was nosing into one of the numerous slips formed by little piers jutting out from the quay like wooden tits. From the oily water in the slip and from the dock itself rose a revolting odour of decomposing foodstuffs. Indeed, there was refuse all about, and delayed or abandoned shipments lay rotting in great masses on the quay. Two native women wearing soiled and tattered mother-hubbards foraged for something to eat. Sharon's nose wrinkled involuntarily and she put her palm to her mouth.

Carlos smiled knowingly and purred, "In Cuba one must take the bitter with the sweet."

"Jove, yes!" put in Hilary Edgecomb emerging on deck. "This is the Havana I remember well. Sights and smells! La Habana — the haven! As the bard of Avon would say, 'A rose by any other name would smell as sweet'."

The quay extended perhaps a quarter of a mile below the Prado, which ran alongside the city wall. From it, leading to Havana proper, were innumerable narrow and irregular streets. They were teeming with ill-clad and hungry-looking natives, amongst whom walked smartly uniformed, well-fed Spanish soldiers, rifles across their shoulders, bayonets suspended from their belts. They regarded with a sort of cool disdain the natives who swarmed about them, pushing queer little two-wheeled carts or carrying carefully wrapped baskets on their heads.

Things moved swiftly once the hawsers had been tossed, mooring the boat to the pilings on the pier. The gangplank was lowered and a crew of black stevedores, naked to the waist, their back and shoulder muscles standing out like great welts in their flesh, set to work unloading the small cargo the *Grover Cleveland* carried — tanned hides from Texas longhorns.

From the confusion of movement on the pier, a tall, rangy gentleman detached himself and boarded the ship. Captain Larribee stepped forth to question him, but after exchanging a few words they both came on deck. The man's face was as brown as a Cuban native's, but his blue eyes and Yankee features distinguished him. Sharon regarded him with interest, noting his hair, bleached white by the sun. Perhaps this was Uncle Clay. The only picture she had ever seen of him was one which her mother left. He was then a serious young man with dark hair and erect bearing.

This gentleman carried himself erect in his immaculate white ducks, precisely creased. The trousers were tucked into high top-boots, laced tight and well oiled. His coat, though spruce, hung open. At his neck he wore a black ribbon cravat tied in a large flowing bow, its string ends falling down across his shirt front. In his brown hands he carried a beige-coloured Equador hat, woven from jipijapa leaves. He was perhaps fifty, sparse, lean, and solemn. The skin over his cheekbones was drawn tight like a drumhead. His white eyebrows, a startling contrast against the deeply tanned skin, lent distinction to his broad forehead.

He followed Captain Larribee in Sharon's direction. Now she knew he must be Uncle Clay, and she ran forward to greet him. But she stopped suddenly, for he was standing stock still, looking at her aghast.

"Grace!" he cried, his voice high-pitched. "It can't be you, Grace!"

Sharon faltered, looked helplessly at Captain Larribee, saw that he was as bewildered as she was, and was about to excuse herself when the gentleman recovered his composure and said hastily, "Forgive me, my child. I'm really sorry. I was carried away for a moment — startled." He wiped his brow with a large clean handkerchief. "I am Clayton Arms. The captain has informed me that you are my niece, Sharon. You are the very image of my sister as I saw her last."

"Uncle Clay!" Sharon cried, throwing her arms about his neck. "I was hoping you'd meet me." She began an excited babble about her trip and Clayton Arms smiled briefly. His first emotion checked, he became brusque.

"Are you ready, girl? We can go ashore now. I have a carriage waiting to take us to the depot. It's nearly five o'clock."

"But I haven't had my dinner, Uncle Clay."

"Well, the train doesn't leave for Santiago until half past six, so we shall have time for some supper."

Captain Larribee stepped forward and removed his cap. "Perhaps we shall meet again some time, Miss Douglass. You will always be a welcome passenger." He offered his hand, and Sharon took it, bidding him an honestly fond good-bye. As she looked back at Uncle Clay she thought there was a disapproving glint in his eyes.

Hilary Edgecomb advanced and bowed. Having melted somewhat in his resentment he grew rhetorical. "The voyage has been truly a pleasurable one and I regret that it must so soon be terminated. May a kindly fate permit our paths to converge again at a time not too far in the future."

Carlos Menendez alone remained silent. But Sharon read farewell in his eyes, and intuitively she knew that she had gained a life-long friend in this Cuban, and that somewhere his path and hers would meet again.

Thor Edmundson had brought her bags on deck and Sharon, taking her hat boxes, let Uncle Clay carry the straw suitcase and the brown leather portmanteau. At the far side of the pier a hansom cab waited with top rolled back. Perched behind was a ragged, dishevelled Cuban boy, a starved, pinched look in his features. Sharon was to come to know this look all too well. Harnessed between the shafts was a mangy brown mule, unkempt and with bare spots and open sores on his back. Around each sore swarmed a hundred flies.

"First of all, girl," Uncle Clay stated as he arranged the bags, "we'll have to get you something to eat. You said you were hungry."

"Famished, Uncle Clay."

"Let us hope not," he replied, frowning slightly, as he took her elbow to assist her to her seat. In Spanish he directed the driver to leave the pier and seek the higher level of the city. The mule set himself a pace which was little better than a slow walk.

"We'll have ample time in which to get acquainted, girl," Clayton spoke, "so I won't press you too hard for details about yourself. You're as pretty as your mother was. And in spite of your grief, too. The news of your father's death gave your Aunt Phoebe and me quite a shock. Surprising enough, considering we hadn't even met the man. And I hadn't seen Grace since some little time before her marriage. It's been a long time since she took that ill-advised step, but all time is as one day with the Lord. Hearken unto that, girl. I guess your mother and I were a bit strained about things after she married that man — a common gambler. I hope you don't take after your father, girl."

Sharon was amazed at this lengthy speech. Judging from his appearance she had taken her uncle to be a man of fewer words. "I don't think I take after either father or mother, Uncle Clay. I think I'm pretty much myself."

"And your mother was a Sunday-school teacher, too," Uncle Clay lamented further, indifferent to Sharon's reply. "Did you get any schooling?"

"Not a great deal — and it wasn't much of a school. I never finished."

"I daresay you got enough. Higher education was not intended for women. Can you bake, girl, or cook a meal, or make a dress?"

"I — well, I declare, I guess I haven't had much practice. Father always had plenty of help around the place and the Chinese cook didn't like me bothering in the kitchen."

"Such nonsense! But Phoebe'll teach you soon enough. Do you go to church regular?"

"I — well —"

"I can see your father was lax all right. You'll begin next Sunday. We don't miss a sabbath, morning or evening. It isn't an elaborate church, but it's the Word that counts. Nearly everybody down here is either a Catholic or a heathen. It's the same thing. A few of us Methodists go to Santiago and hold our meetings in a rented hall. I teach a class and Phoebe leads the choir. Have you been baptized?"

"I — I don't know. I don't think —"

"Well, we'll take care of that. We'll baptize you before it's too late. Never did anyone any harm to be saved twice. We'll be glad to have you about the house, girl. The Lord didn't see fit to bless your Aunt Phoebe and me with any children. It was His will that you be sent to us in our declining years. You'll be a big help to Phoebe in the kitchen and you can teach the native children on the plantation some reading and writing. A little, but not too much. They get out of hand if they get to be too smart. Once a nigger gets out of hand you can't manage him at all. It's quite a task to run a large plantation. I demand absolute obedience and I pride myself that I get it. Just remember that we don't tolerate any nonsense in our household. There's too much of it among young girls to-day. It leads them to paths of perdition. Your Aunt Phoebe and I want to spare you that."

"Yes, Uncle Clay." Sharon's apparent humility was merely a phase of her keen disappointment. The promise of a thrilling life in a new land had already been broken. As Uncle Clay pictured it, life would be nothing but a dull round of duties. But right now food was important, so she lightly dismissed the unpleasant thought of being forced, for the first time in her life, to regulate her conduct according to the dictates of others.

At Clayton's orders the hansom was stopping before a small café on the corner of two very narrow streets. An appetizing odour of frying fish emanated from the open door.

"We'll eat here," he announced bluntly. "The food is cheap and simple, but clean. Come, girl. We have no time to lose."

They spent half an hour in the dark and narrow cubicle which seemed all kitchen and no dining-room. The food was good, but there wasn't nearly enough of it to satisfy Sharon's appetite. She considered asking for more and twice she looked at Uncle Clay with the words at her lips, but something in his face or manner halted her. He looked so smugly satisfied, as if this was all anyone should expect to eat at one sitting.

A cuckoo clock on a shelf over their table

showed it was five-thirty. They would have some time to themselves before boarding the train for Santiago. There was still daylight lingering in the streets, and Sharon glanced about her with revived interest as she climbed back into the waiting carriage.

From somewhere their Cuban had procured an over-ripe banana and sat hunched in the seat eating it. The underfed young native munched with a solemnity that Sharon thought a trifle ridiculous, as if an over-ripe banana was an occasion in his life.

Sharon took Uncle Clay's arm. It was stiff and unyielding so she smiled up at him. "Do let us drive about, Uncle Clay, and see something of the city. We have time before the train leaves. Please!"

"Well, all right, girl, if that will please you." The smile had worked. He turned to the boy and directed him to drive to the Alameda de Paula, but to be sure they were at the depot by twenty minutes past six. The boy nodded solemnly and dropped a lackadaisical whip across the mule's back.

"Lay it on hard!" Uncle Clay shouted as if on the verge of a fit of temper. "He thinks you're petting him. Lay it on!"

The boy laid it on and the mule increased his gait ever so slightly. Uncle Clay shrugged and gave up. He drew his arm closer to himself and Sharon slipped her hand from under it. As darkness gathered she came to notice sounds more and sights less. The creak of the wheels and their rattle on the wooden pavement were insistent on her consciousness and, in a minor key, they sang a dull, vague warning. She dismissed the uncomfortable thoughts with her characteristic "Fiddlesticks!"

They turned, apparently without reason or direction, from one narrow, filthy street into another and another, each street trying to outdo the preceding one in filthiness and irregularity. The buildings were of quaint design, not exactly Spanish, but with a strong Castillian flavour. Most of them were at least three stories high, with a piazza for each floor running across the entire face. They were painted white and the floor-to-ceiling shutters were green. But in spite of this bold colour contrast, and in spite of the brave carving on the railings, there was a discouraged air about them.

Perhaps it was due to the half-starved and bedraggled appearance of the inhabitants streaming in and out with little purpose in their comings and goings, but always on the move. Like living skeletons they walked about, hollow-eyed and with sunken cheeks, their shoulders sagging in dejection. Yet in those hollow eyes there was a feverish gleam. Anyone looking for it could catch this gleam in the eyes of every Cuban in Havana. And it was not a fever that Spanish quinine could alleviate. It was the fever of revolt.

Several times Sharon noticed people shying

away from the houses and into the streets, nimbly dodging the hansom or clumsily hindering its progress. Soon she began to observe that on these particular houses were tacked little squares of black cardboard with white legends in Spanish.

"Uncle Clay, what are those little black cards for?"

"It is the sign of death, girl. Everywhere people are dying of hunger and destitution."

"Oh!" Sharon's voice was tremulous with sympathy.

"I shouldn't worry too much about it. These people populate fast. They are dying at the rate of two every thirty minutes and begetting at the rate of almost three during the same time."

True, there were children everywhere. As hollow-eyed and sunken-checked as their elders, still they laughed and played and overran the patios into the streets. The girls were in grayish-white dresses, worn until the cheap cotton fell apart in rags. Very small boys wore nothing at all, and the larger ones had trousers of soiled white drill. Fighting and wrestling, they presented a tangle of spindly arms and legs and ribs accentuated by emaciation.

From time to time the squalor and meanness were relieved by the grandeur of huge marble buildings and the quiet dignity of the Spanish colonial churches. Great statues of the Virgin on the bell-towers looked sadly and gently down on a pitiful people.

The evening warmth hovered about Sharon like a comforting cloak. She spoke seldom, and then only to ask the name of some church or building.

"That's the Governor's palace," Clayton pointed out, and Sharon throught she detected a tinge of bitterness in his voice. A great, squat building of gleaming white marble, with broad steps and a colonnade of polished pillars, stood in a setting of smooth greensward. In the plaza tall white fountains played. These formed the leitmotiv in the pattern otherwise dominated by the massive building, austere and aloof — the Playa del Rey.

It was a city of contrasts: a city of dirty, crooked *calles* and long, spacious *avenidas;* spruce, well-ordered soldiers and teeming human activity — an exotic city, darkly mysterious and forbidding. Yet in spite of their beaten look, the lowliest streets proclaimed, "Yes, this is La Habana! And we are proud!"

The largest city of the West Indies and the chief seaport, Havana was a city with a body and soul. Her body might be crushed and broken, but always her soul survived, groping, alive. The body of the city sweated and stank, yet the odour was not unpleasant, a mingling of roasting tobacco, boiling sugar, and tropical fruits.

Rounding unexpected corners, the carriage passed through crumbling fortresses damaged by hurricanes, some with new tobacco factories built within their ruins. It was an ever changing picture and Sharon could not get her fill of it. Havana! She said the word several times, letting it roll melodiously over her tongue. Havana! A city steeped in the mysteries of old Spain and permeated with the superstition and voodooism of the West Indies.

And everywhere about the Spanish soldiers marched, singly or in groups. Whenever a company of them approached the hansom the Cuban boy would jerk the mule over to the side of the street; cringing as if struck with his own whip, he reminded Sharon of a beaten cur. She pitied him, but mingled with her pity was a measure of contempt for what she thought cowardice.

The carriage turned abruptly into a street so narrow there was scarcely room to pass. On one side was a school, on the other a tobacco market and clearing-house. The school was jerry-built of crude yellow bricks, scaling and chipped. No glass remained in the windows, and an ivy-vine crept across the door and around the spire like a strangling rope. Sharon thought to ask Uncle Clay why a schoolhouse should be abandoned, but there was a grimness about his face that kept her silent.

The tobacco market also looked abandoned at the moment. There was no one near the auctioneer's block and the great bins of tobacco were open to the air, some containing huge leaves, others the rough cut and the finer grades. As the carriage drew immediately opposite the market Sharon saw that frightened groups of natives were huddled in the shadows of the interior.

The hansom had progressed only a carriage length when a shot rang out. It came from behind a gable on the low roof of the tobacco mart. Chips scattered from the bricks in the school building, and a puff of white smoke showed from where the shot had been fired.

Clayton barked an order to the driver and the boy brought the whip down hard on the mule's back, lash after lash, but the animal kept to its own slow pace.

A shot was fired from the other side of the street and a puff of smoke rose above the schoolhouse. More shots came from the second story windows of the building, then seemed to come from every direction, the bullets whining to their marks and the puffs of smoke hanging lazily in the twilight like grey balloons.

"Quick, girl!" Clayton shouted. "Run into that market!"

He helped her out of the carriage, which still moved on at the same pace, and swinging down beside her grabbed her arm and propelled her into the semi-darkness of the market. They made it just in time. Inside the shelter children whimpered and their mothers told their beads; outside, the street was alive with fighting. Furious footsteps pounded across the roof above Sharon's head. Ragged Cuban soldiers bearing rusty rifles and gleaming machetes leaped to the street, shouting their defiance and crying their challenge to the Spaniards.

In answer, a score of soldiers poured from the door and windows of the schoolhouse. Shots rang out in a fusillade, spattering against the buildings, ricochetting from the pavement and embedding themselves in human flesh. The Cubans, unfamiliar with their rifles, discarded them and began swinging their machetes in wide, ruthless arcs. The leader of the Spanish company gave an order. His men fixed bayonets. In an instant bayonets were battling machetes — not charging and stabbing but, with Cuban tactics, swinging and cutting with the broad surface of the blade as though it were a knife. Amid the defiant shouts and the challenging cries there now arose screams and groans as Cuban rebels or Spanish soldiers fell underfoot.

Appalled and speechless, Sharon stared. A small, emaciated Cuban and a towering Spanish soldier engaged in hand-to-hand combat on the kerb directly in front of her. The Cuban, summoning strength far beyond his puny physique, swung his machete in a powerful circle as the soldier raised his arm to slash with his bayonet. The machete struck first, neatly and cleanly severing the upstretched arm. It fell amid a spurt of blood beside its owner and lay grotesque and twisted on the bricks, a small emerald ring showing on the little finger. The soldier, incredulous and uncomprehending, looked at it, then at the space where it had been. With a wild scream he collapsed at the Cuban's feet. Grinning with satisfaction, the native gloated over his handiwork and made the sign of the cross.

Sharon clutched her uncle's arm.

"You may see more of this, girl," he said. Taking a deep breath, closing her eyes a moment, and setting her teeth, she conquered the wave of nausea that threatened her.

The fighting ceased as quickly as it had begun, and the combatants of both sides fled quickly, leaving their dead and wounded to lie in their own blood. The women and children thronged into the street from the market and the nearby houses, the children to gaze awe-stricken at the sight, the women to minister to the fallen men. Sharon and Uncle Clay followed.

The carriage stood in the street unscathed, the lazy mule still unconcerned about anything more serious than the flies that infested his sores. But the Cuban boy lay sprawled across the high seat of the hansom, one arm hanging down over the side. From a bullet wound in his forehead the blood trickled thickly over his distorted face. In his hand he still clutched the peel of his prized banana. Sharon stared at him, colourless, and then at the sights about her — the fallen soldiers, the blood, the severed arm. She gave a queer little moan and sank gently amongst the billow of her skirts at Uncle Clay's feet.

When Sharon regained consciousness she found herself in the depot of the Havana-Santiago railroad. A woman held a vial of spirits of ammonia to her nostrils and Uncle Clay stood anxiously by with a tin cup of water in his trembling hand. Struggling to clear her head, Sharon heard the woman say in a soothing voice that sounded like the rustling of taffeta, "There we are, precious. Just take another breath and we'll be all right."

Uncle Clay said, "How are you, girl?"

She sat up slowly and pressed her fingers to her throbbing temples. "I'm all right, Uncle Clay. Silly of me to faint away like that. I feel so ashamed!"

"Thank God you're all right," Clayton murmured. "Your Aunt Phoebe would never forgive me if anything happened to you. Now that you're better, let's be getting along. The train leaves in five minutes. I dislike dawdling."

Sharon rose from the wooden bench, thanked the woman, and followed Clayton. How they got to the depot he didn't condescend to tell her, but she supposed he had driven the mule himself. How else could he have brought her there in a dead faint? Following him, she regarded with mingled respect and awe the broad shoulders, the Equador hat, and the great boots. There was something about his general bearing that made it easy for her to understand how he could command absolute obedience. He was a forbidding figure, this new-found uncle of hers, yet capable of the utmost gentleness. The frank emotion he had displayed at their first meeting and his concern when she fainted were oddly at variance with his sternness and brusque speech. She was glad she had came to in the depot and not in that hell-street where men lay dead and dying. She felt vaguely that she had lost face in her uncle's eyes by her weakness, and determined that she would never faint again.

The train to Santiago was like something discarded in the States twenty years before. Behind a ramshackle engine with an outsize cow-catcher and tall chimney were strung some six or seven high wooden coaches, dirty brown in colour. Because of the heat the windows were open, and Sharon surmised that the interior of their car would be black with soot and dust. She was right.

There were few passengers in the coach, and Uncle Clay chose two seats near the front, stowing the suitcases in the rack above and adjusting one seat to face the other. Sharon settled herself on the hard green plush and prepared to enjoy the trip as best she could. With a snort and a series of screeches accompanied by the clanging of the lone bell, the coaches jerked forward individually, decided to pull together, and rattled down the tracks gathering momentum with the chugging engine. The medley died down to a steady click-click of the wheels as they left the shelter of the terminal roof.

Soon they were out of Havana. Through the windows Sharon could see the landscape in soft focus, and the thought struck her that nearly all of her major impressions since leaving Galveston had come to her at sunrise or sunset — Eric pointing out to her the Dry Tortugas, Eric saying good-bye to her in the dawn, and the terrifying scenes she had witnessed earlier that evening. The panorama of Cuba now passed before her, a series of pictures framed in the square window of the dusty railway coach, reminding her of the nickelodeons back in Chicago, which her father had described to her.

There were fertile fields that had been ruthlessly ploughed under. Carlos had told her about these. She reflected with pride that in her own United States nothing like this could ever happen to the land. The train passed through verdant forests, rich in timber, thick in undergrowth. Coco-nut trees, palm-trees, luxuriant thickets — a veritable jungle. Then another clearing, more broad fields — sugarcane fields, fire-swept, desolate.

In the fields the workers, in their long cotton trousers and great straw hats, miserable looking as they were, yet formed a beautiful picture in the sunset. It was not incongruous to associate the idea of beauty with hunger — the physical hunger for food, the spiritual hunger for freedom. She thought again of Carlos and his patriotic fervour for "the land of men and women and children in human bondage".

But, as if jealous of her thoughts, a light from inside the coach reflected on her closed window and she turned her attention to the conductor who was lighting the lamps. She herself was hungry now — hungry for truths. Uncle Clay drew a little leather-bound Testament from his pocket and began to read in the uncertain light, forming the syllables with his lips. Soon he sensed that Sharon was looking at him. He closed the book over his forefinger and smiled gently across at her.

"The conversion of Paul, girl. A story I never grow tired of."

Sharon felt no concern over Paul's conversion. "I was wondering, Uncle Clay, if you could answer a few questions for me."

"If I'm able to, and gladly."

"I met a gentleman aboard the *Grover Cleveland*," she stated, and at her uncle's disapproving glance hastily added, "oh, a very nice gentleman, indeed — a Cuban who was coming back here to live. He said that Cuba lives under a military despotism imposed by Spain. Is that true?"

"You saw this afternoon how Spain goes about quelling a native insurrection, didn't you?"

"Yes, and it was cruel, but —"

"Your gentleman acquaintance was right. The Spanish have everything completely under control here. That in itself would not be bad. Someone must rule, but Spain rules with an iron hand. She is guilty before God of exploitation, not just of land, but of people, and that is an unforgivable sin."

"Señor Menendez said that because you own a plantation you could tell me more than he could. What did he mean?"

"Very probably he means that he knows we Americans living here are having a devilish time existing."

"How so?"

"Girl, you shouldn't trouble your head about such things."

"But I want to know. Please don't treat me as a child."

"Well, for one thing, there are the high taxes for property, the high duties on things we export, the repeal of the McKinley tariff."

"Then for heaven's sake why don't the Americans do something about it?"

"If the Lord had not meant it to be so, it would not be."

"Oh fiddlesticks, Uncle Clay," Sharon cried.

"The Book says there will be wars and rumours of wars. This afternoon was an example. It has been going on like this for many years. I think it is their admired Garcia who keeps whipping them up. They have long felt bitter towards Spain, whose only interest in the island has been the profit she can extract from it. So, as this afternoon, you see outbursts from time to time."

"Yes, Uncle Clay, that's all I heard talked about on the boat. I was bored to tears. I think that's because of the trading issues —"

"And I think," Clayton interrupted her, "that you should stop bothering your head about such things and leave them to men. It is not a job for women. I'm afraid, girl, you are inclined to be headstrong. We must tame that, mustn't we? Besides, I think you should try to get some sleep. We'll be in Santiago all too soon. I expect your Aunt Phoebe'll have Jason down to meet us."

"Who's Jason?"

"Why Jason Earleigh, my overseer. He supervises the help and takes care of the fields while I do the planning and keep the books."

"He must be smart to oversee all the help on the plantation."

"Very," agreed Clayton. "For a lad of only two-and-twenty I have yet to see them come smarter. Like a whip that boy is. But he mustn't know. I shouldn't want it to go to his head. He knows he must obey me. But I have complete confidence in him, else I shouldn't have left the place in his charge even to come and meet you. When I took him in, I —" Clayton caught himself sharply and subsided into silence.

"Oh, was he an orphan too, Uncle Clay?" Sharon smiled good-humouredly.

"Worse," Uncle Clay confided, grimly. "But I suppose his story is a good lesson to a girl of twenty."

"Yes?" Sharon waited for him to continue, wondering what "good lesson" was in store for her.

"His mother was a wanton." He pursed his lips as though the word left an acrid taste in his mouth. "She mockingly attended the same church that Phoebe and I belonged to. I tried to reason with her, but she persisted in her sinful ways and got into trouble with one of the worthless boys who hung about the harbour. Well, Phoebe took her in." He lowered his voice as he touched upon the delicate subject. "I was against it from the start, but who was I to pass judgment on a fallen one? The child was born under our roof and Phoebe insisted on keeping him. We named him Jason."

"And his mother? What of her?" Sharon suspected her uncle of having kicked her into the streets. She wondered if he would admit the truth.

"She disappeared one night and we have never heard from her since. She probably drifted back among her kind. When woman enters into sin with man; the price is always a steep one to pay, girl." Clayton settled back against the seat and closed his eyes.

Sharon peered out into the darkness. "When woman enters into sin with man —" She clenched her fist and brought her other hand to her throat. Beneath her high collar, suspended on a ribbon, hung Eric's Navy ring. She hadn't once thought of last night as being sinful. What would Eric be doing now? Lying in his barracks, perhaps, or would he be at his cabaña reading? Maybe he was just lying on the beach beneath the stars thinking of her. He seemed so far away now — so much had happened since she left him. Even his fine sullen features and his unruly brown hair were vague to her now, but slowly the picture clarified. She held it for a moment before releasing it and giving herself to another memory — Eric lying warm beside her, his ardent lips pressed roughly against hers. Her heartbeat quickened.

As though he had heard it, Uncle Clay opened his eyes and faced her quizzically. "What are you thinking of, girl?" he asked.

She flashed him an apologetic smile. "Nothing, Uncle Clay," she replied innocently. "Nothing at all."

Eric March spent the entire morning in the bay teaching a class of new recruits from Virginia how to right an overturned lifeboat. For five hours he remained fully clothed in the waves of the Atlantic, then dismissed the class for dinner and returned to the barracks. He was tired and wanted only to sleep, having had no rest the night before except the brief hour or so in Sharon's arms. But he got into dry clothes and went to the mess-hall. More than once during dinner he stifled a yawn. When one of the boys tried to make a joke of it he said, "Being in the water a long time always affects me like that."

After dinner the men were granted an hour of leisure. Eric strolled over to the knoll where the flagstaff stood. It was quiet there, and the sweet-smelling grass was lush with clover. Stretching out on his back, he pillowed his neck on his clasped hands, and gazed up into the blue of the sky, watching the lazy white clouds floating across the heavens like a flock of sheep on a rolling pasture. He was alone and contented.

Pictures of Sharon came pleasantly before his eyes and he thanked a kind fate for bringing them together. Having brought them together, would it permit them to meet again? Or was he never to see Sharon again? He covered his eyes roughly with his arm, as if to blot out the possibility.

His grandmother had tried to make his furlough a happy one, but he had been ready enough to get back. Her home in Galveston was comfortable, but she always gave him the impression that she was keeping it up just for him. He was fond of his grandmother, but his independent spirit was irritated by her overindulgence, by the grasping little tentacles she put forth to hold him.

She had so many ingenious devices, this too-kind grandmother, by which she constantly reminded him that it was she who had taken him in as a baby when his parents were killed in the train wreck, and that it was she who had reared and educated him.

As he grew older the apron strings grew stronger. Little gifts from her both pleased and bothered him. He knew they were bids for his affection, and his affection was not for sale. Then his grandmother was always preparing his favourite dishes and making him conscious of her thoughtfulness, and when he showed irritation she would devise a greater kindness to display her forgiveness. Now that she was old, Eric could not bring himself to break the ties completely. Once a year he acted the dutiful grandson and let her fuss over him to her heart's content.

At the age of nineteen Eric fell in love with a neighbour, a woman of forty. Grandmother in some inscrutable way discovered or divined the situation and, treating Eric as a child, tried to break his spirit. Seeing that this had no effect she took to ridiculing the affair throughout the neighbourhood. There was no one more startled than the woman herself when she heard the news. To have this tall, strapping youngster in love with her was highly amusing — something that called for action. On the innocent pretext of borrowing a book she invited him to her home one summer evening. He stepped across her threshold a youth; he left at midnight a man.

From then on he was no longer interested in that woman. His love died like a quenched fire. But he was a lusty young man, and his initiation into the mysteries of sex whetted his appetite. He grew more impatient than ever with his grandmother's fundamentalist beliefs and her apprehensions for spiritual welfare. She took great satisfaction in a series of self-denials which she claimed had fused her spirit into a great driving force against all things of the flesh.

Her Eric, she believed, exemplified the spirit of American youth that made its way in the world through clean living and honest manliness, and could do nothing evil. When at twenty-one he joined the Navy she gave him up tearfully but bravely to the United States.

As usual on this last furlough she had filled him with good food and showed him off proudly at church. She prophesied that her "days of service" would soon be over, though she could get about as spryly as ever. She insisted on going to the dock to see him off and, after bidding him a prayerful good-bye, she watched him board the *Grover Cleveland* to sail away for another year.

Beside Eric at the rail stood a pretty, auburn-haired girl in a calico dress. They had turned towards each other at the same time, as if moved by the same force. And a spark in his eye had met a spark in hers.

"Hello," he said, winking.

"Hello," she replied, startled at his boldness.

"You going far?" He could see that she didn't mind being startled.

"Havana."

"Only Key West for me."

"Really." She had turned away and looked across the water as if no one had spoken.

"Yes. We'll be passengers together for that much of the way."

His voice had pulled her back — he meant it to — and she had looked straight into his eyes as she said, "That will be nice."

Lying beside the flagstaff now he recalled that conversation, remembering her thin-moulded, determined lips and the way she said the words, hardly showing her teeth at all. And he remembered how, on his first night on the *Grover Cleveland*, the knowledge that she was aboard, warm and vital, had tortured him. He had lain on his berth unable to sleep or to think of anything else. He had told himself angrily that he was a fool, but he could not silence the little voice within that kept reiterating that he was again in love.

"That's a hell of a joke," he had muttered aloud. "Just one hell of a joke."

"Oh no!" the voice said. "It's no joke at all. It's something wonderful that's happened to you."

"Don't be a damn' slob," Eric countered.

"Give in and be happy," the voice urged. "Stop fighting it."

"A girl is a girl." He was not ready to give in. "I've had lots of them — white women in Galveston, brown women in Key West, women of all kinds in other ports."

"But that was lust. This is the real thing. Just as it was the first time."

"Yes, I guess so," Eric had finally admitted.

The real thing. Her name, Sharon Douglass, was different. How he had ached that night to lie warmly near her, to feel her in his arms.

Cursing, he had sat up and stared out of the porthole. He had stared until he saw her dancing across the waves, naked, as he desired her. It was no use fighting. This time he really desired a girl because he was madly in love with her. He had feared he would never possess her, and the apprehension had both pleased and hurt him.

Disappointment had conflicted with his sense of decency. Softly he had repeated over and over, "Sharon, Sharon", until he had fallen asleep.

"Now," he thought, lying on his back beneath the tropic sky, "I hope I haven't lost her. I gave her my ring. I promised to write, I kissed her good-bye. Oh, I thought of everything all right — everything except to tell her I loved her." Now he would have to do it in a letter and he felt the inadequacy of it, yet he began to look forward to nightfall with a new intensity. To-night he'd write that letter.

The hour being up, he brushed himself, cast one more glance skyward, and descended the slope to the parade ground where the sailors were lining up stiffly for afternoon inspection.

In the few drowsy moments before Sharon drifted to sleep in the rattling coach she watched Uncle Clay settle himself on the cushion. With his head reclined he had a sturdy, powerful neck on which the cords stood out like knotted twine beneath the skin. In repose his rather stern features softened. His eyes and brows took on a certain benign dignity and his tight lips were now relaxed and slightly sensuous in their fullness. Her uncle was really a handsome person. "His mouth is a great deal like Eric's," Sharon reflected, and that made her smile.

She dreamed in her fitful sleep of Lucky Fred Douglass, for the first time since his death. But here he strode down the aisle of the coach toward her, tall, uncouth, his fine Prince Albert bulging slightly where his gun was strapped. In his hand was the broad sombrero he had worn for years and his long silky hair was now silver. Just as he was about to sit beside her, he was replaced by Carlos Menendez. Smiling enigmatically Carlos sat there saying, "Guard well your tongue. Guard well your tongue. Guard well your tongue", until the phrase merged with the click of the wheels and Carlos was gone.

Again she found herself walking on the beach with Eric. The moon was so bright it hurt her eyes, and the noise of the waves drowned his words; but by studying his lips very closely she could see he was saying, "I've been honest. Are you afraid? I've been honest. Are you afraid?" And the waves took it up as though it were the theme of a great discordant symphony. Afraid, afraid, *afraid.* And the moon was hurting her eyes so.

She awoke to discover that it was the sun emerging, red and glaring over the crest of a hill, and shining directly in her face. The wheels clicked over the rails like a chorus of castanets. She smiled. Stupid dream! Pushing her hair back from her forehead, she sat up in the seat and arranged her petticoats and dress. It was bright and glorious outside, and through the coach window she watched the nickelodeon continue from the night before. Uncle Clay was still asleep, holding the Testament in his hand.

Sharon thought, "Why, this landscape looks

just like our own hill country in Texas. Not great overwhelming mountains, but gentle rolling slopes." The hillocks were the dull green colour of sage, with scattered patches of timber, scrub, and second growth. There was an occasional steep slope on which zigzagging trails and pathways wound downward like pop-corn strings on a Christmas-tree. Sharon wondered how far it was to the sea. Was it just beyond this range of hills, or was there another and another, stretching east and west of her until they were lost to sight where blue sky and blue water met, kissed and were wedded.

The train came to a sudden stop to take on water. The air, gently cool a few minutes before, was now oppressively hot. As the sun climbed higher from range to range, the valleys between appeared lost in shadow, and the hills stood out as clearly to Sharon's view as if she were viewing them through a stereoscope. The sun glared down, bathing the landscape in deep orange and purple.

Across the dry bed of the adjacent tracks there scuttled a land crab, pink and repulsive. It wasn't the colour, however, that attracted Sharon's eye, it was a sense of movement, felt rather than seen. The crab came face to face abruptly with a lizard that had scurried from beneath the train. The lizard's yellow legs were thick and ungainly, and he dragged his ugly green belly sluggishly across the earth.

She breathed a sigh of relief as the train started

again. Now there would be a breeze. But the breeze turned out to be a blast that swept down the aisle sucking away every trace of freshness in the stuffy little coach.

The starting jerk of the coach woke Uncle Clay and as he straightened in his seat the kindly dignity of his brow was lost in a frown. His neck sagged and the powerful cords were concealed by the looseness of his skin. The wrinkles about his mouth intensified and the fullness of his lips turned into hard straight lines, no longer sensuous, but thin and ascetic. The metamorphosis was a little startling to Sharon, but she smiled and greeted him cheerfully.

"Good morning, girl." He spared a brief smile in response to her generous one. "Did you sleep well?"

"Well enough, thank you. As well as one can on a train seat."

"You must get used to privations," he reprimanded.

"Yes, Uncle." Sharon for the moment was meek.

"At home it is our practice to start the morning with a verse of Scripture. Then during the day we pause now and then for meditation. Our souls grow hungry, too, girl. And we must nurture them regularly with the Gospel."

"I'm sure, Uncle Clay, that is a fine idea."

"Inasmuch as I'm not at the plantation now, Aunt Phoebe is taking care of that duty. But there is no reason for us to let our souls go hungry, even on this train, is there?"

"Why, no. I suppose not," Sharon murmured.

Clayton opened the Testament. "I shall read from the ninth chapter of the Gospel according to Saint Mark, verse forty-three. 'And if thy hand offend thee, cut it off: it is better for thee to enter into life maimed, than having two hands to go into hell, into the fire that never shall be quenched.' It is well to remember this through the day, for it means that you are able through the help of the Lord to rid yourself of any temptation that may come to you."

Rid yourself of temptation. Cut it off. Sharon could hear Eric say, "I've been honest. I brought you here for just one purpose." She wondered if this little verse could have stopped her and concluded, with something of relief, that she would have gone ahead exactly as she did. What she had done, she had done, and there was no remorse in her heart. Again she could hear Eric's words, "What I want to do I go about doing", and she resolved that she would make those words her credo, in spite of the Bible and Uncle Clay.

"I see you are thinking it over," Clayton observed. "I'm glad of that, girl."

Sharon had to rid herself of the temptation to laugh. Uncle Clay must never know what she was thinking. As she turned to look at the Cuban countryside again she bestowed upon her uncle a Mona Lisa smile.

Everywhere now there was jungle, and she

wondered what creeping creatures the dark, exotic thickets sheltered. The flowers that lined the tracks were vivid scarlets, blues, yellows — gipsy maidens in a riot of colour. Around them, like gallant protectors of their virtue, grew Spanish bayonets, sage green, pointed, razor-edged blades, standing like cutlasses, hilts thrust into the sand. Still farther back, aloof and regal, stood the Royal palms, infinitely wise monarchs ruling from the thrones of the hills. Overhead, dipping in graceful tribute from time to time, flew brilliant birds, such as Sharon had never seen.

It all formed a composite picture — the wild growth of shrubs and plants, treacherous vines smothering great trees, colour clashing with colour. But the picture would not stay still. It was restless, disturbing. What spider-like menace lurked behind it? Revolt? Misery? Hunger? The vista was as unsteady as a mirage — everything near seemed green and thriving, everything distant black and dense. The landscape was blurred in haze at one moment and sharply etched the next. When Carlos had said that nothing could be really seen when the sun shone brightly it had seemed like a paradox, but now his words had meaning.

Turning from the window to rest her eyes, Sharon leaned her head back on the seat, and felt Eric's ring against her breast. It lay there warmly, as had his hand the night before last. She had travelled these many miles without him and was near the end of her journey. "This is Cuba, my new home," she reflected. "I've reached a new horizon. What, I wonder, lies on the other side?"

2

The Golden Fleece

Jason Earleigh tossed the covers back over the large four-poster bed in his narrow room and lay naked beneath the mosquito-net, letting the cool, before-sun-up breezes play across his body. In the grey dawn that dimly lit the old banjo clock he could see that he had fifteen minutes before it was time to get up. It was a quarter to five.

The fact that Mr Arms was gone hovered about his consciousness, and he trifled with the idea of cheating for half an hour. But he well knew what would happen. The shrill voice of Mrs Arms from her room across the kitchen would set his teeth on edge with, "Jason! Ja-*son!*" Might as well get up now. Still, there were those few extra minutes. He stretched out, hooked his toes under the foot board and, grasping the head board with his long fingers, twisted as though he were on a rack. To vary the exercise he lifted his legs high into the air, balancing himself on his shoulder-blades. The mosquito-net draped over him like a tent and when he dropped his lanky frame back on the mattress the tent collapsed.

Mrs Arms liked to joke about his lankiness. At sixteen he was nearly as tall as he was now and she used to humiliate him by saying to anyone at all, "Jason's growing faster than a weed, only not as gracefully," making him wish he'd been a damned runt.

The fine down on his face was Mr Arms's pet joke. To their neighbour, Mr Floyd, he had said the other day, "Jason's so slow his beard hasn't even got around to growing yet."

Like his face, Jason's body was hairless. His blond thatch was thick enough, but it was faded to the colour of corn silk. Even his pale blue eyes seemed faded in contrast to his sunburned skin. He had no great muscles on his torso and arms, and his over-developed leg muscles were out of proportion. But that was typical of Jason — he felt that his whole life had been out of proportion.

Promptly at five he swung out of bed, poured water into the china basin from the tall pitcher on the chiffonier, and splashed himself well. After drying off with the rough towel he slipped into his brown cotton shirt, its dank odour of sweat reminding him of the twenty miles he had ridden in the sun yesterday afternoon. Stepping into his corduroy breeches, he drew his belt tight around his narrow waist and sat on the only chair in the room to lace his high waterproof boots — necessary in the swamps not only as a protection against water but against snake-bites.

The routine of dressing set his thoughts ahead to his early morning chores: wake Mrs Arms — wake the cook — while cook gets breakfast go down to the cabañas and see that the natives are getting up — feed Jerry and saddle her —

But what was he thinking of? How could he have forgotten that this was the morning Jerry was to be hitched to the phaeton and driven the ten miles into Santiago to meet Mr Arms and his niece? The ride into town would be a welcome change. It meant wearing his Sunday clothes. Unlacing his boots, he pictured Mr Arms's furious reaction if he should take a notion to defy his wishes and appear at the station in these working boots and trousers. Mr Arms had a temper, all right — hot as hell. He could see him now, stern and tight-lipped. Would there be a change now that a girl was coming to live with them? Would it be too much to hope for — that Mr Arms would soften and become a little humanized? What would the girl be like? Sharon was her name they said. Well, it was a nice enough name. But he didn't expect her to be friendly. He had very few friends, and none were girls. He supposed she would be like the other people from the United States he had met — brash, loud-spoken, and always on the go.

As he changed his shirt there came over him, apparently without cause, a feeling of pity for this Sharon who would be under Mr and Mrs Arms's strict surveillance as much as he was. Mr Arms would probably force her to go to church against her will. And she would likely have to be up for breakfast at five-thirty and listen to her uncle expound the doctrine of brotherhood and sweet charity. The picture crystallized Jason's hatred for this foster father, whom he had always called Mr Arms.

There were many bitter memories contributing to this hatred, but two scenes always stood out far above the others. There was the time one of the workers had begged to go home because he was ill, and Jason was letting him leave the field. Almighty Mr Arms, ordering the boy back to work, had said, "He's no sicker than I am, boy!"

"But, sir, even his wife told me he had an awful fever last night."

"I'll be the judge of that. I give the orders around here. Do you understand that? I will be obeyed! And no bastard is going to stand in the way. Get that, boy!"

"What do you mean by that, sir?" Jason demanded hotly, the veins standing out livid on his forehead.

And just because he showed his resentment Mr Arms stood there before the natives and deliberately related the circumstances of Jason's birth. Jason stood beside Jerry, staring at the ground and knowing that every damned Cuban within hearing was grinning at him.

Then there was the time Mr Arms destroyed his books. Jason had not gone to school, and Mrs Arms had taught him all he knew about reading and writing and ciphering. The Armses owned books all right. There was the Bible in various sizes, and of course *The Pilgrim's Progress*, *The*

Life of Christ, and a dictionary. There was an ornate volume of Longfellow's poems belonging to Mrs Arms and a book on the planting and raising of sugarcane. During his teens Jason read and reread these books awaiting the time when he could buy books of his own.

Not until he was twenty-one did Mr Arms pay him wages. But in the first six months he saved enough to buy several books when he was sent to Santiago on errands. How proud he was when he arranged them and rearranged them on top of his chiffonier — Byron's poems, the *Divine Comedy*, the *Odyssey*, the *Iliad*, Shakespeare's *Anthony and Cleopatra*, and the sayings of Socrates as recorded by Plato.

But his pride was shortlived. Mr Arms, entering Jason's room to give him some orders, noticed the books and, motivated by the very wrath of God, swept them to the floor with one sweep of his arm.

"I'll not have books of this sort under my roof, boy!" he thundered.

"But why, sir?"

"Because they're trash. That's what they are. Trash designed to undermine the word of the Lord. I won't have it. It isn't that I don't want you to read, boy. But you'll read what's good for you."

"I suppose you mean that I'll read what you say is good for me!"

"Exactly. And I don't care to hear another word out of you. We won't discuss it any longer." While he spoke Mr Arms gathered the books in his arms and, marching to the kitchen, fed them one by one to the flames.

Even thinking about it made Jason fume. "Damn his hypocrite's hide," he muttered as he donned his tan pith helmet. "Some day I'll get out of here. I'll go to the States. Nothing can stop me when I make up my mind I'm ready to go."

He opened his door, crossed the kitchen, gave a short-tempered knock on Mrs Arms's door. She answered him as shortly and he could hear her stirring about. After waking the cook he took a drink of water from the pail in the corner, tipping the dipper more than was necessary to let some of the cool water trickle over his chin.

Some of the natives were already about when he rang the bell in the yard for them to get up. He could smell the frying of their salted peccary. The air had a pleasant tang about it, something electric — perhaps it was because a newcomer was arriving.

At the stable he slapped Jerry, the roan mare, on the flank and laughed at the surprised look she gave him as she woke. She rose, snorting and neighing.

"Time to feed, Jerry-girl!" Jason called out. "And I'm going to give you a brushing this morning that will make your coat shine like copper. They's company coming, Jerry. A girl." He winked. "And I don't want you getting jealous of her either. Mr Arms says that if she's anything like his sister was, she's a very pretty girl, indeed. So you've got to look your best, Jerry."

While Jerry enjoyed her oats and bran mash Jason hurried back to the kitchen where he found much bustling about. Conchita, the young Cuban girl who helped Mrs Arms about the house, was setting the table, the cook was frying sausages, and Mrs Arms, in a dark blue figured percale dress which revealed her doughy plumpness in front and the top of her corset over her shoulder blades in the back, surveyed all with a terrible eye. In her hand she clutched the worn and familiar book bound in black leather, her personal volume.

Jason hung his helmet on a nail in the kitchen, washed his hands and bade the ladies a good morning.

"Good morning, Jason." There was accusation in Phoebe Arms's voice. "You're two minutes late."

"I had to curry Jerry."

"You took plenty of time to it. Talking to her like a ninny, I presume."

"I always talks to Jerry when I brush her. She stands still better."

"Nonsense. You must grow out of the habit of talking to dumb animals. It isn't natural."

"Yes, ma'am."

Mrs Arms took her husband's place at the table, propped the big Bible up before her and, like a disappearing cannon, sank behind the fortress of its pages.

"Come," she commanded, "be seated, all of you. It is time for our morning Scriptures."

Santiago sweltered under the blazing sun that August morning when the train brought Sharon to her final destination, her new home. The dirty, narrow streets, winding in a complicated maze, were crowded with tradespeople marketing their fish and fruit and vegetables. Among them were a sprinkling of British, some Americans, and a good many Spaniards. The Cubans neither cringed nor looked bitter when a Spanish soldier approached. The soldiers here, as in Havana, were everywhere, but they laughed and joked among themselves and flirted with the Cuban girls — who flirted back with them. Sharon noticed how unlike Havana it was, and wondered why.

Santiago might have been second in importance to the capital city, but to Sharon it seemed first in the spirit of friendliness. The Cubans smiled at her when she stepped from the train; the Spanish soldiers tipped their hats or saluted and grinned, nudging each other. The officials were courteous and from a balcony overlooking the depot a girl was singing. In Havana the soldiers had only leered. Nobody had smiled. Nobody had sung. Yes, it was a different city all right.

Sensing her thoughts, Uncle Clay gave them words: "You're surprised at the difference, eh, girl? Well, so is everybody. Cuba is a small island, but her hatred travels slowly. In Havana hard times and cruelty have brought about hatred and despair. In the country it has not yet reached despair, though General Garcia keeps it at hatred pitch. Here in Santiago the people don't quite understand. They are puzzled and curious, but what they don't understand they dismiss with a smile. I have lived long enough in Cuba to know a Cuban's emotions. They are like children. Sometimes I think it is wisest that they be kept so."

Sharon had read about Santiago back in Texas, had seen pictures of its large land-locked harbour and knew that it was frequently visited by yellow fever. She was excited about it, her excitement enhanced by the knowledge that here was a former smuggling centre, the objective of French and English invaders, an oft-looted city of intrigue and conspiracy. She could see quite a distance down a typical street with its open-air shops, its clutter of carts and its quota of half-naked children running in and out among them.

"Where's that boy, I wonder?" Uncle Clay clicked his teeth in impatience. "I told him to be here bright and early. Oh, there he is."

Sharon looked up at the flustered youth who was running towards them. Uncle Clay set the bags down and, taking the hat-box from Sharon's hand, set it down too.

"This is my niece, Sharon Douglass, Jason. Sharon, this is Jason Earleigh, my overseer."

"I'm very pleased to make your acquaintance, ma'am." Frankly Jason stared at her.

"How do you do, Jason?"

"How-do." And to Clayton. "Was it a hard trip, Mr Arms?"

"Hard enough, boy. Pick up the bags. How is Mrs Arms?"

"Very fine."

"Did you ride the South-forty yesterday?"

"Yes, sir."

"How is Pablo?"

"The fever hasn't left him, sir. Mrs Arms is still giving him quinine."

"I see. Well, let's be on our way."

Uncle Clay helped Sharon into the front seat of the phaeton and she found herself riding between him and Jason. She tried to study the boy without his knowing it, but he fixed his pale blue eyes on her and gazed thoughtfully.

"The house has been turned upside down getting things ready for you, ma'am." He let Jerry wind her own way homeward among the pedlar's carts. A gentle pull of the reins now and then was all she needed for guidance. " 'Spect you'll find things pretty comf'table at Promised Land."

"That'll be fine. I'll be glad to get unpacked. All my things are mussed after the boat ride. And you know how grimy it is on a train."

"I guess I know, ma'am, but I've never been on a train myself. Your brown suitcase is pretty heavy. Did you bring some books along?"

"No, I didn't — not a book. Why?" Sharon looked at Jason now with more interest and less curiosity. "Are you a bookworm too?" She had no sooner uttered the words than she saw Eric standing before his little shelf of books, his eyes beseeching hers for approbation.

"I guess you can call me that, ma'am." Jason brought her back. "Why, do you know somebody else that likes books?"

"Yes, a young — I mean — a friend of mine." She looked hastily at Uncle Clay. He had his head turned away and was engrossed in the panorama of the countryside as they left the outskirts of Santiago behind.

Jerry was a high stepper and the phaeton was light. They moved swiftly past field after field of sugarcane that waved and crackled in the hot breeze as the stalks rubbed against each other. The fields were well kept, and the workers in them sang as they laboured. The occasional plantation homes also had a neat, well-kept look. What a contrast to the plantations near Havana! Uncle Clay spoke only rarely, and then to the occupants of another carriage. To Jason and Sharon he had nothing to say.

But Jason kept up a running conversation all the way to Promised Land. Sharon knew within the first five minutes of the ride that she liked this tall, lean boy with the shock of blond hair and the candid expression. She knew she had an ally now, and perhaps things wouldn't be so bad at the plantation. The five minutes with this boy who could not keep silent for one had dispelled all her forebodings. For all of the ten miles she matched him in conversation, pressing him for explanations and plying him with eager questions.

Jason thought, "I was a fool to worry this morning. We're going to be friends. Things will be different now around here. She's got a nice smile and she's pretty."

"That's the Floyd plantation," he pointed out to Sharon. "They ain't got no truck with sugarcane. They's tobacco planters. Old man Floyd —"

"Mr Floyd, Jason!" Clayton broke his silence, reminding the two that he was there.

"Yes, sir. Mr Floyd, ma'am. Mr Arnold Floyd. He runs a market back in Santiago. And a cigar factory too. He makes the finest cigars on the island, ma'am."

"Do you smoke cigars, Jason?"

He looked at her as though she had asked if he ate three meals a day. "Why, certainly, ma'am. I rightly think that nobody in Cuba smokes anything *but* cigars. Mr Floyd makes the best smokes in the whole world, I guess."

"Jason is given to exaggeration, I'm afraid, girl." Uncle Clay actually smiled at Sharon. He seemed human and friendly out here in familiar surroundings, as if getting home was making a new man of him. Sharon breathed more easily.

"Our plantation's next," said Jason eagerly, "yonder of the bend of the road."

"You mean we're close to it?" Sharon sat up in her seat as Jerry voluntarily broke into a trot. No detail of the landscape escaped Sharon's scrutiny. She scanned the curve of the dirt road, the palms, the large field of sugarcane at the right, the hill to the north, bathed by the sun in a flood of gold.

"Yes, ma'am. We're right next to the Floyds, we are."

"Have the Floyds any children?"

"Well, not exactly children, ma'am. They's got a daughter about eighteen. Name of Libby. They's just the three of them."

"Are you and Libby Floyd sweethearts, maybe?"

Jason flushed to the roots of his hair. "No, ma'am, just acquaintances, I guess. I haven't got any sweetheart. You might like Libby, though. You'll see her in church Sunday. She sings in the choir. Not very good, because she's got a hare-lip I expect."

"Oh." And to relieve his embarrassment at this personal remark, "What's that hill?"

"That's San Juan, ma'am. Nice hunting up there — or it was. There's some talk of the Spanish building a fort on the top of it. Just a short piece further on this road is El Caney."

"El Caney," she repeated thoughtfully. "That's a beautiful name."

"Yes, ma'am. Spanish."

"Do they have any dances there?" She lowered her voice.

"Dances?" Jason didn't seem quite sure of what she meant. "Well, I guess in Santiago they's dancing. You rightly mean a ball, don't you?"

"Yes, that's it. A ball. Where they waltz," Sharon went on enthusiastically, "and dance the cotillion, you know."

"No, ma'am, I guess I don't. I don't know how to dance. Well, here we are. Gee, Jerry, gee! Gee, girl!"

But Jerry needed no instructions. She was already turning into the broad drive of cinders before the front veranda at Promised Land. It was a large white house, trimmed in orange, and the veranda roof was supported by great tall pillars of oak brought from Saint Augustine. A small semicircular balcony overhung the wide doorway. The house, built in the shape of the letter E without the middle arm, stood tall and commanding, facing north in the general direction of San Juan hill. At the rear were the gardens, Phoebe Arms's pride, severely laid out — she was from Virginia — and well tended every moment of the day.

The carriage had hardly come to a stop when the porch was overrun with grinning, dark-skinned Cuban children, the boys in neat suits of white linen, the girls in yellow pinafores. No naked children were going to run about Promised Land if Phoebe Arms could help it. It was apparent that they liked Jason, for they clustered about him, hanging to his arms and hugging his legs as soon as he swung to the ground. A few of them regarded Sharon solemnly, and all hung back shyly at a safe distance from Mr Arms.

Jason laughed and patted a little girl's head. "These are the young brats too tiny to go to the fields yet. This little skinny one, this is Miguel. And that's Tomas and that's Luis. The fat little boy is Mario. He eats too much salt pork, don't you, Mario?"

Sharon laughed indulgently at Mario hiding his head behind a pillar. "How about the girls?" she asked.

"Well, the one with the smooth hair is Maria. She's Mario's twin sister. And that's Dolores, and this is Rosa, and the one with her thumb in her mouth is Juanita."

"You know them all?"

"They're always begging me to play with them, that's how," Jason replied sheepishly.

"Girl! Jason! Stop jabbering!" Clayton turned to the house. "You bring in the suitcases, boy, and then take Jerry to the stables. I'll rub her down myself."

"Yes, sir."

The three stepped on to the veranda and with perfect timing the great front doors with their brass knockers and leaded windows swung open. José, the man-servant, stood aside as Phoebe Arms hustled on to the porch. She wore grey taffeta — very badly, for it made her skin look ashen. Grey curls, looking slightly ridiculous on a woman of her age, clustered about her neck in thick, tumbled ringlets. About her throat she wore a collar of double chins. Advancing on Sharon like a juggernaut, she kissed her lightly on the cheek.

"Now, you may kiss me, niece." She proffered her own grey jowl.

Hesitating only because she had pictured Aunt Phoebe as being a slender, possibly scrawny woman, Sharon did bring her lips to the face that looked like ashes and felt like parchment. "I'm awfully glad to know you, Aunt Phoebe."

"That's a dear child. Your uncle and I are glad to have you with us, I am sure. José will show you to your room. Dinner is at two. You will be prompt. I expect you have a lot to tell us, so you need not help in the kitchen this afternoon. Jason, do not stand there gawking. Help José with the bags. I declare you grow lazier by the minute. Look sharp, José! Clayton, dear, Juan has run away again. Did you have a hard ride? I'll brew you a cup of tea before afternoon prayers. Pablo's fever is worse. I'm afraid it's the Lord's will. Come, do not let us stand here in the heat."

She turned and led the way into the hall. At the far end of this imposing introduction to Promised Land Sharon viewed a great, broad staircase curving gracefully to the second floor. In the parlour at the right a fire burned busily in the hearth despite the heat. At the left was the dining-room, dark and shuttered. Sharon caught a glimpse of heavy silver on the table and thick glass-ware on the sideboard.

"Come, niece, into the parlour." Aunt Phoebe's voice pierced the air. It was pitched an octave higher than nature intended anyone to talk. "We have a fire in the grate. Heat draws heat right up the flue. You'll find it cooler in here."

But Sharon stood in the hall admiring the great chandelier of crystal that hung from the centre of the ceiling. Then Jason came clattering down the steps, two at a time. He stood before her, panting a little.

"I put your bags in your room, ma'am. José is at the well drawing water for you."

"Please, don't call me ma'am any more. Call me Sharon."

"All right, ma'am — I mean Sharon. That sure is a pretty name, Sharon. Well, I have to take Jerry to the stables. I'll be back for dinner." Jason turned and disappeared through the great doors, his spurs jingling against his boots.

Pablo de Barbuda was born on the Isle of Pines. He came to Cuba in 1858 and settled down as a weaver of hats at a town called Jucaro. There, by an aged priest from the mission, he was married to a Spanish girl, and from this union was born a daughter, Conchita.

When the girl grew into her teens, Pablo, then entering into middle life, liked to spend long hours in the sun before his cabaña, dozing or smoking cigars which he made himself. His siestas were disturbed, however, by his fat wife continually nagging him to weave more hats so that she might buy a mother-hubbard of flowered silk instead of the common calico she must wear. He was a good weaver and he sold many hats, but money meant nothing to him. Because he refused to quicken his idle fingers, she ran away with a French sea captain, and so he was not bothered by her any more.

Now and then his daughter, Conchita, gave him a turn. She was proficient in the art of keeping his house and he feared she might marry and leave him alone. She had many suitors in the town — four Cubans, a French lad named Pierre, an English drunkard called Giles, and a chubby, blond fisherman from Holland named Peter Kleef. She flitted from one to the other, driving them all mad with her quick childish laughter, her bright, black eyes with the long lashes, and her lithe, tantalizing body — but she gave none of them an answer.

What bothered Pablo most of all was his fellow Cubans. They were always asking him to come to their secret meetings in the woods, late at night, when the Spaniards slept. He did not like to go. It was not a decent hour to be prowling about the jungle, and besides, the men talked of nothing but making war. They were stupid if they believed they could make war against the Spaniards. When they showed him rifles from a British filibustering ship he displayed only a sleepy interest. When they showed him bullets brought by a freebooting expedition from the

United States he yawned.

"What good are your rifles and your bullets if you do not know how to use them?" Pablo scoffed.

"We will find a leader to show us how," said Pedro, a tobacco worker.

Pablo returned to his hats and his sun. One day a Spanish officer came to him — a young Spanish officer, hardly more than a boy. He had a haughty smile on his lips and a jaunty hand on his sabre.

"Good day, Señor Hat-weaver," he called, leaning down from his horse. Puncturing a hat with his sabre, he swung it aloft. "I do not think this is a good sombrero, señor. See, I can cut it into ribbons." The soldier laughed lustily at his little joke. "I have come for your taxes."

"Taxes?" Pablo whined, shrinking back from the sword. "I do not pay taxes."

"You do not pay taxes, lazy one? I will see into that." The Spaniard drew a sheet of paper from his tunic and studied it carefully. "You lie, Señor Hat-weaver. See, here it is on paper 'Pablo of Jucaro. One cabaña. One daughter. Taxes, twenty-five pesos.' "

"Twenty-five pesos?" Pablo repeated numbly. "I do not have even one peso."

"I shall give you three days, then, to find twenty-five pesos. And see that you find them, señor!" The young soldier flourished his sword. "If you do not I shall rip open your belly from crotch to button with my own sabre, then feed your entrails to my friends, the vultures!" Laughing, he wheeled his horse about and departed in a cloud of dust.

Pablo did not dream in his patch of sun that day. In the evening, a tall man on a white horse stopped there. He wore a homemade uniform and rode the horse as though he were born to it.

"Good evening, Señor Barbuda," the stranger called out. "I am Señor Garcia. I am the leader of your fellow Cubans. Do you wish to fight with me against the Spaniards? I will show you how to use a gun."

"Will I have to pay taxes, señor?" Pablo asked.

"No. That is why we are fighting."

"Not even one peso?"

"Not even one peseto!"

"Then I will fight."

So Pablo marched away to the Valley of Gualmaro and fought under General Garcia for two years. Conchita promised her father not to wed and, keeping her promise, became a waitress in a café at Jucaro.

One day a Spanish bullet struck Pablo and shattered his kneecap. After many months it healed, but he could not walk without the aid of a stout stick. So General Garcia gave him a medal and three pesos and sent him home.

He heard then about a job which a Señor Arms of Santiago had open at his plantation — a job of sorting sugarcane by lengths — and he went to ask for it. Señor Arms was willing to let him try, and Pablo and Conchita moved to the plantation. Pablo slept in the cabañas with the other Cubans, but Conchita served as a maid for Señora Arms and lived in the great white house. They were there four years and Pablo was happy again. When he wasn't sorting sugarcane he could dream in the sun — that was, of course, if Señor Arms did not see him.

One day in August Pablo felt very sick. He tossed all night on the floor of his cabaña, and the next day he could not drink enough water. He was so listless he could barely move; his head ached and his body ached and cold waves ran up and down his legs and back until his teeth chattered. His eyes were glazed and his tongue was as scarlet as the blood-rose. He was cold one minute and the next he was burning up both inside and out, and his skin was hot and dry. When Conchita visited him in the evening with some biscuits smuggled from the kitchen, she saw at once how ill he was and summoned Mr Arms.

Pablo tried to eat the biscuits, but they choked his throat and he could not swallow. He did not even care to eat. He only wanted to drink. In his restlessness as he lay on the floor he thought he saw the Spanish tax collector in his doorway.

"— three days to find twenty-five pesos," the youth was saying, "and if you do not find them, señor, I shall rip open your belly from crotch to button and feed —"

"No, no, no!" cried Pablo, struggling to his

feet and swaying in his delirium. But the Spanish soldier was gone. Pablo went behind the cabaña and vomited, as a child, without effort, a blackish mixture which looked like blood.

On the evening of the fourth day of his illness Pablo sank into a coma. That was the day Sharon Douglass came to Promised Land. Everyone clustered about the cabaña. Phoebe Arms read from her Bible, "Thy kingdom come. Thy will be done —"

Pablo's skin had turned a lemon yellow and was cold to the touch. Mr Arms felt his pulse. There was barely even a feeble action. Sharon stood in the doorway, eyes wide, clutching Jason's sleeve.

"Is he going to die, Jason?"

"Yes," said Conchita, who had not been asked. Conchita eyed Sharon and Jason, her eyes smouldering. Under her stare Sharon dropped Jason's arm. Only then did Conchita look back at her father.

"I'm afraid there is no hope," Clayton Arms said.

"I'll fetch Padre Esteban," Jason offered quickly. "Pablo can't die without the padre." Conchita's face lighted and she looked fondly at Jason.

"Nonsense!" snapped Phoebe Arms. "Heaven is just the same for a Methodist as for — A padre is nonsense. If he's a sinner God, and not the padre, will sit in judgment on him."

"But —" stammered Jason.

"You heard her, boy," Mr Arms dropped Pablo's hand. The Cuban went into a violent convulsion and fell back lifeless to the floor. Mr Arms covered the twisted body with the blanket.

"Jason," he said, "you and I will dig a grave tonight. We will pray God that none of us will be infected from handling this wretched creature. It's yellow fever, that's what it is."

"Yes, sir."

The death watchers departed from the cabaña. Outside the moon shone down with an eerie light upon the fields. Huddled in little kneeling groups were the other workers, chanting a prayer — a weird exhortation to the moon. In the distance someone was beating a drum with slow and measured strokes. Its muffled notes hung heavily over the trees like muted thunder before a storm. Sharon shivered slightly and drew closer to Jason. "The last two days," she reflected, "have been filled with violence and death; and I thought the passengers on the boat were joking about Cuba."

Conchita cried softly, lingering at the door of the cabaña where her father lay. Sharon's heart went out to the girl and, drawing away from Jason, she placed her arms about Conchita's shoulders saying, "Let me help, dear."

Conchita looked up through her tears. When she saw who it was she shrank back and bared her teeth, looking from Sharon to Jason and back to Sharon.

"You leave me 'lone, do you hear? You leave

Conchita 'lone!" Picking up her skirts she fled back to the kitchen leaving Sharon standing beside the cabaña, her hand to her cheek as if she had been slapped.

On the Sunday following Pablo's death the Arms household set out for church. Jason, having hitched Jerry and the gelding Freddie to the phaeton immediately after breakfast, drove Clayton, Phoebe, Conchita, and Sharon into Santiago. It was a bright morning, scorching hot, and the roads were dusty. Sharon and Phoebe carried parasols to protect them from the sun, but Conchita scorned parasols. Not a cloud trimmed the sky, not a breath of air was stirring. The heat was oppressive and the stillness, broken only by the rhythmic trotting of Jerry and Freddie and the subdued conversation between Sharon and Jason, seemed ominous.

Passing the Floyd place they noticed that no one was about, and Jason, pointing to the open gate and the fresh wagon tracks, observed that the Floyds had already left for the service. Occasionally they met another carriage or passed one on its way to Santiago, but for the most of the ten miles the road was deserted.

Prior to assuming its present pious air, the Calvary Methodist Church had been a store. The church board had purchased a block of discarded seats from the Havana Opera House and installed them in the building. These were placed in front for the members, while behind them, for any others who might choose to attend the services, were rows of hard benches. Beyond the altar, which Clayton Arms had built and donated in solemn ceremony, was a rough table for the collection plates, communion trays, and the preacher's hymn book. A baptismal font, highly carved and bearing the words, "Suffer the little children to come unto me", was at the left. It had been brought all the way from the United States. At the right were draped the American and Spanish flags. Across thc front of the altar, crudely carved by Jason's hand, was verse sixteen of the third chapter of the Gospel according to Saint John. The windows of the store had been transformed with cheap paint into a semblance of stained glass. The right window bore a highly coloured representation of Jesus being baptized by John in the Jordan; on the left was a lurid picture of Satan tempting Christ. The small organ, formerly a show piece in Phoebe's girlhood home in Virginia, possessed very poor tonal qualities, but for the purposes of the impoverished Calvary Methodist Church it was satisfactory. Phoebe had donated it, Phoebe played it, and, to its accompaniment, Phoebe led the small congregation in song. To Sharon's ears Aunt Phoebe's singing was atrocious. Never before had she been compelled to attend church by either her father or by her own religious will.

For Sharon did have a religious sense, though she had never been able to confine her religion to one creed. God was so mixed up in her consciousness with blue skies and deep streams and cowboy ballads and bleating calves and saloons and moonlight that she didn't know which she worshipped most — an unknown quantity, Uncle Clay's God, or Nature. She hated being pinned down like this — to state her belief in so many words and have done with it. But she politely endured Aunt Phoebe's soprano; politely listened to Uncle Clay preaching sonorously about sin, his obsession; and politely declined to let her religion become imprisoned by either the songs or the sermon.

Indeed she was too busy looking about her — and trying to forget the death and funeral of Pablo de Barbuda. It had been two days ago, that funeral, but she felt it would be burned on her memory for all time. She could see it so clearly now — the rough wooden coffin that Uncle Clay and Jason had built and which Aunt Phoebe had grudgingly lined with a real linen sheet, the yawning grave that Jason had dug, under Uncle Clay's supervision. Although Pablo had lived and died a Catholic, Phoebe Arms had refused to permit the padre to conduct, or even attend, the simple funeral rites. It was as though she nursed an implacable hatred for all things Catholic. Then that evening Sharon had come upon Jason standing alone at the new grave, his hat in hand. He was saying something in a foreign tongue. She waited for him by the stables.

"What were you doing, Jason?"

"I was reciting some words that Padre Esteban taught me."

"What do they mean?"

"I don't know exactly. They's Latin. Padre Esteban always says them when somebody dies. They probably won't work for poor Pablo because I say them. But I have tried."

"Are you Catholic, Jason?" Sharon asked, a little awed.

He had looked at her squarely for a long time, searching her face as if for understanding. "Yes, Sharon. Only you must never tell anyone. Never. If Mr and Mrs Arms ever found out they would raise the roof, I guess. Sometimes I sneak away and go to Padre Esteban's Mass for the Cubans in the hills, but sometimes I can't get away. And when I tell the padre about it he says that it is what is in the heart that really counts. The padre is the kindest man I ever knew."

"He sounds very kind. He must mean a great deal —"

"You won't tell anyone?"

"Of course not. It will be our secret. You can trust me."

And that was the first of many secrets which Sharon and Jason were to share in this strange, strict household.

As his sermon rose to a dramatic crescendo Clayton mopped his broad forehead with his large linen handkerchief, a gesture that Sharon later learned preceded the end of the Sunday morning service. While Uncle Clay drew his ponderous conclusions about the wages of sin, Sharon caught the eye of Libby Floyd, who sat across the aisle from her. Libby was eighteen, a short girl with straight brown hair and sunburnt complexion. Her shoulders were narrow and rounded and her breasts flat. She had broad hips and thick ankles and wrists. Sharon was sure she had never seen such an unattractive girl, and her sympathy went out to her.

Libby's hare-lip gave her a queer, sneering expression as though she regarded everything with extreme disdain. Her eyes were a medium brown and her small nose did nothing to enhance her appearance. However, she did not seem conscious of her lack of beauty as she sang loudly, almost outdoing Aunt Phoebe herself, though every syllable sounded to Sharon like a plaintive whine. She determined she would be Libby's friend.

Her attention was drawn from Libby to Uncle Clay who was announcing, "And now it gives my wife and myself great joy to tell you, dear friends and followers of Christ, that we have with us a new lamb to add to our flock. My niece, Miss Sharon Douglass, has come all the way from Galveston in the States to live with us. I am going to ask her to rise and show herself."

Sharon felt appraising eyes upon her, burning through her as though she were before the seat of judgment. She rose hesitantly to her feet, smiled on the congregation and at her uncle and aunt, then sat down quickly.

"My niece will become a regular member of the Calvary Methodist Church," Clayton continued, "and next Sunday she will not only be taken into our membership by the confession of her faith, but will also be baptized unto her eternal glory. Mrs Arms will now lead us in the last stanza of 'Abide With Me'."

The organ thundered forth and the voices filled the hall as the Calvary Methodist Church of Santiago de Cuba concluded another Sunday morning service.

Sharon was allowed less than a week to accustom herself to her new surroundings. She was thoroughly unprepared when, on the Monday morning following her first church service, Aunt Phoebe reproached her with, "You're up late, niece."

"Yes, I overslept, didn't I? But the bed felt so good I couldn't resist."

"You will learn to resist. You were not here for breakfast when the bell was rung. Consequently, you shall not have any breakfast now."

"Oh, but I don't want any. That's why I didn't bother to get up. I wasn't hungry."

"In the future, niece, you will rise for breakfast and partake of food with us whether you feel so inclined or not."

"Yes, auntie."

"Please, just address me as aunt."

"Yes, aunt."

"I will inform you now as to your duties in the

household. All of us have our tasks to perform, and if we perform them well the plantation will run in harmony. Your chores will be simple to begin with, I shall expect you to supervise Conchita in her duties. She's still mooning about her father and neglecting her work. You will learn to prepare meals both for our simple tastes and for the somewhat vulgar taste of the natives. The cook sometimes falls ill. In a week or two you will learn to bake bread, and that will become your regular task on Mondays, Wednesdays, and Fridays. Conchita will be doing most of the other work if you keep her at it. And now I will give you your first lesson in cooking. At your age I was an accomplished cook. I do not understand how you managed on your ranch not knowing how to cook."

"We had Lee Wong, a Chinese cook."

"I should think you'd be frightened to death of the murderous creatures."

"Oh, but Lee wouldn't harm a hair of your head. Poor old Lee! He took my father's death quite hard."

"Harder, I imagine, than certain other persons," Phoebe remarked pointedly.

"Aunt Phoebe, father and I —" She was about to tell her aunt that it was none of her business how she reacted to her father's death but she said instead, "Oh, what's the use. You would never understand."

But Phoebe wasn't listening. She was busy at the big wooden table in the kitchen, measuring flour and spices into a bowl.

Sharon worked so hard all that week that each night she tumbled into bed utterly exhausted. She had little time to think of Eric except at night when she undressed and saw his ring lying against her breast. She wondered when she would receive his first letter, and each time Uncle Clay returned from Santiago with the groceries and mail she eagerly questioned him. But each day he answered her with a shake of his head.

She began to wonder what she would do if she should have a baby. In all the novels she had read, the seduced heroine had always borne a child and suffered horrible consequences. By all the laws of fiction, she told herself, she would have a baby; yet somehow she couldn't be concerned about it. She painted lurid pictures of her uncle's wrath, yet she was not in the least frightened.

Early in life Sharon had learned about these matters from an Osage Indian squaw. As the squaw had borne eleven children, each without effort, the prospect of pregnancy never worried Sharon. It was only the heroines of novels who seemed to suffer. None of the women she knew had endured their terrors. Melissa Sanders back in Cardenas had borne a child out of wedlock and nobody seemed to bother much about it. They talked, of course, but the affair soon blew over.

The old squaw also told Sharon how to know

that there wasn't to be a baby so, some two weeks after Key West, she breathed a sigh of relief. Promptly and gratefully she forgot about it all, not because she had been spared disgrace, but because she was exempted from a bothersome task.

But at night sometimes she lay awake, too exhausted to sleep, and the picture of Eric would appear before her — his brown, unruly hair, his ardent lips. Why hadn't he kept his promise to write? Many a night she wanted to cry, but, clutching his ring in her hand, she would hold back her tears and would finally fall into a deep sleep of weariness. Once or twice she thought of confiding in Libby — for seeing each other on Sundays they had become casual friends; but she couldn't bring herself to speak of love affairs to Libby just yet.

It was difficult to supervise Conchita who, after the death of Pablo, wore an air of importance induced by self-pity. Conchita found many ways of getting out of work, and more often than not Sharon would have to perform her tasks for her. Still, after prayers, just before supper, and then later on in the evening, she had a little time to herself, and she spent it acquainting herself with every nook and corner of Promised Land.

One place she liked to explore was the large attic stored with trunks and antiques brought from the States. On the second floor were the large bedrooms, furnished with an eye for prim hospitality. Phoebe had one, Clayton another. Conchita's was smaller and so was Sharon's. The largest of all was the guest-room, though the Armses had not entertained a guest in years. In the spacious parlour on the first floor were Aunt Phoebe's choicest pieces brought from the old homestead in Virginia. Here were the portraits of her father and mother, framed in heavy gilt and standing on easels. The imposing room was furnished with a large plush settee, stiff, straight-back chairs, a small folding rocker, an immense walnut secretaire, a spinning wheel, and — Aunt Phoebe's most prized possession — a century-old harpsichord which she permitted no one, not even herself, to play.

Across the hall was the dining-room which also was never used. The family dined in the kitchen. The curtains in the dining-room were always drawn, the shutters always closed. Yet the table was draped with white linen and places set for six with heavy silverware. The beautiful hand-painted china, which had been a wedding gift, was kept under lock in the sideboard. On the table were two pewter candlesticks.

Sometimes Sharon sat in the darkness and coolness of the dining-room and sometimes she sprawled on the broad steps in the hall and read. The grandfather clock stood guard on the first landing like a sentry, chiming out the hours.

During the next few weeks, in the late evenings, she went on long walks with Jason — down the road to El Caney, or across the fields to the foot of San Juan Hill. They never stayed away long, however, for the watchful eye of Phoebe was always upon them, and Clayton disapproved of the two being together without a chaperon.

Sharon grew to love the sky and the trees and the hills of Cuba, and she liked nothing better than to have Jason with her to point out new sights and explain new sounds. Jason walked beside her with a stride as broad as Eric's, but he lacked Eric's nervous energy. Their walks together were free and easy jaunts. The secret of Jason's birth put him in a fascinating light. But what made her enjoy these walks more than anything else was that she knew they made him happy.

It did not take Sharon long to learn that Jason had been starved all his life for friendship. In her presence he talked freely and told her much about himself. But in the parlour or the kitchen he was reserved and silent, and would sit by himself in a corner, sometimes running his long, sensitive fingers through his hair.

Before long Sharon began to suspect that he was growing to love her. She saw it in the quizzical tenderness in his eyes when she looked up at him from her plate at meal-times, in the hesitant touch of his hand on her arm as they leaped across a small stream or puddle, in the way he watched her sing as he held the hymnal for her in church.

This troubled her, for she knew that it would

lead to heartache for him. It irked her, too, for continually it brought back pictures of Eric. She considered telling Jason about Eric, but decided against it. He never spoke to her of other men she might have known and it seemed best to let that subject lie dormant.

Every afternoon at five, Clayton Arms rang the large bell in the yard, the gong notes reverberating across the fields of cane, a signal for everyone connected with the plantation to gather on the front lawn. Clayton would stand on the veranda until all were assembled, then Aunt Phoebe would lead them in singing a hymn. Clayton conducted the service, and the Cuban men, bare to the waist, lolled on the grass with their women and children, listening to the Gospel, their wide-brimmed straw hats protecting them from the sun.

Clayton was following a series of talks based on Cotton Mather and his puritanical tirades against sin with a series based on the Word of God itself. There was no substitute for the Book, he told his flock. For some days now they had been hearing about the creation and the Garden of Eden. On this particular afternoon Clayton dwelt on the story of Noah and the Flood.

Sharon sat on the grass among the others, Jason on her right, Libby on her left. Libby often walked over to attend the service. On the veranda, partly concealed by one of the pillars, stood Conchita watching Jason with Libby and Sharon, her eyes clouded with the smoke of hate, her lips sullen and defiant.

Throughout the sermon Libby talked to Sharon. Though she tried to keep her voice low, it whined nasally through her hare lip.

"Shh!" Sharon cautioned. "Uncle Clay will be furious."

"I don't care. I haven't had a chance to talk to you since Sunday."

"What do you want?"

"Mamma sent me over to invite you to supper to-night and to spend the evening with us. Will you come?"

"I don't know whether I —"

"Do you have to ask your uncle?"

"I suppose I should. But I'd come if I wanted to, anyway."

"Then you will?"

"Do you want me to, Libby?"

"Yes, of course I do."

"All right, then, I'll be there."

The conversation stopped then. Aunt Phoebe was glaring at the two girls from the veranda. As they sang the closing hymn, Sharon saw Libby looking at Jason very much as Conchita had looked at him that first night.

The service over, Sharon went into the house to help the arrogant Conchita lay the table and to inform Aunt Phoebe and Uncle Clay that she was having supper with the Floyds. Low in the west, advancing to meet the setting sun, storm clouds marched up from the horizon and the wind began to lash the palms with flagellating frenzy. As she placed the heavy plates one by one on the table, Sharon's heart grew heavy and oppressed.

After Clayton had finished the sacred task of administering the Gospel that afternoon, he drew Phoebe aside into the parlour with a restraining hand.

"What is it, Clay? Supper's waiting. Is it important?"

"I consider it so, Phoebe."

"Well?"

He drew an envelope from his pocket. "This letter came by post to-day. I picked it up when I was in town."

"Well —" Phoebe reached up to take the letter but Clayton held it from her. He had words to say.

"It's for Sharon. Apparently it's the one she's been asking for these past weeks."

Phoebe shrugged her plump shoulders in annoyance. "Probably from some friend in Texas. Why don't you give it to her?"

"It isn't from a friend in Texas. It's from a common sailor in Key West."

"A sailor!" Aunt Phoebe repeated the word as if she were pronouncing a death sentence. "Does she know a sailor?"

"Much better than a girl of her years should know a man. I took the liberty of opening the letter and reading it."

"But, Clay, was that wise?"

"Wise or no, I opened it. I can't make much of it, but I got enough to convince me that this friendship must be nipped in the bud immediately. A common sailor! Here, I wish you to read the letter yourself."

Hesitantly but curiously, Aunt Phoebe took the letter, adjusted her spectacles, and read in slow measured syllables:

My dear Sharon:

Please believe me that it took a great deal of courage to address you as such, for I felt that in full respect I should have said 'My dear Miss Douglass' instead. But I didn't, because I wanted you to know my real feelings, and if I had not used your Christian name I am afraid I would not have talked as freely as I wanted to.

I tried to start a letter to you upon more than one occasion, my dear, indeed this is the fifth beginning, but each time my pen becomes choked up like words in my throat, and I have to leave the post and go for a tramp on the beach. It is the only way I have of clearing my head of the thousand and one devils that have been tormenting me since you left.

You should see the cabaña now, my darling, for I have stacked it with books like a library. Grandmother sent me a shipment, and if it wasn't for my oath of allegiance to the United States Navy I'm afraid I would desert and be spending most of my time there on the palm matting where our lips first met.

Even thinking about it now sets my blood tingling, and over my body there creeps a strange sensation that would only be satisfied if I could hold you once again in my arms.

I left so many things unsaid that night. You must have thought me an odd fellow but you must have cared for me else you wouldn't have come with me to the edge of the sea where the whole world was ours that early morning. Do you remember it, Sharon? Have you still my ring? I should have bought you some flowers and I never should have let you return to the ship alone. I hope you have seen fit to forgive me for certain oversights which I committed. Believe me it was only because you took my breath away and sent my head spinning that I was incapable of harbouring sane thoughts. I wanted to weigh anchor that morning and tell you that I loved you, but I didn't, and it seems stupid to say that I forgot. I hope that this letter now and my actions then will tell you what I didn't have the sense to say to you in person.

Do you like Cuba? You must tell me all about your new life and especially when you think you might see me again. I do hope you will answer my letter, but if you are angry with me for any reason or have met another man and see fit not to write to me, I want you to know that I will always think of you and there will never be any other girl for me again.

Things are so uncertain here and we never know when we'll be transferred. As an ensign I sometimes get important news before the rest of the men, and I hear that if the pleas of Northern Cuba and Havana carry any weight in the States, the Navy will be called upon to help quell the insurrections. I don't believe it though. America is for the underdog and I think we'd fight Spain. But that is an empty dream. It would mean a formal declaration of war and I doubt if the United States will ever fight in another war again. The Commodore says we were too soul-shattered after '68 to even think of fighting. Besides, our army is a farce. Of course the Commodore is right. American people can be fooled you know only some of the time, as A. Lincoln said, so I'm not giving it much thought. Do you see much trouble down there?

Yesterday we had a very distinguished visitor and a particular hero of mine. You probably grew tired of hearing me talk about him on the boat but I never tire of talking about Mr Theodore Roosevelt. He spoke yesterday from the bridge of our cruiser. I wish he was a naval man instead of a land-lubber politician in the Civil Service Commission. I could follow him to the ends of the earth or I mean the seas. Did you know he was once a cowboy? He is in politics now, but he is a born leader. He should have been in the Navy. One of the fellows here said that R. wanted to be a policeman and might later on, because he has some connexions with the New York City police department. Can you see him as a cop, Sharon? I can't. I admire him greatly but he'll never hold public office, I expect. You know he was once defeated in a race for mayor.

But I wish I was more like him. He has a dominant personality and possesses great energy and force. Do you know that he remembers everyone he once knew? He knows an awful lot, reads all the time, too, and works like a demon. Besides, he's an adventurer and a student. He'll take a job where all is sweat and hell and no praise and'll handle it like a veteran. There is a man for you! He knows explorers, cowboys, writers, and statesmen. I think he's bully!

But all I've done is talk about myself and R. I do hope you'll see fit to answer this letter but remember even if you don't I'll never forget you. You are constantly in the thoughts of,

Your Obedient servant,
Eric March.
U.S.S. *Philadelphia*.

P.S. — I carved a sail boat for a small Bahaman boy the other evening and he was pleased with it. I named it *Sharon I.* — E. M.

Aunt Phoebe folded the letter and slipped it back into the envelope. "Perhaps we should forbid Sharon to write to him. What does he mean, Clay, about their lips first meeting? Do you suppose — ? Yes, I think you'd best talk to Sharon and cut off this brazen affair before it goes any farther. I see very plainly that she has sinned and needs your spiritual guidance."

"I shall speak to her, never you mind."

"Are you going to give her the letter?"

Clayton shook his head.

"What are you going to do with it, then?"

"It must be destroyed. I forbid you to speak to anyone about this matter, Phoebe." He crumpled the letter and the envelope in his huge fist and strode over to the grate, tossing the ball of paper into the hungry flames.

The Floyd mansion, a solid, square house of yellow stone, was three stories high and was set on the crest of a knoll where it could dominate its surroundings. Clustering haphazardly on the hillside were the servants' cabañas. The palm-bordered drive wound down to the road and there, spanning it, were two heavy wrought-iron gates brought from England a century before, reputedly on a pirate ship. There was no broad veranda across the front as there was at Promised Land. The two great oaken doors, brass-bound, opened directly on the lawn with only a few flagstones to form a threshold. The windows were barred with ornate grilles, and over the doors, carved in stone, was the Floyd coat of arms — a plumed helmet against crossed lances. Above the insignia was carved in Gothic script the name of the estate, "The Grail".

Surrounded by fields of tobacco, The Grail appeared thoroughly modern from the outside, but, entering the reception hall, Sharon had the sensation of stepping back into the Middle Ages. Standing guard on each side of the massive staircase was a suit of armour. On the walls hung odd-shaped shields, long lances, battle-axes and dim tapestries. The rooms were dark and quiet and heavy with time. The servants moved about with guarded footsteps and spoke in hushed tones. As Sharon entered the dining-room with Libby she wanted to raise her head and shout at the top of her voice to see if any sound would echo from the oak-beamed ceiling. Mr and Mrs Floyd talked in strident whispers, and only Libby's nasal whine penetrated the sombre atmosphere like a dull knife.

It was evident that the Floyds had done far better with tobacco than Clayton Arms with sugarcane. While Uncle Clay was apparently well enough off there were no signs of luxury about Promised Land as there were at The Grail. The Floyds sat down to dinner amid medieval splendour. In the brown-panelled, oak-beamed dining-room, Vincente, the servant, moved about with silent tread as he served the meal. The great oak table, long and narrow, was heavily laden with silver — platters, tankards and candelabra. A blazing fire roared in the stone grate at the far end, and there, stretched out on a large bear skin rug, were Falstaff and Lear, the hounds.

Arnold Floyd sat at the head of the table. Though small, and insignificant, he appeared lordly in the midst of this splendour. He was a man of perhaps sixty, bald, dry-skinned, and with shrewd little eyes like gimlet holes in his face. A slightly Hebraic nose divided his sunken cheeks. He wore his clothes badly — they were draped about his narrow shoulders like a sack.

Lavina Floyd fairly towered above her husband. She was such a huge woman that at first glance she seemed all breasts. Her face, fat and round, perched on her short thick neck like a toad's. She was jaundiced and the yellow hue of her skin was ghastly in the candlelight. Sharon had never seen such a sickly complexion on such a robust person. Lavina's hands were coarse, and her wrists thick; but how sedately she wore her gown of rich brocade shot through with threads of gold! It was so stiff that when she stood it seemed to offer perfect support to her bulky figure.

Sharon observed that Libby's appearance was a composite of a her parents' worst points — her father's narrow shoulders and flat chest, her mother's thick wrists and ungainly limbs. Her wide, innocent eyes had a soft, fawn-like quality, but not even the candlelight could soften the dominating hare-lip. Sharon kept her eyes on her plate during most of the meal.

Arnold and Lavina Floyd had been born in England, Libby in Cuba. Arnold's grandfather, a privateer, had been hung with great ceremony at Portsmouth. His father, an American seaman, had been captured during the war of 1812. After fifteen years of imprisonment in a filthy cell in Dartmoor, he escaped and visited his wife, who served ale at a nearby tavern. He stayed with her long enough to sow his seed, was recaptured, and eventually died of dysentery. The seed flourished and married the daughter of the Vicar of Carstairs. They moved to Cuba where, with tobacco, Floyd built The Grail. The people of Santiago sometimes called it Floyd's Castle.

Mr and Mrs Floyd did most of the talking during dinner, tossing words like volley balls across the table at each other, never letting one drop to the floor. As the dinner progressed, Mrs Floyd became the more talkative, while her husband gradually subsided.

"My dear," Lavina said, turning to Sharon who was busy with her dessert of pineapple chunks. "You don't know how pleased we are to have you with us this evening. Libby has spoken of you so frequently. Your poor father —" Lavina stopped to take a bit of pineapple and Arnold took the ball.

"You needn't be ashamed that he was a gambler," he assured Sharon, lowering his voice confidentially. "You know, we have a few skeletons in the cupboard, too. My grandfather, Morgan Floyd, sailed up and down the Spanish Main, pillaging and plundering until he swung from a yard-arm one fine morning, like a pendulum in the sky. Haw, good joke that!"

"And his father, my dear —" Lavina's mouth was full, but Arnold was about to let the ball drop "— was a jail-bird. Dartmoor Prison. Yes, it's a fact. Would you ever?"

"I'm a little surprised," Sharon answered and laughed uncertainly. But she didn't take the pains to explain that her surprise was not at learning that the Floyd ancestry included pirates and jail-birds but at the fact that her host and hostess were so liberal with their family anecdotes, so glib in relating stories that were slightly off-colour.

Libby had little to say. It was easy to see that she felt bottled up in the presence of her parents, whose verbal game of ball was too swift for her. Sharon wondered how many times Libby had heard the stories of her jail-bird grandfather and pirating great-grandfather. But most of all she wondered at the Floyds' knowledge of her own father. She could scarcely imagine those tight lips of Uncle Clay's revealing any family affairs; nor did she think Aunt Phoebe showed a tendency to confide in Mrs Floyd or Libby. Yet the secret was out. Idly she wondered how many of the church members knew about it, and decided she didn't care.

Her thoughts were interrupted with the first fury of the storm battering against the house like rams in the hands of a besieging army. "Mercy!" she cried, rising quickly. "Now what shall I do? I didn't bring my cape, and this dress spots so."

"Our Pedro shall drive you home in the carriage," Arnold soothed.

"Nonsense, Arnold!" Lavina was scornful.

"Pedro shall do nothing of the sort. One drop of rain will ruin her dress. She shall spend the night here in the guest-room."

"Oh, but I couldn't —"

"Of course you can."

"Oh, no, mamma," Libby spoke up, "not in the guest-room. Let her sleep with me so we can talk."

"Very well, Libby. We'll send Pedro over, Sharon, to inform your aunt and uncle that you are remaining here. Then they won't worry."

The thunder rolled like a mammoth across the alley of the sky, and lightning cleft the clouds with long, jagged streaks. Falstaff and Lear rose from their haunches uneasily, sniffing the heavy air, wincing as rain spattered down the chimney, hissing and steaming on the blazing logs. At Lavina's command they lay down again, their cold muzzles on their forepaws, their large brown eyes doleful and disturbed.

That night the two girls lay beneath the wide counterpane on the canopied four-poster bed in Libby's room. Away from her parents, Libby's tongue was loosened. She told Sharon monotonously of her childhood days and of the school she attended in Santiago, where the other pupils shunned her or made fun of her lip. She claimed she didn't care. Sharon was almost asleep when Libby asked, bluntly, "Are you in love with Jason?"

"In love with Jason?" Sharon laughed. "How can you be so silly, Libby?"

"I'm not silly. He's in love with you."

"Oh, fiddlesticks!"

"Think what you like. I know it."

"Well, I'm not in love with him. We're just friends. He's never had a real friend before, so now I'm it. Why, I've never even thought of Jason that way. He's nice but he's not — well, not like someone else I once knew."

"Who, Sharon?"

"A sailor."

"Tell me about him," Libby whined, sitting up in bed and clasping her knees together. "What was he like? Are you in love with him?"

"I don't know. I think I am." And so there in bed, as the storm pelted rain against the windows, Sharon told Libby Floyd everything. Ever since her affair with Eric she had been wanting to tell someone about it — more than ever as the days lengthened into weeks and no word came from him.

Libby stared wide-eyed into the darkest corners of her room as Sharon related her dramatic story. She drank in every word of it, knowing that this might be the nearest she would ever come to having such an experience. If she should take a boat trip, no sailor would speak to her at the rail, and tell her of his adventures, and point out all the interesting places. No, she couldn't hope that some day a fine, handsome young man would offer to be her guide at midnight in a strange city, and take her to an odd eating place and let her wear his coat.

Sharon lay face downward with one arm across the pillow and her cheek resting on the soft, firm muscles as she told Libby about the walk on the beach, the discovery of the cabaña, and of their overwhelming desire. Libby slipped back beneath the covers and lay breathless on her pillow.

"But, Sharon," said Libby, finally breaking her awed silence, "aren't you afraid?"

"Afraid of what?" Sharon turned on her back and drew thc linen sheet close around her throat. "There's nothing to be afraid of. And as far as people talking is concerned, I'm twenty and I think I'm old enough to govern my own affairs. I'd go to that cabaña with Eric again in a minute. I guess I'm pretty fond of him. Give me your hand, I'll let you feel his ring. I never take it off. But I wear it under my dresses — I don't care to answer questions."

Libby released the ring and withdrew her hand quickly as if afraid of this close contact with romance.

Sharon went on, "No, Libby, I'm not in love with Jason. But you are, aren't you?"

Libby nodded in the darkness. "How did you guess?"

"I just happened to remember the way you looked at him this afternoon at prayers. And I added that to the way you questioned me a minute ago."

"I've been in love with Jason ever since we were children. But he'll never notice me."

Sharon controlled an impulse to sympathize. She knew Libby well enough not to say anything that the girl might interpret as pity.

"I'll always love Jason," Libby whispered and there was no nasal twang in her whisper this time. Sharon had to strain her attention to hear her distinctly. "No matter what he thinks of me, I'll always think the world of him. But please don't ever tell him that. Every Sunday when I go to church I feel as though I were going to my lover. If he doesn't know that, I can pretend he feels the same way. You won't tell him, will you?"

Without answering and without needing to answer Sharon took Libby into her arms and let the child sob her heart out. "This is a fine mix-up," she thought. "Conchita who hates me loves Jason. Libby who likes me loves Jason. I who like all three love somebody miles away and now Jason loves me. Damn! I wish Lucky Fred were alive to tell me what to do."

The thunder quieted and the lightning flickered out. Only the rain beat down on The Grail. For the first time since Lucky Fred Douglass's death his daughter cried — and was not ashamed of her tears.

Sharon was fascinated with the fields of cane from the beginning. From her window they looked like row upon row of walking sticks set at angles into the ground. The narrow, grass-like leaves, almost three feet long, spread in two rows like blades from the top section. The first afternoon that Jason took her into the fields she saw at closer inspection that the canes were quite beautiful, their smooth stems notched with bands of orange and orchid.

"Here," said Jason, breaking off a length for her, "chew on it. I rightly think there ain't no better candy on God's earth." And she found the plant to be as he said — sweet and succulent.

Uncle Clay promised her that when they harvested and took the cane to the factory she could go along. There were over a hundred sugarcane factories in Cuba, and the nearest one to Promised Land was a little north of Santiago — a co-operative affair run by the planters. It was a well-equipped, well-managed factory with a capacity for producing a hundred tons of sugar daily. Clayton and the other planters always hoped that their crops would yield an abundance of juice, for regardless of the quality of the cane, the factory upkeep remained the same.

"You see," Jason explained to Sharon as they rode on the big wagon with the first load of cane, "this factory's power is only as good as its capacity to evaporate and evaporate quickly. It can evaporate six hundred tons of water in twenty-four hours. And it can handle at least a thousand canes with a high grade of juice and so, roughly speaking, give us a hundred tons of sugar. But if the crop is poor we don't do so well. With poor canes the factory can only treat about half as many and we only get about fifty tons."

"Oh," said Sharon, tossing the whole ponderous subject aside with a smile, "I think it's easier to learn how to bake bread under Aunt Phoebe's directions. At least she doesn't throw so many figures at me."

"Why, gosh, Sharon, I think it's as simple as gooseberry pie."

The factory, a low building of corrugated iron, was situated beside a small stream now running thick with syrup. Planters were arriving from every direction. Sharon was not the only woman there, for many of the planters had brought their wives along. While Sharon entered the steamy factory with Jason, the other women spread lunches on a long table beneath a clump of palms. There was a fiesta spirit about it all — they were making their trip to the factory a gala affair.

Sharon and Jason shuffled through the layer of shucks and dry blades of cane that covered the ground. The air was heady with a sickly-sweet smell. Each room of the factory was filled with busy Cuban workers, stripped to the waist, their brown bodies glistening with sweat and steam, their industry shaming their more indolent brothers who laboured in the fields.

There were five large rooms to visit — the extraction room, the defecation room, the evaporation chamber, the crystallization room, and the curing room where the sugar was finally prepared for shipment. In the extraction room Jason and Sharon stopped to watch the crushing mill, a roaring, motor-driven machine consisting of a feeder, several rollers, and a hopper that emptied into a carrier. Before the cane was fed to these rollers it was run through another roller device that flattened it ready for crushing.

"Why does that roller jump every now and then?" Sharon shouted at Jason, as she noticed the top roller on the crusher jerking up and down.

"Oh, sometimes a damned cheater sticks bolts and crowbars in with the cane to get more tonnage. Such stuff would wreck the roller if it couldn't hop up like that. Sometimes rake handles get in by accident, so that's taken care of too."

Sharon laughed at his strenuous effort to make her hear over the noise, and followed him into the defecation room.

"This is where the juice is purified," he explained in a normal tone. The tour from there on was bewildering but fascinating. Sharon saw how the purified juice was decanted, the clear liquid running off through a pipe and the cloudy into the stream beside the factory. Jason explained every detail.

"You know this place as well as if you owned it," Sharon remarked gaily. He smiled at her and led the way to the next room.

As the sun beat more directly on the roof and walls, the temperature rose to oven heat. Sharon watched the scum overflowing the defecators and forming a sort of frothy crust on the floor, from which rose the sweetish perfume that permeated the whole building. The juice ran on into the evaporating room to be converted into syrup.

"This is where the power of the factory is gauged," Jason explained in his painstaking way. "See the coal fires under the evaporating pans?"

Sharon squatted to look at the fires, although the heat was oppressive enough without getting any nearer to its source.

"Here is where we find out how much juice we're getting — and seventy-five per cent of it goes up in steam," Jason went on.

"I'm about to go up in steam myself," Sharon said as she led the way to the crystallization room. Here the remaining twenty-five per cent of the juice, now in thick syrupy form, entered the vacuum pans for concentration.

The final process was claying. "You see, Sharon," Jason continued, wiping his brow, "the crystals are placed in these coneshaped moulds and the moulds are capped with wet clay. The water in the clay seeps through the sugar and washes away the last trace of molasses. It leaves the crystals as clean as a hound's tooth. I rightly think this is the best system. It takes a lot of people to do it this way, but after all, that means jobs."

"It's certainly been instructive to me," Sharon said sincerely as they stepped outside. Even the blazing tropical sun felt cool compared to the terrific heat and high humidity inside. Sharon looked at her dress, so damp that it clung to her wretchedly.

"Did I fall in the river?" she asked Jason.

He laughed. "No, but you do look like a wet hen. Let's see if the wagon's unloaded. It's about time we're getting home anyway if we want to make it by supper."

"All right," Sharon agreed. "Supper sounds good to me. I'm starved."

"Here," Jason handed her a length of cane, sticky with sap in the heat, "munch on this."

She looked at it and lifted it half-way to her mouth. Then, shuddering, she threw it from her and wiped her fingers on her dress. "No, thanks," she said, "I've suddenly lost my appetite."

After weeks of wondering why she hadn't heard from Eric, Sharon began to consider writing to him herself. Did his silence mean indifference? If so she would be a fool to write. Had she meant no more to him than a night of pleasure? Being her father's daughter, she determined to find out. Sitting down at the secretaire in the parlour one afternoon she penned him a note. Leaving some leeway for possible accident to his letters, she asked him point-blank, "What are your intentions, Eric?"

She gave the note to Uncle Clay when he went to town. "Uncle Clay, will you please post this for me? It's very important."

Uncle Clay read the address, pursed his lips and pocketed the letter without a word.

"That's just his nature," Sharon reflected.

"He doesn't like to appear obliging to anyone."

She continued her walks with Jason whenever she had the opportunity and this helped to keep her from worrying too much about Eric. She tried to keep her association with Jason on a friendly basis, but in little awkward ways he often demonstrated that Libby was right.

One evening when they started on a walk Jason suggested, "Let's go up San Juan Hill and see where the Spanish are building the fort."

"Isn't that a long way?" Sharon asked, though not unwilling to undertake it if that was Jason's wish.

"We don't need to go all the way. There's a clearing part of the way up where we can stand and see miles and miles away, if we make it before dark."

"And if not?" Sharon was teasing him.

"Then there'll be the stars to see. I think it's going to be clear to-night." Jason was no good at banter.

As they passed the pantry window Sharon caught a glimpse of Conchita peering at them, a confusion of love and hatred in her eyes, sullen defiance in the pout of her lips.

It took the bright edge from Sharon's gaiety as she walked with Jason across the clipped grass and up the pathway of San Juan Hill. Off the road the shrubs became tangled and thick, but Jason walked through them with such a smooth effortless stride that Sharon marvelled at the pace he set — slow enough for her to keep up with him, yet seeming to take them right up the hill in a very short time.

Neither spoke until they came to the clearing and Jason said, "Let's sit down."

"But what about snakes?" Sharon wanted to know. "And all the other crawling creatures?"

"They won't disturb you, I expect, if you don't disturb them. We've walked nearly an hour, and I feel like resting. Besides we can enjoy the view a lot more if we sit down and take our time to it. Don't you think so?"

"I guess." Although darkness was settling there was still enough light to reveal the expanse of cultivated acres before them and a low range of hills dimly outlined against the sky.

Jason found a long stick and beat the grass and brush until Sharon was satisfied that no crawling creature would be likely to remain near. She sat down where the grass was shortest while Jason stretched out in tired abandon.

"Look, put your head on my lap," Sharon offered. "Then you won't get that loose grass in your hair."

"Fine." Jason sighed heavily. "I like that. It's good to have someone to talk to and be thoughtful when you're tired."

"Just rest then," Sharon said gently. She was in no mood for talk. The brown eyes of a girl who coveted Jason's attention looked at her from a window. She wished that Conchita might have Jason's head in her lap and that she, Sharon, might again pillow Eric's head on her arm.

Jason closed his eyes for a few minutes and when he opened them the stars were out. "God, Sharon," he said quietly, "look at the millions of stars. Suppose someone said to you, 'Count every star in the sky by sun-up or else you'll be made into mincemeat,' what would you do?"

"I expect," she answered gravely, "I should be made into mincemeat. But what amazes me is the way they appear so suddenly. It wasn't like that in Texas."

"No? I supposed it was like this everywhere. But then I haven't travelled as you have. There's lots I don't know."

"Do you like to be out like this alone, Jason?"

"Yes. Only we're not alone."

"No? I see no one else."

"I don't think anybody is ever quite alone," Jason replied, turning his head to see her face better. "I think there's always somebody about even if you can't see him. Maybe an old friend you once had. Maybe your other self. The one that says 'don't' when you want to do something you know you shouldn't. Why, I never feel alone even when I'm just out walking by myself. Somebody's always with me. Maybe God. Maybe the Blessed Virgin. I can't tell just who."

"I never thought of it that way before," Sharon said slowly, and then to herself, "Maybe an old friend you once had."

"What was that you said?" Jason asked.

"Oh, nothing. Nothing important."

"Some time I'd like to take you to see Padre

Esteban," Jason announced, boldly, for him. "You'll love the padre. When I'm with him I feel as though nothing could ever possibly harm me. He's a wonderful man. I suppose he talks with God all the time. Sometimes I think maybe I'd like to be a priest. But I'm not good enough, I expect."

"I don't think you have any reason to say that."

"I guess Mr and Mrs Arms would carry on something awful if they knew I ever thought of such a thing. I was brought up to believe I wasn't any good and Catholics weren't any good either. But Padre Esteban showed me where they were wrong."

"Yes?"

"He says that hate is the worst thing there is and that everybody is good in God's sight. So that made him a better person than Mr and Mrs Arms, and it even made me better because they hate the Catholics and we don't hate anybody. That's how it is according to the padre's lights."

"Is it as simple as that?"

"Sure, Sharon. Even Mr Arms preaches about how God is love, but I couldn't make much sense out of it when I was a boy because Mr Arms pretended to be such a godly man, but he was a hating man too. So when Padre Esteban explained how simple it was I was so happy I cried. I wasn't as bad as Mr Arms said I was. You know, Sharon, it's wonderful to be able to talk to you like this. I never had anybody I could really talk to before. You know how I happen to be here, don't you, Sharon?"

"Why, I know that Uncle and Aunt Phoebe took you in just as they did me. Only you were a baby —"

"Is that all you know?"

"Why —"

"It isn't, is it? You knew that I never had a father — I mean, that they weren't married. You know that, don't you? Mr Arms is always telling everybody."

"It doesn't matter to me, or to any sensible person, I think, whether your father and mother were married. What is important is *you* — just as Padre Esteban taught you."

"I didn't think a girl would talk like that."

"Well I talk like that because that's the way I feel about it. So stop worrying about what Uncle Clay says. He told me about it on the train, and I felt then that I wouldn't have been ashamed to have known your mother. I guess Uncle Clay likes to talk about people's pasts. I guess he's told everybody I'm a gambler's daughter. So we're both in the same boat — being talked about. And I don't give a damn, Jason, and don't you."

"Gosh, I think you're swell, Sharon."

"Oh, fiddlesticks!"

"Next time we come up here we'll start a little earlier and try to get to the place where they're digging for the foundation of the fort. It's like a scar in the hillside. It's just on the other side and a little farther up."

"A hole in the ground doesn't sound very exciting but I'll be glad to take the walk with you. I suppose I should be interested in the fort. I expect it will be very important same day."

"It will be. This hill protects Santiago from the land side, you know. I guess they have to fortify it against the Cubans — Garcia's men — now that they are pretty well armed."

"Where do they get their guns?"

"Mostly they're smuggled in by filibustering ships. Some are from the United States. You remember Pablo?"

"I should say I do. You mean the Pablo who died?"

"Yes. He fought with Garcia for two years."

"What's a filibuster ship, Jason?" Sharon lifted his head and changed her position.

"Well, it's when Americans, or other people, try to help out one part of the fighting, usually the losing side, by shipping supplies to them. There was the case of the *Virginius*, in 1873. She was fitted out in an American port and she flew the American colours. She was bringing men and supplies to the rebels, but she was attacked in Cuban waters by a Spanish gunboat."

"What happened?"

"Well, all the crew and the passengers had to face a naval court right here in Santiago, and over fifty of the prisoners were executed. Eight of them were Americans. Back in the States there was an awful row stirred up about it. They claimed that even though the boat had no business helping the rebels the prisoners should have been returned to America. Anyway, it caused so much fuss that Spain sent over Martinez Campos, and he talked the rebels into laying down their arms. That's how the slaves were freed and the Cubans got into government affairs. But you couldn't vote unless you paid twenty-five dollars a year in taxes. The whole thing is a mess, Sharon, but I'm for the Cubans."

"I guess I am too, Jason. Don't you suppose we should be walking back now?" Jason's words had brought back the memory of Carlos Menendez. She remembered he had told her that hell would break loose on the island, and it seemed as if Jason sensed the same thing. But it was very remote now as she rested on the hillside beneath the glorious stars.

"Gosh, it's so nice here I hate to go back to that — that house. I wish I owned a boat and could go sailing away from this place."

"What would you go sailing for?" The mention of a boat and sailing brought back another memory. Sharon shut her eyes tight.

"Why — why for what I'm looking for, I expect. A girl, I guess. She'd have to be a girl like you though. And I'd sail away to a new land — I'd seek a beautiful golden fleece, like the other Jason. You think I'm silly, I expect."

"No, I don't, Jason. No."

He sat up. "You want to go back now?"

"I believe it's best."

"Will you kiss me before we go down?" he asked shyly.

"Why, yes, if you like." Sharon leaned forward and gave him her lips. He tightened his arms about her shoulders suddenly. She closed her eyes and tried to keep her reason — to remember. But try as she would, she could not be Sharon Douglass on a hillside, with Jason Earleigh's lips pressed ever so tenderly to hers. She was Sharon Douglass at the rail of the *Grover Cleveland*, and one Eric March was crushing his lips against hers, then throwing his head back and laughing — laughing and whispering, "Bully girl, Sharon."

"You're the only woman besides Mrs Arms I've ever kissed," Jason said hoarsely and Sharon could feel his hungry eyes upon her.

"Am I?" she asked, and placing her hand on his shoulder she rose and started down the hill.

As Jason joined her he pointed out the twinkle of lights in the parlour at Promised Land far below them. And here and there across the valley other plantation lights flickered and glowed like fire-flies on a summer night.

With the repeal of the McKinley tariff in 1894, the plantation owners suffered severe losses. Until that time Clayton had done well for himself. His fine home was paid for, and he could easily afford a large corps of workers. His broad acres of sugarcane had brought him a good profit from the United States, because under the tariff he had been exporting his sugar to New York duty free.

In the 1895 sugar slump Clayton became harder and harder pressed for funds. Like the others about him, both Americans and Spanish, he grew sterner-visaged every day, more tight-lipped and silent as the months passed by. Sharon often wondered if he had foreseen some of the hell that Carlos Menendez had prophesied, and if this explained the sternness he had exhibited ever since her arrival.

With the bottom dropping out of the sugar market and prices plunging through the floor, the pressing tax demands of the Spanish Government added new furrows to Clayton's brow. New worries weighed on his heart like a great burden that daily became mere difficult to bear, that weekly bent his spirit a little lower.

He began to take an almost fanatical joy in summoning his help to afternoon prayers. Now he preached to them from the Revelation of Saint John the Divine. He would stand for an hour, sometimes longer, on the broad steps, and paint vivid pictures of death and destruction to come — the doom that was about to descend on the whole world. Whereas it had been his wont to laud the glories of civilization and the great promises, taking many of his texts from the inspirational passages of the Psalms, he now went to the opposite extreme and talked only of the end of things.

The parallel was too obvious to escape Sharon's notice. With the transition from the Old Testament to Revelations, the striking career of Clayton Arms seemed to be foretold. His delineation of Judgment Day, so vividly portrayed over and over on the veranda at Promised Land, frightened the servants, and Sharon observed disturbing signs among them — furtive whisperings, significant glances at the fields beyond. Her Uncle Clay had never paid good wages, claiming to believe that placing too much money in the hands of those who did not realize its value was folly. It was well known that Garcia and his lieutenants were enticing every Cuban in the countryside to bear arms. The pay was small too, yet it was more than Clayton's men were getting.

Clayton, when not preaching to his help or his congregation, said very little to anyone. He began to take his meals alone in the parlour where he sat for hour after hour reading his Bible. Phoebe never spoke to Sharon of his odd behaviour. She went about her household tasks as though nothing was the matter either within or without the walls of Promised Land.

It was Conchita's duty to take Clayton his meals and it was a task she tried to avoid. When compelled to carry it through, she would slip into the room and timorously set the tray on the shelf of the secretaire where her master sat engrossed in his book. But Clayton never acknowledged the service. He kept staring at the page, his great, hollow, penetrating eyes seeming to burn through the paper. It was as if he might at any moment spring into a fiery rage. Conchita would slip out as quickly as she dared.

Clayton left the fields entirely to Jason's care, now that the harvest was only about a tenth of its former size. The herds looked neglected, and Sharon wondered how long it would be before this land would resemble the environs of Havana. When her uncle had told her that hate with its subsequent despair travelled slowly, he was wrong. Within the brief space of a year, the terrorism of the north country had spread to the south.

Clayton left his retreat for a weekly trip to Santiago, where he presided over the meetings of the American Plantation Owners Society. This, his daily trip for the mail and supplies, his afternoon prayer session, his Sunday at church and his retirement at night were the only occasions on which he left the parlour.

Sharon hated the conditions prevailing in that hard year of 1895 — the unrest and political terror throughout the countryside, the monotonous drudgery at Promised Land, and the extreme religious fervour. And now she hadn't even Libby to exchange visits, the Floyds having moved to their Havana home. This left Jason as her only friend.

With the drop in sugar prices, Arnold Floyd had suffered his share of the reverses too. Those who dealt in sugar were now unable to support the tobacco trade. Competitors in Havana and Daiquiri undersold him in the American market, his Cuban employees deserted him to join Garcia, and his factory had been so damaged by a street fight that he knew it would take weeks to repair it. Handing over his presidency in the Plantation Owners Society to Clayton Arms, he sent Lavina and Libby to Havana, boarded up The Grail, and followed them a week later.

The streets of Santiago were peaceful no longer. Had Sharon come into the depot now by the Cuban railroad she would have found the city like Havana — in turmoil. Everywhere there were street skirmishes, and Clayton and Phoebe forbade her even to think of visiting Santiago.

In the early fall of 1895 the pent up emotions of the population burst forth into a new and more bitter struggle for independence. Uprisings, poorly organized but effective, broke out all over the island. The months wore on and there was no sign of appeasement. One by one the Cuban workers deserted Clayton Arms to fight with Garcia's scattered troops. Only the women and children remained, and it became a pressing problem to feed them. That year there had been poor crops and no sale for what cane there was on hand. All the money, save a small percentage for household expenses, went to meet the excessive property tax levied by Spain to support her own troops and to cover the terrific losses in her previous wars. Thus Uncle Clay could pay no wages that fall.

Towards the end of 1895 Sharon found herself forbidden to leave the plantation because of the great danger of rape by rebels or loyalists. She was virtually a prisoner, and only Jason's presence made her life bearable at all. Jason was always there to protect her, to listen when she wished to talk, to be quiet when she wished, to leave her alone when she preferred solitude.

In those twelve long months she had heard nothing from Eric. For days at a time she would succeed in forgetting him. Then in the dead of night she would see him again, standing before her at the ship's rail, and she would throw her arm across her face to blot out the picture. She no longer wore his ring about her neck; it seemed a mockery to do so.

The urgent demands of the Plantation Owners Society to the United States Government went unanswered. This was attributed to President Cleveland's strict adherence to the Monroe doctrine. But neither the Cubans nor the Americans nor the Dutch nor the French were to know what hell was really like until the dawn of the new year, when there arrived to govern them a gentleman with sneering lips and a condescending manner. He was sent to them by the Queen Regent of Spain as a somewhat belated political Christmas gift. His name was Valeriano Weyler; his rank, general. He was affectionately called by his friends "The Butcher".

Until the late summer of 1896 rumours had been circulating that General Weyler would make a tour and visit Santiago. The people lived in an atmosphere of tense expectancy for months. Occasionally conflicting rumours had it that General Weyler entertained no desire and no intention of leaving his headquarters at Havana, and that he had no interest in the people themselves.

But the day finally dawned, bright and clear, when General Weyler, riding amongst red and gold and purple splendour in a high carriage drawn by four spanking black stallions, bowed and sometimes even deigned to smile for his people. Santiago donned its finest clothes that morning and the streets were lined with spectators. The Spaniards cheered and waved flags to greet their new leader. The Cubans either openly jeered or stood silent and sullen, hatred showing candidly in their faces. To the Americans it was like circus day. It was not their method to gloss over problems with pomp and pageantry.

Having been assured that there would be no demonstration during the general's visit, Clayton Arms permitted Jason to drive the little family to town — Phoebe, Sharon and himself. Sharon wore the same black dress she had worn on the *Grover Cleveland* two years before. The Armses were so poor that they could not afford to replenish their own wardrobes, let alone Sharon's or Jason's.

When the parade was over and the last cheers and hisses had died away, the Armses' party turned toward their carriage and Jason asked Sharon, "What do you think of the handsome general?"

Sharon grimaced. "Did you see his face? I mean did you really see it?"

"What has his face to do with it?"

"He has the cruelest expression I ever saw."

"Yes? I didn't realize. But I expect you're right."

"Those beady black eyes and the way he scanned the people as if he was handing them their death sentence."

"Oh, nonsense, Sharon."

"Nonsense, my hat! I saw eyes like that in a weasel once, just before it pounced on a rabbit. And those side-whiskers! They looked like jibsails flapping in the breeze."

As they reached the carriage, Clayton, making sure that no one else was in hearing, said to his family, "No good will come of this new regime, you mark my words."

General Weyler had been the Marquis of Tenerife when he fought in the ten years' war against Cuba. Unrestrained in his methods of fighting then, he had no intention of modifying them now. He took well to heart the words of his sovereign when she beckoned him to her throne and said, "If necessary starve the fools into submission, Señor General."

As he sat now in his vault-like office in the governor's palace he toyed with the idea. The ballroom had been converted into an office to accommodate him. The only pieces of furniture were his desk and chair. Dwarfed as he was in these surroundings of tall pillars and over-ornate chandeliers, the general's mind was in no sense overshadowed. Beneath his bushy hair his brain raced towards a scheme of reprisal against all rebels. Stroking his side-whiskers, he allowed the brief suggestion of a smile to flicker across his haughty lips — a smile as cruel as the man himself.

General Weyler's main problem was that Cubans look so much alike. The only difference between the loyalists and the rebels was their opposing allegiances. Segregating the offenders and dealing with them was to be the general's major task. He turned from the narrow floor-to-ceiling window and pulled a bell cord. Immediately an aide-de-camp was at his side, saluting smartly.

"Your orders, Señor General?"

"Take pencil and paper, Luis, and write as I direct you.

"To Her Most Gracious Majesty, the Queen Regent of Spain, the Imperial Palace, Madrid," Weyler dictated, "Greetings!" He stroked his whiskers gently during a pause. "I have conceived a plan, based in part, on Your Majesty's words of wisdom uttered some months before your humble servant departed for these shores. My great difficulty lies in distinguishing one faction from another. However, I plan to herd your rebellious subjects together near Havana and Santiago de Cuba and thus keep the entire population under my thumb. If need be I shall, as you so wisely suggested, starve them into admitting their part in the rebellion against Your Gracious Majesty's most enlightened rule. I shall make a comprehensive report to you from time to time. May the Blessed Virgin see fit to make your days long and generous upon this earth. Ever I remain, your loyal and humble subject, Valeriano, Marquis of Tenerife."

"That is all, Señor?" Luis asked.

"Yes. That is all."

His report to the Queen Regent of Spain safely under way, the general proceeded to convert his plans into action. He knew that the Spanish troops had been lax in the past. That would be amended immediately. Construction soon began on stout fences encircling the small agricultural settlements and on concentration camps near the larger towns. Rough timber barracks were provided for the expected guests and slightly better quarters for the new Spanish recruits coming from across the sea.

Americans in Cuba were aghast at what followed. So were the Dutch and the English, the Germans and the French. Every Cuban who was not directly attached to a plantation suddenly found himself caught in the man-trap with no hope of escape. Then, a little later, it was any Cuban regardless of his employment. If a

Spanish soldier could lay hands on him he was taken prisoner. Whereas before they had at least been free, hungry and oppressed though they were, to wander about their provinces, they now found themselves penned up within great enclosures and foul buildings. They were treated like pigs.

The mortality rate doubled, then trebled. The miserable prisoners, already suffering from malnutrition, were compelled to subsist on putrid food and stagnant water. During the first two months of the new administration over forty thousand persons died in the province of Havana alone.

In his comfortable office Weyler muttered, "They'll soon lay down their arms once and for all. When they're hungry enough we'll know who the offenders are." His scheme was to prevent the raising of any crops. Cuba could thus be starved in less than three months. But the Cubans, growing weaker and gaunter, still uttered threats of revolt. Their deep, hollow eyes still burned with the fever Sharon had noticed in Havana on her first visit there. Their bodies were even thinner now, and their cheeks hollower, but their spirit was as staunch as ever. In every province their voices arose as one chorus shouting defiantly for all to hear, *"We will die of starvation before we submit to Spanish tyranny!"*

The Armses now lived in solitude. The shrubs grew wild on the track to El Caney and the scorpions and lizards sunned themselves in the ruts.

Plantation after plantation was boarded up. Many of them, appropriated by the Spanish Government when their owners could no longer pay the taxes, carried ineffectual signs, "For Sale. Cheap." The Grail, still owned by Arnold Floyd, stood on its knoll looking like an abandoned castle of an age gone by.

Around the bend in the road Promised Land still stood among the canefields. The cabañas, no longer occupied, rotted in the heat. The stables and the house needed paint sorely, but there was no money for paint. Every Cuban worker who had been in Clayton Arms's employ was gone. Some were dead; others were still existing in the concentration camp near the old sugar factory. Weyler had taken the men first, then the women and children. They cried and pleaded and begged the Americans to help them. But Weyler's orders were absolute, inflexible. His men made no exceptions. The American plantation owners had no power against a Weyler command.

Conchita was the only Cuban who remained at Promised Land, and she had to hide every time the Spanish soldiers came down the road on their fine horses shipped from Spain.

The Armses spent most of their time now in the parlour and dining-room. Jason slept in his room beyond the kitchen, Conchita upstairs and Sharon in the dining-room. Phoebe and Clayton slept in the parlour. They kept the shutters closed and the lights dim. They managed to grow enough food to keep them going with what little they could buy out of the fast diminishing savings. Uncle Clay seldom spoke except when reading to his family from the worn leather Bible.

Often after dark the Spanish raiders would come riding up to the front doors singing, cursing, shouting, and pounding until the plantation owners would admit them. When they raided Promised Land Clayton would stand in the doorway of the parlour in his night-shirt and quote the Scriptures, while the heedless soldiers tramped through the halls and ran up and down the stairs, searching for cringing Cubans to pen up with their fellow compatriots.

These raids were always staged at night and Conchita knew her instructions well. She was to slip from her bed and flee to the attic by way of a light-weight ladder which she could draw up after her. By bolting the trapdoor from within she was reasonably safe. Sharon and Aunt Phoebe would take refuge in the dining-room while Uncle Clay stood at the parlour door invoking the vengeance of Jehovah on the vandals.

Jason's attitude toward the trespassers was unique in the household. Indeed, probably no one else in all Cuba displayed such fearlessness. He would prance about the kitchen, his night-shirt fluttering like a flag in the wind, and taunt the marauders with jibes and jests. Because he smiled or grinned throughout his performance they — not knowing a word he said — smiled back and even saluted.

"G'wan, you dirty Spics," he'd laugh, "look hard. You'll find twenty-five *Cubanos* in the flour barrel! You're getting hot now. There's not much chance over there, Señor Pig. Come on, you bastards. Look sharp, you sons o' bitches!"

"Sí, señor. Sí, señor!" they grinned back, exploring all the cupboards.

If the raiders could not find a Cuban on the premises of a plantation they would demonstrate their displeasure by slashing portraits and tapestries with their bayonets or carting away any other treasured possessions they could lay their hands on. They were merciless to Spanish owners, wary of the Dutch and French, and when sober, deferential to the Americans. But as often as not they fortified themselves with more than their capacity of Jamaica rum, and then they delighted in seeing acres and acres of sugar-cane go up in flames. The burning of a barn or a house made a pretty sight, too, and the screaming of trapped animals or human beings was an exciting sound.

One night after about six months of this terrorism under "The Butcher's" omnipotent guidance, everyone in the Arms household was awakened from a troubled sleep by a furious pounding at the door.

"Clay, Clay! Get up!" Aunt Phoebe called in a quavering falsetto.

Deliberately Clay got up. "This will all be

reckoned with in the Lord's judgment," he said, shuffling across the hall. The pounding came more and more furiously and added to it were shouts of impatient command. As Uncle Clay opened the front door, a Spanish officer brushed him aside, announcing, "I am Captain Gomez of Her Majesty's army." Following him were a small company of soldiers, insolent, indifferent to Aunt Phoebe's moaning. They searched the house by the light of their torches, pushing open doors and peering into closets. In the dining-room Sharon stood in her wrapper, beside the china cabinet, not afraid to show her scorn. One soldier stood leering before her and held his torch so close that it singed her hair, but she did not flinch, and they left the room without molesting her.

Bursting into the kitchen, they crowded the room and invaded the pantry. Jason was at his taunting best that night, fairly shouting his insults at them, but ever maintaining his defiant grin. "Button, button, who's got the button?" he called "G'wan you goats. You ain't even warm. Look in the —"

But he was interrupted by a thud on the floor above them. The soldiers looked upward, then at each other. Jason began to caper again, tugging at their lapels. "Ha! Ha!" he laughed, "Let's look in the pantry again. Nothing up there!" He pointed at the ceiling and shook his head. Seeing it was no good, he beckoned them to come to his room and led the way, winking and smiling. But the soldiers of Her Majesty's army were not to be fooled. The youth in the night-shirt was amusing, but something upstairs needed looking into.

They whirled toward the front hall and raced up the stairs, and found in the rear hall-way the hapless Conchita lying stunned and bruised beside her ladder. The top rung was broken. Two of the soldiers picked her up and stood her on her feet. She cowered and whimpered and turned pleading eyes to Clayton and Jason, who had followed the men. But the officer, seeing Conchita's look, turned on his hosts and threatened them with his gun.

"Ha!" he ejaculated, turning back to Conchita. *"Una Cubana señorita, no? Muy hermosa!"* He followed this with a sharp command and the men dragged Conchita back to the stairway, past Aunt Phoebe and Sharon who had also followed, and on down the steps. She stumbled and tried to free herself, but that only caused the soldiers to grasp her arms and shoulders harder, making her cry out in pain. Another moment and they were dragging her through the front door, then the Arms family heard them pounding away in the distance.

Jason was the first to react. "The dogs!" he cried. "The beasts!"

"Hush, boy!" Clayton reprimanded. "Perhaps it's the Lord's will."

"Amen!" Aunt Phoebe's shrill voice resounded.

"The Lord's will, fiddlesticks!" Sharon

exclaimed. And she was about to deliver a sermon the like of which neither Uncle Clay nor Aunt Phoebe had ever heard. But a dull red glow caught her eye. She stood transfixed as she realized it was growing brighter.

Jason saw it too. "Holy Mother! They've set the fields afire!" He rushed out of the door with Sharon only a few paces behind. They ran across the yard and past the cabañas. Here they stopped, helpless to stay the flames and realizing their own danger. The landscape not far beyond was an inferno, with the blaze leaping twenty-five feet at its highest.

"There goes the last of what little crop we had," Jason said, shielding Sharon from the heat. "That's good-bye to everything." Hearing a sound behind them the two turned to see Uncle Clayton staring and pointing at the barn. The Spaniards had been thorough. The dry timbers were submitting to the flames without resistance. It was good-bye to the barn too. "Christ! The horses!" Jason yelled, and streaked off to fight a battle with time.

Throwing open the large double doors he released frantic goats, chickens, and pigs. He could hear Jerry and Freddie pawing and whinnying and he called to them soothingly as he made his way through the sea of smoke. "Easy there, old-timers. I'm coming, Jerry-girl. Stop your pawing, Freddie. I'm coming. Easy now. Easy."

Sparks began to fall from the hay mow like rain

drops and Jason could feel the heat on his body as if he were in a furnace. Reaching the horses he tried to lead them out by their halters but they refused to budge. "Damn fool. That's what I am," he muttered and removed his night-shirt. Tearing it in half he felt again for the horses heads, coughing as he danced in pain from the falling sparks, but he got those makeshift bandages about the horses' eyes and lead them out of the stall. "Easy, Jerry-girl, Freddie-boy," he managed to say between coughs.

Sharon, waiting outside in an agony of apprehension, saw Jason emerging from the barn with the two horses, saw that he was safe, saw that he was stark naked, and gave way to her sense of the ridiculous. She laughed for all she was worth.

Clayton took the horses and Jason, standing there in the brightness of the firelight looked at Sharon stupefied. It was Aunt Phoebe who brought him to his senses.

"Land sakes, Jason!" she cried in her hysterical soprano. "Where are your clothes? You're as bare as the day you were born."

Jason's violent blush rivalled the flames as he cast one horrified glance at himself, stammered some unintelligible words, and made a wild dash into the nearest cabaña.

Conchita, still stunned by her fall and frightened nearly out of her reason by her abduction, knew barely more than that she had been thrown over a horse as if she were a sack of meal, and that she was being carried across the fields, which were burning behind them. She struggled on the horse's back and tried to sit up, but the animal was trotting jerkily and she was weak. She gave up and lay limp. The rider, a young Spaniard scarcely out of his teens, roughly helped her to a sitting position. He grinned.

"The señorita does not find it comfortable riding on her belly, eh?" he said to her in Spanish. She stared ahead of her in stony silence. "Has the weasel got the señorita's tongue?"

"Where are you taking me?" she asked.

"Señorita wants to know too much in that question."

"Goat!" Conchita spat.

"The señorita has spirit. That I like."

The horse leaped across a narrow ditch and Conchita clutched his mane for support. Her blouse, half ripped off in her struggles, fell from her shoulders, exposing her bosom. The young soldier put his arm about her waist and his hand came in contact with her full, round breast. He grinned even more broadly.

"By the blessed Saint Philip," he exclaimed, "would that I had you in bed, señorita, instead of on the back of this horse!"

Conchita half turned and slapped his face sharply.

Below them, in the next valley, lay Santiago. The company of raiding soldiers approached it from the north, riding across the fields and purposely avoiding the roads. In this way there was no need to go through the city itself, for the concentration camp lay to the west.

Hailing the sentry at the main entrance, the officer reined in his horse and commanded his men to halt. Conchita brushed her hair back from her eyes. Her first paralysing wave of fear was gone, and replacing it was a determination to keep her wits about her and hope for the time when she might escape and get back at these dirty dogs somehow.

"Open the gate, Roderigo," commanded the pompous officer. "We have another guest. A lovely guest this time."

"Sí, Captain Gomez." Roderigo opened the gates and allowed the party to pass through to the commandant's quarters. A lantern glowed dimly over the doorway, giving just enough light to show the letters on the wooden sign which read: Casa de Colonel Felipe Martinez. Gomez dismounted and rapped loudly on the door.

After a minute or so the door opened and a sleepy officer appeared. He had the belligerent face of an English bulldog. His trousers were drawn up over his night-shirt.

"Eh —" the colonel had a habit of prefacing his speeches with and an odd little grunt "— er, soldatos, what is the meaning of this?" He saw no delegation of prisoners. He fumbled at his desk for his spectacles.

"Colonel Martinez," Captain Gomez announced proudly, "we have brought another prisoner — this girl. She was trying to hide from us."

"So?" The colonel adjusted his spectacles and looked at Conchita, his face softening. "Eh, let's have a look at her." His almost kindly voice belied his gruff appearance. Conchita willingly stepped forward.

"Sí! You have brought in one whole señorita to-night. Come inside, my dear."

Captain Gomez grasped Conchita's arm as if angry at the colonel's remark and taking it out on her. He fairly pushed her into the gloomy building, and stood beside the desk.

"Eh, sit down, my dear." Colonel Martinez knew just how to speak to frightened señoritas to put them at their ease. His tone was gentle and persuasive. "Over there, child." He pointed to a rough camp cot. Conchita sank down on it. "Where do you live, señorita?"

"On the road to El Caney. With Señor and Señora Arms."

"So? How old are you, my child?"

"Twenty-one."

"And your allegiance?"

"My — my what, Señor Soldier?"

Colonel Martinez smiled as a father might smile at his baby. Conchita could see Captain Gomez smiling too, but his was a cruel smile. The colonel spoke again. "Eh, your allegiance, child — your loyalty."

"Oh, but to the Señor and Señora."

"I know, but to which government?"

"I know nothing about government. My father was a soldier for Señor Garcia. Is that government?"

Captain Gomez's eyes glittered in the poor light. "See, colonel! She's a damned little rebel. It's a good thing we got her."

The colonel answered Conchita as if the captain had not spoken. "Yes, my child. I suppose that is government. Where is your father now?"

"With the blessed saints." Conchita leaned forward and asked innocently, "May I go now?"

"Eh, I'm sorry, but I'm afraid not just now, señorita. You will have to remain here just a little while." He gave a sharp command, and from one of the corners of the room his aide-de-camp appeared. "Take the señorita to Casa F," he ordered.

"Sí, señor." The aide took Conchita's arm and led her into the night where the stars shone peacefully above like thousands of gems on the black bosom of the sky.

Casa F was a low, crude structure beneath a clump of palm trees near the edge of the camp. Colonel Martinez's aide opened the padlock, and drawing the door open just far enough for Conchita's slim body to squeeze through, he shoved her into the inky darkness, shut the door, and snapped the lock. Casa F had no ventilation, and the foul-smelling darkness was almost palpable.

With the first step Conchita took she stumbled against something yielding which must have been an arm or a leg. Trying to right herself she lost her balance and fell over the body, but there was no response and as Conchita sat rubbing her elbow she wondered if the person was dead. Crawling now, she made her way — she had no idea where, but she couldn't stay near a corpse. Her path being unimpeded for several feet, she got up and tried walking again. Coming against a wall she decided to feel along it and get into a corner, as far away from that body as possible.

Again she stumbled on a body, but this one grunted and whispered a curse. It was a welcome sound. Someone was alive.

"I'm sorry if I wakened you," she whispered, sinking to her knees.

"What are you doing, prowling around? Why don't you go to sleep?"

"I just came here."

"Oh, you're the boy they just shoved through the door."

Conchita did not answer at first. She wasn't sure whether to say she wasn't a boy or just to say sí. The man seemed kind, like the colonel. "Sí!" she said.

"Lie down here and rest. There's lots of room in this case. They haven't filled it up with human pigs yet."

Conchita stretched herself painfully on the floor and tried to find a position that would not hurt her bruises. "I'm hungry," she said, wanting to keep the stranger talking. The darkness was so much more frightening when there was no sound. And then she knew the stranger was quietly laughing at her.

He whispered sardonically, "You will get water and dry bread once a day. That is all."

"Madre de Dios!"

"And they won't let you out for exercise. And when you want to empty your belly — even though there's nothing to empty but wind — you crawl over to the far corner. Men and women alike."

"I want to go home!" Conchita remembered that a boy would not cry and she bit the back of her hand in her effort to keep back the tears. She sat up — it was no good trying to be comfortable.

The stranger sat up too and leaned his shoulder against hers. In her ear he whispered so that she could barely hear it. "Perhaps you shall go home, boy. There are ways of doing that."

"What do you mean, señor?"

"Sh! Be careful. Reach behind you." He found her hand and guided it. "Feel this board. It is held by one loose nail. It took me ten days to work that board loose. To-night it is going to work for me. Are you thin or fat, boy?"

"Oh, very thin."

"Thanks to the wretched treatment I've endured I'm thin too. We'll crawl out, then we'll climb one of the palms that leans over the fence and drop down on the other side."

"Oh, but señor, I have never climbed a palm-tree."

"No? What kind of a boy are you?"

"Oh, I'll try. I'm sure I can. I'll try very hard."

"Good. You seem so young to be left in this hell. I feel it my duty to help you, though I may be risking my own neck."

"I'll be very careful." Conchita felt a rush of fresh air.

"You go first, boy. And stand perfectly still when you get outside. Remember, not a sound."

She felt the edges of the opening, outlining it with her hands, and learned that she must lie on her side and work herself through. Her bruises and her shoulder hurt but what was a little hurt? She was getting away. How kind of the stranger to help her. Yet there was still the palm-tree to climb. She must not count too much on seeing the señor and the señora and Jason again. It would even be good to see Sharon. She stood up in the tall grass and at her feet she could hear the soft scraping as her stranger friend worked his way out. He stood beside her.

"Are you all right, boy?"

"Sí." But how her shoulder ached!

"Hurry before the moon comes up — or worse still, the dawn." He took her hand and led her along the side of the building, step by step, cautiously, almost silently. They reached the clump of palms. Conchita could make out the dim outline of the man's spare figure, and she kept behind him so that he would not find out his mistake. As he released her hand to examine the palms the moon peered from behind a cloud. "Quick, boy! Down in the grass!" Without giving her a chance to obey he grasped that aching shoulder and pushed her down. She gritted her teeth and let two tears squeeze through her tightly shut eyelids.

They lay there holding their breath until the moon should be considerate enough to hide behind the next cloud. Conchita shyly drew her tattered blouse across her bosom.

"Well, I'm damned! What do you mean by making me believe you were a boy?"

"I — I don't know. I wanted to get out. I told you I'd never climbed a palm-tree."

"Well, I can't take a girl along. You'll have to go back. I'll take the board down again and see that you get inside all right."

"But please take me," Conchita pleaded, nearly forgetting that she must not speak above a whisper.

"Why should I save a girl? A girl is worth nothing to Cuba. If you were a boy you could fight."

"But I'll fight. I'll fight. I'll do anything. I'm sure I can climb the palm-tree. Please, señor!"

"All right. I will let you try. You can cling to me — but if you fall, don't cry out, because we will both be shot. It is very necessary for me to get away — for Cuba's sake. Do you still wish to try it, or shall I put you back?"

"I want to go with you. I won't fall. I won't cry out."

"I haven't much more strength than I need for myself but — there, the moon is gone. Good!

This is our chance. Come! As I climb you climb too. Hold to my shirt, but don't pull back."

Conchita grasped the slack of his shirt and thanked the Saints that the fabric felt stout. With toes gripping hard she followed the stranger up the slope of the nearest palm. It wasn't as fearsome as she expected, although she couldn't see where the fence was and she wasn't sure of her footing. "If I fall. I must not fall on the fence," she thought, "for then I would surely cry out" But despite her hurts and aches she managed not to be too much of a drag, and they reached the fronds where they had hand holds to steady them.

"This means we've cleared the fence," the señor whispered. "Sit down and place one leg on each side of the tree trunk. Can you do that?"

"Sí, señor. I am doing it."

"I will drop now. Then I will stand up and I will stay right there to break your fall."

"But, señor, I cannot even see you."

"You should thank God for that. Then they cannot see us. Here I go." Conchita heard the swish of his body in the grass and the thud as he struck the ground. Then, "It is not very far. I am safe. Let go with all your muscles and just drop. Don't jump."

"But I cannot see you. I am afraid."

"Then do you wish to stay there?"

"No, no, señor. I will do as you say. Which side shall I drop from?"

"At the left. Just let go with all your muscles. I'm here."

"Sí, I am coming." Conchita swung one leg about so that she sat on the trunk facing into space. She shut her eyes and slid off. In a tumbled heap the two lay on the grass, both slightly shaken but neither hurt by their adventure. They sat up, waited a moment to recover their sense of balance and to be sure that no one had been aroused. Hearing nothing but the sigh of the wind through the palms they got to their feet and the stranger took Conchita's hand again. "Where — where are we going, señor?"

"I must get to Havana. And you?"

"I have nowhere to go except the plantation where they just found me."

"They will find you again."

"Oh, I hope not, señor. You have been so kind to help me."

"It is nothing. We will soon be at the road. There we must be careful too — not to be seen by anyone who might tell." Just before they reached the road the moon came out again. "I go this way," the man said. "And you?"

"That way." Conchita could now see his face. A long, crooked scar on his cheek held her eyes. He was really middle-aged and she had thought him young — like Jason perhaps. "Thank you, thank you! And may the Holy Mother be as kind to you as you have been —"

"I was glad to help you, señorita. It was nothing."

"What is your name, señor? I'd like to know it, for I will be remembering you in my prayers."

"I may need your prayers, señorita. My name is Carlos. Carlos Menendez." He bent over and kissed her hand. But, straightening up, he was a different man. He gripped her bruised shoulder, and this time Conchita gave a little cry.

He relaxed his hold, but his voice was cold steel. "I'm sorry if I hurt you, señorita, but you must never mention my name to anyone. You do not know me, nor where I am going. Remember that. Speak my name to no one! Do you understand?"

"Sí, sí, señor. Only to the Blessed Virgin."

And Carlos Menendez vanished into the darkness.

A few moments after his mad scramble to the cabaña, Jason emerged clad in the ragged garments of a long-departed Cuban worker. He had a sheepish expression on his face, and in spite of the gravity of the situation, Sharon's eyes flashed with merriment at his discomfiture.

The four of them stood in the yard a long time watching the fire burn itself out. Phoebe cried as she saw the fields laid waste and the stables crumbling to ashes on the ground. It was the first time Jason and Sharon had seen her cry and they looked at her with compassion in their eyes. As the last cane was consumed and the fields lay black and barren with little grey puffs of smoke rising from them, dawn smiled on the world as if nothing had happened and the rising sun flooded Promised Land with rose.

A cock crowed mournfully from the charred remains of a fallen rafter and forlorn chickens scratched in the earth, while the goats frisked away in the dewy grass and the pigs grunted their disapproval of everything.

With the fires at rest Phoebe became suddenly conscious of the chill in the air and that she had nothing on her but her flannel night-gown. "Gracious!" she said, dabbing at her eyes. "We shall all catch our death. Come back into the kitchen and I'll brew a cup of strong tea. 'Twill put heart in us."

"Perhaps you're right, Phoebe," Clayton agreed, taking one last, sad look at the blackened fields. "Perhaps you're right."

The disconsolate family trudged back to the kitchen in silence. As they sat about the kitchen table drinking tea and eating bread with guava jelly, Jason quietly stood up. "I want to have a word with the family," he said.

"Well, boy?" Clayton questioned gloomily.

"We're in pretty much of a fix, Uncle Clay. Up to our necks. We have no crops, no stables, no hands. All that's left of Promised Land is a house half boarded up. I think we should have a council of war." It was the first time Jason had made so bold as to talk to Clayton and Phoebe as their equal. It was the first time he had addressed his foster-father by any name other than Mr Arms. Clayton, taken aback, stared at Jason with a light of respect in his eyes which glimmered an instant and died out. Phoebe was as stunned as Clayton. Jason had always seemed so — well, agreeable, and now he was actually taking matters into his own hands. Sharon's eyes glowed and seemed to say, "Go to it, Jason. Tell them."

Jason took heart. "Something has to be done. I don't know what exactly, but it seems to me rather foolish for the four of us to live on here at this house. I propose you put it up for sale sir, and move into town."

Clayton jerked to his feet. "Sell this house? Are you crazy, boy?" he thundered. "It took me thirty-five years to build this place up —"

"And two years for the Spanish to destroy it!" Sharon interrupted. Clayton glared at her but she was determined to have her say. "You told me on the train, Uncle Clay, that these were problems for men and not for women. I'm afraid you were wrong. You men, with your little Plantation Owners Society, have accomplished — nothing."

"Jason! Sharon! Both of you keep quiet," Phoebe admonished. "The idea of you two presuming to talk to your Uncle Clay like that. It isn't proper!"

"Oh fiddlesticks, Aunt Phoebe! For two years I've lived here, working like mad and being proper and — well, what have I got out of it? Absolutely nothing! If you didn't want Jason or me to have anything to say about Promised Land, why did you raise him and why did you send for me? You have us on your hands now and you'll have to listen to us. Your kingdom is destroyed, Uncle Clay, and you know it. For two years you've been drilling absolute obedience into me, and for all your life you've been demanding it of others. That's over now. Jason is a grown man. You'd best listen to him."

At this outburst Clayton and Phoebe sat mute. Never had anyone spoken to them like that. They were outraged, but helpless. Jason of all people — and Sharon. Phoebe bit her lip, and her miserable face, all lines turned downward, threatened to melt into tears and drip woefully down upon her collar of double chins. Clayton's thin lips were as set as ever, and he drummed nervously on the table with his finger-tips.

"Well, boy, what do you think ought to be done?" he finally asked.

"First, Sharon and Aunt Phoebe must leave for a safer place. After what happened this morning even Americans aren't safe. I think they should go back to Havana and stay with the Floyds."

"And leave Clay? Never!" announced Phoebe flatly. "I'll stay with him here if to-morrow is doomsday. Wouldn't be surprised but what it will be."

Sharon tried very hard to be calm, to appear impassive about the decisions to be made. But the word "Havana" was like a magic chord of music to her ears. She had never cared for Santiago, and she hated the life at Promised Land —

the work, the poverty, the restrictions. The only thing she really liked about it was the countryside and her walks with Jason. But even the countryside was unattractive now, and there would probably be more fires to devastate it completely. Havana! The word kindled a flame of memory and she could hardly contain herself at the prospect of going there. Little as she had seen of the city, it held a fascination for her — the narrow streets and contrasting boulevards, the quaint three-story houses, the marble palaces, the splashing fountains and green lawns. She let the scenes race before her mind's eye while she remained outwardly calm. She did not want to hurt Aunt Phoebe or Uncle Clay, but she nourished a wild desire to be free again, and in Jason's proposal she saw a glimmer of hope. Very quietly she said, "If Aunt Phoebe stays, then so do I. Why, I wouldn't think of leaving here and going to Havana all by myself. I'm not as selfish as that. What do you all take me for?"

"But it's the best thing, Sharon," Jason argued. "It's different with Aunt Phoebe wanting to stay with Uncle Clay. They're married."

"Jason is right," Phoebe announced grandly. "Of course you'll be safer with the Floyds in Havana. Clay can go into Santiago and send them a telegram."

Sharon's heart beat wildly. It took all her self-control now to keep from jumping up and hugging Aunt Phoebe. Neither the burning of the fields nor the capture of Conchita could dim the prospect of her trip to Havana. Dimly through her inward happiness she could hear Jason's words:

"The taxes are paid for a year. That's good. We'll board up the rest of the house, you and Aunt Phoebe will live in town, Uncle Clay, and I'll stay out here in one of the cabañas and keep an eye on things. If conditions don't improve you can post the house for sale just before the taxes come due. If things do pick up — and I rightly guess they ought to — we can all move back and take up where we left off."

"Good, boy, good," Clayton said, rising. "If I weren't so tired I'd thrash you for your impudence; but go ahead with your plans. I've done my best. Now you do yours."

"I guess I'd better pack if I'm to make the train for Havana," Sharon said dreamily.

"Train nothing," Jason said, his words bringing her up short. Seeing her quick look of surprise he modified his tone. "They's too much skirmishing going on about the railroad lines to Havana. We're going on horseback."

"On horseback!" Sharon was really surprised at this idea.

"Yes. It's the safest plan. I've thought it all out. I'll go with you as far as the Floyds', then we'll know you're safe. And I'll bring the horses back here. You can ride on Jerry."

Sharon nodded. Jason turned and bent over Aunt Phoebe. Taking her hand in his, he kissed her on the forehead, wheeled toward the door and was gone.

Jason Earleigh had at last come into his own.

Jason, in his new self-imposed authority, decided that they would leave at sundown, ride hard all night and rest in the jungle during the day, when the heat would be too oppressive for travelling. It was well over five hundred miles to Havana and he hoped to make it in five nights. Jerry was to carry Sharon and her suitcase; Freddie would take Jason and the bag containing two blankets, a few utensils and the food supply. It would be heavy work for the horses, he knew, but he would give them frequent rests. Sharon would need to rest too, for she had not ridden since coming to Promised Land and would find so many hours in the saddle tiring. He tethered Jerry and Freddie by a long rope on the lawn at the rear of the house, where there was shade and grass. They would have the best he could give them.

Phoebe helped Sharon pack.

"You haven't been happy here, have you, Sharon, dear?" she asked. Her voice was lower now, as if weighted down with her distress.

"Why, of course I have, Aunt Phoebe."

"No, dear, I'm afraid Clay and I failed somehow. We really did want you with us. We always wanted a daughter. And you did make us both happy."

"Did I? Did I really, Aunt Phoebe?"

"Yes." Phoebe placed a kindly hand on Sharon's arm and looked into her eyes. "If we've made any mistakes — if Clay and I have seemed — well, harsh perhaps, can you forgive us?"

"But there's nothing to forgive." Sharon patted the hand on her arm. They both resumed their packing.

"Clay is so strict at times. And there's no compromising with him. And the running of a plantation is hard, you know."

"I do know that. Now, don't you worry about anything. Jason says everything will be all right. And Jason knows."

"Yes, Jason knows. It's strange. He's been with us since he was a baby, and now, this morning, I've just discovered that he's really with us. Do you know what I mean?"

"Yes, I think so."

"Clay's pride has been hurt, but he'll get over it. I think I shall enjoy living in town again. There won't be so many responsibilities."

Sharon closed her suitcase and began to buckle the straps. She regarded Aunt Phoebe attentively and her heart went out to her. The plump figure seemed to sag all over and the grey curls looked bedraggled. In the kitchen, giving orders, she had always seemed hard and invulnerable, but now in Sharon's bedroom she seemed crumpled and pathetic.

So much happened during the day that they had little time to think of Conchita. Once Clayton remarked that he would go into town and see the authorities about it, but the matter was dropped — at least in conversation. There was so much to think of as they all worked feverishly to have things ready for departure by nightfall.

In the year 1896 the United States of America began to feel its muscles and to think seriously of being a big brother to various surrounding islands that dotted the seas. The people of the Unitcd States had a protection complex. Nothing so pleased them as to step in and polish off a bully. Everywhere the press aroused sympathy with propaganda stories of the cruelties in Cuba. In New York Mr Dana did his share. In California, Mr Hearst did more than his share.

The United States kept a careful eye on the proceedings in the Caribbean. The people might have wished to do something, the press might have willed it, but Grover Cleveland would not budge an inch. So the United States, alternately holding its breath and cheering the underdog from the side-lines, sat back to watch.

The native uprisings had quickly spread to all parts of the island since Weyler's arrival. The Spanish soldiers tried in every way to suppress the rebels, but open fighting was ineffective against the guerrilla tactics of Garcia's men. The insurgents followed Garcia's plans to the letter — never fighting in open battle, but continuing their surprise skirmishes all over the island.

And the Unites States watched it all with

growing concern. News leaked through of the cruelties in the concentration camps. Dispatches about the burning of American property were released, and the press resorted to every trick of the trade — atrocity stories, truthful and otherwise, and — the greatest weapon of all — the human interest story designed to bring tears to the eyes of the hidebound isolationists.

And somewhere in that pattern, in the web of those stories and the fabrication of those dispatches, the burning of the Armses' stables, simple as it was in relation to the whole chaotic picture, found its proper niche.

When dawn finally came that ill-fated day, the sun found Conchita walking along the road that skirted the hills of Santiago. She had never been so far from Promised Land since her arrival six years before, and she was uncertain of her direction. But she thought less of this than of her two conflicting fears — the fear of recapture, and the fear of hiding in the jungle. Between these two she must choose.

At first she braved the danger of being taken back to Casa F. She walked along the road, knowing enough to be sure it would lead her to El Caney. There was a place between El Caney and Promised Land where several roads came together. This was one of them, and if she could just get to that place she could get home. The day grew brighter and the hills began to come to life. Puffs of smoke floated from the cabañas and cocks crowed on the plantation fences.

Every few steps Conchita would look behind her to be sure no soldier was in pursuit. Once, on looking back, she saw a cloud of dust. A moment of listening, and she heard the muffled drum-beat of horses' hooves. They were coming fast. Her eyes darted about quickly. There was only the jungle for refuge. She ran into the luxuriant vegetation, not knowing what serpents or deadly insects she might enrage with her sudden intrusion, and lay down in the tall wet grass.

A centipede darted from beneath her, but she lay very quiet. Purple orchids nodded gently in the mild breeze, their petals still heavy with dew. Spanish moss dripped from the mahogany trees like eerie green mist floating above a swamp. Conchita held her breath while the company of soldiers rode past, sitting erect on their fine horses and looking straight ahead of them.

But she dared not take that risk again. She might not leap into the jungle fast enough or far enough another time. She must work her way through this forest of mahogany and cedar and thick undergrowth, and she must find the road on the other side by nightfall.

She got up and began to fight her way through the brush and ferns. The stubborn vines held her back and the shrubs tripped her. The Spanish-bayonets cut her viciously like razor-blades. Her dress was torn into ribbons and her arms and legs were bleeding. It seemed hours since she had started, but the sun hadn't travelled far. She stumbled and fell; got up and stumbled again. Her hair was dishevelled, her face lacerated.

When a harmless snake wriggled down the trunk of a tree just an inch from her elbow she screamed and jerked back. Her head reeled with the chatter and screeches of the birds. She covered her ears with her hands. The jungle was far more terrifying than the soldiers. What a fool she had been! She could never hope to reach that other road. The only thing to do was to go back and find the one she had left. It was so hot now that she slipped off her scarlet bodice and tossed it aside. It was torn anyway.

Now she was glad she hadn't gone far into the forest. She could soon get back and she would wait at the side of the road until dark. Turning towards it, she made her way only a little further when she came upon a small stream slithering through the jungle like a serpent in the grass. She had not seen this stream on her way in, but it was going towards the road — she was sure of that. And the walking was much easier.

"In a little while now, Conchita, you silly girl, you will be at the road again," she sang softly to herself. When the sun was high above her she left the stream, for it didn't seem to be taking her to the road after all. A little more toward the right should bring her there. How foolish she was to get excited about it. She was tired and she wasn't walking as fast as when she made her way into the jungle. The birds in the cedars and ebony-trees screamed, "Just a little longer. Just a little longer, little Conchita." Now she didn't cover her ears.

At last, because she could drag herself no farther, she stopped to rest and to listen closely. She might hear horses' hooves, or the creak of cart wheels on the road. But she heard only the wind through the trees, the chatter and chant of the birds and — what was that other sound, like music! It sounded like the stream she had left behind. Taking another step she saw it. And at that moment something in the grass caught her eye, a flash of scarlet against the green. It was her cast-off bodice.

"Madre de Dios!" she groaned, sinking to her knees. She was lost. And where was the road? How could she tell? She rose to her feet unsteadily, the green jungle swimming before her as the hot tears flooded her eyes. Then, with a sob, she picked up her skirts and tried to run. No matter what the direction, her tears blinded her anyway. She fell and lay still. When she had spent her tears she got up again and struggled on. She must find that road, though her clothing was nearly torn off, and her legs were red with blood.

The horses were saddled, and Jason helped Sharon to mount Jerry. "We'll take it easy at first," he assured her, swinging into Freddie's saddle and adjusting the straps on the food pack.

"Oh, fiddlesticks!" Sharon laughed. "Don't worry about me. I'm an old hand with horses."

"All right," Jason said dubiously. "But the minute you get tired, you let me know."

It was nearly sundown. Their first objective was Cristo. Then on to San Luis and from there Las Tunas, then Ciego de Avila, San Fernando, Concha, Cardenas and — happy name for Sharon — Havana! Jason had a rough map in his pocket and a compass at his belt. Clayton and Phoebe stood on the veranda to wave farewell. Phoebe's lips trembled as she wished them a safe journey. Clayton's were set in their usual straight line, but in his eyes was the same kindness that had lingered there when Sharon had fainted in Havana.

"Good-bye, girl," he said, clearing his throat, "and God bless you." Then, reaching up and gripping Jason's hand, "Good luck, boy. Good luck."

"Thank you, Uncle Clay. I should be back inside of ten days at the most." He brought his quirt down on Freddie's flank. Sharon clicked her teeth, said "Get up" to Jerry and the two horses loped down the road toward Santiago.

Clayton turned to Phoebe. "Well, there go our children," he said huskily. "A great deal has happened in two years."

Phoebe shaded her eyes with her hand the better to see the rapidly diminishing figures.

It felt good to be in a saddle again. She and Jason talked freely as they rode side by side into the twilight. Darkness soon replaced the twilight, and as they reached the jungle there was enough light from the stars to enable the horses to see the road.

"Tired, Sharon?" Jason asked, removing his hat and wiping his forehead.

"No. I'm not tired."

"A girl rightly ought to be by this time, I expect."

"I've ridden before."

"I'm glad that you have. It'll likely be a hard trip."

"I can stand it. Don't worry about me." Then, seriously, "Jason, I'm proud of you."

"Of me? Why?"

"Of the way you took things over this morning. I waited two years for you to do that. I was beginning to think you never would."

"Somebody had to tell the old folks what to do."

"I know. After all, you practically ran the plantation this last year."

"That was nothing. There wasn't much to run."

"Maybe not, but I know Uncle Clay and Aunt Phoebe got a jolt this morning, and you were the one to give it to them."

"I wasn't aimin' to jolt them."

"You did the right thing."

"Sharon," Jason phrased the words slowly, "do you like Cuba?"

"Why?"

"Well, sometimes, especially when you first

came here, I thought you didn't like Promised Land or us that lived there."

"I've always liked you, Jason." Sharon remembered the time they had sat on San Juan Hill about this same hour and talked of religion. She wondered what Jason was getting at now. "But I didn't always like Cuba. One thing I didn't like was the church in Santiago."

"Neither did I. I think you would have liked Padre Esteban's mission better. I've always liked you too, Sharon, from the very first day I saw you. Do you know, you've never told me anything about you — about — about before you came here."

"Haven't I? There was never much to tell."

"Did you know many other boys?"

"Some."

"Were you ever in love?" he persisted gently.

"Oh, Jason, you ask such questions for a man!"

"Yes, ma'am, I know it." His voice dwindled away as if he thought she was scolding him.

"Well, yes," Sharon answered, deciding to be quite straightforward about it, "I was in love, or I thought I was" — she bit her lip as a painful picture of Eric flashed across her mind — "with a sailor."

"A sailor!" Jason slapped his thigh and laughed.

"Yes. Is that so funny?"

"No, Sharon. I shouldn't have laughed. But it's — well, it's hard to imagine it of you."

"I met him on the boat coming over here. We — he showed me Key West. He was very kind." How Eric would have hated that adjective! It made her laugh now.

"What's the joke?"

"I just remembered something about him."

"What happened?" Jason asked quietly. "Did you stop loving him?"

"I guess that's the joke," Sharon replied humourlessly. "I think he stopped loving me."

"Then it's all over?"

"Yes, I suppose so."

"I shouldn't be talking with you like this, I guess," Jason apologized, "but I have to. You see, Sharon, I — I didn't like Cuba either. I hadn't been anywhere else, but I hated it here anyway. Then when you came, all of a sudden I didn't want to leave here any more. They's lots of people who could say it better'n I could, but they couldn't mean it any more'n I do."

"Yes, Jason?"

"Well, Sharon, I guess it's just that I sort of love you and I'd like to ask you to wed up with me as soon as things is all cleared up."

Sharon realized that he was dead serious. "You mean you want me to be your wife?"

"That's it. Do I stand any chance, Sharon?"

"Well —"

Jason stopped Freddie and reached over to grasp Jerry's reins. Sharon pulled up beside him saying, "Why are we stopping, Jason?"

He swung out of his saddle and offered to help

her dismount. "To rest the horses."

"But they don't need resting yet, do they?" She did not move.

"Perhaps not really. But I want to talk to you. I really must know. Won't you give me your answer, please?"

Preoccupied, Sharon accepted Jason's help and swung down beside him.

"God, if praying does any good, Sharon, you ought to give me the right answer. Padre Esteban told me to pray to Saint Francis and I did. Please, Sharon." He bent over, bringing her palm to his lips and kissing it tenderly, hesitantly. In a moment the two years slipped away from her and she was on board the *Grover Cleveland* at the rail. It was Eric who was kissing her palm that dusk abreast of the Dry Tortugas. She could even hear their words, dreamlike, across the waters of the Gulf.

"Why did you do that, Eric?"

"Because I wanted to, and what I want to do, I go about doing."

Sharon shut her eyes tight and closed her fingers into a small fist. Jason mistook the gesture. "I'm — I'm sorry, Sharon. Are you angry?"

"Oh, no — no, of course not, Jason."

"Then your answer. Can it be yes?"

"I'll — I'll give you a definite answer, Jason, when I come back from Havana. That's a promise."

"Will it be yes? May I hope that it will be yes?"

"It might be."

Jason flung his hat high into the air and let out a joyful shout. Retrieving the hat he went into a little jig on the road bed.

"Oh, Jason!" Sharon laughed a little shakenly. "You're acting like a child."

Jason did not answer, for his attention was now on Jerry. She was shying away from him nervously. Patting her flanks Jason soothed, "There, girl. What's wrong, girl? Steady now." Freddie neighed at something ahead of them in the road. Jason cupped his hands to his mouth. "Hulloa, there!"

"Please don't hurt me," a girl's voice whimpered. "By the Blessed Virgin, please don't hurt me!" And they could make out the half-naked figure of a girl coming toward them.

"Are you — are you soldiers?" she asked faintly.

"No, of course not," Sharon answered. Then she gave a little gasp. "Mercy, Jason! It's Conchita!"

Jason and Sharon were at her side in a moment. Recognition came to her slowly. She stared at them, unbelieving, tears in her eyes. "Is it really you, Señor Earleigh? You, Señorita Douglass?"

"Yes, yes."

"Then you came out to find me! How can I thank the Holy Mother?"

"How did you get away from the soldiers?" Sharon asked, helping her to sit down on the grass.

"A good man helped me to escape from Casa F and the soldiers. I was trying to find my way home. I'm so glad you came for me."

Jason built a small fire by the roadside and in the light of the flames Sharon saw Conchita's cuts. "You poor child! You're bleeding."

"Have you had anything to eat?" Jason asked.

"No, señor. But I am so happy I don't care."

Jason took the pack from Freddie's back and gave the canteen to Sharon. "There's the water. You can wash her wounds while I get her something to eat."

While they ministered to her she told her story, remembering not to disclose the name of her benefactor. With hot salt pork in her stomach, her wounds dressed with torn handkerchiefs, and wearing a percale dress of Sharon's, Conchita rested in the grass. While Jason wiped out the frying pan with water and leaves, Sharon repacked her suitcase. And in that brief time Conchita was asleep.

"What will we do?" Sharon asked.

"I rightly don't know." Jason stood looking at the girl and shaking his head.

"We can't leave her —"

Sharon's words were cut off by the sound of hoof-beats, unmistakably coming toward them.

"Whoever it is we'll stop them," Jason said hopefully. "And if they aren't Spanish soldiers they'll take her back. We can't turn back, and we certainly can't take her with us."

But his hopes were soon dashed. Out of the

night and into the dying glow of the fire, rode Captain Gomez, his fine company of soldiers behind him. He looked from Jason to Sharon and then at the sleeping Conchita, an ugly sneer across his features.

"So!" he exclaimed pompously. "We meet again, señor and señorita." He dismounted as he spoke, and jerked Conchita to her feet. The bewildered girl, recognizing him, turned her pleading eyes to Jason.

"How did she come to be with you, señor?" the captain asked suspiciously. A soldier took Conchita's arm, gripping hard.

"We found her."

"That is not a very good lie, señor. I am afraid you will have to come with me to Colonel Martinez. This girl escaped last night from the camp. We have been searching for her all day. It is my duty to deal with her. And for you, it is not well that you are found protecting her."

"We can't come with you," Jason said. "We are on our way to Havana. We found the girl. That is the truth."

"It makes no difference, señor. You will come with me."

Sharon stepped up to him. "Fiddlesticks," she said with all the venom she could command. "Remember, señor, you are dealing with Americans now. And that makes a big difference. We have done nothing wrong. If you force us to come with you, there will be trouble."

Captain Gomez just looked at her as she stood

facing him. He was not quite sure of his ground. Last night he had stupidly ordered his men to fire the fields of the plantation where these three lived, and his superior officer had reprimanded him for it. He knew it did not pay to fool with Americans.

"Perhaps you are right, señorita," he said politely. "After all, I was only sent to find the escaped prisoner. That is sufficient. You may go."

"But what are you going to do with her?"

"That, I am afraid, is not your affair." He turned on his heel and gave a command to the soldier who held Conchita. She started to scream, but a big hand smothered that and a second soldier helped get her on his horse. Jason stepped forward, but a bayonet flashed out and stopped him, its owner holding him back with the weapon against his chest.

"Everything will be all right, Conchita." The bayonet could not keep him from speaking. "As soon as I come back from Havana I will go to the camp and get you out. I promise."

As Conchita was only crying now and not trying to struggle away from the tight arm that held her on the horse she was free to speak also. "Gracias, Señor Earleigh. Gracias."

Captain Gomez mounted, the horses wheeled about, and the company galloped into the darkness. Silently Jason strapped the suitcase back in place on Jerry's back. Pouring the remainder of the water on the fire, he saw that every spark was stifled. Sharon accepted his hand to mount, and silently rode on towards Cristo.

Conchita stared straight ahead of her. Even when Captain Gomez barked out an order for his men to halt she did not change her attitude.

"What is up, captain? Are we not going on to camp?"

"I have decided against it. You know what will happen. Colonel will say, 'Eh, captain, you found the prisoner. You know what must be done. Eh, deal with her.' "

"That is what the colonel will say, all right. You are a good mimic, captain."

"Gracias. Well, if I have to deal with her, I will do so now and have it off my mind. You, señorita," he said sharply, "jump down!" The soldier helped Conchita carry out the captain's order and several of the men dismounted. Captain Gomez took a rope offered him by one of his soldiers and, seizing Conchita's wrists, he knotted it about them.

"What are you going to do to me?" she cried out.

"I am going to carry out the law for prisoners who do not like our hospitality and try to run away. With the compliments of the Spanish Government you will receive twenty-five lashes. You should be glad to have it over with."

A torch was brought, and Captain Gomez himself tied the pleading girl to a convenient palm-tree.

"Please, señor, please!" Conchita begged. "I'll be good. I won't run away again. Please! I promise by the good Saint Teresa. Please! Please!"

But her words became an agonized shriek as Captain Gomez cut her across her back with a quirt, leaving a welt in the flesh like an angry searing flame. Again the quirt fell — and again and again. "— thirteen — fourteen — fifteen — sixteen —" the captain counted slowly. The screams died down to moans. Gomez stayed his hand and surveyed the sagging figure against the tree-trunk. "What is the matter with her?"

The aide leaped forward and felt her wrist. "She's fainted, captain."

"Damn," Gomez grunted. "Oh well. Untie her and leave her here."

"But —"

"Those are my orders. We cannot be bothered with dead weight."

They mounted, and soon the sound of their horses' hooves dies away. The jungle was as quiet and as dark as before. Conchita's form lay motionless and limp on the carpet of leaves and grass. All night it was so, and as dawn again brought promise to the world it blessed her still body with the warmth of the rising sun.

Far above, like a blemish in the sky, an ugly red-headed bird wheeled and dropped. It was joined by another and another. They flew in great circles, gliding a little lower each time, their eyes fixed intently on one spot beneath them.

Thus did Conchita de Barbuda, daughter of the lazy Pablo, end her days upon this earth.

3

The Dark Room

It was Sharon's twenty-third birthday. She sat in her room at the Floyds', wanting only to be alone — to take a personal inventory, to review her year in Havana. Was she never going to have a good time again? Was the period of turmoil in Cuba never to come to an end?

The Floyds had been glad to see her when she arrived on horseback with Jason, her back aching and her thighs covered with saddle blisters. They seemed glad enough, too, to have her as company for Libby. But life with the Floyds had its drawbacks. She was tired to exasperation with Arnold and Lavina's verbal games and their tedious recounting of past glories. The year had passed so slowly that she almost wished that there would be an honest-to-goodness war instead of the constant flare-ups of petty street riots and skirmishes. Anything for a blessed change.

The Floyds' home in Havana was on the edge of the native quarter and its back lay against the quaint three-storied wooden buildings that had fascinated Sharon on her first visit. It was a brick house of imposing proportions, and the Floyds let out a room to a clerk in the American Consul-General's office, a young man with a slight limp. A mild romance was flourishing between him and Libby.

"Jason will always remain a tender memory with me," Libby had confided to Sharon, "and he'll never know how much I loved him. But I'm twenty-one now and I have to find myself a husband. Why, you and I are practically old maids, Sharon."

"Yes, dear."

"I'm going to capture Glenn if it's the last thing I do."

And Glenn, the young clerk, seemed willing to be captured. At first it was amusing to Sharon, but now even the novelty of "Libby's man" was wearing off and life, she felt on her twenty-third birthday, was pretty jaded. She came to the conclusion that people just didn't dance any more, at least not in this outrageous country. She had been to only one ball — it had been given by the tobacco house where Arnold worked — and she'd been to several concerts given by Lavina's Tuesday Afternoon Club. Her only other entertainment had been a performance of *Aida* at the Havana Opera House and a lecture delivered by a dried-up little man who had journeyed all the way from Schenectady, New York, to speak on "The Dream of the Horseless Carriage and Why it Can Never be Realized". Apart from reading a few insipid novels by genteel women, her only pastime was taking walks along the Prado. Precisely at nine o'clock each night the Floyd household went to bed. Sharon wanted to stay up some night until two or three or four. She wished she dared scream — just once, but good and loud — so that she could enjoy the sensation of a sound other than the discreet whisperings of the Floyds, and the calf-talk between Glenn and Libby in the parlour.

She heard Libby running up the stairs and calling her name. She got up and met her at the door.

"A letter for you, Sharon." Libby was breathless and excited. "It must be from your uncle. It was posted in Santiago."

"Thank you, Libby. I'll read it and let you know if there's any news of interest to the family."

"Yes, Sharon." Libby turned and plodded down the stairs much slower than she had come up. There was some basis for her excitement and curiosity. Letters for Sharon were a rarity. Aunt Phoebe never wrote. She left that task to Clayton. About every two months Jason scrawled a short note in his halting hand. The scratchy pen he used was no help in making it out, but after some study Sharon would usually learn that he was optimistic about the work he was doing at Promised Land. Always he told how he missed her and of the hopes he held that she would let him have the chance to prove himself a good husband.

This letter from Uncle Clay followed his usual pattern:

Dear Niece:

Your Aunt Phoebe tells me that your birthday is approaching and so she and Jason join me in wishing you many happy returns of the day. If things weren't so bad here, we could have done a little something for you in the way of a gift. As it is, however, I am afraid I have to tell you that I cannot continue to send any more money to pay Mr and Mrs Floyd for their kindness to you. I must write him a letter asking him to trust me for the future sums. I wish God would show me some other way, but Jason refuses to let me ask you to come back here. He says it is not even safe for a girl to be out in the streets any more. Jason does all the buying and your Aunt Phoebe is absolutely powerless to take any responsibility. Jason says the soldiers have absolutely no respect for any girl.

It is truly remarkable the way the boy has guided us. I always knew he was smart, but he has been a godsend. As you know, he has practically attended to all the details. He is living in town with us now. He reports that the trouble has died out near El Caney and that the house will be safe. He goes out to look it over every Sunday after church. He rented a small cottage for the three of us and he takes care of all the business. My savings are all gone and that is why I cannot send any more money to you. Jason has a job in a tobacco factory and he gets five dollars a week wages. The poor boy works fourteen hours a day and his salary is all we have to feed us and pay the three dollars rent per month on this place. Our taxes on Promised Land are past due, so Jason is putting up the place for sale. It about breaks my heart to see things turn out this way.

If only the United States would do something not only for us Americans but for the terribly oppressed Cubans back here. Weyler is indeed a butcher. If it wasn't for my interests here, I think all of us should have returned to the States months ago. I know I can talk these problems over with you, for you proved to me in the past that you had a head for them. The United States is deeply involved in Cuba from an economic standpoint all right. So many of us American citizens own plantations and mines and railroads here. Besides, I know that the American people, under the influence of that newspaper man — what is his name? — are outraged at Spain's treatment of the natives. I despaired of help as long as Cleveland was president but now that we have Bill McKinley in the White House, I'm hoping for the best. Cleveland did all he could to keep Americans on the side-lines, but I think that McKinley will show some action, maybe even intervene, if Spain doesn't grant this land a bill of home rule. After all, the United States does have a "moral obligation" as Mr Hearst says.

Well, Sharon, that is about all. Jason and your Aunt Phoebe, along with me, ask for God's bountiful blessing to be upon you. Write, girl, when you have the chance.

Yours truly,
Uncle Clay.

Sharon folded the letter and tucked it into her bosom. She thought about it for a while, then descended the stairs to the parlour where she knew she would find Arnold and Lavina. It was tea time and they had never relinquished their beloved English tradition.

"Mr Floyd," she began with no preliminary chatter, "did my uncle write you a letter?"

"Why, yes, Sharon. He did. But I wasn't going to —"

"Did he mention that he has no more money for my board?"

"Oh, he said something of the sort. Don't worry about it. You are welcome to stay on here, you know, for as long as you like."

Lavina gave her a cup of tea. "Of course, my dear."

"I know I can, and you've both been wonderful to me. But as long as Uncle Clay cannot do any more for me it's going to be up to me to help myself."

"My dear," said Arnold, "we've always disliked the expression 'paying guest'. Indeed, if it were not for our own reverses, these words would be banished from our home for ever. A guest is a guest."

"Nevertheless, I must help out."

"Why, Sharon, what do you mean?" Lavina asked, setting her cup and saucer aside, and devoting herself completely to anxiety.

"I'm going to find work. I'll find myself a position."

"A position?" Lavina nearly choked on the word, "Mercy, what a thought! Of course, you're not serious."

"But I am serious." Sharon sipped her tea with casual unconcern for Lavina's disturbed emotions.

"Go to work? A young lady holding a position? But that's so common. It's — it's — why, it's positively unthinkable! I won't allow it. What would the Tuesday Afternoon Club think?"

"I don't know. But I doubt if the Tuesday Afternoon Club would care to undertake the payment of my board and keep. Therefore I shall have to consider ways of taking care of that myself. Mr Floyd, they have girls working at the tobacco factory, haven't they?"

"Well, yes. Common women of course. Lavina is right, Sharon. It's unthinkable."

"You can go on saying that as long as you like but there's no use in arguing with me. I've made up my mind and when I want to do something, I go about doing it." A little sword of memory pierced her heart as she said the words, but she banished the hurt and went on, "There's lots of things I might do. I could sew perhaps, or tutor. In fact, the more I think about getting out and doing something the more I like the idea. I'm sick of just sitting around singing the same old tune of nothing to do." She put her cup down so suddenly that Lavina's expression changed from worry to astonishment. "Singing!" Sharon stood still for one moment of final decision, then she started for the stairway saying, "That's what I'm going to do, sing!"

"But Sharon!" Lavina's voice stopped her at the door and the huge bulk that was Lavina was coming towards her. "Please, don't be too hasty. We'll manage somehow. The Tuesday Afternoon Club would cut me dead in the street if they knew you were working as a vulgar actress."

"It isn't the stage I'm thinking of, if that's what you mean. I'm thinking of a café. I know the proprietor of a café right here in Havana. I should have looked him up sooner." As she dashed up the stairs she heard two horrified voices echoing the word "café".

El Americano café was situated on a high point of land overlooking the harbour. Its broad, low front with the neatly lettered sign above, EL AMERICANO, HILLARY EDGECOMB, PROP., presented the only clean spot in the entire block. Much to Edgecomb's annoyance, there had sprung up on both sides of his beautiful El Americano a squalid assortment of cheap native shops, their goods displayed openly to the street.

They might have attracted a few customers, but Edgecomb was certain they drew millions of flies into the neighbourhood. The shopkeepers hawked their wares to the passers-by in pleading Spanish, Dutch, and French, and to Edgecomb's sensitive ears the babel was maddening.

He often grumbled about it and said he couldn't understand how he did any business at all with those uncouth vendors hounding his customers to buy, buy, buy. Yet he had a fairly steady clientele of Americans, Englishmen, and Spanish officers, so that he found himself in the enviable position of proprietor of one of Havana's better eating places. The fame was more in evidence than the profit, however, for out of every dollar that he made, Spain extracted almost half for taxes. Only after three years of painstaking service to diners was he beginning to recover his original investment.

The interior of El Americano was as spotless as a clinic. Hilary had it painted white with green trimmings. Paintings of the American scene looked down from the walls and a small orchestra consisting of Spaniards who were either too old or too young or physically unfit for the army occupied during the busy hours a high platform at the end of the room. Painfully they played American one-steps, but the diners seemed to enjoy their music. There was a balcony extending along the other three walls where patrons could dine in privacy. The food was served by Spanish girls dressed in stiff American costumes and looking self-consciously like a group of orphans dressed for Sunday visitors. The menu was as New Englandish as the Boston Tea Party.

The café always opened at three o'clock in the afternoon. At five-thirty Hilary himself would stroll in and conduct a careful inspection of the kitchen floor, the ovens, the coffee urns, the napery. He would brush the inside of a copper cooking pot with the flat of his hand to make sure that it felt as smooth and immaculate as it looked. His help had it that he washed his hands twenty times a day.

One afternoon when he was partaking of tea and wafers while going over his week's bills, the front door opened and a trim young girl in green satin approached. She looked vaguely familiar to him as she addressed the head waiter, though he couldn't for the life of him place her. When Alfonzo pointed him out to her, the girl's face lighted in recognition and she came to his table with a disconcerting look of expecting to be called by name.

"Mr Edgecomb, what a charming surprise!" she smiled, extending a gloved hand. "I was just strolling about for an afternoon constitutional when I saw your sign. I said to myself, I simply can't pass by without saying good afternoon to an old friend."

This gave Edgecomb time to rise and it gave him a little time — though the young lady talked very fast — to rack his brain for some clue. He'd seen her, yes. And he'd talked with her. But where? "My dear girl," he said hesitatingly, "I'm afraid you have the advantage. I —"

"Now if that isn't like a man," she laughed. "You don't remember me?"

"I'm afraid not. I see so many —"

"Think back to '94. The *Grover Cleveland.*"

"Yes?" He was still floundering.

"You don't remember your shipboard friend, Sharon Douglass? Why, Mr Edgecomb, we dined in Key West."

"Jove, yes!" Edgecomb exclaimed. "Of course I remember you. You were travelling from Galveston."

Sharon pouted a little and dropped her lashes. "I'm hurt," she said coyly. "You didn't even remember me. I had to come right out and tell you. And I thought you could never forget me nor our other friend, Señor Menendez."

"His was a sad story, wasn't it?" He was glad enough for a change of subject.

Sharon dropped her injured air. "What happened to him? I haven't heard a thing."

"During my first year here he used to drop in for a game of chess. But two years ago I heard he was killed in a street riot."

"I'm so sorry to hear that," she said sincerely. "I liked Señor Menendez, and I admired his patriotic spirit."

"Forgive me for being so inconsiderate, my dear Miss Douglass. Please be seated, won't you? I take it that you're still Miss Douglass, or have I the honour of addressing a wife and perhaps a mother?"

"Oh fiddlesticks, Mr Edgecomb," she said archly as she took the chair he offered her at his table, "of course I am still Miss Douglass."

"Wasn't there a sailor —"

She removed her gloves and kept her eyes down. "You must mean Mr March. Wasn't that his name?" Then with a little toss of her head she looked at Edgecomb again. "I forget names as easily as you forget faces. I can't imagine what ever became of him."

"And I thought you two cared for each other," he said mercilessly, remembering a certain incident that had humiliated him very much. She was the same Miss Douglass all right. A little older in looks perhaps, her eyes not quite as sparkling as before, her waist a little thicker, and her hands — well, they were rather rough for a young lady who had nothing to do in the afternoon but take a constitutional. But no matter, she was the same vivacious girl all right. After three years she had walked into his life again. The world was indeed small.

"Care?" she was saying. "Why, he was just a common sailor, anybody could see that."

Her mind raced. She must play every card carefully. He mustn't think she had come here with a purpose in mind. She said rather indifferently as if only making casual conversation, "You never hear of him, I suppose?"

"No, I'm afraid not. What a charming dress

you're wearing, my dear!"

"Isn't it? A gift from my Uncle Clay," she lied. It had taken her a week to make it for the opera party. She had converted it from a cast-off bedspread that Lavina let her have. "He had it sent from Paris. They're so far ahead of us, you know."

"You'll have some tea with me, won't you?" Edgecomb offered.

"Why thank you. I mustn't stay long, though. I'm playing in a croquet tournament this evening and it's growing late. I'm visiting with friends here this fall and winter. Plantation life is lovely, but I craved a change."

"And how is your uncle?"

"He has sold his plantation since I came to Havana, and he finds time weighing heavily on his hands in Santiago, poor dear. He says it's tiresome just being a gentleman."

"I can imagine." They had a little laugh, slightly forced.

"Mercy, you have done well for yourself, haven't you?" Sharon exclaimed, looking about her appreciatively. Yes, he looked prosperous enough. The linen was fine and white, the waitresses knew their places. Everything was right — now if she could only bring up the subject tactfully enough. She prayed for an ounce of the fortune of Lucky Fred Douglass.

"Oh, in a modest way," Edgecomb replied with a hint of a smile. "It's certainly pleasant to have you visit me, Miss Douglass. And I saw

Captain Larribee a month ago. He's still making the run from Texas through the gulf — fatter than ever."

"Oh, is he? I suppose he still stops at Key West then?"

"I presume so."

"Do you remember that perfectly hideous hole in the ground where we ate that night?" She tried to give her inflection just the right touch of scorn.

"Well, rather!"

She let her glance fall on the orchestra platform. "Oh, you have music!" She rose and pirouetted about her chair.

"Dinner music," Edgecomb explained. "It's done in the best New York restaurants, you know. Child's, Delmonico's."

"Really? You know I heard the other day that society is singing for a lark. One girl has positively scandalized her family by singing in a café. Shocking, isn't it?"

"I suppose it helps business though. If a pretty girl like you —"

"Why, Mr Edgecomb, are you suggesting that I — ? Well, my uncle wouldn't hear of it, that's all."

"Oh, please don't misunderstand me, Miss Douglass, I merely meant —"

"But I'm not offended, Mr Edgecomb, really. I think it would be fun, myself. My uncle need never know."

"You mean you would want to sing — here?"

"For a lark, of course. I like your place."

"But can you sing?"

"I think I can sing as well as any society girl. I'll make you a business proposition. I'll sing for you each night — except Sundays of course — if you promise never to tell my family."

"Would you expect to be paid?"

"Oh, that — the thought is a little unsavoury, isn't it? I mean, I'd prefer doing it without any thought of pay — my means are substantial. Still, a small stipend to make the arrangement more — shall we say business-like?"

"Miss Douglass, you are a woman of ideas. Let us hear you sing. Alfonzo!" he called. And as Alfonzo approached from the front he explained, "Alfonzo is my general factotum. He plays the piano and oversees the waitresses and ejects any guests who become offensive."

"Sí, señor," Alfonzo stood at attention.

"Play something on the piano to accompany Miss Douglass."

"Sí." He led the way to the platform and stood aside for Sharon to precede him. She had no idea whether she had a good singing voice or not, but she would soon find out. The music for "Daisy" was on the piano. Alfonzo asked, "What shall I play, señorita?"

"Just play 'Daisy'," she said, and handed him the music. She stood with one hand on the piano and the other holding her skirt daintily.

Daisy, Daisy, tell me your answer do,
I'm half crazy, all for the love of you.

Edgecomb's face was passive. She wished he would react in some way — even a frown would be better than that mask.

It won't be a stylish marriage,
I can't afford a carriage,
But you'll look sweet
Upon the seat
Of a bicycle built for two.

Still Edgecomb stood like a statue.

"Play it again," she said to Alfonzo the moment she ended. And on the next rendition she left the piano and danced, improvising the steps, but letting herself respond to the rhythm with all her pent up hunger for dancing and gaiety. Edgecomb's face was still a mask, but there was a twinkle in his eyes now. Finishing with a flourish she awaited his applause and he was generous with it.

"Jove! That is indeed fine!" Edgecomb exclaimed. And then, as Sharon sat down and crossed one knee over the other, his eyes were caught by her shoe and held there for a horrible moment. Why couldn't she have remembered not to cross her legs, especially with that left foot over? It was the boot that had that awful hole in it — as large as a cavern's mouth; and Edgecomb had seen it. "Come down to the table again," he was saying. He stood with his back to her until she reached the table, apparently deep in thought.

"Yes," she said to break the tension.

"Why didn't you tell me you needed a job?" He took her hand.

Jerking away from him, she said, "Don't be presumptuous."

"You lied to me. Why?"

"Pride. Why else do people lie about such matters? But do you think I can help your business? Did you really like my singing? You won't back out, will you? I do need a job."

"My dear Miss Douglass, 'the quality of mercy is not strained'. Of course you may sing here. But tell me, what has happened?"

"It's been awful!" It was good to be able to tell it. Edgecomb listened patiently and politely and she let him have the summary of the unhappiness and hardships she had experienced in Cuba. Only one important phase of it did she omit — her longing for Eric. That lie must stand. It was none of Edgecomb's business, anyway.

"Then you'll come back and sing for us to-night?" he asked.

"Indeed I will."

"Then I'll give you an advance. You may wish to buy a pair of dancing slippers to match your beautiful green gown."

"Thank you, Mr Edgecomb." Sharon took the money, said her good-bye, and hurried out, breathing a fervent, "Thank you, Lucky Fred."

The Floyds were properly horrified by Sharon's announcement that she was going to support herself by singing in a café. Only Libby was thrilled by the idea.

On her first appearance at El Americano Sharon was as nervous as if she had been facing a firing squad. The café was patronized by Spanish officers from the nearby barracks and by sailors from the Spanish fleet moored in the harbour. Like Edgecomb, they did not respond heartily until they came under the spell of Sharon herself; but soon they were applauding and shouting bravo and even tossing pesetos at her feet. Within a week she felt quite at home and pleasantly sure of herself, weaving about among the tables patting a sailor on the shoulder, waving to an officer, stopping at another's table to sing part of her song especially for him.

"Aren't you afraid of standing up before all those men?" Libby asked one evening as Sharon dressed to go to the café.

"Not at all, goose. I'm not afraid of any man. The only thing I'm afraid of is that they'll discover I can't sing and then I'll be out of a job. I can't afford that."

"I do wish mamma would let Glenn and me come to hear you; but she won't hear of it."

"They were there themselves last week. Why don't you tell your mother you're old enough to go anywhere she does?"

"Oh, I wouldn't dare."

"Where's your backbone?" Sharon pulled a white drill middy over her head and Libby helped her arrange the large black silk tie. "Are you going to be a child all your life?" Pinning on a sailor hat, Sharon was nearly ready.

"You're so brave, Sharon. I wouldn't have the courage to wear bloomers on the street." Libby referred to Sharon's heavy blue serge cycling bloomers. "Perhaps Glenn could persuade mamma and papa."

"I've got to fly now, Libby. Good-bye."

From the carriage house in the rear Sharon wheeled out her bright new bicycle, the first thing she had purchased with her precious pesetos. Her salary covered board and room and it was amusing to see Lavina accept it with repugnance and yet with alacrity. The patrons had become so generous that she was able to buy a taffeta gown in addition to her cycling outfit and, more than that, she soon saved the magnificent sum of eight dollars and sent it with her love to Uncle Clay and Aunt Phoebe. She announced that she expected to be able to do this each week, explaining that she was doing some genteel tutoring in English and mathematics. The answering letter from Uncle Clay was so grateful in its tone, so full of thanks on Aunt Phoebe's behalf, that Sharon was glad she had lied.

At the café that evening, in her little dressing-room off the passage to the kitchen, Sharon made ready for her first entrance at nine. Hilary Edgecomb entered without knocking and found her applying the last touches with her curling iron. He placed his hands on her bare shoulders and looked at her in the mirror.

"Good luck, my dear," he said.

"Thanks, Mr Edgecomb. Are there many diners?"

"The room is filled, thanks to you."

"Oh, fiddlesticks! You're the one who has brought *me* the luck."

"Have it your own way, my dear."

She rose from the dressing-table. "How do you like my gown?" she asked. "Wait, this goes with it." Picking up a small ivory fan shc paraded before him in the few paces the room permitted. The salmon-coloured gown, exposing her shapely shoulders, was trimmed in lace and velvet bows. The bustle had bothered her at first, but she quickly accustomed herself to it and was mightily pleased at the admiring glances she and her new gown attracted. Pirouetting before Edgecomb, she held the skirt up daintily with one hand and flourished her fan with the other.

"Jove, it's beautiful!" Edgecomb said. He grasped her shoulder as she glided by him. She stiffened as hc prcssed his lips to the round slope of her back. "But it isn't half as beautiful as you," he murmured.

"I'm not beautiful, flatterer," she smiled, "and you know it."

"To me, you are beautiful. I am very fond of you, my dear."

"Well, I'm fond of you too, Mr Edgecomb."

"How much?"

"Ask no questions —" She broke off listening

for her cue, her hand on the door knob. As the cue was struck she picked up her skirts and swept out of the dressing-room, through the passage and into the dining-room, waving her fan languidly.

The white walls and the gleaming linen gave the place a glittering brightness. The chandeliers, each with seventy gas-jets, cast a glow on the polished floor and the instruments of the orchestra, reflected the sparkle of the jewels worn by the officers' ladies. As Sharon stepped into the room the men all rose and gave her a salvo of applause.

"Thank you," she said, bowing graciously when the applause subsided. "For my first number I shall sing 'Tell Me Pretty Maiden Are There Any More at Home Like You'." As the music took hold of the song and she entered into the spirit of the singing she felt that she had been born to sing in a café. She waved her fan gaily as she went into the chorus and decided that she felt so much at home here, simply because as a little girl she had sung tender bar-room ballads in the saloon at Cardenas.

Before the song was finished she noticed Glenn and Libby entering, and saw Alfonzo bow and escort them to a corner. She waved but they were too timid to acknowledge her gesture. Poor Libby looked as scared as a calf ready for branding; and even Glenn looked as though he expected someone to pounce upon him.

The guests demanded an encore of the chorus

and Sharon gladly complied. But that was not enough. They clamoured for more, more. So she gave them "Jeannie With the Light Brown Hair", and bowed her way out amid furious applause. In her dressing-room she found Edgecomb waiting.

"Marvellous, my dear," he said, lighting his pipe. "The only fault I have to find is that my customers are paying more attention to the entertainment than to the excellent food I serve."

Sharon was standing at her dressing-table with her back to him. She whirled. "You mean you don't want me to sing any more?"

"Oh, my dear, of course not, of course not. Have no fear I want you to sing for me as long as you desire to. The peculiar thing about it is that you really haven't a voice at all. You know that, don't you?"

"So, you realize it now. I wondered how long it would take. Just let the customers come to the same conclusion and then —"

"Nonsense, my dear. Nothing of the sort. It isn't your voice the guests admire, it's you. And I don't blame them."

"Well," Sharon said dubiously, "it's nice to know they appreciate me in spite of my voice. And now, if you don't mind, I'd like to be alone and have my dinner in here."

"Very well, I'll send a kitchen boy to take your order. The waitresses are so busy with that crowd of patrons you've brought us."

Sharon ate slowly, reflectively. So Hilary was going to require some tactful managing. She believed she could keep him at arm's length. Would it be wise to confess to him that she loved Eric? Just thinking of Eric now brought a slow burning anger to her breast. Why must she cling to her foolish love at him? Why must she long for his rough kisses and his groping hands when he was indifferent to her? When the *Grover Cleveland* had put into port two days before, she had gone down and asked Captain Larribee — casually and discreetly, of course — about Eric. Beyond informing her that the last he heard was that young March had been transferred to a different base, the captain had little to offer. He couldn't even recall which other base it was. She supposed she could find out by writing to the proper authorities in Washington, but she had written to him directly once and the letter had not been returned, so she would not make a fool of herself again. His ring was tucked far out of sight in the bottom of her brown portmanteau.

Her reverie was interrupted by a gentle tap at the door.

"Yes?"

"It is I, Jaime Perez," a thin voice announced on the other side of the door.

"Come in."

The door opened and a short, incredibly slender man crossed her threshold. His hair was white as frost and his skin was brown and wrinkled like parchment. He wore a neat white suit, and a black string tie. Taking a pair of spectacles from his coat pocket and adjusting them on his nose, he peered at Sharon myopically.

"Ah, yes, it is just as my friend said. You are rather pretty — perhaps not beautiful. My friend knows the fine point of distinction and spoke especially of your auburn hair."

"Well!" Sharon gasped. "Who are you, may I ask? And what do you want here?"

In answer the little man took a shabby, crumpled card from his coat pocket and presented it to her.

JAIME PEREZ Y VESCARRO
Instruction in Voice, Piano, Violin, Cello, Palmistry
Numero 25 Avenida de los Arbores Verdes

Sharon smiled as she read it. "What can I do for you?" she asked pleasantly. This Jaime Perez seemed harmless enough, and his list of accomplishments was impressive. "I hope you don't expect to teach me voice, señor."

"Ah, no." Perez returned her smile and clucked like a squirrel nibbling at an acorn. "That would be impossible. Your voice, señorita is, shall we say, slightly bad? You probably sing worse than anyone I have ever heard. No insult intended, señorita."

Sharon laughed. "I know my own shortcomings," she said.

"My friend says that you are the most sensible

woman in Havana," Perez went on in his thin voice.

"Your friend? Who is this friend? Do I know him?"

"Sí, señorita, but I did not say whether my friend is a he or a she."

"Well, who is it then?" Sharon was growing impatient.

"That, señorita, I cannot tell you — yet."

"But why do you come to see me?"

"I came to ask you if you would, out of the kindness of your heart, take a message to my friend. Conditions are such that I am unable to take it myself. My friend said you would not fail me. Will you do this for me?"

"Why not?" Sharon asked, her curiosity aroused. "I am through singing at midnight. Is that too late?"

"Not at all. My friend knows your every movement. He expects you after midnight." Perez withdrew an envelope from his pocket and handed it to her. "Please deliver this envelope to this address." He indicated the face of the envelope. "I might explain that this is no ordinary mission. When you come to the house you will find it darkened. The front door will be ajar. Walk in, but do not show a light. The gas is disconnected in the house. Walk straight ahead three steps and then two steps to the right. There you will find a door. It too will be ajar. Walk in and go forward four steps. In front of you will be a table. My friend will be seated at this table.

Hand him the envelope and leave immediately. To-morrow night I will call upon you again. Is everything clear?"

"No, none of it is clear, but as I see you are not going to tell me what is behind all this I must find out for myself. If you will give me those instructions again I will follow them exactly."

Phrase by phrase her caller repeated his instructions waiting after each few words for her to parrot them. He bowed, opened the door a trifle to peep down thc passage-way, and slipped quickly away. She could not hear his steps, and, just to make sure he was gone, she opened her door to look. There was no one there. But he couldn't have been a ghost for she held the envelope in her hand. The address was the same as the one on the stranger's card — Numero 25 Avenida de los Arbores Verdes. "The front door will be ajar — go forward four steps — leave immediately — to-morrow night —"

The orchestra was playing her cue. She slipped the envelope into the front of her dress picked up her fan, and made her second entrance.

At half-past twelve Sharon found herself pedalling over the cobblestones of the dark, narrow street which was the Calle de la Reina. The flickering gaslight cast eerie slanting shadows, making the three-storied houses on either side of the street seem to lean inwards as if coming together in a vaulted roof far above her. A sudden chill possessed her, but she did not think of turning back. Occasionally she saw a light in one of the windows and heard a baby crying or a guitar strumming softly. Tacked on the door of at least half the houses was the black sign of death with the white letters. When men stared rudely at her, she pedalled faster. But now a soldier stepped in front of her abruptly so that she had to stop or run into him. She stopped. He leaned towards her and steadied himself on the handle-bar of her cycle.

"Señorita, where are you going at this time of night?" he demanded. His breath reeked of rum.

"Home," Sharon said shortly.

"And where have you been?" He leered suggestively.

Sharon laughed. "Señor soldier would not stop a poor girl from making a little money, would he?"

"No, señorita." He poked her lightly in the ribs. "How was business to-night, señorita? I know a whore, señorita, who says business in Havana is sick. You are a pretty one, though. I'll wager you have no trouble —"

Sharon slapped him smartly on the cheek. "Señor soldier talks out of turn."

"You — you she-devil," he cried, "you come with me."

"You're drunk," she countered, holding her ground. "I warn you. I am an American. Go home to bed and leave me alone."

The soldier peered at her closely. *"Americano!"*

"Sí."

"Muy bien," he said meekly, and with a hiccough, "you may pass."

Some ten minutes later she reached the end of the street. Veering sharply to the right was a narrow alley-way. In its centre glowed a feeble gas lamp. Beneath it was the sign — she could barely make out the letters — Avenida de los Arbores Verdes. And not a tree in sight! Dismounting, she walked along, wheeling her bicycle beside her until she came to Number Twenty-five.

Just as Jaime Perez had said, the house was dark, but the door was ajar. She leaned the cycle against the wall beside the door. It was a two storied house of white adobe, built flush with the alley-way. A balcony across the front made a roof over a part of the street.

The shutters were all closed. The street, the house, the air itself seemed ominous — silent as death. But she opened the door and entered the black void. She could hear nothing but the furious pounding of her heart.

"Well," she told herself, "there's no sense in standing here." But the thought failed to give her the courage she hoped it would. Just a few steps inside this house was a stranger — Perez's "my friend" — a man or a woman — sitting at a table — waiting for her, "the smartest woman in all Havana". Why the darkness? Why the secrecy?

She advanced straight ahead — slowly — three steps. Now, two steps to the right. There should be a doorway. Reaching forth a curious hand she touched wood, and the wood receded. She pushed the door open as far as she could without moving from the spot. Four steps forward. Now what?

"You have the envelope, señorita?" a voice hissed directly before her.

"Yes."

"Give it to me."

Reaching into her dress. Sharon brought forth the envelope, her fingers trembling ever so slightly. She held it straight before her. It was snatched from her hand. She turned and retraced the four steps to the door.

"One moment, señorita. Won't you sit down? There is a chair at your left." The voice was a man's.

"My instructions, sir, were to leave immediately."

The voice assumed a normal tone. "That is right, señorita. You have proved that you can carry out instructions. That is all I wished to know." A match was struck and a candle on the table was lighted.

"Perez! You?"

"It is I, señorita," Perez chuckled in amused satisfaction.

"But I don't understand. Why do you have me deliver a message to yourself?"

"Only to see if you had as much wits about you

as my friend said. He is right — yes, my friend is a 'he'. You are capable of carrying out instructions to the letter. But there is one sad mistake you made this time which you must never repeat. Never try to hide anything between your breasts. It is the first place a man will search. There are other places, señorita, where you may hide a small folded message. But we'll leave that to you. This time it was not such a sad mistake, after all, because it happens the message itself is unimportant. See?" He ripped open the envelope and drew forth a blank sheet of paper.

"But I still do not quite understand, señor," Sharon said.

"I do not expect you too, just yet. But presently you will understand everything. My friend will explain it all. He is in that room." Perez pointed to a door opposite the one through which Sharon had entered. "He is waiting for you now."

She walked across the room and knocked on the door.

"Enter."

Pushing open the door she stepped into a bedroom. Reclining on the four-poster, pulling at a cigarette, was Carlos Menendez.

His shirt and collar were open. His boots lay sprawled grotesquely on the floor.

"Señor Menendez!"

"Are you surprised to see me, Señorita Douglass?"

"But of course. I thought you were dead. Mr Edgecomb said —"

"Mr Edgecomb and most of the Spanish army think me dead. How have you been, señorita? Well, I hope."

"In excellent health, señor."

"Good. We shan't waste time in talking over trivialities."

Sharon regarded him closely. He had changed. Now his eyes burned with the fever that glowed in the eyes of all Cubans. He was thinner, a great deal so, and his hair was thinning. Where were his polished manners? And why was his speech so clipped and decisive? As she remembered him on the *Grover Cleveland*, he was given to a leisurely drawl and flowery language.

"You find me changed, señorita?"

Startled from her reverie, Sharon managed to say, "A little," with the proper degree of deliberation.

"You have changed too. You must have worked hard."

"I am not ashamed of it."

"If you were, señorita, I would have nothing to do with you. I have watched you closely, I know exactly how long you have been singing at El Americano. Do you remember our talks on board the *Grover Cleveland*?"

"Yes, certainly."

"You know, of course, where my sympathies as a Cuban patriot lie?"

"I think so."

"At that time I had reason to believe, after talking with you, that your sympathies lay in the same direction. If they have changed, you had best leave here immediately, and I warn you that it would not be well to remember this address. If you feel the same as you did then, you can be very valuable to both Cuba and myself."

"Señor Menendez," Sharon replied evenly, "my sympathies have not changed. I and my friends hate Spain for all that she has done to your people and mine. If you could see what is left of my uncle's plantation, you would know why I say I am ready to do anything you ask of me."

"Good, señorita. Good!" He paused. "It is still Señorita Douglass?"

Sharon smiled. "I have had no luck in changing it to anything else." They both laughed and the three years that separated them rolled aside as though their last meeting had been yesterday. They were old friends again.

"I will have my servant, Jaime, bring us coffee," Carlos said.

"Your servant? You mean the voice teacher?"

"Ah, he is no more a voice teacher than I. He has been a faithful retainer to the family of Menendez for two generations. I lettered the card he presented to you. It was all carefully prearranged, my dear."

After an hour of reminiscing over coffee and crullers, Sharon rose to go.

"Mr and Mrs Floyd will be beside themselves

if I don't get home soon. It must be nearly two o'clock."

"I wish it were possible for me to be seen on the streets so that I might escort you back. But I can't. A safe journey to you. Will you return to-morrow night?"

"Yes, of course. Good night, señor."

The following midnight Sharon returned to the dark room as she had promised.

"Come in, señorita," Carlos called from the bedroom. A candle was on the table and some five or six maps were laid out on the bed before him. They were traced and retraced so many times that the paper barely hung together at the creases.

"I cannot stay long," she said, dropping in a chair and removing her hat, "for Mr and Mrs Floyd were put out because of last night. They can't seem to understand that I am capable of taking care of myself."

"I will come to the point immediately. Once you asked me not to speak in parables and said that you had more respect for plain facts. Do you still feel that way?"

"Señor Menendez, I am essentially the same girl you met on shipboard. If my eyes seem tired it is because they have seen so much suffering. If my spirit is not as lively as it was when you first knew me it is because Spain has helped to deaden it."

"Then the fact, señorita, plainly and simply

put, is this: I want you to become a spy for the rebel army."

Sharon jumped from her chair. "A spy!"

"Yes, and please do not shout. One never knows which wall is listening. I want you to be a good spy, and a good spy is a discreet one."

"I understand, señor, forgive me." Sharon sank back into her chair and pondered his words. A spy! Why, that didn't really happen except in fiction.

"Do you remember, señorita, when I once told you that I was returning to Cuba, where I could do the most good for my people?"

"Yes, I remember it well."

"I found that that good lay in espionage. I became a spy for General Garcia. But now I am no longer useful in that capacity. So I am asking you to take my place."

"But why me? And why are you no longer useful?"

"The answer to the first part of your question is that you are less liable to be suspected. You are young and a woman. Men do not think of young women spying on an army. Then, too, you have courage, señorita. I told you that three years ago. Again, I think you like adventure, and if you like the work you will do it well. But the most important factor is that you are an American and therefore above suspicion for the time being. The answer to the second part of your question is that I have once been caught and imprisoned. I escaped. But I cannot use my freedom for Cuba because I would be recognized. So General Garcia has appointed me head of the espionage service, whence I can direct operations in comparative secrecy."

"I understand."

"Of course you realize, señorita, that you do not have to do this for me if you do not wish to."

Sharon considered. Then she said, "I will do what you ask of me, señor."

"Good. We'll get down to business at once. You will not have to leave the city at all or change any of your daily habits. Your post of operations will be El Americano."

"The café? Then is Mr Edgecomb — ?"

"No! He has nothing to do with it. I wouldn't trust that man farther than across this room. He would probably be as lamentable at espionage as he is at chess. Señor Edgecomb had best continue to think that I am dead."

"I understand. But why the café?"

"What better place could we choose? I am pleased to think that fate was trying to make amends for some of her unkindness to Cuba when she led you to sing there. Even these ageing eyes can see that you possess certain — shall we say, charms? And there is no café in the city more popular with the Spanish officers than El Americano. You are to employ your charms to the best advantage on any Spanish officer that we name. You will receive certain explicit instructions at regular intervals. They must be obeyed to the letter."

"May I employ my — as you say — charms in the manner I think best?"

"Of course. Your job will be to extract information from certain men we designate. It will not always be easy. The Spanish officers are not stupid. You may lose some of your friends because of your actions. You may have to entertain men in your room at the café. You may have to drink with them. You may have to —"

"I think I can prevent it going so far as that, señor."

"That, of course, is up to you. On Mondays and Thursdays you are to come here at midnight unless you are — entertaining under our orders. In that case you will return at any time on the morning after. That would be Tuesdays and Fridays. I will not be here at any time but your instructions will come from me. There will be no hint in them that I know you, no friendly word of greeting, nothing save official instructions. Yet I want you to know always that I wish you luck and that I will be with you constantly in thought. Jaime will be here on the nights I mentioned. If you come then he will hand you your instructions. If you come on the following morning you will find instructions in this room. Examine the rug beneath your chair and you will find it is double. At the edge next to that wall is an opening. In that pocket you will find my messages. Do you clearly understand all these directions?"

"Quite clearly, señor."

"The door of this house will always be unlocked. On its face will be tacked the black sign of death, so that no outsiders are likely to enter. There will be no instructions for you to-night. General Garcia's army lies to the west of here — waiting. They will make no move until they learn the intentions of the Spaniards. You will report here at midnight next Tuesday. Jaime will give you your first instructions then. I believe that is all, señorita."

"All right."

"Oh yes, one thing more. If you make a mistake, if you are caught, I must warn you that you cannot expect any help from us. We cannot stand behind you. Also, if you are caught, I must warn you not to reveal whom you work for and where you receive your instructions. Our entire cause might be lost if you did."

"You can trust me, señor."

"I know I can."

Sharon rose to leave. "Good-bye, Señor Menendez."

"*Hasta mañana,* señorita."

On the following Tuesday at midnight, Sharon again turned down the Avenida de los Arbores Verdes. At Number Twenty-five she leaned her cycle against the wall. There was a light now in the window downstairs. The shutter was thrown back for all who passed to look in. Sharon peered through the aperture into the room where she had first delivered the envelope. Now a cot was before the window at an angle, and Jaime lay upon it, covered with blankets.

Sharon hurried to the door. It was closed, and tacked on it was the death sign. Hesitating only an instant, Sharon pushed open the door and walked through into the larger room where Jaime lay, groaning.

"Enter, señorita."

"Señor Perez!" Sharon stepped quickly to his side. "What is the matter? What's happened?"

Jaime propped himself on one elbow. "Come closer, señorita, and be not alarmed." Then in an undertone, "I am only feigning sickness. There were two Spanish soldiers here this morning on inspection. We must be careful." Taking her hand he said aloud, "My medicine, little sister, take the bottle to the apothecary and have it refilled."

"But — but my instructions," Sharon stammered. "Señor Menendez said —"

"Instructions? What instructions! What are you talking about? Your instructions are to leave at once for my medicine, sister."

Sharon stared about the room and began to question her senses. But it was the same house — the same room — and this was surely Jaime Perez pretending to be sick and babbling about medicine.

"Señor Perez," she ventured, "I —"

"Leave, you fool," he whispered. "Take the medicine bottle with you. Go home with it. Be sure you are not followed. And never mention certain names around here again. You are never to be surprised at what might be going on here. Now leave."

Sharon nodded, grasped the medicine bottle and said aloud, "Yes, brother, I will fetch your medicine."

She left immediately looking neither to the left nor right, mounted her bicycle and pedalled back home. She was relieved to find the house dark. Her insistence that the Floyds stop worrying about her must have taken effect. Slipping into the room she shared with Libby she found her sound asleep in their large four-poster bed. This was good. Under the gas jet and with her back to Libby, Sharon sat down and uncorked the medicine bottle. There, rolled into a tube, was a small slip of paper. Using a hairpin as forceps she rolled the paper still tighter and withdrew it. She looked again at the sleeping Libby before reading the message:

1. Memorize these instructions and burn this paper immediately.
2. At the first opportunity dispose of the medicine bottle by tossing it into the harbour.
3. To-morrow night captain José de Azules will dine at El Americano. His reservation is table five.
4. You will recognize the captain by the following: Black hair clipped short. A scar

above his left eyebrow. He smokes cigarettes rather than cigars.
5. The captain is particularly fond of Scotch whisky. He is a devout Catholic. Use that to the best advantage. We think he is unmarried. He speaks English.
6. You are to learn from him the *total number of Spanish companies stationed in Cuba.*
7. Record only that number on a slip of paper. *No other writing of any kind.*
8. In two days a stranger will appear before you and will identify himself with the word *beef.* You will hand to him without question the slip of paper with the number on it.
9. In the event that you have been unable to obtain the desired information, you are to let the stranger know by offering to sing for him.

Going over it thoroughly again and taking another cautious look at Libby, Sharon touched a corner of the paper to the flame and held the opposite corner until there was nothing left of the message but a feathery grey fragment that fell apart as she dropped it.

"Now, please go, Mr Edgecomb, and let me rest," Sharon said on the following night as she stood in her dressing-room preparing to change her costume.

"Very well, my dear, if you wish it," Edgecomb said affably. "Jove! Those officers like your singing! How they applaud!"

Sharon's answer was a mirthless, impatient smile.

Edgecomb lighted his pipe and said, "Naturally, if you prefer to be alone, I shall respect your wishes, but I do wish you'd dine with me."

"I'm sorry, Mr Edgecomb, but my job is to sing for you and that is all."

"Quite so. You drive a hard bargain." He closed the door gently behind him.

Sharon lay down on the small couch that was crowded into her room. Everything was going wrong. She had made her three appearances on the hour and now there was only the midnight performance. And still table five was empty. At her eleven o'clock appearance she had scanned all the officers and found that none of them bore a scar over the left eyebrow. Fear that she had misread the instructions obsessed her so that she sang dreadfully off key and in her anxiety even forgot some of the words.

As she lay on the couch trying to reassure herself that she had read and memorized the instructions accurately she heard the strains of "Waltz Me Around Again, Willie". That was her cue. She picked up her fan and made her entrance. As she began her song Alfonzo dimmed the lights.

Weaving and gliding among the tables she winked at this officer and that; favoured one by sitting in his lap for just an instant; and flustered another by flirting with him outrageously in front of his wife. She could usually tell whether the lady was wife or sweetheart. If excessive attentiveness indicated sweetheart she would leave that table alone.

At table seven was a regular patron, fat Hans Pheigg, the tobacco trader, with his mistress. A pock-marked youth was entertaining the notorious Madame Le Fevre at table six. Influenced by his fifth bottle of rum he grasped Sharon's wrist and reached for her shoulder. But the Madame drew him into her own embrace.

Sharon stopped short at table five. Then with a pirouette she sang with renewed enthusiasm, "Around, around, around". There were three men seated there. Two of them were nondescript in appearance, but the one in the middle was swarthy in a stalwart, commanding sort of way and his jet-black hair was close clipped. And — yes, there was a scar over his left eyebrow. Between his fingers a cigarette rested carelessly.

Sure of their attention, Sharon concentrated hers on Captain de Azules, smiling at him slowly, provocatively, and cutting off the smile with her fan — except for her teasing eyes. She strolled away and back again nonchalantly brushing the ash from his cigarette with her fan. The captain smiled politely, rose and bowed. As he sat down very slowly she sang the rest of her song to him.

Alfonzo turned the lights up again and the patrons resumed their dining. Before making her exit Sharon — quite by accident — dropped her fan, and quite by accident it fell at the captain's feet.

She gave him no time to retrieve it, but hurried to her room to change into her new flowered kimono, a rose-coloured silk patterned with morning glories. Seating herself at the dressing-table she took down her hair, applied two drops of costly French perfume, and began languidly to comb out her curls. With a shawl of auburn hair about her shoulders she stepped into the corridor and called across to the kitchen, "Alberto!"

The Spaniard dressed in immaculate white stuck his olive-skinned face around the kitchen door. "Sí, Señorita Douglass."

"I believe I dropped my fan, Alberto, while I was singing. I think I must have dropped it near table five. Will you fetch it?"

"Sí, señorita."

She returned to the task of combing her hair. A few moments brought the expected knock at her door. Without turning she said, "Come in, Alberto."

The door opened and closed.

"Lay my fan on the couch and leave quickly."

"The señorita is most unkind." A vibrant voice spoke. "If the señorita were polite she would ask her caller to sit down instead of bidding him leave."

"Oh!" She had no idea she could be so fluttery. "It is *you,* señor!"

"Yes, it is I. You will pardon me, I hope, for

begging the liberty of returning your fan in person. Your Alberto was doubtful, but I was insistent."

"That's quite all right. It was very stupid of me to drop it."

"Not at all. I'm glad you did drop it, else I should not have had the pleasure of returning it."

"Is it so great a pleasure?"

"Indeed, señorita."

"Please be seated, señor. I am honoured to have you call. But your friends at the table, will they not miss you?"

"They are well trained," de Azules said blandly. "They will wait. They hear and see nothing."

"Then we are free to — shall we say — visit for a time?"

"Quite, señorita."

"Good! I am finished singing for the evening. If the señor hadn't already dined I would ask him to dine with me here in my little nook. It is tiny — but private."

"I'm so sorry, señorita, that I was committed to eat with my lieutenants. And if I had known that I would have the opportunity of dining with the señorita, I would not have eaten one morsel. But we might partake of some light refreshment, perhaps?"

"Of course. Only you will have to suggest something. I am so stupid when it comes to liquor, unless of course I order what my father always used to drink —"

"Your father? Perhaps I know him."

"Hardly, señor. Lucky Fred Douglass turned in his chips three years ago in the States." Sharon looked very sad.

"Turned in his chips?"

"That means he died, señor. American slang. Forgive me."

"Forgive me for being stupid. I'm sorry about your father."

"Lucky always said there was no drink like good old Scotch whisky."

"Ah, Scotch whisky! Your father was a discriminating man."

"Alberto!" Sharon called.

"Sí, señorita."

"Bring Scotch whisky and one glass."

"Sí, señorita."

Closing the door, Sharon sat down beside the captain. He eyed her pleasantly, taking in at one glance her figure, delicately outlined in the clinging folds of the kimono. His eyes lingered momentarily on her lips, her throat, the upsweep of her breasts, the curve of her thigh. She went cold under his scrutiny, and hoped he wouldn't be difficult.

Like an unwelcome guest the vision of Eric intruded itself on the fringe of her consciousness, making her wish herself back on the companion-way of the *Grover Cleveland* with a sailor's eyes, not a Spanish officer's devouring her figure and making her feel naked before his gaze.

As if something should be done about this silence between them, de Azules rose stiffly. "I am afraid I have the advantage over the señorita. In the dining-room all the talk was of you. I couldn't help but learn your name. It is an unfair advantage. You should know my name. Allow me to introduce myself. I am Captain José de Azules y Lapiz, of Her Majesty's Army."

"Such an impressive title," Sharon responded graciously. "I am overwhelmed. May I call you just plain José?"

Smiling warmly the captain sat down, took her hand, and said, "Please do."

Alberto's knock at the door interrupted this gesture. Taking the tray, Sharon informed him that she and the gentleman were not to be disturbed, not even by Señor Edgecomb himself. With a doubtful look Alberto departed, muttering something about not being responsible for Señor Edgecomb.

Sharon set the decanter on her dressing-table and poured Captain de Azules a glassful of the Scotch.

"Señorita, señorita," the captain objected, "Please! Not so much at one time."

"No? This was how my father drank it."

"Your father must have been a better man than I, señorita." The captain's eyes twinkled mischievously as he swallowed the whisky in one long gulp, then poured himself another half-glass and downed that. He resumed his seat on the couch, decanter in one hand and glass in the other. Sharon sat opposite him on the chair.

For the next half hour Sharon talked of nothing but her work, the way she occupied her spare hours and the places she had been. While she talked the captain drank. When his speech thickened and the bottle became unsteady in his hand she slid on to the couch beside him and ran her fingers through his bristly hair. Very deliberately the captain set the glass and decanter on the floor and less deliberately threw his arms about his hostess.

"Señorita, señorita," he whispered hoarsely, fumbling at the neck of her kimono. She took his hand in hers and lifted it away. "Wha's th' matt'r?" It was all too plain that he was intoxicated now with lust as well as with alcohol.

"José," she said as if talking to a little boy, "how can I do what you want me to do when I've just been to confession this evening?"

"Confession?"

"Yes. For my sins. I did penance for a full hour and the padre warned me to behave, else the Blessed Mother will be angry with me."

The captain faced her with eyes blinking and shoulders squaring in an effort to get hold of himself. In awed, hushed tones he said, "Forgive me, señorita. I did not know. You are different. You are good. One meets so many bad girls in the cities and when you let me come to your room I thought it was because you were a bad girl. Now I can see you just wanted to be — to be friendly." He paused to gloat over the perfect word, his face triumphant, and very silly. "You are sweet, señorita, like my wife."

So the pig had a wife. Her next smile was infinitely tender. "Do I — do I remind you of her?"

Captain de Azules would not have wished his lieutenants to see him then. There was no military precision in the way he buried his head in Sharon's lap. She stroked his hair compassionately. After all, he was behaving quite well considering his state of intoxication; and compared with that beast of a captain who took Conchita away he was really a gentleman.

"Señorita, señorita," he groaned, "the soldier's life is a hard one. It makes men into wicked beings. My dear mother, may the blessed Saints comfort her soul, used to hold me like this and hear my confessions through the week, before I would go to the good padre in Valencia for forgiveness. I pray you will forgive me, señorita, and I shall make a novena to Our Lady at the first opportunity I have."

"Of course I forgive you, José, you are a good soldier. You are only tired after your day's work. You just lie quiet, José, and rest — just rest." She crooned the last few words and kept on stroking his hair. Very softly she hummed a lullaby.

"So — so tired," he murmured.

"Of course. After commanding so many men all day long, anyone would be tired." She said it gently, soothingly.

But he raised his head and looked at her, wideawake. "How did you know, señorita, that

I commanded men?"

"Why — why, I guess anybody could tell," Sharon stammered, "you're twice as soldierly as the rest who come here to eat. The moment I looked at you I said to myself, 'There is a man who is a born leader'."

"Did you, señorita?" he answered, blinking a little foolishly.

"And besides, you mentioned your lieutenants." Why hadn't she thought of that before? The head sank back in complete satisfaction and blissful relaxation, a benign smile on the swarthy face. "You are a leader, aren't you?" she asked. "Please don't disappoint me."

"Sí, I have a great company of men, all fine soldiers."

"They must be splendid, having you for a leader."

"They are splendid soldiers and *companeros.*"

"Do you have many fine soldiers and *companeros* in your company?"

"Why?" The eyes opened and glinted at her suspiciously.

"Because the number of soldiers you have is the number of your loyal friends — and I know you must have many loyal friends. You are so good to your friends."

"Oh," The captain was a little muddled now. That was better than being suspicious. "I have a full company strength of loyal friends, señorita."

"It is nice to have so many, José. I wish I had a loyal friend."

"I will be your friend, señorita," Captain de Azules said huskily.

"You are kind, José, to a poor friendless girl. But I am afraid my dear uncle would be very disappointed if he saw me with a soldier. You are very sweet, José, but you must not come to see me again." She raised his head in her arms, and leaning down, kissed him on the brow. She remained like that for a moment, her breast pressing against his shoulder. Before she could let him get away she must get the information. If the whisky, her nearness to him, her flattery, her faked religious precepts would not accomplish her end, to what could she resort? She would leave that decision until the time came.

José's arms went about her waist and he raised his head so that he could brush the exposed swell of her breast with his lips. She straightened up again and with a little sigh the captain sank back. "Señorita is an angel," he whispered.

"And she feels so safe with a soldier," the angel whispered. "Such a brave soldier with so many brave soldiers fighting for him. It is so romantic. I'll wager there isn't another company of men as fine as yours, or with so brave a captain."

"Oh, sí, señorita. There are. We are a brave Army."

"But, I think you are the bravest. Why, what could the others do? A few little companies! Bah! I'll wager the Queen is proudest of you."

"The Queen doesn't even know of my existence," the captain said petulantly.

"Then shame on her, I say."

"And there are many more companies besides mine. How could she know about me only?"

"I think you joke, José. You are modest like a real gentleman. I'll wager there aren't even five companies besides yours."

"The Queen would not like to think that. She thinks there are seventeen companies all told — and she is right."

"Seventeen?" Sharon pouted. "Then I lose my wager. The forfeit will be a kiss." She leaned down and kissed him, this time full on the lips.

"Señorita is a better singer than a gambler," Captain de Azules muttered. And his head felt heavier than before on her lap.

"José," she whispered. "José!"

There was no response. She straightened up and lifted his arms from about her waist. Frightened, she slid from beneath his head and called Alberto in.

"What's the matter with him, Alberto?"

Alberto, after a cursory examination, grinned and said. "He will be all right. He will sleep through it. He is only, as your Americans say, cock-eyed drunk."

"Oh. Can you take him out of here? His friends are waiting for him."

"I know, señorita. They are beginning to be concerned about him. I will take him." And Alberto easily took the limp form over his shoulder. Sharon held the door open. As soon as they were gone she took a slip of paper from the drawer of her dressing-table and wrote in the centre of it the number seventeen.

The following afternoon the postman handed Sharon a letter from Clayton. She clutched it eagerly and hurried upstairs to her room where Libby sat in the window-seat embroidering a pillow-slip for her hope chest.

"Didn't I get any mail?" Libby whined. "I thought surely somebody in Santiago would remember me." She sighed disconsolately and as Sharon was too occupied to answer she went on, "Once Glenn and I are married and move to New York or Chicago or Saint Louis or some place, then maybe we'll get lots of letters."

"You goose, why do you want to live in any of those cities? What's the matter with Havana?"

"I'd like to see something of the United States. And so would Glenn — he talks about it all the time."

"I bet all those cities aren't what they're talked up to be anyway," Sharon said absently. "I bet Galveston's as good as any of them." But something Libby had said struck her. She looked up from the letter and regarded Libby intently. "Did you say you and Glenn were to be married?"

"Yes." Libby was demure.

"Oh, Libby! Did he ask you?"

"Yes," Libby sat up importantly. "Last night."

"What did you tell him?" A proposal was always exciting.

"Well, I sort of led him on. You know how I mean. I didn't want him to think I was anxious. And he was so funny, so serious, that I could hardly keep from giggling. Then he asked me right out to be his bride and right then I remembered Jason and, Sharon, what do you think? I started to cry!"

"Libby, you didn't."

"Yes, I did. I could hardly understand it myself, but Glenn was so kind. He took his own hankerchief and wiped my tears and swore he'd always want to wipe my tears away, and that made me cry all the harder, and I said yes I'd be his loving faithful wife and he had me blow my nose and we kissed."

"When is it going to be, Libby? I'm so happy for you."

"When is what going to be?"

"Why, the wedding of course, you goose."

"Oh, maybe not for a year yet. I haven't told mamma or papa. They might not like it. Glenn is trying to arrange a transfer back to Washington or some other city, and when that's definite we'll announce our engagement." Libby resumed her work. "What does your uncle say, Sharon, dear?"

"Things are working out fine, he says. He inquires after the affairs of your father and mother and asks about your health. Jason is still working. Shall I read it to you? I've only skimmed over it myself."

"All right. Since I don't get any letters I guess the next best thing is to listen to yours. Curl up on the seat and make yourself comfortable. Here, there's plenty of room."

Approaching the window-seat, Sharon read, " 'My dear niece, God has been so good to me these last few weeks. The money you sent from your new position as a tutor has been a blessing indeed. Your Aunt Phoebe —' " but she had no sooner made herself comfortable than Lavina entered the room without knocking. She smiled at the pair.

"Ah, sewing, Libby?" she asked.

"Yes, mamma."

"And reading, Sharon, dear?"

"Yes, Mrs Floyd. A letter from my Uncle Clay."

"How nice. But I'm afraid you must put it up for a few moments as you have a visitor downstairs. He appears quite gentlemanly."

"I have a visitor?" Sharon repeated, giving herself time to think over the short list of those who might know where she lived and have reason to call on her. "It isn't an army officer?"

"Heavens, no! An army officer? God forbid! Sharon, you know the strangest people. I confess I can't understand it at all — singing in a café — if your uncle knew —"

"Yes, but he doesn't know. And you aren't going to tell him."

"Sometimes I feel it my duty —"

"Fiddlesticks, Mrs Floyd. I'm old enough to take care of myself. But I mustn't keep my caller waiting." She slipped her letter back into the envelope, excused herself and hurried downstairs.

Seated on the divan in the parlour was a small, erect gentleman wearing a walrus moustache, a monocle, white gloves and pearl-grey spats. He carried a Malacca cane. On one knee he balanced his derby hat. As Sharon entered he rose, removed his monocle, squinted at her, adjusted his monocle and regarded her appraisingly.

She felt like a racehorse being considered for the auction block and had to down an impulse to ask, "Will I do?" when the gentleman cleared his throat and proceeded.

"Ha-rumph! Miss Douglass, I presume?" His accent was English.

"You presume rightly, sir. I am Sharon Douglass."

"And I am Sir Geoffrey Wheeling, Miss Douglass," the little gentleman explained, "lately affiliated as the Master of the Ballet with the Havana Opera House."

"Yes?" Sharon sat down.

"Perhaps you have read about us in the paper." He resumed his stiff posture, sitting so near the edge of the couch that Sharon was uneasy. "And perhaps you haven't. Ha-rumph. A certain group of British gentlemen and gentlewomen on Cuban soil are arranging a jolly pageant to be presented on the fifteenth of August and to be entitled 'A Day at the Seashore'. It has come to my attention that you sing at — at a café, or restaurant, I believe."

"That is right." She smiled deprecatingly. "I sing at El Americano."

"According to reports which have reached my ears you are a bit of a sensation, my dear Miss Douglass, ha-rumph!"

"Well, I try to please."

"But, no matter about the deuced details. Let me ask you bluntly. Would you care to sing at our pageant, what?"

In the moment it took Sharon to frame a reply Lavina burst into the room, extending a gracious hand and casting Sharon a sweet but challenging look.

"Oh, my hostess, Mrs Floyd, this is Sir Geoffrey Wheeling."

Lavina beamed at the caller, facing him like a Saint Bernard having a conference with a toy Boston bull.

"Charmed," grunted Sir Geoffrey, as if he felt as insignificant as he looked.

"It's such a rare pleasure, Sir Geoffrey, to have you visit us," Lavina cooed. "Would you care for tea, perhaps?"

"No, thank you," the little man replied, backing away to keep from being completely overpowered by the mammoth presence. "I'm afraid I have an appointment. So sorry. Ha-rumph." He eyed Sharon studiously. "Perhaps, Miss Douglass, we could conclude arrangements for the pageant at the café where you sing. If you care to join with us you can tell me there."

"That will be quite satisfactory," Sharon said, extending her hand. "You can come there to dine and we can talk business afterwards."

"Perhaps not to dine," Sir Geoffrey said. "I always dine at an English café in the British quarter. It is the only place I know where — ha-rumph — I can really get good beef prepared the way the English serve it."

Sharon stood electrified. Clearly she had heard the word. How clever he had been — or had Carlos prepared the speech? Everything he had said left a perfect loophole in case she did not have the information and there was even the allowance for outsiders being present. Her look flashed understanding to Sir Geoffrey.

"I know how you English like your beef," she smiled. "My father used to joke about it with his British friends. Do you know where El Americano is, Sir Geoffrey?"

"I'm not sure that I do."

"It is on the boulevard — just a moment. I'll write it down for you." At the secretaire she scribbled the address; and when that slip of paper changed hands there was another slip of paper folded within it.

Back in her room she found Libby still waiting to hear the letter from Santiago.

"Where did we leave off?" Sharon curled up on the windowseat again.

"You had just read the words 'Aunt Phoebe'."
"Oh yes. Here it is:

"Your Aunt Phoebe and I are overjoyed at your good fortune and at ours. Jason, who is such a comfort to us now, such a strong staff for us to lean upon, has proved to be a blessing to us too. But I believe Jason realizes how sorry I am for my lack of understanding in the past, and I hope the good Father above will see fit to forgive me for my sins.

"Jason asks me to send you his love. He talks about you constantly. He still works, but now his salary is his own and I believe he is saving some of it, thanks again to your kind help. It is more than enough to supply our humble needs. Children of God do not need fine raiment or costly foods.

"So far there has been no prospective buyer for Promised Land. We hope for one of two things — either that we will be able to sell the plantation before the Spanish Government takes it from us in lieu of taxes, or else that we will be able to obtain some money somewhere and pay the taxes.

"It seems to me that the time for action has arrived. In about a week I am coming by carriage to Havana to see Fitzhugh Lee, our Consul-General, and to enter a formal plea for aid from the United States. The newspapers can no longer keep silent up north and several gentlemen, notably Mr Hearst and Mr Roosevelt, are extending their sympathies to Cuba. I am coming to Havana as president of the American Plantation Owners Society. There is to be a conclave of the society there. Our first attempt was a failure. I didn't mention it before, but last June we in Santiago made a formal plea for help straight to the Secretary of State, Sherman at Washington. It did no good, for I see by a Boston paper that even though Sherman did act on 27 June, and did send a note to the Government at Madrid protesting against Weyler's monstrous rule, it was of no use. This Boston paper states that the Spanish Foreign Minister replied that Valeriano Weyler had behaved in Cuba with no less regard for human feelings than our Secretary of State's own brother, General Sherman, in his famous march to the sea during the Civil War.

"So it looks as though this time we are going to have to make our plea over the heads of the Government and straight to the hearts of the people. I am quite sure they will demand that justice be done. A true American never lets a brother American suffer.

"You may expect me then perhaps in a week. I shall stay a week or two to visit with you and my dear friends, the Floyds. I trust that Arnold's affairs are working out well and that he and his good wife and daughter are in excellent health. To-morrow I will write them announcing my visit. It will be good seeing you again. May God ever guide you in the paths of righteousness that you may be a good influence over your pupils."

"Viva Weyler! Viva Weyler!" A portly Spaniard, his hair hoary, his knuckles knotted with age, feebly shook his fist at the Americans in the throng that lined the Boulevard of Havana. It was General Weyler's farewell parade.

Contrary to Clayton Arms's expectations, the note from the White House to the Spanish Minister for War in Madrid, written on 27 June 1897, and signed by the Secretary of State, did have some effect. After a great deal of grumbling and a few heated exchanges of notes, General Valeriano Weyler was recalled from Cuba by the Queen Regent of Spain.

"God damn President McKinley," another Spaniard shouted.

"Viva Weyler! Viva el Generalissimo!"

"Pigs of Americans! Stupid dogs, all of them!"

There were angry mutterings from some of the more daring Americans in the crowd. There were very few Cubans to be seen. Those who were not herded into concentration camps kept to their homes on the back streets. But there were enough other nationalities to make up for them; Spaniards, British, French, Dutch, and Americans jammed the pavement. Next to the Spaniards in numbers came the Americans.

While there was joy in their hearts at the sight of Weyler leaving Cuban soil, there was also uncertainty that the next man would be any better.

The Spaniards were unrestrained in their cheering of the general and did not hesitate to show their contempt for the Americans. They too were uncertain about their hero's successor. He might not let them have as free a hand as had Weyler. They knew well that the Americans in Cuba had been instrumental in having their leader recalled.

"To hell with President McKinley! Long live Weyler! Ten thousand curses on the United States!"

Sharon and Uncle Clay watched all this with suppressed emotions. They did not join the French and the Dutch in their cheering, but kept quietly inconspicuous, as did all the more discreet Americans. They knew that this was merely the beginning. It would be an empty victory if they progressed no farther.

Uncle Clay spoke as they worked their way toward Sharon's cycle. "I have made up my mind. I am calling on Mr Fitzhugh Lee this very afternoon. He can't ignore the demands of the Plantations Owners Society for ever, and I can't keep on here much longer. I've let him put me off for two weeks now, and I'm thinking I've been too patient with him."

"I hope you can pin him down and make him listen, and that it does some good," Sharon replied as they reached the clearing where her cycle was resting. The streets were still too crowded for her to ride it, and soon she would have to leave Uncle Clay. They walked along at an easy pace. Neither spoke for some time.

Sharon compared this view of Weyler with the one they had had of him when he "honoured" Santiago. There was the same piercing quality in his black eyes, the same flagrant scorn in his expression and the same disdain in the haughtily curling lips. He might be a little fatter — and why not, with the best of the land at his fingertips? She was glad to see the wind taken out of his sails and she hoped it might mean the release of the poor *reconcentrados*, especially the women. In Jason's last letter he had written that he despaired of ever finding Conchita. The camp near Santiago had denied any knowledge of her.

"I turn off at the next corner," Sharon said, "and you go two blocks farther before you turn."

"I know the way all right by now," Uncle Clay replied petulantly. "But I was wondering if you wouldn't go with me. Do you have to dine with your pupil's family every night?" And as she nodded her head, "Oh, well. I suppose if you must do so, you must. Good-bye, girl."

Sharon said her good-bye, and waved back at him as she pedalled away. He had aged horribly. She was shocked at her first sight of him in over a year. His burning eyes were sunken, and his face, once weather-beaten and tanned the colour of mahogany, was now an unhealthy ivory. The vision of how he and Aunt Phoebe must have deprived themselves before the small sums began coming in from her "tutoring" brought tears to her eyes.

She reflected on the lie she was living and laughed to herself at the thought of Rudolph, her imaginary pupil. She couldn't help being a little proud of her creation. Rudolph, a very special boy of sixteen, was the son of Anton Glock, the night chef in one of the fashionable cafés, who did not wish the family stirring in the mornings when he must get his sleep. In the afternoons Rudolph studied pianoforte and cello. His music teacher, having been engaged before Sharon, had the preference as to lesson time. That left only the evening hours in which Rudolph could devote himself to his English and mathematics, a subject in which he had always been slow. Mrs Glock spoke just enough English to take an unholy glee in talking it by the hour. It was she who kept Sharon so late, telling her all about her girlhood in Denmark and Germany, her two former marriages, and her extensive travels. The Glock family were so real to Sharon that she would not have been surprised to meet the three of them strolling along the street some afternoon.

At twenty past twelve, Sharon approached Number Twenty-five. Leaning her cycle against the wall, she approached the doorway, barely noticing that the house was dark and apparently deserted, so accustomed was she now to the twice-weekly excursions. Even when Jaime Perez was not there to slip her the instructions, she did not hesitate. She knew where to find them. To-night would make her eighth assignment and she did not even worry or wonder about it.

Assignments were becoming routine, although every one of them had been as exciting as the one with Captain de Azules — and as successful. On 24 July, two days after her meeting with the captain, the Cuban army increased its companies to nineteen in number. On 26 July the wisdom of this increase was proven. One Spanish company was slaughtered virtually to the last man because they were outnumbered by three to one. Perhaps by accident, it turned out to be the company commanded by de Azules.

On the afternoon of 25 July, Sharon went sailing with Lieutenant Arturo Velasquaz. The lieutenant was rewarded with three of her kisses and shared with her a bottle of wine. It was a peculiar coincidence that the company to which Lieutenant Velasquaz was attached was unexpectedly engaged in combat a week later in the nearby mountains and was nearly annihilated. The lieutenant, unfortunately, lost his life in this engagement.

On the Sunday following, Sharon attended mass with Captain Luis Balbo, stationed with the Spanish Medical Sector as a staff surgeon. She partook of communion with him and prayed with his rosary beads. Oddly enough, the next

Wednesday the base hospital quarters of the Spanish army was burnt to the ground. In the conflagration seven staff officers, twelve male nurses, four surgeons and seventy-three wounded soldiers perished during the night. With the surgeons Captain Luis Balbo went forth to meet his patron saint.

On the evening of 29 July, Sharon sang her songs so liltingly to Private Roberto Nego that he begged her to walk with him in the moonlight. She allowed herself to be coaxed, and listened rapturously to his tales of old Spain and his boyhood in Barcelona. Three days later the ammunition base for five Spanish companies was blown to atoms, and not a trace of young Private Nego, who was stationed there as a guard could be found.

Similarly two Spanish gunboats, stationed along the coast of Cuba — not in Havana harbour — were sunk one night with no loss of life, but complete destruction of the ships. Three nights before, Sharon had danced with Romanzo Geyal, a sailor on one of the boats. When they questioned Romanzo, along with a number of other sailors, regarding the sinking of the ships, the poor youth became so addled and frightened that he jumped into the sea and drowned himself.

And so it went on. The life of a spy fully gratified Sharon's adventurous spirit. And the fact that she was an American girl gave her a feeling of security. She had been valuable too. She knew that. Though she never heard from Carlos except officially she learned through Jaime that her services were satisfactory. Once she had asked how the information she received was translated so quickly into action and Jaime cautioned her not to ask questions, but dropped a sly hint that the rebels were well supplied with perfectly trained carrier pigeons.

So entering Number Twenty-five now, she felt no fear, only the keen prickling that always ran up the back of her neck as she pushed open the door of the dark room. Blackness enveloped her.

"Jaime," she called softly. "Jaime," then stood listening for a moment. "It is I, Jaime, your little sister bringing fruit for you again. How is the sickness, Jaime?"

No answer.

She stepped forward without hesitation. She knew every inch of the floor by this time. In the inner bed-room she locked the door behind her and lighted the candle on the table. Moving the chair she lifted the rug and from the pocket drew forth a rifle cartridge. Unscrewing the cap she poured the powder out on a little sheet of paper. There, tucked in the bottom of the cavity, was a folded square of tissue paper which she removed with a hat-pin.

Holding it near the candle flame she read the instructions and committed them to memory:

1. Continue to entertain Colonel Vincente Mares in your room. Take plenty of time for

this assignment. It is an important one.
2. Above all be careful. Mares is nobody's fool.
3. Plans are altered somewhat. Instead of learning when Mares plans to make his next attack, *concentrate on learning when further troops are expected from Spain — and their number.* We have reasons to believe Mares will not attack until aid arrives.
4. You will be contacted in the usual manner. Destroy these instructions and the cartridge.

Rereading the third section, Sharon touched the tissue to the flame, burnt the gun cotton, dumped the powder into her hand and burnt the paper which had held it. She picked up the metal cap and, with all that remained of the shell in her hand with the powder, she blew out the candle.

At the doorway she paused to call back into the dark room, "Good-bye, brother, I will come again with more fruit. Sleep well."

On the street again, she mounted her cycle and rode away into the darkness. The breeze whipped the powder from her hand when she opened her palm, and as she crossed the bridge over the canal leading in from the harbour a soft splash told her that the rest of the cartridge had landed in safe oblivion.

Shortly after Sharon's conversation with Sir Geoffrey Wheeling she received an envelope through the mail containing one hundred and fifty pesos and a paper marked simply "Beef". She hadn't really expected any pay, but she was willing to accept the money, because she knew that it might at any time be very much needed. After each assignment came an envelope with the same amount and with the new word of identification. Shrewdly she started a bank account, and before a month was up she had the comfortable knowledge that she possessed over a thousand pesos, and that if the emergency arose she herself could save Promised Land from the Spanish Government.

At times she longed for the quiet plantation, though the peacefulness had bored her. Already the thrill of helping Carlos Menendez help Cuba was wearing off; already the edge of excitement was dulling. Here on the frail couch in her dressing-room lay Colonel Vincente Mares, even as Captain de Azules had lain, stupefied and drowsy, except that the colonel was so heavy she feared that at any moment the bamboo legs of the couch would give away. No longer was she alarmed when her guests became dead drunk. With her experience in enticing them to drink excessively she knew what to expect.

But none of them had been quite so brutish-looking as this Colonel Mares, with his jaw gaping and his stringy hair clinging to his moist brow and getting into his eyes. Those bloated cheeks, that paunch with the tunic rumpled across it. She was beginning to hate the sight of men — portly pompous officers like Colonel Mares, men as tired and wasted as Uncle Clay, priggish men as mincing as Hilary Edgecomb, fussy and talkative men like Arnold Floyd. She would welcome the sight of Jason again, tall and rangy, not a spare ounce of flesh on his body, shy of manner, and as much a part of Cuba as the hills surrounding Santiago.

And at night the dreams of Eric! The only man who had possessed her and the only one she could not possess. If she could only dismiss him from her dreams and know that he would never torment her again. Sometimes he would flash across her mind with the swiftness of a bullet, and even for that fleeting instant the picture would be so sharp, so poignant, that it would leave her aching with desire for him.

Liquor did not loosen Colonel Mares's tongue as it should. Nor, while sober, would he let even a hint of a military secret escape his lips. He seemed to consider it his natural right to come to Sharon's dressing-room whenever he chose. There was that standing offer that she become his mistress which she had neither declined nor accepted. Perhaps that was why he continued to make himself at home in her room each night.

She sidled up to him and sat very lightly on the narrow edge of the couch. "Sleepy, dear one?" she whispered.

A grunt was the only answer.

She was tired of trying to bleed him for information and getting nowhere at all. If he would not nibble at her bait perhaps he would play her catch for fair if she gave him all the line. Impatience goaded her to the point of folly. She bent close to his ear, affectionately caressed his cheek and whispered, "Dear one, please talk to me. I get so lonesome when you lie still like that and don't speak. Of course I know you are tired. I would be, too, if there were so few soldiers that I had to do two men's work. When do you expect replacements from Spain, dear one, and how many will there be?"

A moment of silence while Sharon felt the colonel's body grow tense, and the atmosphere in the room, charged with suspense, ignited. Vincente Mares leaped to his feet, pushing Sharon aside, and she found herself staring into a pair of cold, calculating, and wideawake eyes.

"So, at last, señorita, you come out with the question I have waited for. For seven days I hoped you would ask it. I didn't think your patience would endure for ever."

"What do you mean?" Sharon asked, backing against the door.

"Just what I've said. You were very clever, señorita — almost too clever. Sometimes you had me thinking I was the fool, but I was the more patient one and I found you to be the fool, señorita." He advanced toward her, arms outstretched.

"Keep away from me, you drunken pig," she warned.

"So you think me drunk, eh?" Gripping her

wrist in the vice of his fist he twisted her arm and growled, "Well, I'm not drunk! Nor was I drunk last night, nor the night before. And at last I find you to be just what I've always suspected — a spy!" He looked at her in gloating triumph.

"A spy!" Sharon curled her lips in scorn. "How ridiculous! Let me go at once, you simpleton!" with her free hand she clawed at the fist that held her arm against the door.

But the colonel grasped that hand too and pinioned her by both arms. "Let you go," he taunted with malice in his eyes, "so that you can return to Numero 25 Avenida de los Arbores Verdes, eh?"

"How — did you know about that?" Sharon stammered.

"Oh, so now you don't think I'm so simple, eh, señorita? I've been watching you for a week. I've watched the house at Numero Twenty-five. I've checked back on some of your recent friends — Captain de Azules, Private Nego, Captain Ralbo, and Lieutenant Velasquaz. I've checked on their companies and what befell them. Everything fits. It will make a pretty story when I take you before the Generalissimo, Señorita Spy! There is only one present for such as you and that is a wall and a ditch. And it will be my great pleasure to see that you receive it."

"No, no!" Sharon cried, desperately struggling to release herself from his grip. And seeing that that only made him tighten his hold she tried a pleading tone and leaned limply against the door, putting herself at his mercy. "Please let me go. You are mistaken. I have done nothing. I swear it by Saint Catherine."

"Stop your whining. You know no more of the Saints than I do. Yet you tricked Captain de Azules with them, didn't you?"

"Very well," Sharon said quietly but with menace in her tone, "I warn you that you had better let me go. I thought I could appeal to your sympathy, but I see you have a heart of lead."

"Lead! That's a good one!" Colonel Mares had to laugh. He released her left arm and held only her right. "Soon you, too, will have a heart of lead — and a belly full of lead." He laughed.

"I am an American. I demand that you release me."

"Shut up. I do not give a damn for Americans."

"I'll call for Señor Edgecomb and he will have you thrown out of here."

This convulsed the colonel. "Who?" he guffawed. "That little nincompoop?" He even released his grip on Sharon's right wrist.

With a power born of terror she jerked herself loose, struck him across the face with the bracelets of her left arm, and brought her knee up sharply against his stomach. He fell crashing to the floor. This gave Sharon time to snatch the key from the door, get out, and lock the door from the outside.

She headed straight for the dining-room and

could hear her guest pounding on the door. Mercifully the orchestra was playing loudly enough to prevent the sounds reaching the diners. But she could not go through there. The dining-room was flanked with Spanish officers on both sides. They must be expecting her. That would mean the kitchen door would be guarded too. There was one other way — the roof. Parallel with the corridor was a narrow stairway leading to the balcony. A ladder led to the roof. As she sped up the stairs she heard Mares roaring, "Let me out of here, you nameless bitch!"

Holding her skirts high and hoping the darkness would protect her, she emerged on to the roof. There was another ladder from the roof of the souvenir shop next door to the ground. But there must be five feet between the two buildings. She couldn't make the leap with her gown on. She tore it off. Her petticoats whipped in the breeze. Slipping out of them, she stood in her camisole and pantalettes. With one foot she explored the edge of the roof, got her bearings, took six long paces back, taking a little run, leaped into space, not knowing whether the next moment would bring blessed safety or a crash to the stones of the patio forty feet below. It brought — except for a scraped arm and a bruised knee — safety.

In five minutes she was pedalling furiously down the boulevard. In half an hour she surprised Uncle Clay and Arnold Floyd at a chess game in the parlour. Libby was almost hidden in the mist of her wedding veil, on which she was sewing yards of lace.

"Why, Sharon!" she choked. "Where are your clothes?"

"I haven't time to talk," Sharon gasped, looking out through a crack in the shutter. "Quick, Libby! Get me a dress. Any dress. And throw some of my things in a suitcase. I have to get out of here right away. Hurry, you goose."

"What's the matter, girl?" Clayton demanded, stepping up to her.

"Please, Uncle Clay. I can't tell you now. I'll send word. All I can say is, they're after me."

"Who's after you?" Arnold asked, grasping her arm.

Sharon winced and hid the arm behind her. It was the one she had hurt. "The Spanish soldiers. They found me out. I was a spy for General Garcia."

"What?" Clayton was incredulous.

"Oh, my goodness," Libby said, sitting down in the middle of the stairs, her wedding veil trailing beneath her.

"Oh, hurry, Libby! Please! This is no time to lose your wits. I can't go upstairs myself because —"

Her words were cut short by the sound she dreaded. Men's voices and that awful pounding again on a door. The front door.

"There they are," she groaned, "but I may make it by the back door." On her way she shouted back, "Say good-bye to Mrs Floyd for me."

"But mamma's at the Tuesday Afternoon Club's Saturday night social," Libby called in bewilderment.

Sharon cautiously opened the back door, peered out and fled into the surrounding blackness.

In the parlour, Vincente Mares thundered at Clayton Arms: "Where is the señorita, señor? You had better tell us. The Generalissimo wishes to see her and he bids us have no patience with those who stand in the way of his wishes."

"I tell you she isn't here. My niece has not returned."

"You lie, señor. We traced her here. She was riding her cycle in her underwear." He turned to his men and barked, "Search the house!"

Two of the soldiers burst into the girls' room and found Libby cowering on the window-seat, her wedding veil still in her hand.

"Is that she, Tuan?" one of them asked the other.

"No. That is not the singer. The one who sang was pretty. This one is as plain as a cow and, see, she has a split lip." Tuan turned to go.

But his companion detained him. Looking slyly from soldier to girl and winking at the soldier he said, "Why go? She is a woman." He nudged Tuan in the ribs. "Let us mix a little fun with our work, eh?"

"Bah," Tuan pushed his friend playfully. "I don't like her split lip."

"Need you look at her lip, my friend? Can't you cover her face with your sombrero? Besides, it is not those lips I am interested in, anyway. Come on. I may need some help. She is fat and scared. That's the way I like them."

The two soldiers advanced towards the quivering girl and with one jerk of his fist Tuan's friend ripped Libby's dress open, tearing it from her body. Tuan helped by doing the same with her undergarments. He cupped one of her breasts in his rough hand.

"Bah!" he said. "She is as flat as a day-old omelet."

But his friend was occupied with gripping the struggling girl's ankles and forcing them apart. Libby found her tongue and screamed.

As the sound penetrated the parlour walls Arnold Floyd and Clayton both leaped forward in an attempt to get to her. But the men on guard were ready for them. If bayonets would not stop them, guns would.

"What are they doing to my daughter?" Arnold raged.

"What are your men doing to that girl?" Clayton demanded more calmly, though the veins stood out in purple designs against his white forehead.

"Playing with her, I expect." Colonel Mares grinned.

It was a cunning, vicious grin and it maddened

Clayton beyond restraint. Leaping forward with clenched fists, he lunged at the colonel. "By the Eternal," he croaked hoarsely, "if your men harm a hair of that innocent's girl's head, I swear I'll send you all to hell myself. I'll —"

Deliberately raising his pistol, the colonel still grinning maliciously, fired one shot. The assailant fell at his feet, a bullet hole in his temple pouring forth blood. The limbs jerked convulsively in the final spasm of death.

Lavina returned from the social at about eleven as usual and, as usual, she let herself in the front door. The lights were on in the parlour. The men would be playing — who was that crying? She plunged into the room to find Arnold huddled in a corner moaning like an insane thing and pointing. Her eyes followed the line of his arm to the body of Clayton lying on the floor, his head in a pool of blood.

"Arnold!" Lavina's voice was tense but controlled. "What happened?"

"Shot — soldiers — Spanish soldiers — after Sharon in her underwear — shot — she was a spy — they shot —"

He pointed again at Clayton and then shakily lifted his arm upwards until his trembling finger indicated the girls' room. Lavina, as she tried to run upstairs, heard him moaning again and she distinguished the one coherent word, "Libby".

"Libby!" she called brokenly. "Libby, dear!"

On the window-seat, naked and lifeless, lay

Libby's bruised body. There were tooth marks on her abdomen; her eyes were blackened; a gash in her arm dripped blood. In her hand she still clutched a torn, blood-stained remnant of her bridal veil, the treasured symbol of her chastity.

Sharon looked neither to the right nor left as she ran, terror-stricken, through the streets, still clad only in her camisole and pantalettes, her hair streaming out behind her, her footsteps beating out a frenzied accompaniment to her turbulent emotions.

On a strange avenida she slowed down, not only because of the pain that stabbed into her side like the searing of a branding iron, nor because every breath she drew burned in her throat like a scalding liquid, but because she felt that here she was comparatively safe. There was no one to be seen in either direction. Everything was unfamiliar. A row of dingy houses lined the street stiffly on either side like ill-turned-out soldiers standing at sloppy attention.

Hearing steps she darted into a doorway and hid there until the person passed. It was filthy and smelly, but it was dark. It was as good a place as any to stop for breath and to think over her plight. She had time now to be ashamed of her wild panic and the terror-cold fingers that clutched at her heart. She had never known such fear before and she blamed it on the soft life she had been leading in Havana. But that shouldn't be. Life in Cuba was no bed of roses and, if anything, it should have given her strength to face any ordeal. She needed at this minute all the courage she had ever developed riding the range alone. Perhaps she wasn't the strong-willed girl she always thought she was.

As soon as possible she must try to get word to the Floyds. Uncle Clay would be so worried about her. He wasn't the strong-willed person he once was either. Cuba did awful things to people. If she could only get away. But that looked hopeless. She could hardly fancy herself walking into the bank — like this — and asking for her thousand and eighty pesos. The bank would probably be notified anyway, and be ready to seize her.

What she would do when daylight came she could not foresee. Staying here would get her nowhere. She must do something. When she had rested a long time and the sounds in the houses and street had all died completely away, she stepped forth to see what she might find, but there was a sudden clatter of hoof-beats and there was just time for her to jump back into her doorway before a party of soldiers came by. Their leader held a torch which he thrust in all directions, and as it lighted his own face Sharon could see that he was no one she knew. Fortunately the torch defeated its own purpose, for instead of revealing Sharon it only cast deeper shadows on her. Like some eerie ballerina it cast dancing silhouettes back and forth across the street and only confused the scene.

With the soldiers gone, Sharon ventured out again. She felt safe with them ahead of her. They weren't likely to return, and, besides, she couldn't be positive that they were looking for her. "After all," she reassured herself, half aloud, "lightning never strikes twice in the same place."

She walked slowly, keeping in the shadows of the houses so that the moon would not pick her out. The pain in her side was gone and the wild terror that had rolled over her like a tide was retreating. "Stupid girl," she berated herself, "no matter what happens from now on you are going to stand up to it. What would Lucky Fred think of you being so scared?"

She had walked perhaps an hour when she came to the street's dead end. Another street led her to the left. Coming to a feeble gas-lamp she saw there was a street sign and approached it to see where she was, though for the life of her she couldn't see that it made much difference. Dully she read and reread it. Only with the third reading did full consciousness seize her. *Avenida de los Arbores Verdes!* But it wasn't familiar to her here. She glanced about her and started walking much faster. She could see no numbers but if she kept on walking she would reach Number Twenty-five and she would be able to recognize it.

She came to it sooner than she anticipated. And it was easy to recognize, for all the gas-lamps were turned on full. As she stood in the shadows across the street, making up her mind as to the best way to approach the house without being too noticeable, she breathed a sigh of gratitude. Why hadn't she thought of this before? Why had she left it to chance — or a guiding hand — to bring her here? Jaime must be there and perhaps others. They could hide her. She was about to step forward from the shadows when, to the accompaniment of curses and loud laughter, the door was flung open and some five or six soldiers dragged out a stumbling little man with snow white hair.

The soldiers brandished their rifles and the man flourishing a sabre was Colonel Mares. He gave a command, the soldiers marched forward and tied Jaime Perez's hands behind his back. Then facing him, the colonel demanded, "Do you still refuse to speak?"

"Sí. I know nothing," Jaime replied calmly, but with a sneer. No cry for mercy came to his lips; no grovelling plea disgraced his eyes. It was simply, "I know nothing" and, in the light of a torch, his face was placid, his posture stoic.

"Where is the señorita?" Mares roared.

"Quien sabe?" Jaime shrugged.

"Then where is your superior?" Mares held the torch closer.

Jaime grinned impudently. "Señor Colonel speaks in riddles."

"Very well. We have given you a chance to talk. Now you'd better pray to God for mercy."

Colonel Mares stepped aside, raised his sabre

high and gave a curt command. The little band of soldiers sprang into formation, a straight line, facing Jaime. And Jaime faced them squarely.

"Ready." The colonel's voice was calm now.

The guns were raised shoulder high, the cold moonlight glittering on the polished metal of the rifles.

"Aim!" The voice had a higher pitch and a decisive ring.

The soldiers sighted, both eyes open; the long barrels sought out the heart of another Cuban patriot.

"Fire!" The voice rang out in arrogant triumph. The sabre dropped. The six shots were fired as one and Jaime Perez slumped to the cobblestones.

Sharon could not quite catch the next few words from Colonel Mares, but his riflemen turned and marched up the street, leaving Jaime to lie grotesquely in his own widening pool of blood, and Numero 25 Avenida de los Arbores Verdes to shed its light on the pavement. If other eyes than Sharon's witnessed the sight, if other ears heard the deathly sounds accompanying the stark tableau, there was no sign. The neighbours knew better than to meddle with Spain's military justice. Or perhaps they no longer cared.

But it was too much for Sharon. In spite of her sturdy resolution not to give way to panic again, she gazed at Jaime's slender body and let the horror of the scene paralyse every fibre of her being. Her heart pounded wildly against her ribs like a tomtom beating out a voodoo message to her brain, spelling out, "Run! Run!"

With a sobbing cry she threw her arm across her face to blot out the sight and, turning back the way she had come, fled down the street, stopping for nothing, paying no attention to directions, running madly on and on, with the blind terror tagging at her heels. And ever beating through her mind were the stern words of Carlos Menendez: *"If you make a mistake, if you are caught, I must warn you that you cannot expect any help from us. We cannot stand behind you."*

When she could run no longer because of the pain in her side and her bursting lungs, she dropped into the shelter of another doorway. Noticing dully that the door was partly open she looked inside. Far off in the distance — a distance that seemed many miles — she could see candles burning at an altar. A church! Here she would be safe. Pushing the door open she stumbled down the aisle, clutching the seats for support, genuflecting not for obeisance but because her legs were so tired she could hardly stand. Finally she sank to her knees on the cool floor, buried her face in her arms and gave way to long, wretched sobs.

As the sobs subsided she heard a woman's voice from out of the darkness. "What's the matter, honey? Somebody steal your clothes?"

Sharon looked up, straining to puncture the

darkness. Gradually, from the surrounding gloom and into the light of the flickering candles a figure in pink calico emerged. Sharon regarded the woman quizzically. "I thought I was alone," she said, sitting up. The tension in her breast was eased by the sobbing.

This stranger was about her own height and surely not much older. Her dress was elaborate with ruffles and ribbon, and the hat she wore was a large floppy affair with feathers curled over its crown. About her neck was a feather boa, and over her arm a large hand-bag of patent leather. She smelt of cheap, strong toilet water. Her face and frowsy blonde hair looked washed out in the wan candlelight. But Sharon attached no significance to the girl's features and dress. She accepted her simply as a woman and instinctively as a friend.

"M'gawd, honey," the woman said, sitting on the kneeling-rail beside her. "I thought the cops were after you the way you came racing down the street. I was standing outside and I thought if the cops were coming I'd better duck in here and, gawd, honey, you did too. Are you sure they ain't after you?"

"No, there aren't any cops. Just soldiers."

"Oh, them's the ones that tore the clothes off you. I know how they are. Just because a girl's in business, honey, they think she's open twenty-four hours a day. They just ain't got no consideration at all hardly for a working girl. That's what I say."

"In business?" Sharon asked.

"Say, you ain't new to the streets are you, honey? Don't you know the one-two-three?"

"How do you mean?" Sharon thought of waltzing.

"I mean you ain't in your regular territory now, are you? I know how you feel. I ain't in my own district either."

"I've had an awful scare and a terrible shock to-night and I'm afraid I don't quite understand just what you're talking about," Sharon explained.

The stranger in pink calico gripped her shoulders hard and pulled her up into the candlelight to look at her face closely. "M'gawd!" she declared. "If you ain't a gringo like meself! And I thought you was one of these native 'toots. You ain't been in trade long, have you, honey? Well, it don't matter much I always say. You'll soon be sorry you've been in it this long."

Sharon, dazed by all that had happened and distracted by the pain that persisted in her side, was about to ask the woman point blank what she was talking about when the meaning of the fancy wardrobe dawned suddenly upon her. "You — you're a bad woman, aren't you? I mean —"

"Well, some says yes and some says no," the stranger replied, laughing easily. "It all depends on how you look at it — say! you don't mean to tell me you ain't?"

"I certainly am not," Sharon replied.

"Then what are you doing in the streets this time of night, missy? And, m'gawd, in your bloomers too."

Sharon looked down at herself and burst into tears again.

"There, there," the woman comforted, "don't take on so, honey. Pearl's going to help you. Pearl can always think of something to do." Taking Sharon into her arms, she pressed her head against her ample bosom and let her cry it all out. As the tears abated she told Pearl her story. Pearl listened to it all, was quiet a moment, and then said, "You can come home with me, honey. It ain't much of a palace but it's clean and it's big enough for two. You can hide out there till it's safe to come out again. I ain't gonna let it be said that I didn't help out a fellow American when I got the distress signal. Come along, honey. We'll go home and rustle up some chow."

"Did you say your name was Pearl?" Sharon asked, wiping the last tears from her face with the hem of her camisole.

"That's right, honey. Pearl Davis from Elkhardt, Indiana."

"Mine's Sharon Douglass. I'm from Cardenas, Texas."

"That's great, honey. Pearl's my regular name, but most of the boys around Havana call me 'the madonna'. I guess it's the maternal instinct in me. Great kidders, the boys. Well, come along, honey. Let's skidoo, now."

—

After two weeks in the refuge of Pearl's rooms, Sharon's first agony of apprehension wore off, and she determined to get out to see what she could learn about Uncle Clay and the Floyds. They would be as anxious about her as she was about them. All she had to wear was a cheap native dress that Pearl had dug up for her. The Madonna, being so generous of bosom and so broad in the beam, hadn't a dress in her wardrobe that Sharon could wear.

Pearl was asleep when Sharon decided to venture out, and Sharon waited for her to wake up so that she could explain and say good-bye.

"Don't be silly," Pearl cautioned and rolled out of bed to strip off her ruffled nightgown and get into her business clothes. "They'd spot you in a minute — even with those clothes on. Here, tie my corset strings."

"But I've got to find out about my Uncle Clay and the folks." Sharon tugged and tightened the strings and tied them neatly, tucking the knot in so that it wouldn't make a lump through the snug dress Pearl was going to wear. "I can't stand it any longer."

"Then let me go. I'll bring back information or die trying. Where do your Uncle and these people live?" Pearl wriggled into her princess slip, the only petticoat she wore. Sharon scribbled down the address and helped her into the dress. "I'll be back this afternoon and I ought to have some information, or I don't know me own abilities. Just trust me, honey." She began to apply her vermilion lip rouge.

Sharon put a gentle hand on her arm. "You don't need so much in the day-time, do you?"

"Maybe not, honey. I forgot I was just going on a social call."

From a hamper of soiled clothes beside the dresser she jerked a knitted undershirt and modified the contrast of red and white. She was as lavish as ever with the toilet water, but Sharon let that go unmentioned. Stepping out of its aura she said, "And could you — would it be asking too much for you to go to El Americano? I'd like to know about Mr Edgecomb. I'd appreciate —"

"Sure thing, honey. Anything you want. We're both Americans, ain't we? Just leave it to Pearl when it comes to handling the menfolks."

Pearl left Sharon smiling at that remark about the menfolks. It brought back what Pearl had said a few days before: "I can see where you weren't meant for trade, ever, honey. But I don't mind for meself. The business is all right excepting when the boys get rough. Then I slap 'em on the hinder and tell 'em not to be so playful. I make 'em behave. It's all in a day's work, I say."

And Pearl was good-natured. She talked with Sharon by the hour about a mythical dream prince. She had him down pat in her mind and was almost convinced that he actually existed. When she met him she would be instantly transformed and he'd take her to Indiana and they'd live in a cottage and she would belong to the Ladies' Sewing Society and he would be a director of the bank and their children would grow up to be the most respectable ladies and gentlemen in the whole state of Indiana. She even had Sharon convinced.

She was a good listener too. Her willing ears were always ready for tales of life on a Texas ranch, of episodes on a steamboat, of an adventure in Key West, of a long, lanky farmer boy and his timid love-making, of a girl getting a job singing when she couldn't sing worth a nickel. Sharon wondered now as she waited — and she smiled again — at what Aunt Phoebe would say about her living with a "woman of the streets". It was distasteful at first accepting food and shelter paid for with the money Pearl earned by night, but Pearl was the soul of hospitality; and there was no choice. To walk out even now would mean just about the same as standing up before a firing squad.

While waiting for Pearl she paced the floor until she was worn out. Then she tried reading. Pearl subscribed to the Elkhardt paper, and Sharon picked up a late copy and found an item that caught her eye.

U.S. CONSUL-GENERAL AT HAVANA BEGS PROTECTION SHIP

It has been disclosed by Consul-General Fitzhugh Lee of the United states of America in Cuba that the street skirmishes among the Cubans and Spaniards are growing worse daily and are threatening American property to such an extent that aid has at last become imperative.

Lee, a nephew of Robert E. Lee, as an army officer, led a confederate cavalry troop in the battle of Shenandoah. He also served against the Comanche Indians in Texas. His demands as conveyed to the secretary of the Navy the Secretary of State, and the President by round robin official communication have become insistent. It is necessary for the protection of American interests, claims Consul-General Lee, that a battleship be commissioned to stand guard in Havana harbour.

To-day Congress appointed a special committee to consider Lee's request and word is expected from them by the latter part of the week.

Sharon tossed the paper aside. Debating the issue — appointing committees — as you do for a Sunday-school picnic. Word expected by the latter part of the week. In the meantime her uncle and his friends could lose their property and businesses which had taken them years to build up. Why didn't those stupid politicians back home do something? Why —

She sprang up from her chair at the sound of Pearl's key in the lock. Opening the door, she asked tensely, "What's the news?"

Pearl dropped her hand-bag on a chair and tossed her hat on the bed. "M'gawd, it's hot, Sharon. Let's have some tea. It'll cool us off."

"What did you find out, Pearl? Hurry, tell me!"

Pearl put the tea kettle on the oil stove and reached for a match. "Maybe if you have some tea in your tummy it'll give you more strength."

"Strength? Strength for what? Bad news? What is it, Pearl?" She clutched Pearl's shoulders, her knuckles showing white. Pearl laid the match aside.

"Take it easy, honey. It's about your Uncle Clay."

"What happened to him?"

"He's passed on to his reward, honey. There wasn't anybody at that address you gave me, but the lady next door told me. The soldiers shot your uncle that night you had to leave. He was dead when Mrs Floyd came home."

Sharon sat down again, her heart numb with despair. After a century-long moment she whispered, "What about the others? Mr Floyd and Libby?"

"The girl's dead too, kiddo. It was awful, the lady said. They raped her. Can you imagine?"

The horror did not penetrate Sharon's mind at first. "And Mr Floyd?" she repeated dully.

"The lady says his mind went cuckoo on him. He's been mumbling to himself ever since it happened. Gee, ain't it awful, honey. I feel terrible sorry for you. Mrs Floyd sold everything as quick as she could and took her husband to England. They just left a couple of days ago. And the lady says they gave your uncle a real nice funeral and his wife and a boy was up from Santiago. The boy was inquirin' all over town for you, she says."

"That was Jason," Sharon said, stupefied.

Pearl sat down on the edge of the chair and put her arm about Sharon's shoulders. With a violent shudder, Sharon released the floodgate of her overflowing emotions.

"Aw, come on, honey. Don't take it so hard. Things'll work out all right. Don't take it so hard. Gosh, I have to go to work pretty soon and I can't leave you like this."

"I'll be all right in a minute," Sharon assured her, straightening up and wiping her eyes. "There aren't many tears left, I guess. But I just happened to think about Libby. Pearl, you never saw a homelier girl, but that night she was sewing on her wedding veil her eyes were so shiny that she looked almost beautiful. And to think — !"

"Sure. Those Spic soldiers stop at nothin'." Pearl patted her shoulder and took up the tea-making where she had left off.

"What about Edgecomb? Did you get —"

"Oh sure! I forgot to tell you about him. Sure, I went there and I asked him for a job — singing. You should've seen the look he gave me — he said he never wanted to see or hear another singer." Then she imitated Edgecomb's precise, womanish speech, " 'The last singer I had left me flat with the whole Spanish army on her heels.' Honest, kiddo, I thought I'd die. I almost laughed right in his face."

Sharon laughed too, then gripped Pearl's arm. "You didn't tell him anything about me, did you?"

"What do you think I am? I went out to get information, not to hand it out. I should say I didn't tell him anything about you. I wouldn't have told him anything if he'd offered me his whole shebang."

"Good for you. A friend of mine said he wouldn't trust Edgecomb across the room. Not that he's dishonest, but he might not be smart. And even if he could help me, how could I get to him? I know I was a fool to think of going out. How do I know Mares isn't still on the look-out for me?"

"That's why I say you can stay here just as long as these Spics keep kicking up a fuss. You know you're welcome, don't you, honey?"

"Yes, and you don't know how much I appreciate it, but I can't let you support me altogether. I've got to do something to help. I'll write to Jason. Maybe —" She paused dubiously.

"Maybe what, honey?" Pearl relaxed on the bed.

"Oh, I was going to say maybe he could help, but he'd be only too willing and then I'd feel that I had to marry him. I tell you what. I'll go out with you to-night and you can show me the one-two-three." Sharon poured the tea. "I'll wear my native —"

Pearl jerked to her feet and pulled Sharon around facing her. "No you don't kiddo. You'll do nothing of the sort. Little Pearl will bring the bacon home that way. A sweet kid like you thinking of a thing like that! Why, it ain't even decent, I say. Over my dead body you'll go out to-night."

Sharon smiled her gratitude.

"Aw, gee, honey," Pearl went on, "don't say things like that any more. Somebody around here's got to be a lady."

Pearl brought home a gramophone and cylinders that next week. "Here, honey, this'll help cheer you up while you're cooped up here."

"That's sweet of you, Pearl."

"I thought you'd like it. And if there's anything else you want, just holler."

"If you think of it sometime I'd like some stationery. I hate to ask you for anything, but —"

"Aw, forget it, honey. I'm doing all right. Maybe things'll clear up and you can go out pretty soon."

"Yes, this can't last for ever."

But it lasted for five desolate months. Day after day the routine was the same — Sharon slept while Pearl was out on her beat, and in the daytime cooked American meals that were a delight to Pearl; she sent to the *Ladies' Home Journal* for patterns and made a dress for each of them; she did all the washing and ironing and what little housework the two rooms required.

Writing long letters to Jason helped shorten the hours, and the letters she received from him were gratifying. Even Aunt Phoebe wrote a note now and then. According to Sharon's instructions each letter from Santiago began "Dear Pearl" and was addressed to Pearl Davis. She treasured Jason's letters. Over and over again he avowed his love and begged her to let him come to Havana for her, begged her to marry him.

He was again carrying the burden of the expenses, but it was not a heavy one, for they were living in a modest little cottage close by the Calvary Methodist Church and Aunt Phoebe, having been prevailed upon by the handful of faithful members, had conquered her grief and was now its pastor. Later came word that Promised Land was sold — at a great loss, of course, but there was the satisfaction of cheating the Spanish Government out of their coveted chance to pounce upon it. With the money Aunt Phoebe bought the little cottage they were living in and took a great interest in gardening.

Sharon kept in contact with the world through the newspapers Pearl brought home. Sometimes Pearl teased her when she asked for papers from New York and Boston and Chicago and read them avidly, but Sharon convinced her that they were living in a great period of history and that they should be thrilled by it.

The United States was beginning to show

more concern about the bloodshed between Spaniards and Cubans. Clara Barton brought forth her Red Cross again to do what work she could for the relief of human suffering. Sharon read this news with eager enthusiasm. Clara Barton was a great woman. Having organized the Red Cross in America to serve in the Civil War she was now active again, getting supplies to the soldiers and seeing that nurses were stationed where most needed, acting as a nurse herself when the occasion arose. Sharon supposed that she was the most efficient woman alive with her Missing Soldiers Bureau, her cool head, and her ability to command men as well as women. She was headed now for Key West on the *City of Texas*, with helpers and supplies. One reporter wrote that she looked like a little old lady on a holiday excursion as she waved good-bye from the rail of the boat, clad in her customary black silk and poke bonnet. Yet one had the feeling that she was itching to get into white linen. She was ready for any contingency that might arise. Yellow fever? There was the Florida epidemic of 1887, a victorious chapter in her book of experience. Flood? Johnstown in 1889 had known her as the angel of mercy. Famine? The people of Russia had been talking about her since 1891. Bloodshed? Ask her about the 1896 massacre in Armenia.

Pearl caught some of Sharon's enthusiasm and began reading the papers herself. While Sharon devoured everything, including the advertisements for patent medicines and kitchen cabinets, she concentrated on the latest styles — the large flounces on the dresses, the piping in contrasting colours, the full skirts and open-necked blouses; the new hats, leghorns and pictures, with satin ribbons and clusters of flowers and grapes. There was colour in everything, even men's shirts — purple, maize, mauve, magenta and sky blue.

And everywhere in the United States, Sharon noticed, a building boom was reported. Almost overnight great new houses were erected — shingle and brick and clapboard. Mahogany furniture was going out and golden oak was coming in. Plush was still good. Portieres were fringed and tasselled. Pillows were embroidered with flags and anchors. There were bay windows for huge rubber plants and ferns in wooden containers or flamboyant jardinieres. Paintings of ancestors stood on easels. Pianos, walls and mantelshelves were crowded with photographs of friends and relatives. If you had a telephone you were somebody.

Maude Adams was captivating the theatrical world in *The Little Minister*. DeWolf Hopper was packing them in with "Casey at the Bat". People said, "Have you read *Quo Vadis*?" Soldiers marched to "El Capitan". Sousa had his own band. Someone wrote a song that raised the rafters from one end of the country to the other — "There'll be a Hot Time in the Old Town To-night".

It was an era of high living — good whisky, fine food, fat cigars. If you liked politics there was always someone to take you on for a heated debate — scandals in the capital — our foreign policy — the rush to the Klondike. The World's Fair of '93 was still being talked about.

One night in '98, at the end of January, Pearl came home early. She burst into the room with surprise and excitement animating her face and tumbling her words pell-mell. "Guess what, honey. It's happened, and it's about time, I say."

"What on earth?" Sharon asked laughing.

"It ain't on earth, it's in the harbour. Can't you guess?"

"An American battleship?"

"Yes! Everybody's talking about it. The *Maine.*"

"Oh, grand! When did it come?"

"It passed by Morro Castle this morning and it's anchored next to the *Alfonso XII.* Gee, honey! You know what it means don't you? With sailors in town will I clean up! There's nothing like a nice clean sailor boy for a good time, I always say." Then as a shadow clouded Sharon's features. "Aw, gee, honey, I didn't mean it that way. Honest to gawd, I clean forgot about your sailor boy friend."

"That's all right, Pearl. He doesn't mean anything to me any more. But do you know what I'm going to do? I'm going out to-night."

"Do you think it's safe, honey?"

"Oh, fiddlesticks. I can't think of that with an

American battleship in port. I've got to see it. Just think! It'll have the good old Stars and Stripes flying on it. Besides, I don't think the Spaniards will be after me to-night. Five months ought to be long enough for a person to be forgotten. I've got to go out and celebrate, or I'll bust!"

"I know how you feel, kiddo. And I don't blame you a bit. Wear your Cuban dress and that big hat that goes with it. I guess it's worth the chance all right. I won't mind seein' those old Stars and Stripes meself."

Sharon walked the streets of Havana for the first time in months, confident and unafraid. Nearing the harbour she quickened her pace, not from fear — surely no one would recognize her — but because it was so good to breathe the ocean again. Even the signs of death on the houses could not depress her.

When she came to the harbour she stood transfixed by the trim, stern outlines of the *Maine* silhouetted against the fiery sunset. And the flag! She wanted to salute. As she stood there watching it wave in the breeze, there drifted across the smooth water the notes of a bugle playing "Retreat" and the flag began its evening descent. She scarcely breathed.

After that she simply walked along the pier revelling in her freedom, not caring about time or direction, scarcely even noticing that darkness was settling about her. From the wharf-front shacks came shrill laughter, soft guitar music, and the shouts of children. "I'd better be turning towards home," she finally reminded herself. "This is no place to be out alone at night."

Her thoughts were corroborated by the approach of a column of Spanish soldiers, and she decided to quit the pier immediately, before anyone recognized her. Being very careful not to appear in haste, she walked quietly away. A few squares farther on a foursome of sailors overtook her.

"Here's a Cuban wench," one called to the others. "She might be open for business." He stopped and grabbed her by the shoulder. "How about you and I getting together, señorita?"

"Aw, come on," one of the three urged, "I'll take you to a place where we'll know what we're getting."

That voice! Sharon's heart stopped beating for a moment. She snatched off her straw hat and stepped up to the speaker. There was just enough light to reveal his unruly brown hair.

"Well, I'm damned!" he said. "You fellows go ahead. I've got some tall talking to do." He grasped Sharon's arm and escorted her brusquely away from his astonished companions.

"Please let me go," she said. "You're hurting my arm." She tried to pull herself away from him and to make her voice sound cold and indifferent.

"Wait, Sharon, please! I've got to talk to you."

"Are you sure you haven't made a mistake?"

"No, Sharon, please. Don't you remember me?"

"Yes, but I'm surprised that you remember me."

"But, Sharon, how could I help it?"

There was an earnestness in his voice that robbed her of the determination to remain aloof.

"Well, Eric, it's been a long time hasn't it?"

4

The Spark

At the side of the quay there was a small hut of rough boards that had once been used as a fish market but was now deserted. Eric sat down on the threshold and drew Sharon down beside him. They were not likely to be bothered here. She looked at him steadily in the light of the rising moon, and after a long minute repeated, "It's been a long time, Eric."

He took his pipe from the breast pocket of his middy and slowly filled it with tobacco that had a sweetish smell. He puffed a moment thoughtfully, his brow knitted, his hand on hers. "Nearly four years, Sharon."

"Or is it four centuries? I thought you'd forgotten me long ago," she said coldly, withdrawing her hand from his.

"Why?" he smiled at her quizzically. "You've been in my thoughts every day and night of those four years — or centuries. Yes, centuries is more like it. No matter what I did to forget you'd keep bobbing up again. Hell, Sharon, if you knew how goddamn hard I tried. The guy that said drinking helps you forget was a big liar. I saw your face in every beer glass and whisky bottle I tipped between here and Brooklyn."

"I like the way you showed how very much you thought of me." The irony of her words and the resentment in her voice struck across Eric's consciousness like a whip.

His own voice hardened with impatience. "Why didn't you answer my letter?"

"What letter?"

"I wrote you shortly after you left. It was a long letter, too. I mailed it to the address you gave me. It was never returned, so you must have received it. You couldn't have cared so very much."

She sought the depths of his eyes in the moonlight. Lips may lie but eyes do not, she told herself. Eric's eyes looked back at her, calm and level and honest. "I never received a letter from you, Eric. I watched the mails every day. I kept telling myself that the letter was just delayed or maybe you were sick. I cried when I finally came to believe you would never write. I thought you didn't care. Uncle Clay went for mail every day and —" She halted her speech and gripped Eric's hand. "Uncle Clay! He was the only one who ever got the mail! I wonder —"

"I don't know what you're driving at," Eric said. "All I know is I wrote and received no answer. I tried to tell myself there was some mistake but after a few weeks of saying that over and over I decided you didn't care."

"Didn't care! Oh, Eric, I did — I did! When I couldn't stand it any longer I wrote to you."

"I never received yours."

"That's very strange. Or is it? I gave it to Uncle Clay to mail. Do you suppose — he was so strict, Eric, you can't imagine. I just wonder."

"Let's not worry about it now, Sharon." Eric slipped his arm about her waist. "I've found you again and that's all that matters. I swear to God I've never forgotten. You must believe that. I loved you back there in Key West that night. I love you now. This time we must never part." His arm tightened about her. "We must forget about the centuries, my darling, the time in between, and start all over again from the moment we kissed good-bye on the beach at dawn."

"Yes," she whispered. She burrowed her head in his shoulder but he drew her chin up and found her lips. The four years dropped away and they were alone again before his cabaña. They had no desire to return to the present.

With the first fervour of their reunion expressed they went over the events of the period of separation. Sharon told Eric of her arrival at Havana, meeting Uncle Clay, the street skirmish, the trip to Santiago. She told him of Jason and Libby and of Promised Land. She told him of the sugarcane depression and the burning of the stables and the disappearance of Conchita. She spared him no details of the heartlessness of the Spaniards. She related to him the story of her flight to Havana on horseback, the struggle of Uncle Clay and Aunt Phoebe and Jason, which resulted in her getting a job singing, and how that led to becoming a spy. She told him of the double tragedy on the night she was caught and of how she met Pearl. Yes, and even of her five months in Pearl's rooms. When she had finished he sat staring at her incredulous.

Then his thoughts found three words. "You poor kid," he whispered over and over again. "You poor kid." It was his way of expressing the welling of tenderness that flooded him.

Sharon then drew from him the story of how he had been stationed at Key West for another year before being shipped to Brooklyn. She learned that he was now stationed on the *Maine*, a lieutenant, junior grade. His hurt at not hearing from her had progressed through anxiety and resentment to disillusionment. More than once he had drunk himself into unconsciousness trying to obliterate her image from the bottom of the glass. There was a girl too, he hinted bitterly, but Sharon placed her fingers on his lips and would not listen.

Now that they had explained away the years it seemed that there had been no separation at all. But Sharon clung to Eric as though she feared some force might tear them apart again. She felt the hardness of his body through the heavy middy. She stroked back his hair and the very texture of it was dear to her remembering fingers. Time was not. She was back in Eric's cabaña, and he was reading her body with the exploring fingers of a blind man. Their lips fused; their bodies were warm together; their senses whirled in the vortex of consummation, all reality dimmed by the miracle of finding each other again.

As they emerged from the hut Sharon walked in step with Eric, their hips touching, his arm firm about her waist. On the Havana streets reality and a sense of the present returned to them. They tried to make plans and be sensible. Sharon remembered that she was in danger with every step she took.

"What shall I do?" she said cautiously, "I can't go back to Pearl's house. I simply can't."

"I should think not," he answered hotly. "Living with a whore! You bet that's got to stop."

"No, I don't mean for that reason, Eric," she insisted. "Pearl has been wonderful. You really don't know. It's just that I can't stand the inactivity any longer — when there's so much going on. I want to be doing something."

"We've got to figure this thing out before morning." Eric pondered for a long moment, made a decisive gesture with his pipe, and said, "By damn! I've got it! The very thing!"

"What, Eric? What?"

"The Red Cross! I know they're organizing here because our commander told us about it. They're in an old convent just off the harbour. They're getting things ready for Clara Barton so if hell breaks loose they'll be prepared."

"But how could I —"

"They'll need nurses, don't you see. They'll teach you. I know they'll be willing to take you on. And you'll be safe there. No one'll think of looking for you in a convent. You'll be safe as hell. And — you'll be close to me. I can see you nearly every evening."

"Oh, Eric! You must have been inspired when you thought of that. Which way is it?"

But he was already turning her around and guiding her towards the harbour.

In the United States the presses were busy working the people to a fever heat over the situation.

Theodore Roosevelt, Assistant Secretary of the Navy, urged everyone to be prepared — much to the official embarrassment of Secretary Long. Roosevelt stormed in his office, pacing back and forth like a caged animal, just waiting for President McKinley to signal Congress to set off the fireworks. Just one spark was needed, that was all. Just one spark to set off the powder.

"That — that creature, McKinley — even if he is my president — has no more backbone than a damned chocolate éclair!"

Energetically he laboured to place the United States on a fighting basis. And with his jingoism he easily convinced the people that he was right. His odd appearance, his colourful speech, his abounding enthusiasm, his vitality, and his love of battle helped him win a following that was numberless. His unyielding championship of the little man's rights caught and held the imagination of the citizens — and he who could hold their imagination could be their leader.

Men spoke of him as a "hell of a fellow", but in their eyes was the light of admiration and their voices carried the tone of respect. Those few who claimed he was all talk and bluster were reminded by "Teddy's" loyal disciples that it took more than talk and bluster to step in and clean up the New York Police Force. A business man, a student, a cowboy — who had ever heard of such a man? He was afraid of nothing and no one — least of all Secretary Long.

In his own castle in N Street he indulged in his flair for conversation, put long hours in at his desk, read volume after volume from his library, corresponded with ranch-hands, district attorneys, and congressmen, all in the course of carrying on his shoulders the burden of a gigantic governmental department. He attended dinner parties and related uncalled for and unfunny jokes. At the drop of a hat he would talk about anything or anybody. He met and talked with all manner of people and recited verses for his children and their playmates. He trotted on horseback and took long hikes along the Potomac. He sparred, wrestled, played basket-ball, and did his daily dozen. Cartoonists poked fun at him; he was a household word.

But Secretary Long kept Teddy in his place

until it happened that he was forced to leave his office for a time. He left it, as was the accepted procedure, in charge of his assistant. And that was his mistake. The assistant followed no accepted procedure. With characteristic enthusiasm, Roosevelt set the office humming.

With a stroke of his pen he sent tons of coal to Key West, the Dry Tortugas, Charleston, Savannah.

Another stroke of his pen and the two cruisers, *Columbia* and *Minneapolis*, were placed in commission along with the *Monitor*, *Miantonomo* and the ram *Katahdin*.

A shipment of five-inch rapid-fire guns left the navy yard at Washington for the *Chicago*.

Case after case of projectiles was sent to New York from Monroe. Ordnance was shipped in carloads from the Watertown arsenal to New York; twelve-inch projectiles from the Albany arsenal to New York; completed guns sent to Sandy Hook for testing.

Still another stroke of the pen — a bill drafted by himself — and it was made possible for over a thousand more men to enlist in the Navy.

And when Long came back there was hell to pay. Under secretaries scurried about the capitol cringing from his wrath. Teddy showed the grin that the cartoonists loved.

"That — that imbecile!" Long croaked. "That egotistic son of a — pardon me, gentlemen, but that firebrand — that militarist! He'll be the ruin of this department!"

Roosevelt discreetly stayed home that day and wrote a letter to a cowpuncher, a former comrade.

A surly aide said to Secretary Long, "He talks too much. Somebody ought to take the wind out of his sails."

"Somebody will some day," Long prophesied with satisfaction.

Roosevelt chafed with impatience for somebody to just try to take the wind out of his sails. If his office would only let him present Cuba's dilemma straight to the people. He cursed the red tape that bound his hands. Full of passionate sincerity and addressing no one in particular he gave vent to his opinions in his home one February morning. Head thrust forward, eyes flashing, teeth clicking, voice slipping into a familiar falsetto, words breaking into choppy syllables, he smacked his fist into his palm. Even the walls trembled.

"Why isn't that creature, McKinley, doing something?" he demanded. "No more backbone to him than an oyster. Well, if he won't do anything, I will!"

The Convent of Our Lady of Sorrows stood on a small hill overlooking Havana harbour.

It was a long, low structure, rambling across the crest of the hill and painted gleaming white. For two hundred years it had nestled in its grove of tamaracks. The grounds, gently sloping, were well kept by the old gardener, Pietro. Quaint wood carvings of the Virgin adorned the portico, and the lawn was dotted with marble fawns, caught in frozen capers and looking coldly docile.

The nuns were cloistered in the left wing, while the right wing served as a hospital. It had once been a school for girls, but this had been discontinued as the timbers rotted away, and with them the prestige of the school had disintegrated. It was much more fashionable now to send one's daughters directly to Valencia or Madrid.

The good sisters who had administered to the needs of wounded Spaniards and Cubans alike were now making way for the Red Cross vanguard sent to Cuba by Clara Barton, and working beside the Americans in the common cause of alleviating pain.

Madre Isabela, the Mother Superior, was very kind to Sharon when Eric brought her to the convent. She was only too glad to welcome a strong, willing young woman, despite inexperience. And so Eric left Sharon there in her new world of antiseptics and bandages and human suffering.

Madre Isabela herself conducted her about the grounds and outlined her duties. "We rise at six every morning, my child, and Padre Cristobel says the Mass. During your first few days here I will see that one of the sisters instructs you in the tying of bandages and cauterizing wounds. We haven't many doctors and as a nurse you will therefore have to perform many exacting duties."

"I learn very fast," Sharon said. They passed through the peaceful grounds where only the nuns, sweeping across the grass, their habits billowing in the breeze, supplied movement. It was truly a sanctuary. Madre Isabela led the way back into the main corridor and indicating a door said, "This will be your room, my child."

"I'm sure I shall like it, madre." Sharon took in the spare furnishings of the cubicle at a glance. A small cot and bureau, a chair and clothes-hamper and a picture of Jesus on the wall were all the furnishings the cell-like room contained. There was one very small window and it was near the ceiling. On the bureau was a new candle.

"This was Sister Teresa Luisa's room. She went to her Christ last week." The madre's voice was reverent.

"Oh, I am so sorry." Sharon thought she was saying the right thing.

"We are not. She is blessed."

"I'm sure of it."

The madre's voice took on its business-like tone. "You must never come into your room at night without a lighted candle." She shut the door and they moved on.

"I shall remember that, Madre Isabella, but may I ask why?"

"Because of the scorpions. They are very

deadly. Your candlelight will make them scurry away."

"Thank you." Sharon was humble and sincere.

The madre was a dumpy little woman with small gimlet eyes set in a chubby face. Her cap cut into her jowls so that her cheeks puffed out like yellow apples. She invited Sharon into her own tiny room for a talk. Her eyes were kindly and serene as she looked into the eyes of her new student nurse.

"It is not an easy life you have chosen," she said. "Even in peaceful times a nurse must be able to stand on her feet hour after hour, and be as alert the last hour as the first. In war she must not even think of being tired. And you will be exposed more abruptly than the peacetime student nurse to sights and sounds and smells that will test the very last atom of your fortitude. You will learn to take a deep breath and hold it while you conquer yourself. You will go on and do as you are told, as if nothing had happened. I will say a prayer for you daily, my child. Be strong and be faithful. I know you will be good."

"Thank you, Madre Isabela. I will try."

And so Sharon entered her new life.

Her five months' rest enabled her to be stronger than she could have anticipated. She learned to hold her breath and go on and on though she must listen to the grating of a saw on the femur of a leg smelling to high heaven with gangrene. She learned to shut out the sound of moaning, sobbing, screaming, raving men and boys. She learned to ignore the stench while cauterizing a wound. She learned to stand on her feet from seven in the morning until six in the evening with only a few minutes off now and then.

At first they only let her clean up after the other nurses and she had all she could do then to control her stomach and prevent an upheaval as she carried trays of bloody bandages, clotted with bits of rotting flesh, to the ovens to be burned. In her dreams she saw miles of red bandages and white; she became tangled in them and they choked her. Then she would wake and find herself twisted amongst the sheets and fairly smothering in the small, close room.

As she showed her willingness to spend herself without stint they let her help with the cases. She learned to apply and adjust a bandage on any part of a man's body, quickly and neatly, and to change a dressing that was stuck to a raw, gaping wound without causing the soldier too much pain. She lived intimately with stark, raw life and intimately with horrible, pain-racked death.

But Eric came for her every night he could get shore leave and took her away to a secret retreat and held her in his arms and comforted her until she forgot the stench of putrefying blood and the sight of dying men. Time after time their intimacy carried them both far away from this tortured land of bloodshed.

"My darling, my darling," he would whisper to her, "was ever a man so blessed!"

An hour or two was all they could allow themselves. Then she would have to tear herself from his arms and return to her cot to fall heavily asleep until six o'clock in the morning.

One of her new friends at the convent was Estrallita, a young Cuban novice who lived for the day when she was to take her vows. One afternoon they were working together changing the dressings on the shattered shoulder of a young Cuban.

As the native soldier winced, Estrallita placed her small brown palm on his forehead and stroked his brow with soft, sympathetic fingers. The knitted brow relaxed and a tired smile came over the patient's features.

"The señorita's touch is like the breath of angels." He sighed and lay quiet while Sharon carefully applied the new bandage around his biceps, over his wound, under his back and across his chest. Estrallita took the discarded dressings away. As Sharon turned to go, the soldier placed restraining fingers on her wrist.

"What is the señorita's name?" he asked, his eyes almost happy.

"My name is Sharon Douglass."

"No, no. The other señorita. The one with the cool hands."

"Estrallita is the other señorita's name."

"Estrallita," he murmured to himself, playing softly with the word on his lips. "Little Star."

"But she is going to be a nun," Sharon admonished gently.

The soldier's voice rose to fever pitch. "She cannot become a nun. She cannot! Tell her to come back to me."

Sharon patted his hand, and when he relaxed she said, "All right. I'll tell her."

Overtaking Estrallita in the hall-way she said, "Here, let me take these to the ovens. The soldier back there — the one with the bad shoulder — wants to see you. I think you'd better go to him."

The little smile that flitted across Estrallita's face vanished quickly and she said, "Do you think I should, señorita?" as if Sharon's yes or no could make it right or wrong.

"Of course I do, goose. Run along."

That night after Sharon had retired, a timid knock at her door aroused her. She rose drowsily and opened the door. Estrallita slipped into the room looking guilty and apprehensive. She had not undressed.

"Why, Estrallita, why aren't you in bed? What is it?"

"I had to talk to someone, señorita — someone whom I can call my friend. You are my friend, aren't you?"

"Of course. Sit down. Now tell me what it is."

"It's about the soldier."

"But there are so many soldiers, dear."

"I mean the one this afternoon. The one

who called me back."

"Oh, yes of course. I remember. What about him?"

"His name is Benito. He says he is in love with me."

"Yes?"

"But don't you see, señorita?" The distraught girl tried to convey the seriousness of the situation. She gripped Sharon's arm and her face was a mask of worry. "It cannot be! It cannot! I must not give my heart to any man. It belongs only to the Christ. Only He may have it."

"Do you like the soldier — this Benito?" Sharon asked.

"Oh, very much. Yes, I do like him. When he called me beside his bed this afternoon, he was so kind. He told me about his house at San Pablo and of his mother and young brother who is a *reconcentrado.* And he said that when the war is over he wants to take me home to his mother." Estrallita creased the folds in her robe with taut fingers.

"What did you tell him?"

"I told him he must have a fever to talk so. I told him that if Padre Cristobel knew that I listened to such talk he would be furious."

"But Padre Cristobel doesn't know," Sharon said mischievously.

Estrallita's worry became horror. "But, señorita! I must confess."

"Why?" Sharon's calm was not in the least disturbed.

"Because — because I must. I have offended the Saviour!"

"Have you? Is it so wrong for a woman to hear a man tell her he loves her?"

"What shall I do, señorita?"

"I know what I'd do. I'd listen to my heart and do what it told me."

"If I did that I would be going to the ward now to see if Benito is all right."

"Then what are you doing here? Go to him, goose!"

Estrallita looked dubious and smiled. "Perhaps it will be sinning to do so, but you don't make it sound sinful. I will go as a nurse to see if the patient is comfortable."

She slipped out the door as furtively as she had entered but there was a sparkle of adventure in her eyes which had not been there before.

Later that week Eric brought good news. Having called on Hilary Edgecomb and made discreet inquiries, he learned that Edgecomb considered Sharon dead and had passed that information on to Colonel Mares. Apparently the official board had accepted this information as fact for, Edgecomb reported, they had not bothered him since.

This meant that they could feel free to stroll along the Prado and even appear in public places. In a side-street they found a modest café where they might sup and talk in comparative privacy. "I took your message to Pearl, too,"

Eric told Sharon. "She was glad to hear from you, and hopes you can come to see her some time."

"Oh, good!" Sharon said. "I feel now that everything is straightening out beautifully. I'm dead tired, but I'm happy. Even that riddle about our letters is cleared up."

"Yes? Did you hear from your aunt?"

"Yes. And I almost feel sorry for her, she's so repentant for what Uncle Clay did. She said she stood right there and watched him burn your letter after he had read it, and that many a time she wanted to confess but was afraid of 'arousing his ire', as she put it."

They had a little laugh, and Eric ordered coffee.

"Do you know," Eric began philosophically, "we're like a married couple, aren't we?" There was a humorous twinkle in his eyes and the laugh lines wrinkled towards his temples.

"Are we?" Sharon parried.

"Well, we're enough in love, I guess, and we're happy together."

"Are you happy this way, Eric? I mean completely happy?"

He puffed his briar thoughtfully. "No," he said at length. He took her hand across the narrow table. "Damn it all, I want to be a husband and a father, Sharon."

"Oh, I'm glad you said that, Eric. I was beginning to wonder if you ever would. I'd be proud to be your wife."

"Will you marry me right away, Sharon?"

"Of course I will, darling."

They laughed self-consciously over their coffee. "I should like to be married by the padre at the convent, if you don't mind. I know neither of us is Catholic, but —" She studied his face.

"I had hoped for a navy wedding on shipboard," he said slowly, "but as you wish, my darling."

She smiled gratefully at him and he patted her hand.

The wedding date was set for the sixteenth of February and Sharon got a day's leave to shop. Her major purchase was ten yards of white nainsook for her wedding garments. There was little else to buy other than a pattern, thread, and buttons, for there was little money to spend. She still dared not apply for her money at the bank.

In the afternoon she called on Pearl. On her way there she thought of Aunt Phoebe. Better not tell her about the wedding until it was over. And she thought of Jason. Poor Jason, it would be a blow to him. And Lucky Fred Douglass. He would be glad she was doing what she wanted to do.

Pearl was still asleep when Sharon knocked. Her eyes were dull and she blinked as she opened the door.

"M'gawd! It's *you*, honey! Come on in here and let me look at you. You haven't changed much except you look kind of tired. Well, sit down. Whatcha got in the bundles? How've you been?"

"Oh, I'm fine, Pearl. How've you been?"

"Oh just so-so. Workin' pretty hard while the *Maine*'s in. Why haven't you been to see me sooner? I'd come around to see you but you know how it is. I don't suppose they'd let me come within a mile of the place. Let's see. What'd you buy?"

Sharon unwrapped the bundle. "For my wedding dress."

"Sharon! The sailor?"

They hugged each other and as they broke away Sharon brushed her eyes and giggled foolishly.

"Gee, I'm glad for you. He's a real nice fellow. I could tell that in just the few words he said to me. Gee, kiddo!"

"Will you help me cut it out?" Sharon unfolded the long pattern pieces and handed the smooth white material to Pearl.

"Sure, kiddo. Gee, this is new to me. Workin' on a wedding dress. Say, it took you an awful long time to get word to me. I nearly went loco that night when you didn't come back. I didn't sleep all day. And when your cute sailor boy friend did finally get here he didn't have much to say. I think he was embarrassed."

"That doesn't sound like Eric," Sharon remarked and smiled. "But there wasn't much to tell. I just walked right into the convent and they put me to work and I tried to learn as much as I could and now I'm a full-fledged nurse!"

"You don't mean it? Here now, this is all folded lengthwise. Let's see, we need some pins, don't we? I'll get the pin-cushion."

"Do you think I can get this done in two days?"

"Is it so soon?" They laid material and pattern on the floor.

"The sixteenth."

"Sure, we'll get it done. I'll help all I can before I have to leave." She handed Sharon the shears.

"Oh, Pearl! What would I ever do — what would I ever have done — where would I be — if it wasn't for you?"

"Aw, forget it, kiddo. We're both —"

"Pearl!" Sharon straightened up on her knees, shears in hand. "Pearl! I just thought of something. I want you to be my bridesmaid. I want you to and they'll have to let you. I've worked my head off there and it's going to be my wedding and I'm going to have some say about it. Will you, Pearl, will you?"

Pearl stood there with the pattern envelope in her hand. She looked at Sharon blankly. The envelope dropped from her fingers, she took a step towards the bed and, throwing herself on it, she sobbed uncontrollably. Sharon, when she recovered from her amazement, put both arms around her and tried to get her to explain.

"Don't you want to be my bridesmaid?" she asked, perplexed. "I know it isn't going to be a very big wedding. There probably won't be anybody there at all but Eric and a friend of his and you and me and the padre. But I don't mind not having a big wedding."

Pearl wiped her eyes on the corner of the bed sheet. "It isn't that, honey. It's just that — that — well, it's so damned sweet of you asking me to be your bridesmaid. I can hardly believe it. I never told you, but I was kicked out of a wedding once because — well, because of what I —"

"Oh fiddlesticks, Pearl! It doesn't matter about that. I've never had a better friend than you, and so why shouldn't you be my bridesmaid? That's the way I want it and that's the way —"

"You're sweet, Sharon. Most people have nothing but a kick or a dirty word for a whore."

"You're my friend," Sharon said stubbornly.

"All right, honey. If you can arrange it, I'll be there."

"And I'll be proud to have you." Sharon kissed Pearl and returned to her cutting. "I wouldn't have anyone else in the world."

She returned to the hospital very late that night and in the morning Madre Isabela gave her a reproving glance, but she did not care. Her wedding dress was nearly finished and tomorrow she would become the bride of Eric March. Lieutenant Eric March. And she would be Mrs Lieutenant Eric March! Mrs March! As she wrapped bandages and irrigated wounds with alcohol, her movements were mechanical.

Daily the wounded had streamed in. From the prairies and the mountains and the forests of Cuba, from wherever Spaniards fought Cubans. They came on litters and on horseback. Some came on mules draped across the animals' spines like sacks of meal. And as they were lifted off and placed on the crude stretchers they groaned or screamed or, worse, they simply stared in agony or bewilderment, their eyes numb with pain.

Sharon would sometimes press her fingers to her temples, close her eyes for a moment and wish she could shut out the picture of bleeding, torn bodies, but she would open her eyes and find them still there. She would find herself automatically ripping away a shredded tunic or a tattered loincloth and fighting back her nausea at the stench and the sight. If the wound was very bad she would call, "Surgeon! Surgeon!" and move wearily on to the next stretcher.

And the faces were always changing. Sometimes a soldier would die in the middle of the night, but by morning his bed was always occupied by a new one, with a new bewildered and pain-ridden face. But to-day Mrs Eric March-to-be saw them all as through a dense fog. Not one of them penetrated her consciousness.

She moved like an automaton that morning, except when she saw Padre Cristobal coming from the bedside of a dying soldier. She ran up to him in the hall-way.

"Padre Cristobal!"

"Yes, nurse."

"I am to be married to-morrow and I wish you to perform the service. Just a simple —"

But the padre was shaking his head. "I don't believe you are a Catholic. I cannot perform a service in the convent unless both you and the young man are of the faith. And, as you know, I am too much in demand here to go outside for the purpose. I am sorry."

"It is all right, Padre Cristobal. I am sorry too." She tried not to show her disappointment too keenly. She went on with her work and the disappointment faded away. Eric would think of something. Maybe they could have their navy wedding as he wanted it.

She met Estrallita on the way to the chapel. The novice carried an armful of wild-flowers. "Look," she said, her eyes beaming. "These are to decorate the altar for to-morrow."

"Thank you, Estrallita, but we won't need them. The padre will not marry us."

But Estrallita did not look the least bit disappointed. Something else was making her eyes sparkle. "Sharon, he — he kissed me to-day. I let him. I did it because my heart told me to. He loves me."

"Who?" Sharon asked vaguely.

"Why, Benito, of course. He has asked me to become his wife when he is well. And — and I told him I would. I told him I would leave the convent and go with him. My heart —"

"Forgive me, dear, for not paying attention," Sharon said. "I'm afraid my mind was far away."

"That is forgivable, since to-morrow is your wedding day. You must not pay attention to me."

"But I am happy for you," Sharon looked into the shining eyes and smiled. "I'm sure Benito is a fine man. Have you told Madre Isabela yet?"

"No, not yet." And Estrallita hurried on into the chapel with the wild-flowers, evidently forgetting that they would not be needed.

Some of the nuns baked a huge cake and when Eric called for Sharon that evening they teased him about it.

He only laughed when Sharon told him about Padre Cristobal. "That's fine," he said. "Now we can be married by Captain Sigsbee. That is, if you don't mind." He looked at her soberly.

"Mind? Oh my darling, how could I mind when I know how much it means to you. In fact, I think I prefer being married on the *Maine.* I think it will be something to tell our children about, and maybe our grandchildren."

"Darling!" He squeezed her hand so that it hurt. "All my shipmates will be on their toes to give us a real wedding. They were quite put out when I told them we were going to have it in the convent chapel. They said I was cheating them."

"I almost feel like running back and thanking Padre Cristobal for refusing me. I didn't realize it would make you so happy."

"Are you happy too, Sharon?"

He found his answer as she pressed her body to his and her arms stole about his shoulders.

—

At half past nine that evening Eric climbed aboard the *Maine*, his arms aching pleasantly with the memory of Sharon's presence. Tomorrow at this time they would be no longer just sweethearts. They would be husband and wife. His heart sang as he climbed over the rail and went forward.

"Who's there?" He was stopped by the forward watch.

"Lieutenant March coming aboard."

"Aye, aye, sir."

Eric knocked at Captain Sigsbee's door.

"Come in." The captain's voice was as firm as his features, but when talking of informal matters he had a kindliness that was almost paternal.

"I was wondering, sir," Eric stated flatly as he entered the cabin, "if you would perform my wedding ceremony to-morrow after all."

"Why, of course, lieutenant, I'll be glad to. What made you change your mind?"

"Oh, things just didn't work out as we planned, sir. Besides, I'd rather have it Navy through and through."

"I know how you feel, lieutenant. The Navy gets in your blood. Take the word of an old sea-dog."

"Thank you, sir."

"Not at all, lieutenant. We'll do the job to a T."

On deck, Eric stopped to look across the harbour and let his emotions come to rest in the stillness of the ship as it lay at anchor on the placid water. On shore, the lights of Havana shone like rhinestones twinkling on a dusky maiden's throat. Far to the left, the dim outlines of Morro Castle arose to meet the black sky like a silent, immobile sentinel — watching, waiting. Eric decided it would be good for his nerves to take a turn about the deck before hitting his bunk.

The small service craft had been hoisted on deck, nearly all the crew had retired, and the anchorage watch was scattered about. The sentry on the forward deck paced back and forth as Eric approached him, strolling easily along the gunwales.

"Is all well, Larkins?"

"Aye, aye, sir."

"You can spread the word about, Larkins, that my wedding will be held here on deck tomorrow."

"Aye, aye, sir. Allow me to congratulate you, lieutenant."

"Thank you, Lar—"

The word was wrenched from his teeth as throughout the *Maine* there flared a blinding flash of white, glaring light and as thunder follows lightning, there resounded a dull, rumbling roar. The timbers in the bottom of the ship groaned in agony.

"Good God Christ Almighty!" Eric yelled, jumping to the rail. "What's happened?"

"It must be the end of the world," the forward

watch shouted back and fell to his knees.

Great gusts of black smoke belched from the ship's belly and fragments of wood, bits of jagged steel, and chunks of cement rained down.

"Get up, Larkins," Eric commanded, "and get out of the way or this god-damned stuff'll land on your head."

But Larkins was deaf to the command. With hands clasped in supplication he chanted through clenched teeth, "Our Father which art in heaven —"

With a mad bellow the ship lurched and the funnels snapped from the forward cabin.

"Look out!" Eric screamed. "That son of a bitch is going to fall on you!" But his cry came too late. The huge funnel, rolling off the sloping roof of the forward cabin struck the kneeling Larkins square in the back. With his spine crushed and blood gushing from his mouth, he fell heavily forward and lay inert.

From the forecastle came the groans and cries of trapped men, hoarse strident shouts for help, screams of pain. While the ship trembled and lurched, Eric tugged at the door of the forecastle. But rigging that had toppled across the jamb when the ship listed was so wedged that he could not budge the door either in or out. His head reeled and pounded with concussion. The smoke choked him and now there were flames licking at the deck and rigging. From the other side of the forecastle door came the curses and the cries of the trapped men. Gasping for breath he tried the door again, hurling all his weight against it, but that only sent a paroxysm of pain through his lungs and he fell limp on the tangled rigging.

Captain Sigsbee appeared on deck, cool and collected, giving his curt orders to those sailors who were able to carry them out. Although trained to be fearless in battle, they were stunned by this catastrophe. There was no enemy to fight, yet death hurtled down upon them from all directions. There were only a few who had not lost their heads and escaped injury.

A young midshipman staggered past Eric, his trousers torn from his body and his entrails falling about his knees. Faintly he called, "Mother, mother, help me, please."

At Eric's feet an older seaman lay rapidly bleeding to death, both arms severed from his body. Through whitened lips he muttered over and over, "The bastards, the bastards, the bastards."

Eric struggled to his feet and, through the roar and hiss of steam he could not distinguish how much was real and how much of it was the ringing in his ears — he heard Captain Sigsbee's calm voice giving the order to abandon ship. Dimly his blurred consciousness grasped the meaning of the order. It meant every man to the life-boats. That was his job — to direct the lowering of the boats. He left the forecastle and the cries of the trapped men still rang in his ears.

Half running half crawling, stumbling over

those who lay dead or writhing in convulsive spasms of death, he made for the life-boats. His feet slid in the pools of blood. He fell and in getting up slipped back again into the gore. Cursing he rose doggedly and kept on until he reached a boat. Other staggering men were making for it. Men leaned maimed and helpless against the rail waiting for some level-headed sailor to give them a lift.

Eric got enough of the able-bodied ones together to help lower the boat, but they could hardly get it over the railing, the *Maine* was listing so. "We've — got — to do it!" He tried to wipe the sweat from his brow, but only smeared his eyes with blood. "Got to — get to — Sharon. Got to" Each word was a panted breath, each breath a stabbing hell.

They were about to get the boat over the side when the planking beneath Eric's feet buckled as a new explosion in the hold wrenched and strained at the ribs of the ship. His knees surrendered to the almighty god of the blast and he fell in obeisance. He tried to push back the floor which rose up to slap him in the face but his bloody hands only skidded across the splintered planking. He cursed the imaginary lash that was flogging him across the back.

Darkness closed about him and the outlines of the deck grew dim. He wondered if someone had turned off the gas-jets. A great, satisfying peace stole over his body. He could breathe again. Soft amorous arms — Sharon's arms, surely —

caressed him. His conscious world grew smaller and smaller until he was suspended in space and came at last to blessed rest.

5

"Remember the *Maine*!"

On the morning of 16 February 1898 the sun arose on a Havana shore lined with people — morbidly curious Cubans, frankly appalled Europeans, outraged Americans. There in the harbour was the twisted corpse of the once proud battleship, the *Maine*, a shambles of shapeless steel and shattered wreckage, a gutted hull. A pall of smoke hung over the scene like a veil of mourning.

Sharon stood on the hill-top beside the Convent of Our Lady of Sorrows and regarded the scene with sleepless eyes. Somewhere on that ship or somewhere in that shallow harbour grave must be the body of —

The last boat of survivors and dead had come ashore, a little huddle of sailors, some with gaping holes where there should have been arms, some with dried trickles of blood from their lips from haemorrhaged lungs due to concussion. She had looked at these men vacantly, knowing somehow that Eric would not be in this last load. What was the use of even hoping? Why hope for something that was beyond hope?

She knew that if her soul should be damned no hell could surpass the past eight hours. Standing in the doorway scrutinizing the grisly human wreckage on stretcher after stretcher, she had left her post only when she was sure no more sailors were to be brought in for some time. In these tense intervals she would help unload the stretchers that they might go out again and return with new cargo, cargo to be patched and sewn and cut until the wards ran red with blood and even the surgeons staggered out with horror in their eyes.

The sisters and nurses went about on feet that screamed for rest and with aprons and habits wet with dark stains that eventually dried to rust and stank. Sharon had resumed her vigil at the doorway whenever a new group of sailors was brought in, peering at each white face, agonized or still. If it was too bloody to be recognized she would wipe the brow or cheek with her damp apron and watch to see if the face that emerged would be Eric's. And if the entire figure was covered she would lift the corner of the sheet, dreading to see cold surly lips and bloodclotted brown hair. The thought of Eric dead had stabbed into her brain like the sharp, quick thrust of a dirk, and her mind had screamed in recoiling denial. He must not be dead! Yet to see him maimed like one of these — that would be worse. Before the night was over she was praying that she might find his face under a sheet.

It was Madre Isabela who had summoned her from the door after a dozen stretchers had come in bearing dead and horribly dying young Americans, none of them Eric — yet all of them Eric. She had stood there in a stupor, hearing nothing but that awful explosion as it had thrown her from her chair when she was sewing the last button on her wedding gown, until Madre Isabela's words took form: "My child, the doctors need your help."

"All right, madre." Her voice was empty with despair.

"You must not stand in the doorway and sicken yourself. It is not good to grieve against God's will."

"I know, Madre, but to-day we were to be married."

"But, my child, it would be much better were he with his Blessed Saviour, Christ Jesus."

Sharon had turned on her vehemently. "I don't want him with his Blessed Saviour. He's mine, not Christ's. He's mine, I tell you."

"Our dear Christ bore His cross with courage, my child. We must learn to bear ours the same."

"I'm sorry, madre. I didn't mean it." She had followed the madre back to the ward and taken her post beside the long oak dining-table where the surgeons were amputating. Whenever she could snatch a spare moment she went from stretcher to stretcher, again peering at each face lest she might have missed one. Some of the men were in repose, drugged by their pain, others, still in the throes of torture, beat on the floor or the walls with their fists, or tore at the sheets with gritting teeth.

Ministering to them, she had suffered their pain. When they died, she died, until her body was like an empty shell moving from operating table to stretcher and back to the table again on ghostly feet. They were so pitifully young. Like Eric they had slim, hard bodies that had pulsed with the joy of life. Now they were crying for their mothers, hurt with the wrenching pain of concussion, and hurt with the incomprehensible pain of, "Why? Why? Why?"

Towards dawn Captain Sigsbee had come to the hospital and in his eyes, too, was the pain of bewilderment. As Sharon met him at the door there was a spark of hope in her voice. "Captain, have you any news of Lieutenant March? Is he hurt?"

"Lieutenant March?" Sigsbee repeated dully. "I don't know. Isn't he here?"

"No," Sharon answered hoarsely, dread creeping back into her tones. "No. I've looked at every man at least twice. And he isn't here."

"Who are you?" Sigsbee asked in his dull monotone.

"I am Sharon Douglass. I was to be married to Lieutenant March to-day."

"Oh yes. Well, if I see him I'll tell him you've been worrying." Although sympathy modulated his words they were of little comfort.

Nevertheless Sharon said "Thank you sir," with sincerity.

It was then that she had deserted her post and crept out on the lawn. On her way she met

Estrallita coming from the chapel. Seeing that Estrallita too had anxiety on her face she asked, "How is Benito?"

"He is not well, Sharon. I have just been praying for him. I am so worried."

"Madre Isabela says that we must bear our crosses with courage, remember."

"Yes. I try to remember. But they had to move Benito to make room for the sailors and he was not ready to be moved. Will you say a prayer for him?"

"Of course I will. And I will say a prayer for you, too." And on her way to meet the dawn and to look upon the grey skeleton that had been the *Maine*, Sharon had entered the chapel.

Now, wearied by her hopeless vigil, she returned to the convent.

Three more sailors had been rescued from floating debris and brought in for treatment. One kept lifting his head to stare at the empty space where a few hours before there had been a leg. The other two, suffering from minor injuries and shock, were able to be on their feet, and even to help a little. Sharon asked them about Eric. No, they had not seen him since that last explosion. They had been helping him to lower a life-boat when it happened.

When the casualty list was posted on the convent door, the name of Lieutenant Eric March headed the list of missing. Among the curious who had gathered to read the list there was one whose words clarified themselves in the babble of tongues. "Missing," the voice said as if speaking only to Sharon, "that means they're either blown to bits or drowned like rats in the bottom of the harbour, poor devils."

In the darkness of the convent hall she met Madre Isabela and sought the shelter of her pudgy arms. Together they walked toward the chapel. Through the open door came the sound of uncontrollable weeping. As Sharon's eyes grew accustomed to the darkness she saw that it was Estrallita who was crying her heart out. The novice was prostrate across the kneeling rail.

Sharon turned to Madre Isabela. "Why is she crying?"

"A soldier died just now."

"Not Benito?"

"He is the one. I told Estrallita that he was better off, but she is taking it quite hard."

Sharon ran down the aisle and in that moment when she touched Estrallita's shoulder her own soul came back to her. Here was a heart-broken girl who needed her. Encircling the novice's waist with her arm she slipped to her knees beside her and drew the sobbing girl to her breast.

Madre Isabela seeing the two girls rocking to and fro in each other's arms smiled inwardly and raised her eyes to the crucifix. She padded out and closed the heavy oak doors leaving the girls to their grief.

The grievous hours became a day. And when the day turned to darkness Sharon said to Madre

Isabela, "Please let me stay on duty to-night. I know I can't sleep. I wasn't much help last night and I want to make up for it."

"Good, my child. We shall need you. And the Saviour will bless you for your service."

All night Sharon helped the surgeons catch up with the regular patients who had been neglected in the onrush of urgent cases. Madre Isabela came to her early in the morning and said, "Now, my child, you have done your share and more. I insist that you get some rest."

"All right, madre. I believe I am tired enough now to sleep."

"Sleep as long as you like. The Red Cross is sending a contingent of nurses and doctors to-day."

"Thank God for that," Sharon breathed and dragged herself to her room.

In the heavy twilight that preceded sleep she made a decision. If, when she awoke, there was still no word from Eric, she was going back to Santiago.

Sleep took her into dusk of that day. She remembered her decision the instant she awoke and hurried with her dressing. On her way to find Isabela she met new nurses in new uniforms, and in one of the wards she saw a young doctor whose face was fresh and unlined.

Madre Isabela was having her supper in the small dining-room reserved for her and Padre Cristobal and the doctors. "Come in, my child," the Madre called.

"Thank you, Madre Isabela. No word yet from Lieutenant March?"

"No word."

"Then I am going to leave you, madre. I am going to my aunt in Santiago."

"My dear child! How will you get there? The railway is very hazardous, especially for a woman. Even the roads are not safe. You'd better reconsider."

"No, madre. My mind is made up and when I make up my mind to do a thing I usually find a way of doing it."

"I believe that to be true. We are very fond of you here. We shall all miss you."

"Then I have your blessing, madre?"

"It is not my place to bless you, my child. But I pray that the loving Saviour may do so. There is something I feel I should tell you, though it is an unpleasant subject —"

"About Lieutenant March?"

"No. It is about another person. Shortly after you went to bed this morning she called."

"Oh. I know. A girl about my own age but larger in build."

"Yes. And of a different world. That was obvious. She did not wish to have you disturbed, nor did we intend doing so. She said she had seen the list and wanted to know if she could be of any service to you. Of course, she didn't put it in just those words."

"But you were kind to her, weren't you, madre?"

"It was Padre Cristobal who talked to her. He was kind enough. As soon as she was gone he went into the chapel to offer a prayer for her. You'd better get to the kitchen for some supper before everything is put away. And think this matter over a bit more, won't you?"

"Yes, madre." It was the easiest answer to give. As Sharon entered the kitchen she knew that the more she thought the more determined she would be. All her happy memories of Eric would be transformed into empty mockeries here. A nun gave her a bowl of lukewarm broth, some cheese and bread, and a piece of cake.

Sharon looked at the cake and asked, "Is this the cake?"

"Yes," answered the nun sadly, "that is your cake. The last portion."

Two Cuban boys worked at scouring the copper pots, scrubbing the heavy wooden tables and sweeping the floor. "My cousin is leaving for Santiago at daylight," one of them informed the other.

"Your soldier cousin?" his friend asked casually.

"Yes. Ramon. He is on the troop train now. The train is their barracks. In a few more months I will be sixteen too and then I can fight for Spain."

Sharon ate her cake slowly. Troop train — Santiago. At the far end of the convent lay the dead soldiers and sailors awaiting burial or identification — some would never be identified —

some wore Loyalist uniforms. Troop train — Santiago. Some wore Loyalist uniforms. Some would never be identified.

Back in her room Sharon changed into her native costume. She wrote a short letter to Pearl and a note for Estrallita asking her to mail it. These she left on her bureau. With her scissors she cropped her hair short and laid the long auburn strands in the same drawer that held her wedding dress. Folding a blanket diagonally she used it for a shawl and, making sure no one was looking, she dodged into the supply room where she snatched a roll of bandage.

At the door of the morgue she found a new orderly in charge. She asked his permission to look over the soldiers. The door was open and she could see that a few of the bodies were honoured with candles.

"All right miss. You may go in." He pushed the door wide for her and followed with a large candle to better light the faces.

"No, that is not he. No. No." But at the fourth corpse she stopped, grasped the young orderly's hand for support and said, "That is my brother. Oh, Juan! Juan!" Then making a show of self-control she let go his hand and added quietly. "I will make arrangements in the morning. You — will you kindly leave me here alone with him — just a few minutes?"

"Yes, miss." The orderly stepped deferentially away from her and slipped out of the room, closing the door very softly on the mourner.

Quick! To strip a Loyalist of his uniform. This next man was a Loyalist. But he was so very tall. Here was one farther down the line. There was a candle burning beside him but there was no time to lose seeking one who was unidentified. His coat first. His shoes. His trousers. Not until she had arranged the compact bundle under her shawl did she look at his face.

Benito!

Forgive me!

Forgive me, Estrallita. I cannot make amends.

She opened the door slowly and not too wide. "Thank you, orderly," she said and dabbed at her eyes with a corner of the shawl. "Thank you for your kindness."

In the jungle just beyond the outskirts of Havana six cars stood on the railroad tracks waiting for daylight. A scorpion scuttled across the tin roof of the second car, making little telegraphic sounds. Mingling with the rustle of palm fronds was the heavy breathing of sleeping men. The door of the third car stood wide open.

In the half-light of the night's waning the shadowy figure of a youth in an ill-fitting Loyalist uniform, with head and face swathed in bandages, detached itself from the other shadows of the jungle and proceeded resolutely towards that third car.

At the edge of the door was an iron ladder its rungs clammy with dew. Sharon clambered aboard and sat in the opening a minute to let her eyes adjust themselves to the darkness. Perceiving that there was a vacant space at one end of the car, she stepped gingerly over the sleeping forms and lay face downwards, pillowing her head on her arm. In relief at so much success she permitted herself a few tears. And before dropping into an exhausted sleep she thought of what would happen if her success did not hold through to Santiago. Her last fading vision was of Jaime Perez, a mere sliver of a man standing insolently before the overbearing Colonel Mares.

Raucous voices wakened her. Several of the men were singing and the dissonance set the others laughing boisterously. She lay there with her face to the wall and took stock of what was going on. It was daylight, and from the way the car was swaying and jerking from side to side they must be moving at a pretty good clip. From somewhere near her came the insistent tones of men talking above the other noise. There were three of them.

"Ah, how glad I will be to get back to my home in the valley," said one. The voice was soft and girlish. "I wonder if my mother will remember me."

"You are homesick, Ramon," another said. "That is no way for a soldier to be."

"Yes, I am homesick," Ramon answered softly. "And are not you too, Roberto?"

"Well, maybe." Sharon pictured Roberto shrugging as he spoke.

"I admit I will be glad to get home," the third asserted. "As soon as I arrive I will eat a good meal, take a bath and climb into bed with my woman."

"I shall skip the meal and the bath," Roberto bragged. "What is your woman like, Pedro?"

"She is fat — built like an old sow. I like my women that way. You know that there is really something solid beneath you. But right now I would not be particular. Even a skinny woman would do. What is your woman like, Roberto?"

"Bah, you would not like her even now. She is as skinny as a tent's ridge-pole. I am always afraid I'll get a splinter from her."

"Oh, you two are always talking about women," Ramon remonstrated in disgust.

"Some day, boy, when you're old enough to have a woman you'll talk about them too."

"I am old enough now," Ramon defended stoutly.

"Listen to the boy talk, Pedro," Roberto jibed. "And he's barely weaned from the bottle."

"There is a girl at home waiting for me," the girlish voice went on defensively. "Her name is Carmen Rosa. We used to take walks together in the Valley of Camaguey. She has promised to wait for me until the war is over."

"Is she fat?" teased the practical Pedro.

"She is very pretty," Ramon replied. "She used to put orchids in her hair and play the guitar and sing to me."

Sharon turned over cautiously, shielding her

bandaged face with her arm. Her body ached from the hard floor. Her limbs were paralysed from holding the same position too long. From beneath the protecting crook of her elbow she glanced at the three soldiers. She could tell at once which one was Ramon. He was the slight one with the black hair that was all rumpled. His eyes were filled with longing for his pretty sweetheart, yet his smooth young jaw was set in the hard lines of hatred drilled into him by his Spanish superiors.

"Ramon, have you a cigarette?" one of the other two asked. Sharon could not tell yet which was Roberto and which Pedro.

"No."

"You, Pedro?"

"You know I haven't. You asked me half an hour ago."

Roberto grunted. "I must have a cigarette." His eyes pounced on Sharon. "Hey, soldier, have you a cigarette?"

She did not answer. She tried to breathe evenly; tried to quiet the pounding in her breast.

"Lazy one with the bandaged head! Have you a cigarette or do I have to search you for it?" There was a boot prodding her ribs.

She shook her head emphatically.

"Bah! Why didn't you say so in the first place? Such soldiers they give us. Look at him! He isn't even as big as Ramon. And Ramon's only half-grown." He laughed, and there was a resounding slap on somebody's back.

"He is hurt," Ramon offered. "I got hurt once and had to be bandaged. I didn't feel like talking either."

Roberto uttered his contemptuous "bah" again. Sharon relaxed as the three returned to their pet jokes and lewd conversation, only occasionally drowned by the shouts and singing of the men at the far end of the car. Roberto got a cigarette from one of the others and she was apparently forgotten.

Havana to Santiago! Her second trip! And when she made the first trip she thought she was uncomfortable! She also thought then that she was in danger! Oh Eric, Eric! What if these men found her out? There would be a few brief words before the Loyalist officers in Santiago and a volley of shots. That would be the last sound she would hear on this earth. But Santiago was still a long way off. What if Roberto or Pedro should discover her before the train arrived?

Trying to dispel thoughts of Libby from her mind she turned to the wall again, though her side ached from the constant lurching of the car. She was getting nearer to Santiago and farther from the scenes where she had been happy with Eric.

Soon she was again losing herself in a fitful slumber. The click of the wheels and the drone of the conversation grew dimmer and dimmer until it seemed that she was alone in the car.

Jason, stooping to avoid bumping his head, emerged from the door of the attic stairway into the small kitchen of the little house near the Calvary Methodist Church. He had a dusty old telescope suitcase. Aunt Phoebe was bustling about nervously.

"Is this the one you wanted, ma'am?"

"Yes, Jason, thank you. And to think I nearly left it behind! It's a good thing Conchita was the same size as Sharon. Now fill that kettle with water again and keep the fire up well and get me some towels from the top bureau drawer."

"Yes, ma'am."

"Well, get a move on you. The poor girl's cold and hungry, and you stand there helpless not knowing which way to turn. Just like a man."

"Let's see." Jason with some effort collected his wits. "Towels. Gosh! I didn't even know her when she first came to the door."

"Of course, you didn't," Phoebe answered in her shrill voice. "How could anyone tell it was our Sharon? We must be thankful she got here safe and sound. Only the Lord could have brought her to us again."

"I am thankful." Jason poked the fire unnecessarily. "Gosh, Aunt Phoebe! Even in that soldier's suit and with her hair cut short she was still as pretty as the devil —"

"Jason!" Phoebe's voice was hoarse with reproach.

"Yes, ma'am. She was as pretty as the dickens."

"Yes, yes. Did you refill that kettle? You'll have to pump some more water too."

"Yes, ma'am. I'm tryin' to remember all you said, but I keep thinkin' of the way you came to the door and she started cryin' and you cried too and I didn't know what to do. Gosh, I get flustered like the dev— like the dickens when I see a woman cry. I rightly think she'd be so happy gettin' back home she wouldn't consider cryin'."

"You don't know us women, Jason." Aunt Phoebe looked very solemn as she tested the water in the bigger kettle with her little finger. "We always cry and laugh at the wrong time."

"I guess maybe you're right. Gosh, Aunt Phoebe, isn't it grand to have her back?"

"It's very wonderful, Jason. And we have Him to thank." She cast her eyes to the ceiling and let them dwell there for a moment.

"Yes, ma'am," Jason replied reverently, following her gaze and squinting at the cracks in the plaster.

Aunt Phoebe took a kettle from the range and plodded towards the bedroom. "Here we are," she said, closing the door behind her. Sharon sat in a wooden tub in the middle of the room massaging her body with a sponge and revelling in the extravagance of a wealth of suds. "Here's some more hot water," Aunt Phoebe cooed, "and some clothes of Conchita's."

"Oh, thank you, Aunt Phoebe. Don't go away.

I want you to pour the water in for me. I've been waiting on other people for a long time. Now I want to be waited on."

Aunt Phoebe smiled with gratification as she poured the water carefully around the edge of the tub. Sharon sighed with the luxury of it.

"It's wonderful to have a real bath and plenty of time to enjoy it. Here, you sponge my back, auntie."

"Gladly." Aunt Phoebe dropped to her knees beside the tub, grunting with the effort. "It sounds sweet to hear you call me auntie."

"There was a time when you didn't like it."

A shadow crossed Aunt Phoebe's chubby features but she quickly replaced it with a smile. "I really wanted you to, Sharon. I even liked it that time you did, but I was just an old humbug."

"Just for that I'm going to call you aunt for the rest of my life." They laughed fondly at each other, and as Sharon rose from the tub Aunt Phoebe poured clean warm water over her, rinsing off the last bubble of suds. She stepped out on to a towel, her skin glowing pink, and let Aunt Phoebe help rub her down. "I feel like a new person," she exulted.

"I can't get over your being back with us. I think these petticoats will be just the right fit. There — as if they were made for you. I'm sure Conchita would be happy to know you were wearing them."

"I wonder."

But Aunt Phoebe didn't ask Sharon why she

wondered. She prattled on about the time when she herself could have worn those twenty-two inch waist-bands. "Some folks used to say I was very pretty," she added wistfully.

"And I bet they were right." Sharon kissed her on the temple.

For a moment Aunt Phoebe stood there and beamed, but all of a sudden she bustled with efficiency again. "Mercy, girl! You must be starved. I've everything nearly ready. Jason and I can hardly wait to hear all about your adventures."

At the table Jason could hardly keep his eyes from Sharon. "And weren't you frightened in that box car with all those soldiers?"

"Scared to death," she admitted frankly. "But I didn't need to be afraid because I didn't have a bit of trouble. I guess I was pretty lucky, all right."

Aunt Phoebe spoke reprovingly. "You aren't forgetting His help, are you, Sharon?"

"Of course not, auntie," Sharon assured her.

"Now tell us everything you did while you were in Havana. We didn't get much from those letters signed by your friend, Pearl. Did you see the *Maine* after it exploded?"

Pain flashed across Sharon's eyes. "Yes, I saw it. And I saw much more. If my story is topsy-turvy it's because there's so much to tell I get mixed up myself. Suppose I start with the day I got Uncle Clay's letter saying that he could no longer pay the Floyds for my board."

And so, lingering long after the meal was over,

Sharon told Aunt Phoebe and Jason the story of her life in Havana. In clear, level tones she even told them of her love for Eric, how they had met — although she modified a few of the details — and of their wedding plans. Her voice was under complete control when she told of the explosion and her search for Eric. The only hint of her emotion was that she closed her eyes when she recounted the incident in the morgue.

Jason and Aunt Phoebe sat entranced as if trying to believe that all this had happened to their Sharon. When the story was finished she said quietly, "Then I was standing at the door and Jason was looking at me with his mouth open and his eyes half popping out of his head and you, Aunt Phoebe —" but she could say no more. She tried to laugh, but Aunt Phoebe saw what was coming. Rising hastily she took Sharon's head to her bosom and let the tears flow on to her starched shirt-waist. Jason rose awkwardly and stood looking on in helpless embarrassment.

When Aunt Phoebe had gone to bed Sharon and Jason sat in the kitchen near the stove. Only the red glow of the fire-pot illuminated the room, until Jason removed a stove lid and the flames sent shadows darting across the ceiling in futile chase.

"Sharon," Jason began uneasily, "I'd — I want to say something to — I want to say something to you."

"Yes, Jason, go ahead." But this was not easy

for him. She had to wait for him to gather courage. Yet despite his speechlessness his words expressed themselves in his eyes. He still loved her.

"I'm just no good at all when it comes to saying something important."

"Oh, fiddlesticks! How you go on, Jason."

"Well, this is very important. Anyway, to me it is. And I'm hoping it might be to you too. That is, I mean important to you. It's about — it concerns the things I said to you when we rode to Havana. Only I'm afraid — maybe it's too soon to talk about them now."

"Don't be afraid, Jason. You may say whatever is in your heart."

"Thanks, Sharon." He swallowed and made a valiant effort but again he was speechless.

"You still want to me to marry you. Isn't that it?"

His eyes shone in the firelight — shone with gratitude. "You make things so easy. I don't know why I should be afraid to say anything to you. I do still love you, Sharon. And I do still want you to be my wife — that is, some day when we have waited a decent period of time."

"That isn't necessary, Jason."

He looked at her a little stupidly. "But don't you still love him?"

Sharon looked up at Jason in simple candour. "The important thing is that I wish to forget him as quickly as possible. It is true, Jason, that I do not love you, but I believe I can learn. And I shall try to be a good wife to you. But oh, Jason, please, please marry me soon!"

Jason did not kiss her. He took her hand and gave it a slight pressure. A tear glistened in each of his eyes, and Sharon somehow knew that she had made him happier than he had ever been before.

"Remember the *Maine*!"

Everywhere in an aroused United States the slogan resounded. Incensed voices raised the cry. Angry lips carried it along on a wave of hatred and indignation. Smouldering eyes read the papers. President McKinley appointed a naval court of inquiry to investigate the disaster. The Chocolate Eclair was forced to action at last. Promptly — almost too promptly — the first findings came back: "We ascribe the tragedy of the *Maine* to an external explosion, but are unable to place the responsibility upon any person or group of persons."

The nation read the astounding report across the breakfast table. Cups of coffee poised in mid-air. Voices lifted in protest.

The first report was elaborated upon: "There are three possibilities: First, it might have been an accident. Second, it might have been sabotage on the part of some anxious-to-please Spanish soldier. And, third, it might have been the work of some Cuban patriot desperately trying to embroil America in war!"

Rumblings. Dark looks.

"What does Sigsbee say?"

"Come on, Captain Sigsbee. You ought to know something about the blowing up of your own ship. Speak up, Sigsbee!"

Sigsbee's report to the Naval Department was cautious, bewildered, lengthy: "The Honourable Secretary Long . . . public opinion should be suspended until a thorough investigation can be made . . . it is better to know than to surmise . . . I am, sir, your obedient servant, Sigsbee, Commanding."

But there was no suspending of a public opinion, already well formed and in many minds crystallized. Idealistic Sigsbee! This disaster was no accident. The *Maine* was torpedoed.

Torpedoed, hell! Didn't you know that the explosion was caused by a submarine mine with wires running to Morro Castle ?

Mr Hearst's great hungry presses ate up the rumours and were voracious for more. "Remember the *Maine*!" "Our brave boys!" "To hell with Spain!" "Avenge the *Maine*!"

Congress deliberated. Their reaction was more genteel. They let the people wait.

And the people waited for their President and their Congress to say something, to do something — either to deny the rumours or to take definite steps to punish the guilty.

And the President waited for public opinion to clarify itself and show him the way the people wished him to move.

People said, "Spain is guilty." "McKinley

doesn't know his own mind." "Our national honour is at stake." "It may mean war."

At another breakfast-time the nation read the report of the McKinley naval inquiry. It was complete, but brief — and extremely significant: "Thorough investigation of wreck now completed by means of diving operations . . . the ship was blown up by a mine on the port side . . . external shock caused explosions of two magazines. *Signed:* Captain William T. Sampson, U.S.N."

As the report of the investigation was circulated and the headlines lent their sixty-point persuasion, readers answered, "That's all we wanted to know." And other readers echoed, "We've taken enough!" Cities that for thirty-five years had nursed their Civil War animosities were now staunch friends — Boston and Tampa, Detroit and New Orleans, Chicago and Atlanta. What do you mean by North and South? Slaps on the back. Hell, this is a union. One against Spain. Remember the *Maine.* Right the wrong. Fight now. Our nation's pride must be upheld. Fight now!

But the Chocolate Eclair was still uncertain. In front of the White House he quietly addressed a multitude. "The thought of human suffering that must come to thousands oppresses me."

Someone in the crowd grumbled, "The son of a bitch is just putting us off," and there were murmurs of assent.

The tired voice from the balcony continued, "I

am requesting from Spain an armistice in Cuba, as the beginning of peace parleys to be held with myself as perpetrator. Perhaps by this I may secure independence in Cuba, a desire which we Americans feel very strongly."

Well, what good would that do the boys of the *Maine*?

Yes, what good?

Then you think war is the only solution?

Yes, yes. Mr Hearst says so.

"Oh, come now, boys. Don't quote me." Mr Hearst was so modest.

So on 11 April 1898 this message went to Congress:

> Honourable gentlemen: At this hour of despair the country is calling for action. I had hoped that peace could be kept with honour, but the call of my countrymen seems to be for intervention and war. Because of this war fever I have been receiving telegrams from all over the nation. No more does the nation wish to hold a palaver. There seems to be no alternative other than that I go along with the tide. We of the United States, I am sure, do not have the intention of exercising sovereignty, jurisdiction, or control over the Cuban people, save for their pacification. I hereby assert my determination that if Congress decides to take measures of intervention, I will see that the government and control of

> the islands are left to its people.
>
> I am a peaceful man, but for the sake of humanity, for the protection of American lives and property and for the purpose of ending a needless and costly war, I recommend intervention in Cuba. I hereby ask that Congress respond with resolutions implying the use of force on behalf of Cuban intervention and that measures for immediate mobilization of American troops be granted.

A formal declaration of war!

And Mr Theodore Roosevelt in his parlour in N Street, eyes flashing, teeth gnashing, smacked his palm with his fist. The Chocolate Eclair had come through. The time for a glorious adventure was at hand.

6

A Hot Time in the Old Town To-night

Mobilization was exciting. The Department of War was in chaos. Aides scurried about; attachés got in each other's way. Everybody wanted something of the distraught Secretary Long. Even his efficiency was unavailing in this muddle of demands and questions and doubts and requisitions.

Cheers resounded across the nation and echoed back again. Bands played and pulses quickened. Flags unfurled and hearts responded. The American people drank long and deep of a potent draught as the whole country went on a patriotic binge.

The call to the colours! Already a hundred thousand men had answered the call and were stationed in camps in New York, Virginia, Tennessee and Florida. There were not enough tents for all the new soldiers and there was not nearly enough food. The officers, although their fathers had fought the Civil War, seemed to have learned nothing from their sires. It was a job for Ulysses S. Grant.

At Tampa, the point of embarkation, the regiments poured in daily until there was no more room for them in town and they had to camp on the sand. There was thrilling confusion everywhere. And still the trains kept bringing the hordes of eager young Americans, their souls thirsty for battle, their hearts yearning for adventure. But there was no one to tell them where to go. Supplies arrived — food, blankets, cots, knapsacks, canteens, pup-tents — and no one was assigned to distribute them. Food was piled high on the docks and along the tracks. But it was unclassified and unlabelled. Nobody knew where anything was. The men said, "We signed up to fight, not to starve", and somehow their superior officers blundered through until it was June and the temperature was 110° in Tampa. The men drilled in the merciless sun awaiting the word to go over.

General Shafter, obese, mule-headed and hopelessly incompetent, surveyed it all with a sad shake of his head.

"What a disgraceful sight," he muttered in his headquarters tent. "But it's the country's own fault for not spending more money on the army. Ever since '68 Congress has appropriated no more than enough to keep our army alive. An army must march on its stomach, and it looks like this one will have to limp."

But at last the army was on the move. The command came to move on across the gulf, and at Tampa's single pier over ten thousand soldiers tried to make the transfer from the trains to the boats. Long double rows of men marched with order and dispatch. Preceding them on board went the pine boxes — freshly made, newly varnished.

It had taken a lot to start this army on its way, but the war was popular with the nation from the beginning and there was still an abundance of enthusiasm. Bond issues were floated as fast as they could be launched and no bond issue was permitted to sink. Every ship came back to port. Taxes were levied but the people never flinched.

The cigarette tax. People smoked and avenged the *Maine*. The liquor tax. Men drank to the success of our brave boys. The medicine tax. What does it matter? We must all do our share, sick or well.

And in the White House McKinley debated the wisdom of including Puerto Rico and the Philippines and Guam in his annexation plans. The Church was in favour. There was missionary work to be done. The Secretary of Commerce urged the annexation of the Philippines for business reasons. "If we don't, Germany will," he prophesied. "She is our chief rival for trade in the Orient."

Thus did the President begin to see the feasibility of Roosevelt's naval policy. It was plain to be seen that the naval arm of the nation was soon to be of prime importance; that the military arm, in this campaign against Spanish aggression, would play second fiddle.

But now that the army was assembled it had to be put to work. Get it on the move! The men were restless! On to Santiago! They had drilled long enough! If there was a Spanish armada coming our way we were ready to meet it. To hell with Spain!

Slowly, majestically the transports pulled away from the harbour, flags unfurled, the decks thronged with eager-eyed youths. In rows of three the ships nosed out of the gulf, every one of them a magnificent sight, from the battleship *Indiana* to the cruiser *Detroit.* Between and around them darted the destroyers, keeping close watch over their charges and looking like minnows in a lake.

And all over the nation the fever of war expressed itself in the hit song, "There'll be a Hot Time in the Old Town To-night", and the people sang it at the top of their lungs.

When the news that America had at last intervened came through to Cuba, the Americans there and the rebel Cubans went wild. But their delirium had plenty of time to relax into impatience before the first American soldier set foot on Cuban soil. After deciding to follow Roosevelt's general ideas of naval conquest, McKinley took it on himself to do the job correctly — to start with the Philippines. He ordered Commodore George Dewey to take his fleet from Hong Kong and capture or destroy the Spanish fleet at Manila. And Dewey, trained under Admiral Farragut, carried out his orders with bravery and dispatch.

Americans sat back and read the news with relish. Here was a man, this Commodore Dewey. Knowing that the nearest home base was thousands of miles away, he sailed straight into the bosom of the enemy. On 30 April 1898, as twilight gathered over the deep waters of the Pacific, Dewey's squadron, with all lights extinguished, approached the mouth of Manila Bay. His six cruisers *Olympia*, *Raleigh*, *Petrel*, *Boston*, *Baltimore*, and *Concord* sneaked quietly in.

Lurking in the waters beneath them were submarine mines, and as the *Olympia* sailed in two of them exploded directly in front of her, hurling a spout of water high into the air but falling back harmless. Dewey's lips pursed in anger. Facing the captain of the *Olympia* he said, "The time for action has arrived, captain. You may begin firing when you are ready."

The captain was ready. Shells burst overhead and all around. The water hissed and steamed as the fiery explosives fell to the waves. Stripped to the waist, the sailors stood at their stations awaiting orders and shouting "Remember the *Maine*!" The guns on the *Olympia* roared and the timbers of the ship groaned under the strain. Like echoes came the growls from the *Raleigh* and *Concord*.

The Spanish fleet fell back at the suddenness and intensity of the attack. The *Don Antonio de Ulloa* promptly sank with a self-conscious air, and the *Reina Cristina* keeled over until her decks were awash. All night the battle raged. The flames from the guns lighted the sky with a devilish glow, and the blazing ships were colossal torches held in the hands of Destiny.

By noon of 1 May, Dewey had annihilated the entire Spanish fleet and not one American had given his life.

America rocked back on its heels and stuck its thumbs in its armpits.

The time to help little defenceless Cuba had at last arrived.

On to Santiago!

The American army sailed from Tampa for Daiquiri. And what an army it was! Red tape had a strangehold upon it. The transports were packed to suffocation. The commander-in-chief, General Shafter, was totally inefficient. Most of the time he was bedridden with his gout. When up and about he amiably waged his war despite obesity and unfitness, but resting always on the laurels he had gained in the Civil War. Behind his back the men called him "The Cup of Custard".

And so the army went on to Santiago, sweating and stinking in the overcrowded transports. Because winter-weight uniforms were always issued in the spring for use during the following autumn the men wore heavy army blue — woollen underwear for the tropics! It was not a splendid uniform, but it had its merits. It was neat and serviceable — tan trousers, blue shirt, grey hat. And the men must carry their blanket-roll, knapsack, canteen, and rifle.

The rifles were up-to-date, Krag-Jörgensens, the powder was smokeless. In the hands of an American soldier they were deadly. In the hands of a Cuban they were useless. The Cubans could hit nothing with them, but at close range the loud report scared the devil out of the enemy. So the Americans gave them old and decrepit Springfields. And every Cuban rebel must have his American cartridge-belt. The belts fascinated them as if each belt were a medal of valour. Sometimes a Cuban could do fairly well with a Long Tom Carbine, but his real worth lay in his ability to handle the machete.

The harbour at Daiquiri was in reality a half-moon in the rock-bound shore. There was a small strip of shimmering white sand and beyond the rocks were the wooded hills. Closely crowding the strip of beach was the disordered village, its main street extending on to the steel pier far out into the water. It was here that the devil-take-the-hindmost army from America arrived to rescue Cuba from Spanish oppression.

From a distance the harbour seemed to be crawling with maggot-like craft: naval boats, rowboats, blunt little launches, and tugs towing long streams of barges through the shimmering azure water. The narrow, writhing streets disappeared snake-like into the hills beyond the village. Red-necked vultures, their gimlet eyes ever darting in search of prey, flew in wide circles above the huts built of driftwood and thatched with palm fronds.

The American soldiers wanted action. When was the big push to start? When the pier became so crowded with transports that not another one could dock, they anchored beyond the breakwater and the soldiers were sent ashore on launches. They shouted and cheered and sang, and in spite of warnings about barracuda they stripped off their clothes and swam in.

This foolhardy stunt was not to get the war started sooner, but to reach the reception committee on shore. Those comely Cuban girls! They welcomed the American soldiers with open arms, with kisses and caresses and invitations. They wore roses of red, white and blue.

The big push had finally begun. On to Santiago!

And back home, the girls they left behind them were wearing brooches and buckles of red, white and blue.

At breakfast the next morning Aunt Phoebe chattered about the church members and her garden, but she soon stopped to say, "My, but you two are awful quiet this morning. I've hardly heard a word out of either of you."

She looked from one to the other, and Sharon looked at Jason. He was studying the design of his plate and his cheeks were more than usually red. Nudging him, Sharon said, "I think Jason has something to tell you, Aunt Phoebe."

"Aw, you can tell her better than I can," he demurred.

And when Sharon told the news Aunt Phoebe clapped her hands and said, "Oh, bless you both!" and cried. As soon as she was a little calmer she ordered Jason up to the attic to bring down "that little raw-hide trunk with the rounded top".

"It has my wedding dress in it," she explained to Sharon while he was gone. "I think you can wear it — or don't you want to wear it?"

"Oh, I'd love to, auntie. What made you think I wouldn't?"

"Well, you didn't look very happy —"

"Never mind me. I just wasn't planning on having much of a wedding at all."

"But you only get married once. You should have a wedding. We haven't had a wedding in the church since I was ordained."

"Is this the one you want, ma'am?" Jason held the dusty trunk.

"Yes, Jason. Just set it down there. And tell me, have you set the date? Because if you haven't, I'd like you to be married on my wedding anniversary. It'll be my twenty-eighth. Uncle Clay and I were married the third day of June 1870." She looked to Jason for an answer.

"I guess the bride always sets the date," he said awkwardly.

Sharon said, "Surely, Aunt Phoebe, I'll be glad to make it on your wedding anniversary. Now let's see the dress."

But that evening, strolling with Jason along the quiet lane leading toward the hills, she confessed to him that it was not her wish to be married in the austere Methodist Church by Aunt Phoebe. "Do you remember telling me one night that you would take me to meet Padre Esteban?"

"I do remember. It was the night Conchita's father died."

"Jason, if you had your way you'd have him marry us, wouldn't you?"

"Well, Sharon, yes. But if —"

"No. We aren't going to give into Aunt Phoebe in everything. I can handle her all right. I'll wear her wedding dress and I'll wait until the third of June, but for some reason I feel that I want to be married in that little shrine you told me about — that is if Padre Esteban won't mind me not being a Catholic."

"He won't mind. I know that."

Aunt Phoebe made no effort to hide her disappointment, but she did reluctantly consent to attend the wedding. "But how shall we go?" she asked petulantly when the time drew near. "If we had Jerry and Freddie —"

Jason's face lightened. "I have it. Mr Harkness! I think he'd be glad to lend us our team."

"But the phaeton has a broken shaft."

"Then we'll borrow his wagon, too."

"And we can ask him to go along." Sharon put in happily.

So they borrowed the wagon and the two

sway-backed mares from their next door neighbour and invited him to join the party. He was only too delighted.

Padre Esteban's flowing white hair tumbling down his back and about his shoulders gave him the benign look of Saint Peter. His garment of grey wool with the broad cape-like collar and flowing skirt was girdled with a knotted rope from which hung a large wooden crucifix.

"My son, my son!" he cried, warmly shaking Jason's hand. "It has been so long since I've seen you. I thank the Blessed Father that He has guided you to me once more." Then, noticing there were others, he took them all in with a look of hospitable welcome in his rheumy old eyes. "It isn't often that we are privileged to have lady callers all the way from Santiago. Am I right?"

"Yes, padre. We're all from Santiago."

"Allow me to help you down, señora," he said, offering Aunt Phoebe his hand.

She answered with a cold stare. So this was the famed Padre Esteban whom Jason had for ever pestered her about as a boy? But Sharon was nudging her. "Don't sulk, auntie. Be nice and smile."

She took the padre's kindly hand and smiled of her own accord, not because of Sharon's prompting. It was the warmth of his smile that did it. She might have listened to Jason all those years if it hadn't been that Clayton was so strict. From him she had absorbed a hatred for all things Catholic, yet now it seemed quite fitting to attend Jason's wedding here. Surely no one could hate a man like this old padre.

"I've heard so much about you from my foster-son, father. I'm glad that I at last have the chance to meet you."

"I am glad too for the opportunity to meet Jason's foster-mother. He's often told me about you." The padre next offered his hand to Sharon. Jason helped too, as the wedding gown impeded her usual freedom of movement. "It looks to me as if you two have come for a wedding ceremony," he observed pleasantly.

"Yes, padre. This is Miss Douglass. I've also spoken of her."

"Indeed you have. And I shall be happy and proud to marry you. And this is —"

"Mr Harkness, a neighbour." Mr Harkness did not seem to mind having to introduce himself.

"Good. And now I want you to see my little church. There is no hurry about the ceremony. We will rest ourselves first. I always like to be rested before I perform any important task."

He led them into the roughly built church. Half of it was a natural grotto in the side of the hill; the other half, built of tamarack logs, housed the double row of rustic benches, the small altar rail, and the chancel. In the rocky grotto were the nave and the sanctuary. On natural pedestals of rock were crude wooden statues of the Virgin Mary and Joseph, and around the sides of the shrine were primitive wood carvings at each Station of the Cross.

"Why, it's beautiful," Aunt Phoebe whispered. For a moment she seemed to settle her thoughts on some distant object, as if comparing Padre Esteban's little shrine to the Calvary Methodist Church. In the shrine one felt drawn towards the Creator of all that is good and beautiful, the Author of Peace, whereas in the church the garishness of the painted windows and the stiff austerity of the bare walls gave a sense of the breach between God and the congregation.

"I'm glad you like it, señora," the padre said, smiling modestly. "You see I built it with my own hands, and even though it is dedicated to the magnification of our Blessed Saviour, I cannot help taking a personal pride in it when I see others admiring my handiwork."

"You built it yourself!" Aunt Phoebe looked about her with new interest and admiration in her eyes.

"You see," the padre continued, appreciative of an audience, "When I first came to Cuba from my native province of Aragon, they offered me the largest and most congested parish in Havana. I have always been a peaceful man. I used to spend many happy hours walking alone in the fields of Spain, and the crowded life in the city only oppressed me. So I asked for a church in the country. They told me there was no such church, so I said, 'Then I will build one.' " The padre spread his arms in an inclusive gesture and smiled. "And this is it."

"You see, Aunt Phoebe," Jason said quietly but very proudly, "I always told you the padre in the hills had a beautiful shrine."

Padre Esteban fingered the cross at his belt. "Jason used to see me often when he was a boy. And he told me some very fine things about his foster parents. I always expected — at least I always hoped — that he would come to me for his wedding ceremony."

"Yes, padre." Jason grasped Sharon's hand and the padre laid an affectionate hand on his shoulder.

"But there is plenty of time. You must all be tired from your journey. Won't you come into the cabaña and have some tea? I have it made from herbs I gather. I find it strengthens me."

"Thank you, padre," Sharon said. "We'll be glad to join you."

A door at the side of the shrine opened upon the cloister that led to the cabaña. This structure, too, was a primitive affair of clapboards and palm fronds, yet its interior imparted an atmosphere of culture. The simple decorative pieces were burnt-wood drawings and statuettes. On the floor was a smooth covering of palm matting and, in the centre of the room, a sturdy table. A few chairs were placed conveniently about.

On the wall hung the padre's vestments — his stole, biretta, cassock, and surplice. A rope with a gaily patterned blanket hanging from it was stretched from wall to wall. Noticing Aunt

Phoebe's eyes resting on the blanket, the padre said, "You see, señora, I can make two rooms of my cabaña." He drew the blanket half-way across. "I sometimes hear confessions in here." He opened the door. Outside an aged woman tended a barbecue fire. On the bayonet spits were thrust spareribs of wild peccary, the juices sizzling as they spattered on the hot coals. "That is Señora Mantez," the padre indicated, as the woman turned towards him a face wizened with the furrows of great age. "She comes each day to straighten my house and prepare my meals."

A little boy came running up to the padre and looked over the guests curiously. "And this is Francisco." Padre Esteban placed his hand on the tousled head. "He is Señora Mantez's great-grandson. He is also one of my altar boys and sometimes he is very good, but at other times his conduct leaves much to be desired. To-day you will be very good, won't you, Francisco?" The youngster looked up at his beloved padre with a roguish grin, nodded, and ran to his great-grandmother. She gave him a bone to smear over a face that already looked as if it had never been washed.

After a satisfying repast of spareribs, coarse bread, and strong herb tea, the guests drifted back into the cool, quiet shrine while the padre prepared himself for the ceremony. When he entered in his vestments he led Francisco by the hand. The urchin's face was still unwashed and his hair uncombed, yet in his little surplice he had a celestial look.

"Are we all ready?" Padre Esteban asked gently, and Jason looked to Sharon for her nod of consent before he said, "Ready, padre." They took their places before the altar and after that nothing seemed quite real to Sharon. She heard the gentle voice as from a great distance; the Latin words were mountain echoes. She thought she heard Aunt Phoebe crying, but of only one thing was she sure. Jason's hand on hers was real. Yet even he was worlds away. She must be there being married to him, although she also stood aside looking on, watching someone else being married to Jason and wearing Aunt Phoebe's wedding gown.

Over her body crept a weariness and as her strength ebbed away she tightened her grip on Jason's hand. He was still there. To help steady herself she fixed her eyes on Padre Esteban's benign features. Entranced, she lost herself in a haze of memory. And before her dulled vision the padre's waxen face moulded itself into the gross, worldly features, at first blurred, then very clear, of Colonel Vincente Mares! Oh God, had he caught up with her? But now the face merged into the effeminate simper of Hilary Edgecomb — then Carlos Menendez, his machete scar showing livid — Captain Larribee — Arnold Floyd. She closed her eyes with a numb dread of what she might see next. No! No! It couldn't be so. These men were alive. Eric was dead. Eric lay at the bottom of the harbour.

She opened her eyes by the force of her will, and there in place of Padre Esteban's uplifted eyes were Eric's taunting ones. He was winking at her, and the surly lips were moving. (Steady now, don't faint.) The words became audible, coherent.

"Do you take this man to be your — ?"

"I do," she answered mechanically.

"— in sickness and in health, till death do us part?"

"I do." (Oh, Eric, stop! Please stop!)

But the words went on and she closed her eyes and her ears for relief until she heard distinctly — and it was the padre's voice — "I now pronounce you man and wife." She was herself again. Aunt Phoebe was crying, Padre Esteban was smiling, Francisco was running away, and Jason was waiting for his kiss.

"On to Santiago!"

Once the soldiers embarked at Daiquiri they lost no time in setting out for their objective. Slowly, doggedly, they beat their way through the jungle towards the hills that guarded it, keeping going by sheer will-power.

Santiago de Cuba, by its position, controlled the entire western end of the island, and military manoeuvres had to be planned with astuteness. Four distinct but co-ordinated operations were laid out — the Spanish troops on the island were to be conquered by the army; the navy was to blockade the shore lines so that the troops might neither escape nor receive reinforcements from the mother country; the shore line of the United States was to be protected from Spanish attack by troops remaining at home; and both the army and navy were to besiege Santiago itself.

Part of this army, the "Rough Riders", had its beginnings in Prescott, Arizona. In military annals it was designated as the First Regiment of the Arizona Cavalry, and Colonel Leonard Wood was in command. Second in command was Lieutenant-Colonel Theodore Roosevelt. It was he who incited them to patriotic fervour over the sinking of the *Maine*, and he was the real leader of this dramatic and heterogeneous organization.

A crack regiment at home, they seemed a little lost in Cuba. The jungle was such a contrast to the desert; even the heat was different. And since the greater powers at home had decided against shipping their horses across — except for a few for the aides and officers — they disconsolately faced their trek across the island, a crack cavalry troop on foot.

"We'll be lost trying to take Santiago without our horses," one of the men opined.

"Leave it to Teddy," another cheered him, "he'll know what to do."

The men all knew that Colonel Wood was the more scientific militarist of the two; they knew that although Teddy possessed a keen, alert mind he was inclined to act rather than think. They knew that with Wood it was plan first and then follow through with clear-headed patience. Both men had an iron determination, both loved adventure, and they knew soldiers and their ways equally well; but one was hot-headed and the other cool-headed. It was, as one of their men expressed it, "a hell-rarin', jungle-bustin' combination".

But no one knew better than Roosevelt how well suited Wood was to assume command of the Rough Riders. He had spent two years in Mexico and Arizona, on foot and on horseback, routing Indians. This experience had taught him the Indian methods of fighting, the technique of the ambush — valuable lessons in this crisis of 1898. And he was well liked for his vigorous and steady will, and for the pleasant smile he had for everyone. Yes, the men liked Wood, but they loved Teddy.

And just as Roosevelt recognized Leonard Wood's ability, Wood realized that he had Teddy to thank for the fine men he had under him. They were all hand-picked by Roosevelt himself. College athletes, unschooled cowboys, loyal Indians, restless ranchers, and business men who thirsted for adventure. And if they had no experience with horses before they met Roosevelt he soon saw that they got it. He put them through rigid cavalry drill and, without a press agent, got them talked about and written about more than any other regiment in the entire army.

And so, with the prodigious Roosevelt leading them on, the Rough Riders, their Winchester rifles slung over their shoulders, their .45 Colt pistols hanging at their hips, left Daiquiri confident of the success of their "On to Santiago" campaign. But somehow, as they fought their way through this unfamiliar jungle without their mounts, that confidence dwindled.

"How far is this Santiago, anyway?"

"What good is a rider without a horse, Gawd dammit!"

"Maybe you'll get your chance to be a hero anyway!"

"Buck up. Teddy will know what to do."

On they trudged and stumbled toward the enemy lines, their feet weary and flaming with blisters, up another hill and down another winding trail which appeared to lead nowhere. The seasoned Colonel Wood set a fast pace. Roosevelt, riding one of the few available horses, kept a close inspection of the lines, seeing that there was no loitering along the trail. They advanced in columns of two when there was room and single file when there was not.

When their canteens were dry they cracked open coco-nuts and let the cool milk trickle down their parched throats. There was no time to dig a well or seek a spring. Other regiments might take a little extra time, but not the Rough Riders. They would pass a regiment at ease and ignore the hoots and jibes. Perhap they were a sorry sight marching so intently through the thicket, and shrubs and vines, but what did it matter? On to Santiago. Get there first and show the world how good the Rough Riders really are, horses or no horses.

"So them's the Rough Riders!" a soldier at leisure shouted.

"Hey, sonny! You forgot your saddle!" another yelled at a boy in the regiment.

"God damn him," the boy said. His boots scuffed heavily.

Roosevelt, riding near, said cheerfully, "Pay no attention to the creature. And a gentleman doesn't use that sort of language," he chided, "unless it's absolutely necessary." The beribboned spectacles did not hide the twinkle in his eye.

When the men were lolling about the camp-fire that night, at last resting, Colonel Wood informally addressed them. "Men, I have just received word that several other regiments, under the direction of General Shafter, have taken Siboney. The Spaniards retreated without firing a single bullet."

The cheer that went up had little hint of fatigue.

"Not only that," Wood continued with his genial smile, "but they're showing the Spaniards how things should really be run. A base hospital has been set up and barracks established. Once the city is habitable more transports will come to Siboney. Men, it won't be long before Cuba is ours."

Another lusty cheer and much back-slapping.

"Men, we will continue to advance toward

Santiago on this trail. When we reach the hill we will camp quietly and await General Shafter's orders."

The response to this announcement was a groaning protest from Roosevelt. "I'm for taking it right off, Len."

"You'll wait for orders with the rest of us," Wood replied, grinning affectionately.

The next morning they passed by the abandoned camps of regiments that had gone on before them to branch out and take Siboney. Among these were the infantry — the 8th and the 4th, the 6th Massachusetts and the historic 71st of New York. They had already seen action. The Rough Riders must march steadily on and await orders.

As if she sympathized with their impatience, Fate marched them straight into a column of Spaniards retreating from Siboney. It was hard to tell who were the more surprised, Spaniards or Americans. But Wood acted with the speed of a Mauser bullet.

"Load rifles!" he sent the order back. "Ambush formation."

In answer came the metallic clicks of the rifle blocks and the rifles were raised for firing. At Wood's command and under Roosevelt's energetic directions, the soldiers broke rank and took ambush formation at left and right of the trail. But the Spaniards were also swift in recovering from their surprise. They were the first to fire.

Roosevelt led his men into the very muzzles of

the Spaniards' guns. As they plunged on, man after man doubled up and pitched to the earth. The others followed on, catching his enthusiasm and yelling as a Spaniard clutched at the air with wild, groping fingers before falling, or blindly ignoring a fellow Rough Rider clawing at the undergrowth while blood streamed from between clenched teeth.

Neither the precision of the return fire nor the bravado of the oncoming Rough Riders repulsed the Spaniards at first. Yet Roosevelt riding upright and brandishing his six shooter like a policeman's night-stick, was right there in the midst of the fire shouting "Bully for you, men!" at the top of his lungs. Apparently Destiny protects her favourite sons.

It was not until another few steps would have meant hand-to-hand combat that the firing ceased. The Spaniards who survived fled this way and that, leaving their dead and dying behind them. Only the groans of the wounded now disturbed the quiet of the jungle. Over everything was the stench of blood and the acrid odour of powder.

A soldier came up to Roosevelt, saluted weakly, and said, "Sir, there is a report that Colonel Wood has been killed."

"What!" Roosevelt ejaculated. "Impossible! They couldn't have killed Woodsy."

"You're right, Teddy," a quiet voice broke in. "They can't kill Woodsy." And the colonel himself stepped forth from behind a clump of trees, and as he stood before his men they all sighed with relief.

Immediately he set them to cleaning up the mess, digging the necessary graves and rendering first aid to those who needed it. And when they resumed their march, though bruised, bleeding, and reduced, they were still in the lead. The Rough Riders had proven themselves. Having had their baptism of fire they were sure of their salvation.

But eventually their sureness gave way to complete exhaustion, and even the indomitable Teddy could not deny that they had well earned a rest. A sprucely uniformed regiment marched by, singing and jesting, and with guidons flying high. The Rough Riders tossed back jibe for jibe, but half-heartedly. Their own uniforms were torn and bloodstained. They hadn't had them off for a week.

Roosevelt commiserated with them for a while, then, mounting his horse, he boosted their morale with a talk and with his own example of unflinching determination. "I know you look filthy, men," he said, "and I know you're hungry. But what if you haven't had a square meal in forty-eight hours? I say bully for you! You are men! Tested by battle and found fit and courageous. You aren't tin soldiers dressed up to show off. What you're going to do is to march on and show them all up."

Halting and stumbling, they got to their aching feet, sustained by their own fighting spirit and Teddy's. They fell back into line — columns of two, columns of four. On the march again they grinned and jostled each other. It was this sort of thing they expected when they joined the Rough Riders. They knew it wouldn't be any ice-cream social. On to Santiago!

With death behind them and death still imminent, someone started singing:

A shower, a shower, Jesus Christ on high,
A shower, a shower, the Judgment Day draws
  nigh
What shall we do to keep our flannels dry?
There'll be a hot time in the old town to-night.

And it was perfectly timed. Before the song was finished the heavens unleashed a downpour of tropical rain.

In saturated uniforms, in soggy boots, their blanket-rolls sodden on their aching shoulders, they sloshed on through the mud. There was relief in the rain — it soothed their wounds and cactus scratches — and they sang even louder. And they got their chance at the regiment which had passed and hooted at them before. These men were huddled under the trees waiting for the rain to stop. The Rough Riders hurled a volley of good-natured taunts at them and hurried on. On to Santiago.

"I don't know what we're in such an all-fired hurry for," a Rough Rider growled, "if all we're going to do when we get there is to wait."

But there was no answer to this, for the order came down the line to march single file. They were in Spanish patrolled territory where snipers might be concealed anywhere. They were following a wagon road now, the Siboney road. At the San Juan River it turned, and it was here that the Spaniards opened hell-fire and many a Rough Rider crumpled where he stood or, mortally wounded, crawled on hands and knees to get away from the relentless rain of shot.

Led by Wood and Roosevelt the survivors plunged into the shallow river and half swam, half stumbled towards the opposite side. Some accepted the river as their grave; the others forged on. They named that spot Bloody Bend.

Roosevelt found he was mistaken about the troops they had to pass. In addition to the two cavalry regiments, there were still the 9th Regulars. They were not as good-natured about this race for Santiago as were some of the others. They refused to split their lines and let the Rough Riders through. Roosevelt and Wood put their heads together, commanded their own men to split columns, and in double time, yelling their contempt and sarcasm, the Rough Riders passed around the 9th Regulars as if they had been boys playing marbles.

Thus did they reach San Juan Hill — and on the other side lay Santiago. Colonel Wood gave the command to halt and said, "Men, we have reached our goal."

A cheer broke loose that resounded throughout the valley. Roosevelt said, "I'm sure if they heard that yell in Santiago, the Spanish fleet would turn tail and clear the harbour without even looking at us. When do we take the hill, colonel?"

"When General Shafter orders us to take it. His troops must surely be on the other side of the town, to the east."

"I don't know why we should wait," Roosevelt fumed. "Why not —"

"Don't get impatient," Wood said sternly, though his eyes belied his pursed lips. "We can block the land all right from here. Men, we are at the eve of perhaps the greatest battle of history. Who knows? I am sure that all of you will acquit yourselves creditably to the United States of America. That is all."

And again the resounding cheer, and in it was a note of challenge. The Rough Riders had won the race to Santiago.

If William McKinley thought the army was going to play second fiddle to the navy he soon learned that the army had other ideas. Although reports were infrequent and often delayed, they left no doubt that the army was on the job. The troops had left the transports at Daiquiri. They were on the march through the jungle. General Garcia was co-operating to the fullest measure. Siboney, the strategic city, was taken. And then — what a cheer went up in the United States — the soldiers were through that awful jungle and camping on the slopes of San Juan Hill! They were ready to take the fortress! Even the Navy Department had to concede there was nothing second fiddle about that army. The American fleet had still not reached Santiago harbour. Through the treacherous channel where the Gulf Stream joins the Atlantic the fleet was making its way towards Cuban waters as fast as the turbulent currents would permit.

The harbour at Santiago de Cuba is formed much like a huge rum bottle and is entered through the neck, a long, narrow passageway. In 1898 it was guarded with arrogant vigilance by a Spanish fort on one side and by heavy batteries on the other; and in the water were innumerable mines. Protecting the fort and the batteries from an attack by land were a series of barbed-wire fences, forming a deadly network in the jungle.

Before the American fleet arrived, the Spanish armada of four mediocre ships was guided into the harbour. Their admiral, Pasquale Cervera, knew that Santiago had direct railway connexions with Havana, and it was his plan to remove his relief troops to the capital city in record time. What he did not know was that the United States army had captured Siboney and was now in control of that railway. When he found out, it was too late for him to proceed to Havana by the water route. The American fleet, with seven fine, big boats and one outmoded one, was spread in fan-like formation just beyond the mouth of the channel.

The stern grey battleships were alive with

action as the sailors prepared them for battle. The United States Navy had not been given a real chance to prove itself since 1812, and now every man on the *New York*, the *Indiana*, the *Iowa*, the *Brooklyn*, the *Oregon*, the *Massachusetts*, and the *Texas* was ready to make up for lost time. This would not be any ordinary battle — not if they could help it.

Admiral W. T. Samson ordered the *Merrimac* abandoned and they sank it across the harbour mouth. That was a part of the cat and mouse game he was playing. Although it was seven ships against four, Admiral Samson — older than Commodore Dewey and more conservative — knew better than to run the gauntlet of that guarded channel and attempt a surprise attack. Let the Spaniards come to meet them. If the *Merrimac* failed to block their passage — or if it did not — the other seven ships were ready for battle.

Aunt Phoebe was a good manager and Sharon helped in every way she could, but the little money Jason earned was insufficient to provide for the three of them.

"I'm going back to work, Aunt Phoebe," Sharon announced decisively one afternoon. "I ought to be doing my share."

"But what will you do, Sharon dear?"

"I'll go back to singing in a café."

"But you told me yourself that you were no singer," Aunt Phoebe complained.

"I know, but if I fooled them once I can fool them again. Both of us need things and Jason does too, but he can't buy them with prices so dear. I'm not finding fault with him, auntie. I know he's doing the very best he can. And when the war is over I'm sure he'll find something better, but right now —"

"Yes, when the war is over," Aunt Phoebe chanted wearily.

"But it can't last much longer. I hear the American troops are just on the other side of the hill."

"Where did you hear that, child?" Aunt Phoebe's voice became instantly sharp.

"I was talking to some Americans at the newspaper office this morning. They claim that the American fleet is just outside the harbour, too."

"And did you believe them?"

"I'd like to believe them. And they might know, because they said they got it straight from the editor."

"Straight from the editor! You know Padraic O'Shea's reputation. He has never co-operated with the Church to stamp out vice in this city. His paper is noted for its lies."

"I knew you felt that way about the paper. That's why I wasn't going to tell you I went there looking for work."

"The very idea of working for a man like that!" Aunt Phoebe put on her hat and thrust the hat-pins viciously through the crown.

"But it would be honest work. And I used to

send reports of ranch parties to the Cardenas paper and often got them published. Anyway, Mr O'Shea seemed to have other things on his mind and I didn't have a satisfactory interview, so I've made up my mind to try earning something at singing, and I'm determined."

"Very well, Sharon." Aunt Phoebe took up her Bible. She was calling on a parishioner who had suffered a stroke. "I learned long ago that when you make up your mind it's no use opposing you — only I hope you can work in some good old gospel hymns with your singing."

There was one dress of Conchita's which Sharon had never worn — the black lace, which the child had kept for going to church on Sundays. It would be just the dress to wear for an interview with a café proprietor. The very thought of coins being thrown at her feet again made Sharon hum a little aimless tune as she slipped out of her dress and put the curling-iron to heat in the chimney of the oil-lamp. In Conchita's telescope suitcase there was a mantilla that went with the dress.

Sharon knelt beside the suitcase, loosened the straps, and removed the top section. Her humming stopped. There, on top, lay Benito's uniform. It was carefully washed and pressed now. These tasks she had performed in atonement for the wrong done to Estrallita. Lifting the mantilla from the bottom of the suitcase, she laid it aside and replaced the top. Estrallita — the convent — Madre Isabela — the wedding cake. But she must not let herself become maudlin. She snapped the buckles and sprang to her feet to test the curling-iron. She must think forward, not backward. She must think of Jason. Poor Jason. She must try to repay his love. He was so considerate of her — always doing little things to make her smile, pathetically trying to make her happy.

As she wound the short strands of hair about the iron and held the ends down with sensitive fingers, she thought a little humorously of their wedding night and of Jason's clumsy gestures to lessen her fear; of how she responded demurely to his naïve advances and made things easier for him without letting him suspect that she was actually much older in wisdom than he. She placed her arms about his back, biting her lip for a moment as his smooth, hard muscles felt so much like Eric's. Holding him close to her she had prayed, "Dear God, he's such a little boy. Grant that I may never hurt him."

She repeated the words aloud as she prepared herself to return to singing. "Dear God, he's such a little boy. Grant that I may never hurt him." How fortunate she was that she could wear Conchita's dresses and that Conchita had kept the black lace one in good condition. With the mantilla and her crown of tight little auburn curls just showing under the scalloped edge she looked the part of a café singer. She should get a job easily enough. At least she was not going to give up until she had seen every café proprietor in Santiago.

When she was on her way downstairs the front door opened and slammed and Jason was calling excitedly, "Sharon, Sharon, where are you?"

"Here I am, dear," she answered in anxious tones.

Bounding up the steps he met her on the landing, paused a moment to catch his breath, kissed her and looked her over with loving admiration bright in his eyes. The kiss was a gallant one. The words of a prayer crowded anxiety from her mind and through her thoughts she heard him say, "How beautiful my wife looks!"

"But, Jason, you're home early. And you're out of breath. What's up?"

"Mrs Earleigh, you are now looking at a soldier in the United States army." And now the brightness in his eyes was pure pride. "I enlisted this afternoon."

"Oh, Jason! How did you happen to do a thing like that?" Sharon's legs went weak under her. But before Jason could notice anything wrong she sat down on the stairs simply and naturally, pulling him down beside her. "Tell me everything."

"Well, when I came out at noon to-day to eat my sandwich I saw a crowd gathered around the newspaper office."

"Yes?"

"I crowded in, and there was a notice in the window signed by Padraic O'Shea himself. It said that the American army was on the hill and the navy was just outside the harbour."

"I heard they were. I told Aunt Phoebe. But go on."

"Then there was a telegram from President McKinley calling all American men over twenty-one to the colours. The Consul-General was right there helping Padraic O'Shea sign the boys in and I — well, it was all over and done with almost before I realized I was enlisting. That's how it happened. But — it was all right, wasn't it? You aren't angry?"

"Oh, Jason. Hold me close. Of course I'm not angry. I'm so proud I could cry. But I'm not going to — only I'm going to be worried every minute. And Aunt Phoebe and I are going to miss you terribly."

"But it won't be for long. The Consul-General himself said so. And I'll be earning three times as much as I am now. I just had to take it — for your sake, my dear."

"Of course you did. It just came so quickly, I guess I'm a little confused. My husband a soldier!"

"Yes, dear. And I've got to leave right away."

"Oh, no!"

"That's the way war is. We have to report at General Shafter's headquarters before the Spanish hear about us and block our march."

"And you can't even say good-bye to Aunt Phoebe? She's on a sick call."

Standing he drew her up and gathered her into his arms. "No. I can't even stand here and hold you as I'd like to. I must go this minute." He was already transformed into a dominating character. There was no trace of shyness or boyishness in this kiss. Then he was breathing against her cheek. "My dear, dear Sharon. It won't be for long. They can't keep me from you for long. I'll try to get back to see you whenever I can. Oh, Sharon, my dear."

"You will take care of yourself, won't you? Promise me."

"Of course I will. And you must do the same." He swallowed hard and his voice was low, his words halting. "But if anything should happen to me, Sharon. If — if I shouldn't — I mean if I couldn't come back — I want you to know that — that the month you've given me as my wife has been the happiest time I've ever known. I could die without any regrets."

"I'm so glad to hear you say that, Jason. And you've been wonderful to me."

"But you've been heaven itself. There's never been a man happier than you made me." And his lips were upon hers again, tender this time, and sweet with the honey of his words.

And then he was gone.

And Sharon was sitting on the landing, weak and shaken. Her last picture of him swinging loosely down the staircase, his lanky frame rhythmic as lusty verse, was as dear to her as remembered kisses.

She pulled herself up very slowly and, lagging on each step, she found herself at the front door before she realized where she was going. The hall mirror reminded her. Need she go now? Jason would be making three times as much. Yes, but the need now might be even greater than before. Wiping her eyes and lifting her chin, she left the house.

7

The Splendid Morning

The horses were flecked with foam as the small band of volunteers from Santiago rode into General Shafter's camp. There were eighteen young men, most of them in their early twenties and all of them, like Jason, born of American parents on Cuban soil. Padraic O'Shea rode hard ahead on his big bay horse, looking as cocky as a rooster. No one knew exactly why he had left Brooklyn twenty years before and settled in Santiago, but there was a recurring allusion to an escapade with a policeman's daughter. The English-speaking people in and about the city read his paper and, perhaps because there was no competitor, it thrived. He liked the newspaper business, but there was going to be a fight and he was Irish.

"Sure, an' if ye be General Shafter, ye're the man I'm lookin' for," he declared heartily as a corpulent, flabby man pushed aside the tent flaps.

"I'm Shafter. Who are you?"

"Th' Saints be forgivin' me, but I'm Padraic O'Shea of Santiago an' I'm bringin' ye the foinest lot o' lads ye've iver seen, no less. Faith, an' I wish ivery one o' them was me own flesh and blood!"

"What brings you here? Were you followed?"

"The bastards didn't dare to follow us!" he proclaimed. Then in calmer tones he related the news of the fleet in the harbour and quoted McKinley's telegram. "Faith an' there weren't a great lot of volunteers," he went on, "but look at them, gineral! Ain't they foine now? They's only eighteen, but they'll make up for three times the number of the ordinary run of soldiers."

"Good, good," Shafter said. "We can use them all right. I'll see that they're all quartered comfortably and issued with equipment." He beckoned to an aide. "See that these horses are rubbed down and watered and fed," he commanded in his easy-going manner, and to another aide, "Have these men sign pay vouchers, issue them with equipment and get them assigned to a company."

"Golly," Jason said to himself when he got into his new outfit, "there's no finer lookin' uniform in the whole damned world. I wish Sharon could see me now." He was adjusting his cap at different angles and trying to get the effect in the little tin mirror when he heard his name called. Stepping out of the tent he said to the aide, "That's me. I'm Jason Earleigh."

"Report to General Shafter at once."

"Yes sir." Quaking for fear this meant a reprimand, although he had done nothing wrong that he knew of, he followed the aide to the headquarters tent. It held a small crude desk, a cot, a lantern, and a board hanging behind the desk with nails driven through it to hold official communications. General Shafter sat bull-like on a creaking chair behind the desk.

"You sent for me, sir?" Jason asked and swallowed uncomfortably.

"Are you Private Earleigh?"

"Yes, sir." He swallowed again.

"I have your enlistment record here." Shafter bowed his leonine head over the sheet of paper. "And I observe that you once lived on the El Caney road near San Juan Hill."

"That's right, sir." He breathed more easily now.

"That's very fortunate. All the other boys in your contingent were raised in town. None of them know the El Caney road. You should be familiar with San Juan Hill too. Are you?"

"I've walked its slopes often, sir. My foster-father's plantation was right close by."

"Good. Good. I'm going to have a little mission for you to perform, Private Earleigh. If you're successful it will mean a commission in the army for you."

"Thank you, sir. What do you wish me to do?"

"There are several companies encamped on the jungle side of San Juan Hill just awaiting my orders to attack. If I know Colonel Wood — or rather, if I know his lieutenant, Teddy Roosevelt — as well as I think I do, then Wood's company, the Rough Riders, will be in a position to lead the attack. They aren't likely to let any other regiment get ahead of them."

"I see, sir. I've read something about them."

"Do you think if I gave you a fresh horse you could get a message through to Colonel Wood by dawn?"

"Yes, sir. I'm sure I could, sir."

"Good. Good." There was a smile of satisfaction on the fat features. "To-day is 30 June. I want this attack to be made to-morrow, 1 July. You are to remember what I say because I don't care to risk it on paper. Deliver the message to Colonel Wood in person. He is to take command of both Santiago and El Caney until I can march my men in and occupy them. Do you understand the message and can you remember it?"

"Yes sir. I'm sure of myself, sir." And to prove it he repeated the message word for word.

"Go to the mess tent and get yourself something to eat before you leave. And good luck to you." General Shafter offered his hand. Jason was surprised at the strength of his grip. His own hands were perspiring as he left the tent, and the pit of his stomach felt remote. But he ate because the general had suggested it. His mind was in Santiago. If he took a direct route, which would be the only logical way to go, he would ride a little way along the edge of the city, but not through it. It would be dark by that time and he would need every minute in order to make his objective by dawn. Even at that he would have to ride hard. By riding even harder he could take the risk of being captured in the city and he could stop long enough to speak to Sharon and perhaps kiss her — just once. She could see him in his uniform; she could know how important he was to the American campaign. With his knowledge of the streets there was little chance of capture. And he didn't mind how hard he'd have to ride. The general was giving him a fresh horse. He left his biscuit half eaten, wiped his mouth, and went to see about his horse. That message must be delivered. The fate of Cuba depended upon it. The horse they gave him was a beauty, and high spirited too. Jason patted him on the nose and making sure the orderly wasn't hearing he said, "Cuba is going to have to hang in the balance five minutes. You're taking me to Sharon."

It was midnight in the Little Egypt Saloon near the docks and it was Sharon's second night of singing there. So far she had been successful, although the Little Egypt was scarcely the type of place she had in mind when she started out to get a job. It was a violent contrast to El Americano, but the proprietors of the better cafés in town, after hearing her sing, had shaken their heads sadly and said they were very sorry.

Finally in desperation she had drifted down to the waterfront. And the proprietor here, Destination Smith, had said, "Yes, we can use another entertainer," and she had started at once, leaving poor Aunt Phoebe to sit up worrying until after midnight. Where Destination Smith got his name, no one knew. He had come into the world with two things against him — a blighted face and a deformed figure. The left side of his face was as impassive as if petrified, while the right side flexed in meaningless twitches and jerks. Dwarf-like, he hunched behind the bar serving drinks to the obstreperous crowd.

His customers were Spanish labourers who, because of the war, were finding the mere battle for existence almost a Waterloo; deck-hands off boats from Rio and Pernambuco and Bahia, now quarantined in Santiago by the Spanish officials; and the drifters always present in waterfront saloons. Then there were the Cuban whores who depended on men such as these for their few pesetos.

Sharon sang as well as she could, and the boisterous crowds were not too unkind, but neither were they complimentary. "Who let the frog in?" was their favourite jibe, and from the way they stamped their feet and yelled when they applauded a song she was never quite sure whether they liked her or just liked making fun of her. One big hulk of a man with black, matted hair and ape-like arms — probably a coal stoker — grabbed her around the waist and said, "The señorita could do better for herself if she took her clothes off and kept her mouth shut." Knowing that he could crush the very life out of her if he chose, she cajoled him into letting her go by twisting his ear playfully and telling him the boss wanted her to keep moving.

She heard him laughing above all the noise as she moved swiftly away and found a table where two American sailors sat. How they had come here she didn't know, but they were a welcome sight, and she hovered near their table. They were entertaining two French girls lavishly, and roaring with laughter at their broken English. All four of them were quite drunk. Between the snatches of her song Sharon could hear some of their talk.

"We're from the *Texas*, mamselle," one sailor said to his lady, winking laboriously and pinching her thigh, "out on a li'l French leave."

"Even the admiral doesn't know we're here," his companion volunteered in confidential tones which Sharon could barely hear over the discordant music. "We jus' got tired of sittin' on our arse waitin' fer sumpin t' bus'. We ain't goin' back till morning either. We got lots a time to do anything we —"

Sharon caught the eye of Destination Smith, and he nodded his head sideways meaning that she should circulate around the room. She hoped the boys would not get too drunk to make their way back through the jungle and the barbed wire. She sang louder because she wanted to run and scream. She wanted to be at home with Jason. What would he think if he knew she was working in a dive where prostitutes openly solicited their business? She wondered if the troop had reached headquarters safely and she hoped Jason was sound asleep in the camp. She must never let him know she worked in such sordid surroundings.

Finishing her song, she walked over to the bar. Destination Smith leered at her over the taps. "Not bad, not bad," he said blandly. The mobile half of his face went into a spasmodic grimace.

"I'm a little tired of singing," she said wearily. "Do you mind if I stop now?"

"Not at all. Not at all. Sit down at the corner table there and rest. Maybe one of the boys will buy you a drink."

"Thank you, Mr Smith, but I'd rather go home." She turned towards the door.

"Here! Here! You aren't going home early again to-night!" He hurried around the end of the bar and headed her off. "I just let you go home early last night because you said your aunt would worry. Our girls never go home before daylight. I thought you understood."

"Understood what?" She looked him straight in the eye now.

"Don't pretend to be a little schoolgirl. I was going to give you the best room in the house to start off with. You heard about our Mayme that died from poisoned rum? Well, she had that room and she did quite well with it. Now, be reasonable. I'll see that the girls throw a little business your way. Charge what you think you can get and roll 'em when you think you can, but remember —" he shook a talon-like finger at her — "I get half of everything you make. If you don't want to entertain a drunk in your room, you can refuse. That's a lady's privilege at my place."

Sharon shrank away from him, hardly believing what she had heard. Did he think she was like the girls who sat around his tables enticing the men upstairs.

"I'm afraid you misunderstand, Mr Smith." She looked at the corner of the mantilla which she twisted in her hands. She couldn't bear to look at that face again. "I came here to sing and nothing else. I won't be back to-morrow night. I'll take my money, please."

He shrugged, and shuffled behind the bar, where he took two bills from an old cigar box and pushed them towards her. She slipped them into the bosom of her dress and hurried away without once looking back.

As she turned into the walk of Aunt Phoebe's darkened house she heard a faint "hsst" in the bushes. Frightened, she turned quickly and said, "Who's there?"

And into the faint aura of light from a nearby street lamp stepped the figure of a man.

"Sharon."

She caught her breath, faltered, and stepped back, bringing both hands to her cheeks. It couldn't be! He was at her side holding her to keep her from falling.

"Sharon, Sharon."

She leaned against him, limp, her arms hanging at her sides. Then she began to cry, her lips trembling against his cheek.

"Sharon! It's me, Eric."

But she could not control her weeping. The sobs racked her body convulsively against his and he simply held her arms and shoulders and hair until, regaining her self-control, she stood facing him. Drawing his handkerchief from his middy pocket, he wiped her face as he would a little child's.

She spoke to him in a hushed whisper, "You can't be Eric. He's dead." She passed her hand over his face, scarcely touching it. "I'm tired and nervous. I'm imagining this. You aren't —"

"Here, darling, pinch me." He pressed her finger close to his cheek and released her hand to let her make sure for herself. The doubting quality of her touch made him laugh, and by the familiar sound she knew that he was real. She was in his arms again, but clinging fiercely now. She must never let him go.

"Oh, Eric, can it be true? God brought you back to me once; I didn't think He would do it again. And now He's brought you back to me — but it's too late."

He prised her gripping fingers from his shoulders and stood back from her, mystified, apprehensive.

"Sharon! What —"

"Oh, Eric. What are we going to do? I've got a husband. I married Jason. I told you about Jason in Havana, remember?"

"Married!" He echoed the word hollowly and she nodded.

"I — I thought you were dead. Oh, Eric, my darling, you know I couldn't love anyone but you. Jason's fine, but I can't ever love him as I love you. But he wanted me so badly, and I wanted to forget you. Don't you see, it was my chance of forgetting you —"

"Forgetting me? Oh, Sharon!"

"I was going through the pain of death every time I thought of you. Did you expect me to go on enduring that torture for the rest of my life? I had to try to forget. I admit it didn't work very well, but it helped. Jason's been wonderful to me. But Eric, what are we going to do?"

"I don't know yet. But we'll think of something. We belong together. Perhaps if we both talk to your husband he will see it that way and give you up. He'll have to give you up. I won't have it otherwise." He drew her to him possessively.

"There's so much to tell you. Come into the garden where we can sit down." She led him down the little path and noticed he was walking with a decided limp. "Darling, what's happened? You're hurt!" She offered to help him sit down on the arbour bench.

"Oh, I'm all right now. But I'm afraid I'll have to walk like this for the rest of my life. My leg was broken and wasn't set right. You see, when the *Maine* blew up —" He hesitated, and she could read into the moment of silence all the horror that the blast had been.

"Don't tell me if you'd rather not," she whispered.

"I wouldn't want to tell you all I saw and went through, but the last I remember was the deck rising up and meeting my face. I guess we met, because everything went black after that and when I came to I was in the ocean. It must have been the water that brought me round. I was clear of the ship, and all I could see of it was the flames leaping into the air and some floating wreckage. My leg felt as though it had been pressed in a vice, and I could hardly move it. But a person can do almost the impossible when it's life or death. I saw two men hanging to some wreckage, but my lungs hurt me so badly when I tried to yell that I gave up; and I don't know how I ever did it, but I paddled and floated and swam little by little until I reached a Spanish boat. It was the *Alfonso XII.* They took me aboard and took care of me, after a fashion."

"They didn't report you to Captain Sigsbee?"

"No. I found that out after I'd been there about a month. I made myself a pair of crutches and got out as quickly as I could and went to the convent, but you were gone. Madre Isabela said you spoke of going to Santiago, but no one knew how you went or if you got there. So I called on Pearl."

"How was she?"

"The same as ever. She gave me your address."

"Then what happened? I didn't hear from you."

"I wrote, but the letter was returned to me — addressee unknown. I was assigned to the *Texas* because I wasn't quite disabled enough to be sent home. They let me rest till my leg got better, and I'm as good as ever now except for the limp. When we came here I couldn't wait to look you up. Three of us dived overboard and swam to shore. We've got to go back the same way and be on ship for duty in the morning. I'll have to leave in a minute."

"Then you have to go through that awful jungle, don't you?"

"Yes, but what's a little thing like that compared to seeing you again? I'd go through a thousand hells —"

"Oh, Eric! We're forgetting —"

"No, we aren't. But we're doing nothing wrong. I still love you and I promise you we won't be separated again. Somehow we'll work this out together." He rose, and because there were no more words to be said he took her in his arms and their lips met, dispelling for the moment all thoughts of Jason. Sharon gave herself completely to Eric's kiss.

Jason entered the outskirts of Santiago shortly after midnight and let the horse slow down to a walk. "You've been a good fellow," he murmured, stroking the sleek mane. "I'm going to let you rest a little while. You deserve it. And I guess I've got a right to kiss my own wife."

He would let himself into the house quietly, tiptoe up the stairs and step into their bedroom. How Sharon would rejoice to see him — even for a few stolen moments in the middle of the night. He tethered the horse a few yards from the front gate and approached noiselessly up the board walk to the front steps. But as he was about to place his foot on the first step he thought he heard voices in the garden. Who could be out there at this time of night? Intruders, undoubtedly. Well, he'd soon find out.

Walking down the path he caught the sound of a woman's low voice — Sharon's. And then a man's. Standing transfixed in the path he involuntarily focused his eyes on the arbour from where the voices came, and as his eyes became more accustomed to the darkness he saw two figures sitting there. The man was saying, "— and I promise you we won't be separated again. Somehow we'll work this out together."

And as he rose and drew Sharon up beside him, Jason could tell he was a sailor. Eric, of course. But how? And why? He made no attempt to answer the confusing questions that crowded pell-mell into his mind. But Sharon was his wife and would be true to him now. Then the heads of the two figures came together and there was a portentous silence in the garden.

Turning cautiously and leaving without a sound, Jason tried to persuade himself that this was only a chance meeting, that Sharon was temporarily carried away, and that she would be true. But he remembered that she was dressed up when he came home yesterday afternoon, and he remembered her saying to him before they were married, "I still love him, but maybe I could learn to love you, Jason."

By the time he reached his horse his mind was made up. Sharon had been a good wife to him. His heart told him that. Her happiness must come before his own. The man Sharon really loved was the man she should have. He did not need Sharon's words to tell him that Eric was that man. With a heavy heart he mounted and galloped his horse towards San Juan Hill.

On and on he spurred the obedient animal, urging from him every ounce of speed. The first streaks of light were already grey in the east when he made a slight detour for another unauthorized stop — Padre Esteban's shrine. He thought of waking the padre, but decided it was better not to, for the dear padre would be sure to try to dissuade him from his intention. So he entered the deserted little candle-lit shrine and journeyed the Way of the Cross alone. Going back to the altar, he fell on his knees and prayed. Then he lighted a candle and placed it before the Virgin. At the door again he dipped his fingers in the holy water and crossed himself, murmuring, "Father, forgive me for what I am about to do."

When he rode into Colonel Wood's camp he was immediately surrounded by an excited crowd of men. What was his message? Was there any news?

"I've got to see Colonel Wood personally," he announced. He was escorted to where the colonel was shaving before a little mirror attached to the trunk of a tree.

Standing at Wood's side was Teddy Roosevelt, itching for battle. He was tired of doing nothing, tired of sleeping in the mud, tired of digging latrines. He was sick of swallowing quinine tablets. He wanted action. What good was a uniform and a campaign hat if there was no occasion to wear the uniform and no campaign to justify the hat? He hoped this recruit was bringing their orders.

"General Shafter says to attack this morning," Jason said quietly, "take the hill, and command Santiago and El Caney. Then General Shafter will come and occupy the town."

"Great jumping Jehoshaphat!" Roosevelt yelled, flinging his hat wildly in the air. "That's good news, boy! Good news!" And he grinned as only he could, with the deeply-etched lines shooting up at the corners of his mouth and other wrinkles creasing the bridge of his nose, while his ruddy cheeks fairly glowed with vitality and good humour.

Jason stood by waiting for an opportunity to speak to Colonel Wood again. The colonel was proceeding with his shave. There was nothing in his manner to indicate that the news was good or bad; or even that there was any news.

"Sir," said Jason, "I should like to engage in this battle. General Shafter did not give me any orders about returning to my company there. May I have equipment and be one of your men, just for this engagement?"

"Give him a gun," Colonel Wood said to an aide, and deliberately wiped the lather from his face. Regarding himself in the mirror, he spoke to Teddy much as he might ask what they were having for breakfast. "You may pass the word along, Teddy, that we will charge the hill in precisely half an hour."

"Up the slope, by God, and give 'em hell!"

The battle of San Juan Hill was on. Roosevelt had discarded his coat, and his blue shirt was shredded and ripped so that it was a marvel that it hung on at all. The polka-dot bandanna, wet with sweat, hung about his neck like an old sock. His campaign hat rested at a careless angle on the back of his head; his arms and legs were cut and scratched by the cacti and Spanish-bayonets; his breeches were caked with mud. Every now and then he stopped to breathe on his glasses and meticulously wipe them with his handkerchief. Adjusting them on his nose again, he would wave his hat to the men behind him and yell, "Up the slope, by God, and give 'em hell!"

They crawled through the tall grass on their

hands and knees, stumbling, dodging from tree to tree and from rock to rock. In front of them was their mobile battery of four cannons. It was unlike any charge ever made in history. No Balaclava this; no six hundred riding into the jaws of death. No Thermopylae with legions doomed in the narrow trap of a pass. It looked more as if a corps of cowboys was rounding up a herd of mavericks for branding. Far ahead were a score of men. Here and there was a man on a horse.

From the top of the hill came a flash of flame and the first roar of heavy guns. But the Rough Riders barely halted. The Spaniards hadn't got their range yet, and the real battle wouldn't begin until they reached the top of that hill. They did assemble themselves a little closer together and they sang, "There'll be a Hot Time in the Old Town To-night".

By the time they reached the barbed-wire fences, Roosevelt was on a horse. How he got it nobody knew and nobody cared. And how he was not hit by a Spanish marksman as he came into range nobody could guess. That barbed wire was as mean as hell. It had to be lifted for men to crawl under, or cut away for a horse to get over. First they let Teddy over and remarked that it was a wonder he would even wait for the wire to be cut. He was here, there, and everywhere.

There was a river to cross, but the thick brush on either side concealed them. And by now the 9th Cavalry was catching up with them, and over at the left the 10th and the 6th. Grinning, cursing, yelling, singing, they pushed on. "Up the hill and give 'em hell!" A volley of gunfire from the fortress and they would lie on their stomachs to take aim and fire back. A few kept going straight ahead, taking no time to fire but intent on reaching the top of the hill. Jason was among the first of these, making his way through the tall grass, swinging his rifle like a mop.

"Hey, Teddy!" somebody shouted. "You'd better get off that horse. You make a target as big as a buffalo."

But Teddy only grinned and charged on, most of the time only half-seeing where he was going. His spectacles kept getting befogged with perspiration. It had been his obsession to take that hill and he was doing most of the taking. Another barbed-wire fence? What of it? No time now to do any cutting. Jump the horse over it. Trample it down. Up that hill! Past a little shrine. The Spaniards, the ruthless devils, had blasted the roof off with one of their poor cannon shots. Maybe it had been riddled a bit by American guns, too. Standing at one side, staring in bewilderment, was the old padre with his long white hair waving in the wind and his grey habit whipping about his thighs.

Jason saw it too. His heart went out in compassion to Padre Esteban, but this was no time to stop. He would like to say good-bye but — Up that hill! Give 'em hell! The Spaniards were getting their range right enough now. But the

Rough Riders made it. The Spaniards leaped out of their trenches and took to their heels. The other regiments followed in from different directions. Colonel Wood jabbed the first guidon into the side of the hill and the other companies followed suit.

Then someone planted the Stars and Stripes on the summit, and Jason's cheers went up with the others. But the battle had just begun. There were more trenches. Rifle fire blasted across the slope and overhead the shells broke deafeningly in mid-air. Jason charged into the very teeth of the fighting, near where Teddy Roosevelt was. It couldn't be much longer. "Forgive me, father, for what I am about to do."

Other men were falling. Their screams drowned the roar of the cannon and the sharp zip-zip of the Mauser bullets. Jason climbed to the top of a ridge. This was old territory. He should be able to see Promised Land from here. This was where he had often come to find peace, but now there was no peace. Jets of flame shot out from the cannons. The Rough Riders had the Spaniards on the run again. Yet as they ran they turned back and shot wildly. And there was still another trench where other Spaniards were holding out and firing for dear life.

Jason stood straight up scanning the landscape in an effort to find Promised Land.

"Get down, you damned fool!" another soldier yelled. But he was heedless. He was still looking for Promised Land. And there it was, the same as ever. He could even discern the site of the burnt barn and the — a bullet furrowed across his forehead. Blinded by the blood, he jerked forward, and heard above the screams of the fallen a shriek overhead and a terrific explosion. Earth and pebbles showered over him. He was flat on his stomach and half buried.

Conscious only of a smothering sensation, he tried to dig himself out, and in one moment of awful clarity he knew that he had no hands to dig with. "Sharon, Sharon," he murmured faintly.

"Yes, Jason. I've been true," he heard her whisper.

"If somebody told you to count all the stars before sun-up or you'd be turned into mincemeat, what would you do?"

"I expect then I'd be turned into mincemeat."

Sighing, he nestled his head into the fresh earth and was willing now to sleep.

"Boy, boy, can I do something for you?"

His darkening eyes caught a glimmer of glasses and a sandy moustache, and he said, "You're Mr Roosevelt, aren't you?"

"Those who like me call me Teddy. What can I do for you, boy?"

"Just leave me alone. But you can deliver a — message."

"Of course, son. Of course."

"To Mrs Jason Earleigh, 122 Avenida Santa Maria, Santiago. Tell her — tell her — to — love him always. Tell her Jason — said so."

And then he found his peace.

Roosevelt brushed a tear from his eyes as he straightened up. But he vaulted back into his saddle saying, "Damned glasses. They smudge too easy." He cleared the last barbed-wire fence and joined the concentration of troops pouring over San Juan Ridge. The Spanish flag was coming down from the fortress, and as the Stars and Stripes were hauled up his whoop was the loudest from all those powder-choked lungs. The shells no longer screamed; the rifles were idle.

And there below him in clear and brilliant focus lay Santiago, shimmering in the bright sun of that splendid morning.

Just before dawn Eric swam with the other two sailors back to the *Texas*. They climbed aboard and waited their opportunity to go below. When the sentry's back was turned they slipped across the decks one by one until they were safe in their bunks again.

But there was no sleep for them that morning. They were scarcely settled in their bunks when reveille was blown and Eric had to take his station in the watch-tower. He could easily distinguish the Spanish blockhouses in the mountains, and through his glass he could make out the puffs of white smoke. Following each puff came the rumble of the gun. Santiago was plainly doomed. But there was still the Spanish fleet to be dealt with.

His thoughts went back to Sharon and their

problem, but his attention was caught by several columns of black smoke and he riveted his eye to the glass. It was the Spanish fleet coming out of the harbour! One by one the *Maria Teresa*, the *Vizcaya*, the *Oquendo*, and the *Colon* steamed into full view, their yellow and scarlet ensigns bright against the verdure of the Cuban shore, their black hulls ploughing through the white-caps as they came defiantly down the bottle-neck. Would the sunken *Merrimac* stop them? It didn't. Eric groaned inwardly. All that work for nothing. Cervera was coming right through.

Eric clambered down the rigging and reported what he had seen to Captain Smith. "Four ships ahead of us, sir, bearing southward, heading south by south-south-west."

The alarm was sounded on the gongs and the *Indiana* picked it up. The *Oregon* passed it on to the *Iowa* and so on from ship to ship. Simultaneously the signal for action was hoisted and every man raced to his post. Bearings were taken at the cannons, muzzles swabbed, shells arranged for instant use.

Shouts went up from the crew of the *Texas*. "Here they come. Here they come!"

The firing signal.

The battle was on.

The decks rocked under the series of concussions. Admiral Cervera turned his four ships westward and tried hugging the coast. But the relentless shells burst all around them. The *Maria Teresa* was the first to catch fire and head for the shore. Soon she was aground on the reefs, wrecked and burning like an enormous bonfire. Now that first blood had been drawn the American Navy really got down to business. Eric was at the guns, stripped to the waist, helping load the shells. All around him were his kind — hard, sweating youths with bulging muscles, who went about this business of battle with cool efficiency. Volley after volley burst from the American guns until the boats rocked in the sea like corks bobbing in a pan of boiling water.

The *Oregon* and the *Texas* and the *Indiana* began to close in on the *Oquendo*, now hugging the shore and trying in vain to hold back the three overpowering American ships. At the rail of the *Texas* Eric stood grinning as the *Oquendo* suddenly blew up, scattering a shower of steel and cement and hurtling bodies high into the smoky air. For a moment the grin faded as he remembered the *Maine* and what it felt like to be on a boat that was being blown to hell. But that was just it. That was why he was here. "Remember the *Maine*!" was right. And "To hell with Spain!" was right.

The *Vizcaya* withstood the onslaught forty minutes before turning into the beach with her decks aflame and her crew leaping overboard. The *Colon*, in a desperate effort to run the blockade, sailed down the bay full steam ahead. But the *Brooklyn* and the *Oregon* and the *Texas* gave chase. "Will we catch her?" Eric wondered. "We've got to catch her!"

Inch by inch they overtook her, and at a quarter past one that afternoon the *Colon* hauled down her colours and hoisted the white flag. The battle of Santiago de Cuba was over.

The *Texas*, the *Oregon* and the *Brooklyn* lay in a semicircle about the *Colon*, their engines at rest. Cheers went up from the American sailors and came echoing back from the mountains. From the *Oregon* came the strains of "The Star-Spangled Banner".

— what so proudly we hailed
At the twilight's last gleaming.

Some sailor on the *Brooklyn* shouted, "Three cheers for the *Texas*!" and the cheers went rocketing across the waves.

— o'er the ramparts we watched
Were so gallantly streaming.

"Three cheers for the *Oregon*!" another sailor proposed and the whoops and the hip-hip-hoorays went rocketing back.

On board the *Texas* every sailor was jubiliant, yet Captain Smith stood at his post on the bridge, silent and reserved. "Call all hands aft," he said to his orderly. A little later five hundred men, wearing only their trousers — what was left of their trousers — their torsos blackened and sweating, stood on the quarterdeck facing their captain.

"I want all of you," Captain Smith said quietly, "officers and crew included, unless there be those among you who have conscientious scruples against so doing, to offer your silent thanks to God."

Every man stood reverent, head bowed.

"Three cheers for Captain Smith!"

Santiago had fallen. Cuba was free. It was time to sail triumphantly into port.

The crowds on the piers were yelling themselves hoarse. Closer and closer the *Texas* drew until Eric could discern Sharon jumping up and down and waving her handkerchief. She had not seen him yet, but there was something in her manner that told him all was well with them. He waved both arms in a frantic semaphore until she was able to pick him out from the hundreds of other men crowding the rails.

The sides of the hull were nudging the piles, the ropes were thrown out and the gangplank lowered. To hell with the gangplank! Eric leaped over the rail, and his ankles screamed at their shattering impact with the pier. He worked his way towards Sharon as best he could, and when they met, the pressure of the crowd pinioned their arms to their sides. Sharon had been crying, and as Eric kissed her they were oblivious to the throng of cheering, weeping, hysterical people.

"Thank God, Eric! Thank God you're safe." Her voice shook.

Eric led a path for her out of the crowd. They sat on a huge coil of rope. "And Jason — ?"

She bit her lip. "He was with the Rough Riders in the charge of San Juan Hill. How he got there I don't know, but he isn't coming back." They sat holding hands and in a moment she went on. "I found it out just half an hour ago and rushed here to meet you. An officer came and told me. He was riding a horse. I didn't ask him his name, but he was a big man and he wore glasses and had a moustache. I don't know why I'm saying all this. It hasn't anything to do with us — only I don't think I remembered even to thank him."

"But Jason must have sent him."

"He did. And the strangest part about it all is that Jason sent him to say that I must love you always. 'To love him always and tell her Jason said so' was the exact message."

Until the crowd was dispersed and forming parades in the streets they sat there with fingers interlocked, saying very little.

From somewhere a band was formed and the marching, cheering people fell in behind it, their voices failing to drown out the blaring notes of the Old Hundredth. Sharon smiled up at Eric. "I feel equal to walking home now," she said.

They turned and fell in step with the surging throng. Far ahead of her the purple hills on the horizon seemed to smile down upon them, gladly granting their silent benediction. Sharon searched beyond the hills, again seeking a new horizon, not for herself this time, but for Eric too. But what lay beyond mattered little now. The nightmare of the past could soon be forgotten; the present meant only Eric; and all she asked for the future was Eric by her side, never to be parted from her again.

His hand upon hers was his silent promise, and together they disappeared into the crowd.

The employees of G.K. Hall hope you have enjoyed this Large Print book. All our Large Print titles are designed for easy reading, and all our books are made to last. Other G.K. Hall books are available at your library, through selected bookstores, or directly from us.

For information about titles, please call:

(800) 257-5157

To share your comments, please write:

Publisher
G.K. Hall & Co.
P.O. Box 159
Thorndike, ME 04986